Betray the Night

A Novel About Ovid

Benita Kane Jaro

Bolchazy-Carducci Publishers, Inc.
Mundelein, Illinois USA

Editor: Marie Carducci Bolchazy
Contributing Editor: Peter Sipes
Cover Design & Typography: Adam Phillip Velez

**Betray the Night
A Novel About Ovid**

Benita Kane Jaro

Bolchazy-Carducci Publishers, Inc.
1570 Baskin Road
Mundelein, Illinois 60060
www.bolchazy.com

Printed in the United States of America
2009
by United Graphics

ISBN 978-0-86516-712-4

Library of Congress Cataloging-in-Publication Data

Jaro, Benita Kane.
  Betray the night : a novel / by Benita Kane Jaro.
    p. cm.
  Includes bibliographical references and index.
  ISBN 978-0-86516-712-4 (pbk. : alk. paper) 1. Women--Rome--Fiction. 2. Rome--History--
Augustus, 30 B.C.-14 A.D.--Fiction. 3. Ovid, 43 B.C.-17 or 18 A.D.--Fiction. I. Title.

  PS3560.A5368B48 2009
  813'.54--dc22

                                                                        2008052061

For Lou, whose ideas are in it, and for Marie, who wanted it to be about a woman—and for MAJ, as always

"non ego deserto iacuissem frigida lecto,
    nec quererer tardos ire relicta dies;
nec mihi quaerenti spatiosam fallere noctem
    lassaret viduas pendula tela manus…"

Heroides I.9.

Then I would not lie down alone in a cold bed
Nor complain how slowly the day passed
Nor would I betray the endless night
With warp hanging from widowed hands…

INTRODUCTION

Naked, the princess danced. Under the shadow of the Rostra and out onto the moonlit stones of the Forum, she stepped and swirled in silence. Her dress lay in a heap in the speckled darkness by the sacred fig tree, and her hair, loose from its ribbons, flew to the rhythm of her feet. Behind her trailed a group—several men, an elderly woman, one or two younger ones—some dressed, some with half their clothes discarded as they went. Now and then they stopped to drink from a cup they passed from hand to hand, and presently, as they drew near the statue of Marsyas again, someone began to sing…

PART I

It was an evil morning. The city rattled with discontent under a spiteful December wind: I could hear it all over the house. The servants coming back from the market said that the grain allowance for the poor had run out, and the hungry and disappointed were wandering the streets.

My husband Publius Ovidius Naso was out of town: the house echoed with his absence, and it made the drafts seem worse. In the weaving room someone had left the boxes open and the wool had gusted into a tangle; when I tried to comb my daughter's hair, it flew away from the comb and fanned into her face, until we were both weeping with frustration.

Presently bands of starving beggars began to show up at our house. I gave them what food I could, but it was not enough, and they cursed and muttered. I tried to explain, but what I needed was the authority of a magistrate, like my husband's, to send them away quietly.

Around the middle hour the day suddenly became first much better, then much worse. There was a commotion in the hall: servants were hurrying through; voices were raised. I came out of the atrium where I had been trying to reason with one of Naso's clients. The wind was blowing from the open front door.

"Oh, heaven, what now? If it's the beggars again, tell them…tell them there's no bread left in the house today."

"No, not beggars. Unless you count Cotta and me." It was my husband, appearing suddenly in the doorway. Disheveled and travel stained, he managed still to look elegant and I felt myself begin to smile.

At fifty he was a slight man, only beginning to grow a little solid around the middle, and a little grizzled over his ears. He flashed me his ironic smile from under the amazing architecture of his nose. "No bread? Cotta and I need food. We've been in too much of a hurry to stop."

I peered around a porter bustling past with a box of books. Out in the street Cotta Maximus, his tall young friend, was directing a swirl of secretaries and chair carriers.

"Not much, but I saved some back. And you'll want some soup. It's a cold day. But what are you doing home? I thought you two were staying at Cotta's on Elba until the Saturnalia."

He put his arms around me, but it was like being embraced by a stranger. It was not his familiar scent: now he smelled of the road, and his unshaven cheek scraped my lip.

"Ah, my dear, couldn't it just have been that I missed you?"

He meant it lightly, but his voice trembled on the edge of his control, threatening to fall of its own weight.

"I missed you too," I said, with truth, "but to cut short a condolence call, and especially for Cotta's father…Oh. Something's happened, hasn't it?"

"It's nothing. It's a joke. A mistake. I'll tell you sometime. Did you say soup?" He turned to the street. "Cotta. Cotta, come in and have some soup."

Cotta went on giving directions to the carriers.

"Cotta?"

Cotta glanced quickly at us, then away. "Go out to him," I urged. "Tell him it's no trouble. He's such an old friend."

But Naso only stood where he was. He looked shocked and I wasn't sure he heard.

"Something has happened, hasn't it?" I said. "What? What's the matter?"

"Nothing. A mistake." He shook himself like a dog waking up. "Where is my secretary? Loricus? Where is that man?...Ah, there you are. About what I told you: go ahead. I want them burnt. All of them."

"All of what?" I was really alarmed now.

"Nothing. Just a few words."

"What words? Yours?"

"Just a few. Some small things. It's nothing."

"Your...your poems?"

"Just a few."

"But why? They're good. Everyone loves them—"

"Pinaria, my dear, where is that soup? And I had better change my cloak." He lifted his head and called for his dresser. "Toga, please." Then, to the street: "Cotta? Cotta, are you coming with me to the Palatine?"

Cotta smiled. He took a step back. And another. He smiled again, made a small vague gesture that might have been a wave, and in a moment he and his servants had disappeared.

"So," my husband said. "So it's like that."

"Like what?" I asked. "What is happening?"

I doubt he heard me; he was speaking to himself. "Very well, then, if no one will come with me, alone it will be. Toga."

"Why?" I was practically shouting. "Why do you need your toga? Where are you going?"

He had emerged, draped in the heavy white wool garment of a Roman citizen on formal business. "My dear, it's nothing. A small summons. Just a mistake."

"What kind of summons? Why is it a mistake?" But there could only be one kind of summons to the Palatine Hill. My husband was going, in his best toga, to see Caesar Augustus.

5

He gave me a smile. It tried to be what it had always been, but it did not succeed. Puckered and stretched like weaving when the thread is pulled too tight, it was too short to reach his eyes. "It's nothing. Nothing at all. Keep that soup hot. I'll need it. If no one else does."

Halfway out the door he remembered something and turned back. "Oh, and see that Loricus does a good job burning those books, will you? He knows which ones: just a couple of poems, little things. See he does a good job."

He lifted his head and squared his shoulders. And suddenly he didn't look like a substantial member of the equestrian class, a businessman with large holdings, a magistrate on the Board of One Hundred, a poet of world-wide fame. He marched out our door like a child expecting to confront a bully in the street.

"Wait," I cried. "You don't have to go alone. I'm coming with you."

As always when we walked somewhere in the city, people recognized my husband. But today, though many had come up to walk with us, more turned away without a greeting, as if they had not seen him at all.

"Naso," I said, "What is going on? That was Sosius, wasn't it? Why didn't he speak to us? And wasn't that one of the Metelli brothers? They're avoiding us, aren't they?"

"You know Rome. There are rumors, I suppose."

"Rumors? About what?"

"Nothing. Nothing, really, just a word here and there...."

"What words? What are you—Heavens, what is that noise?" The street was loud with hammering. We had come down into the Argilitum: a wide space behind the Forum where books and other items were sold. Some of the Praetorian Guard was in the street. They were nailing up a shop.

An old man, feeble as a cricket, was pleading, wringing his hands, filling the air with thin cries. The Praetorians paid no attention, merely shoving him aside as they directed the public slaves with the hammers and boards.

Naso said, "That's Audasius."

"Audasius? But I've been to his shop. He sells your poems."

At that moment the old bookseller heard us or saw us and came running. The first person he saw I think was me, for he tried to kiss my hands. I felt his trembling fingers catching at my sleeves like thorns. "Beautiful lady. Gracious one. Please. Help me. They are saying I have conspired—"

"Conspired to do what, Lucius Audasius?"

"Never mind," Naso said, quickly stepping up and taking Audasius' hands in his.

Audasius turned to him. "Epicadus...he and I...You know. Asinius Epicadus. They are saying we—"

Naso smiled at him gently. "Never mind. It's just some kind of mistake. We'll take care of it." He put his arm around Audasius' shoulder and led him, still crying out names, toward the Praetorians.

Behind me my husband's slave-secretary Loricus caught his breath. One or two of Naso's friends exclaimed. Someone among them was shuffling his feet uneasily, and a couple of them backed away until they reached the Temple of Janus, where they disappeared.

Let them go, I thought, my eyes on the scene by the shop.

It was like a mime in the theater, only it made less sense. The Praetorians watched my husband approach with insolent eyes, and as soon as he was near enough, one of them reached out and pulled poor old Audasius out of Naso's grasp, thrusting him behind them into the arms of the slaves. The old man began to tremble and weep again.

Naso said something sharp.

The Praetorian shrugged.

Naso said something again.

The Praetorian contemplated him for a moment, then turned his back and shouted something at the slaves. In a moment they had all marched off, virtually dragging Audasius with them, and Naso stood alone before the boarded up shop.

Slowly he walked back to us.

"What was it?" someone asked.

Naso said nothing. His eyes had hardened in his face, and he hardly seemed aware of us.

"Master?" Loricus, anxious and distracted, took his arm.

"What? Oh. It was nothing. Just some mistake. I'll straighten it out when I see Caesar Augustus." He tried to smile but no one wanted to look at him when he did.Then without another word he took his place at the head of the little line we had made and led us through into the Forum.

The Forum was full of smoke. It swirled along close to the ground, choking and stinging, a peculiarly acrid fume, smelling of hide and paint and wood, meeting us as we came around the Curia into the open space.

Naso's remaining friends wiped streaming eyes and muttered among themselves. One of them leaned forward. "It's not a sacrifice, is it?"

"No," said Loricus.

Naso tried to smile. "At least, not in the usual sense."

Whatever it was, the sky was rejecting it. The wind off the river was forcing the smoke downward, so that the Forum was thick with it. It was hard to make out what was going on.

It seemed to be the Praetorians again, a lot of them. They had massed themselves in a semicircle in front of the Rostra. From it they stared outward with their usual hostile glare. In the middle, behind their backs, wood lay heaped on the stones, and piled on it books curling and blackening in the invisible bite of flames. The air shimmered above and smoke tumbled and poured across the open space. A huge crowd stood watching them, coughing and muttering in the reek.

"Whose books are those?" Naso lurched heavily against me. Loricus put out his arm to let him lean against it.

No one answered him.

"Loricus, go find out," I said.

I saw him politely bowing among the crowd. Presently he came back.

"Titus Labienus' books, Pinaria Ovidii," he said.

Beside me Naso let out his breath.

We made our way slowly through the Forum. It was full of citizens, angry ones. They met the Praetorians' glare with sullen looks of their own, and now and then as the slaves poked up the blaze there were murmurs of rage. People from all parts of the city kept coming in, and few were leaving: rich and important men in their chairs and litters or followed by their entourages; tradesmen, workmen, even idle slaves; senators with their friends on their way to the Curia; aristocratic women trailed by servants carrying packages. I saw my cousin Marcia sweep through, and a number of our closest acquaintances among some knights clustered near the Lapis Niger, pretending not to see us as we passed. Most of the crowd was coughing and swearing but almost all of the men and women in it had paused and turned toward the Rostra.

Behind the long structure a small disturbance had begun. In a moment a man appeared on the top, like the moon popping over the rooftops. A big man with a bald head set strongly on sloping shoulders, he settled himself in the posture of an orator, echoing the statues among which he stood.

"Cassius Severus," the friend said.

"You might as well burn me alive too," the big man cried into the wind. "I know all of Titus Labienus' works by heart." He thumped his chest. "There. Burn that too."

He began to chant. The little wind off the river ripped and tore among his words and I could hardly make out what he was saying. He seemed to be declaiming—it sounded like a history.

"He's reciting Titus Labienus' book, isn't he? Can you hear what he's saying?" I said to my husband.

"Not very well." He lifted his head so that his powerful nose hid his eyes from me, but under it his long mouth was chiseled into his face.

We made our way—a little handful of people now—to the stairs at the base of the Palatine Hill. Naso started to climb. I put my foot on the step beside him.

"No, Pinaria," he said. "I have to go alone now."

"Why?"

"This is not for you. This is men's business."

"I can go to the door, can't I?"

"Thank you. No." He reached out his hand to me. I smelt the warm scent of his body and felt his rough lips on mine. "Please," I murmured into them.

His arm tightened around me. His fine deep eye was filled with light, but its socket looked bruised. Reluctantly he let me go. His hand was cold. "Pinaria, go home. Take the servants. Go home."

He started up the stairs. The wind tugged at his fine white toga, insistent as a child. It was all that accompanied him.

I watched him all the way to the top growing smaller and smaller until he disappeared.

The little wind fretted and tore. Behind us the voice on the Rostra went on reciting. But near at hand under his breath someone was singing.

"New recruit to the arms of Venus,
This will be our rule
This is our order:
First, deploy your force to meet your love,
Second then to win her heart.
Third, campaign to make love last.
This is the terrain our chariot will mark,
This is the limit our wheel will touch…"

It was Loricus, my husband's slave.

"That's something of my husband's. *The Art of Love*, isn't it?"

"Yes, mistress."

His white hair stood up around his head and his brows were pulled down in anger. An odd expression for a servant.

"Loricus, you were on Elba at Cotta Maximus' with my husband. What is going on? Why are you reciting *The Art of Love*?"

"Mistress, I apologize. I did not mean to offend."

"I'm not offended. I like that poem."

10

"Do you? Some consider it frivolous, even obscene. And perhaps a woman would find it…disagreeable?"

"It's meant to be amusing, Loricus. And it is."

"Yes, mistress. I think the best critics agree. Valerius Messalla, young Cotta's father, for example." There was something in his voice that compelled my attention. "Valerius Messalla deeply admired *The Art of Love*. And he knew poetry. Rome has lost something now that Messalla is dead."

From the Forum I could still hear the orator, repeating the condemned history, far on the edge of sound. The servant cocked his head, as if he were listening.

"Oh. Oh, I see. Caesar summoned Naso because of *The Art of Love*. Is that what you're saying?"

"No, mistress. I am not saying that. Ovidius Naso has said nothing to me about why he was summoned."

"But you guess."

"No. No, of course not. It is not for me to do that. Perhaps you would prefer to wait in greater privacy? Would you like me to escort you home?"

I looked up at the top of the stairs. People were passing in the street above, some were coming down, but none of them was Naso. All of them stared at us.

"No, thank you. I will wait."

We waited a long time. Down in the Forum, a roar of rage and pain went up, followed by a kind of heavy silence, in which I imagined I could hear breathing and the shuffling of many feet. Presently the smoke seemed to thin a little. People began to trail through, a few going up the steps past me. No one came down.

The sun slid a little further in the sky, the shadows crept out from their hiding places under the walls to stretch themselves across the stones, the smoke cleared and the sky arched over us, violet-blue, empty and cold. It was getting on for evening. Still I stood there, with the secretary and a couple of the footmen, alone at the bottom of the stairs.

Even so, it was Loricus who saw my husband first. "Ovidius Naso, mistress."

He was staggering down the steps, his eyes staring straight ahead around the huge slope of nose. His hair was disheveled, his toga dusty. Along his cheek ran a smear of dirt. I ran forward, reaching him just as his knees buckled on the lowest step.

If an actor had wanted to portray a man who had lost a contest with a god, he would have put on a mask as stretched with terror as my husband's face.

"My dear, my dear, what happened? Did you see Caesar? What did he say? Was it all a mistake?"

He did not speak. That in itself was strange. He was never silent: words meant everything to him, more than bread, or wine, or love itself.

He looked at me out of stiff white eyes. I didn't think he saw me.

But his lips were moving. At least he was trying to speak, though I had to lean closer to hear him. I thought he said, "It was red."

His hand went up to his cheek, and he stared at the color on his fingers. It wasn't dirt, it was blood.

'Oh, I see. You mean your wound." I dabbed at it with the corner of my sleeve. He looked at me blankly. He must have staggered against a wall or a doorway. He could hardly stand upright now. "Don't worry, my dear," I said, holding him like a child. "It's not bleeding now. It will be fine."

Behind me the slave touched my sleeve.

"Yes, Loricus, we have to get him home. Here. Take his arm."

So the two of us and our pathetic little band of servants half-dragged, half-led Publius Ovidius Naso, knight, magistrate, the finest poet in Rome, through the Forum. The orator had left the Rostra. At its foot the books made a layer of ash and smolder. The stinking smoke still coiled in threads near the ground, but it was thinner. The Praetorians had gone, but amid the long shadows a crowd still muttered.

We were nearly across, almost at the corner of the Basilica Aemilia when we heard the blare of music, followed by chariots rumbling across the stones. A terrible silence fell on the crowd. No one moved. Slowly every face turned to the open space.

Through the Forum came a funeral procession. Women wailing, mimes wearing ancestor masks, statues propped up in the chariots, weeping friends and dependents: a distinguished man. Then the veiled widow, supported by her sons, their togas pulled over their heads.

"Who?" I shouted into the terrible din.

"Titus Labienus," a man behind me said.

"How—how did he die?"

No one answered.

Slowly the funeral car rolled across the Forum. A togaed man was propped upright in it, eyes fixed straight ahead. As he passed people cried out in horror. Some averted their eyes or pulled their cloaks over their heads. Naso began to shake. Even the slave Loricus gasped and shuddered.

The air was suddenly cold, the day too bright. "He's alive," I whispered, but the silence was unbroken. I could see the man in the chariot breathing, though he did not move. Not even to look down at the burnt mess of his history as his wheels ground over it.

Tears forced themselves from my eyes. All over the Forum people turned away or stared at the stones. Many made signs against ill luck, and more than one started for the temples.

The funeral procession wound away, carrying the living man. We stood there until the last sound died into silence, trying to recover from the unluckiest sight we had ever seen.

"Come, my dear," I said. "We'll go home."

In a ghastly voice Naso said, "No."

"But you need rest, food—"

It was desperate but it was a command. "No."

"What then?"

There was life in his eyes now, and the beginning of a fight. "We will go to Fabius."

When Paullus Fabius Maximus married my cousin Marcia, he built a house to take her to on the Oppian Hill, near the Gardens of Maecenas. It was a new neighborhood, and newly fashionable, built by Maecenas over a vast paupers' cemetery Maecenas had filled in. The neighborhood was very elegant, looking over the Forum and across to the Palatine Hill, and many important people built there.

Fabius' house was among the largest. Its steep blank face ran nearly the whole length of the street, with a little dome in the center. Inside lay a complex of gardens and ponds, colonnades, fountains and paths, all overlooked by balconies, and decorated with flowering shrubs and the constant flutter of birds. I knew it well, for my parents died when I was young, and Marcia's family took me in. I was married, twice, once from their own house, and the second time, to Naso, from this one. A beautiful house, in every way suitable to Fabius' position and Marcia's: she is a cousin of Augustus Caesar.

Now, under the gathering darkness the house was full of shadows and I found myself wondering, for the first time, where exactly the cemetery had been, and though I knew they had been moved I kept feeling that the bodies were still there, a long way under our feet.

Fabius' library was shuttered against the sunset. The servant who showed us in made to lift the latches, but Naso, slumped into a chair, waved him away. His eyes were closed and his face was gray.

"Bring us some food," I said. "My husband hasn't eaten all day. Some soup, if the kitchen has it."

"Yes, mistress."

"No," said Naso. "Take away the light."

"The light, master?"

"I don't want it."

"Take it away," I said. "Can't you see? It hurts his eyes."

The servant bowed his way out.

It was very quiet, and without light time did not pass. In the air was a perfume of leather and wax and cedar oil. I could hear Naso's ragged breathing, and a drumming that after a time I recognized as his fingers on the arm of his chair. His weight shifted, the chair scraped restlessly along the floor. I reached out and took his hand.

Presently his breathing calmed.

"What—what did Caesar say?" I ventured. "Was it a mistake?"

With a flash of his old irony he said, "Oh, yes. But it appears the mistake was mine." He laughed, but I didn't understand the joke. It didn't sound very amusing.

"What do you mean? What mistake?"

In the darkness I could feel him shrug.

Presently he squeezed my hand. "Pinaria, I have bad news. I must leave Rome."

"Leave? Where are you going? You mean to your family in Sulmo, or something like that? Why? Is someone ill? Is that what Caesar wanted to tell you?"

"Pinaria, you must be strong. I have been sent away."

"Sent away? You mean—exiled?"

"Something like that. Exiles may go anywhere as long as it's not Rome. I am relegated. I have to go to one place and stay there." His voice was sharp with bitterness.

"Where? Why?"

Again in the dark the sense of a shrug.

"I must leave by morning."

"By morning?"

"That's right."

Words began to pour out of me. "That's impossible. Why? How would we do it? Let's go later—after the Saturnalia. That would be better, wouldn't it?"

"You don't understand. I have to leave by morning. If I don't—"

"Yes, I do understand. It just can't be done—there's too much to do. The packing, and the servants…The weaving room… Just closing up that takes days…"

I knew I was talking nonsense. Slowly I got command of myself. "What—what happens if you don't?"

He did not answer. His breathing was steady, but shallow and tense, and he had taken his hand from mine. I knew he was staring into the darkness.

Finally he began to talk.

"Listen, Pinaria. This happened to my father around the time when I was born. When the Civil War that followed Julius Caesar's death had been won by Mark Antony and Lepidus, and the young man who was then called Octavian."

"Caesar Augustus," I said.

"That was later. Then he was Octavian and one of the original three. The triumviri, they were called. The Board of Three. When they had won the war and come back to Rome they set themselves to eliminate any opposition. All over the city, men who had been on the other side were arrested or murdered or disappeared, and their families too sometimes. My father went to a dinner party, here in Rome, in the home of a man called Salvius, who had been a tribune. Salvius was famous for his parties: he was said to have the most beautiful dining room in Rome.

"That night he offered a toast: 'to the last of the dinner parties'." He said he didn't think there would be many in the future. Unlucky words. The soldiers came. They ordered the guests to remain still. Then they took Salvius by the hair, and over his own table they cut off his head.

"They what?" For some reason I was having trouble hearing what he said.

"They cut off his head. Listen, Pinaria. This is important. They cut off his head. The blood shot out across the room. The food, the tables, the guests were soaked. It was disgusting. Imagine the smell alone." I think I missed a few words. When I could hear again, he was saying, "...picked up Salvius' head to take with them, and ordered everyone not to move: no one did. To have disobeyed would have put them on the lists too."

"Why—why are you telling me this?"

His voice came to me calmly now. "I have to. Pinaria, you are too young to remember but you have to understand what is happening. And what might happen."

"No. I don't want to hear—"

"Yes. You have to. You must understand. My father and the others reclined there all night, watching the blood spout from the severed neck, then trickle, then dry. Most of them cried. One or two were sick. My father, when he got home, bathed himself for hours. After that he removed himself to a darkened room and would not speak to the household. My mother kept him alive on wine. He wouldn't eat. I don't suppose he actually could. It was a long time before he could forget enough to join them at a meal, and then, my brother said, he would eat nothing but gruel, like a child. At night, sometimes, even years later, we would hear him shouting in his sleep. And though he sent us—afterwards when things were quiet—to be educated here and to make our careers, he never came to Rome again.

"And he was lucky. He said that it was only that he had supported Mark Antony so publicly in the war that saved him. He had been the one to open the gates of our town to Antony's army. But there were many who had done as much, and they were killed. All over the city and in the country towns, thousands died, knights and senators mostly, but rich plebeians too—anyone whom the triumvirs hated or feared, or who had something they wanted."

"But that was a long time ago. And Augustus isn't like that any more." I swallowed, fighting an urge to finger my own neck. "Is he?"

In the darkness a soft laugh reached me. "Do you want to find out?"

So for a time we sat in silence again. I had no idea how long we waited. Perhaps it was not as long as I feared. I kept thinking that by dawn he had to be gone.

Presently light burst in on us, along with bustle and noise. The shutters crashed open, revealing the garden beyond, scarlet with the stain of the sunset. A draft of evening air swirled the curtains toward us. Someone began to straighten the desk and more servants scurried in carrying lamps. The room sprang to life.

It was a large room, full of beautiful objects lovingly cared for: a testimony to civilized living and the efficiency of my cousin Marcia's servants: Blue walls starred with gold; white bookcases to shoulder height, marble columns polished and gleaming like moonlight, a high ceiling draped and hung with lamps on long silver chains. In the middle a great, carved pearwood table as large and shiny as a lake floated on gilded feet in its own reflection on the floor.

Around the room busts of prominent poets ranged along the top of the shelves: it always gave me a start to see my husband's sightless eyes staring back at me from one of them, though I had seen it many times before. Beneath them, in the cases, every cubbyhole was filled with rolls, all bound in fine white leather and labeled with gold tags as thin as the paper. A fortune in books, more than the worth of apartment buildings or a factory full of slaves.

In the midst of this richness and beauty Fabius swept in, his toga still billowing around him as his attendant, lost in its thick woolen folds, struggled to keep it off the floor. At last the servant bowed himself out, and Fabius turned to us, his back to the pearwood table with his hands grasping the sides. He was as slim and as tense as a strung bow. He was a dark man, with an elegant head like an exercise in geometry, the fine prominent triangle of his nose balanced against the wedges of his cheekbones.

His family had been important in Rome for hundreds of years. For one of them, Fabius Maximus Allobrogicus, the first triumphal arch in the Forum had been set up: it was still there, we had passed it on the way to the Palatine, to the incomprehensible disaster our lives had become.

He himself had been consul, and proconsul of Asia, then legate to Spain and though he was a little younger, he was Augustus' friend. When Tiberius, Caesar's former son-in-law, was divorced and living in Rhodes in some kind of self-imposed exile a few years before, they had said in the Forum that Fabius was the only man Augustus trusted.

My husband stood up, to show respect. But Fabius with a warm glance at me, came around the table and embraced Naso, patting him gently on the shoulder several times, as if he were a horse.

"Forgive the delay. My boy is ill. But I heard about your trouble," Fabius said. He had pulled a silver tray across the table and was pouring wine into little silver cups decorated with vine leaves. All his gestures were short, sharp, and nervous and he smiled at Naso as if he thought Naso would have to see it from a long way away.

"It's absurd," said Naso, "a new thing: a god making a mistake."

"I'm glad to see that you are making jokes. Still, jokes about Augustus' godhead don't seem to be a good idea just now."

"No? Why not? You don't believe that nonsense either."

"That is irrelevant," Fabius said austerely. "It's a political question, don't you see, my friend?"

"That's why it's a joke."

Fabius gave him that distant smile.

"Look Fabius," Naso said. "We are civilized men. What do you expect me to do—howl?"

"No, of course not. Well. Where is he sending you?"

"Tomis."

"On the Black Sea. At the mouth of the Danube."

"Tomis?" I cried. "But that's not even in the Empire, is it? It's all wild tribes, and fighting and—"

Fabius caught sight of my face. "There's a Roman garrison. Nearby anyway. It ought to be safe enough. Nowadays." He caught sight of my face. "Don't worry, Pinaria. They've resettled a large number of the worst agitators down in Thrace. It's much quieter there now."

Fabius' hands had found something to occupy them: an arrow, long and black in the shaft, feathered in rusty red. In all that elegance and beauty it looked crude and dangerous. Some relic of his wars, I suppose. I wondered why it wasn't out in the atrium with the rest. "So, there's not going to be a trial. Pity. I would have spoken for you."

"Thank you, Fabius. I know you would."

"What exactly is he sending you away for?"

"For *The Art of Love*."

"I see."

"You do? It doesn't make any sense to me."

"Well, you know how insistent he's been about morality lately. Urging citizens to marry, and all that. Speeches in the Forum. Making examples of his own family. You can't exactly claim that your book is—elevating, can you?"

"*The Art of Love* has been out for ten years, Fabius. Why now?"

"You wrote it when you were going to Messalla's a lot, didn't you? Caesar wouldn't have touched Messalla. He tangled with him once and lost badly."

I knew that story too—Cotta's distinguished father had been appointed city prefect—an office Caesar created. When he resigned in a few days, saying he couldn't imagine what the duties might be and implying that whatever they were they were unconstitutional, Caesar was forced to accept the insult. In the end Messalla supported Caesar, but perhaps Fabius was right and Caesar had learned to leave him alone. Perhaps too, now that he was dead we had lost a protector that we had not known we had.

"All right, there's *The Art of Love*," Fabius was saying. "That's it? That's all?"

"He said it was something I saw."

"Something you saw?"

"That's what he said. And that he was a father."

"A father. What did he mean?"

"That the Senate voted him the title Father of His Country, I suppose."

Fabius arched his eyebrows. "Really? You must have done something…"

Naso glanced over at me. "You know what I've been doing, Fabius. My wife will tell you. Nothing but see my clients, go to Board meetings, talk to other people—you know, people in the mining and smelting business like us, neighbors in the country, that sort of thing. Write a little poetry. I have a very ordinary life, Fabius."

"Yes, I suppose so."

"Fabius," I said, "you told us you'd heard about our trouble. Are they talking about us in the city?"

He shook his head. "I've just come from the Palatine: Caesar told me."

"Ah," said Naso.

"Well, maybe he said why?" I asked.

"No. Naso was on a list, that's all."

Naso smiled grimly. "I see. A list. It's like the old days, isn't it?"

"Who else was on the list?"

"Audasius the bookseller."

"I know about that. Saw him today as they were nailing up his shop."

20

"I see. Then there's Junius Novatus—a letter purporting to be from Caesar's grandson in exile. Caesar says it's a forgery. And there's Cassius Severus—"

"Cassius? You mean for Labienus? How could he know about that? It only just happened."

Fabius shook his distinguished head. "Pamphlets. Caesar calls them libels on important men and women. He means Livia and Tiberius and all that Claudian connection."

Naso's face had tightened again. "He's been writing those things for years. He has a right to say what he wants. He's a Roman."

"Now it's treason."

"Words? Words are treason?"

Fabius lifted his shoulders in a graceful little shrug. "He wants me to prosecute Cassius for it."

"For treason?"

Maybe it was a warning to Naso that Fabius was conveying, because Naso looked terrible. His face looked like something made of wood, and his nose was stuck on with plaster. He stared at Fabius.

"Does he think—does he think I've committed treason too?"

Fabius gave the sort of smile a doctor does when the news is bad. "I hope not. Probably he'd have said if he thought that."

"I suppose so." It came out like a croak.

I was having trouble with my throat again. It must have made me miss a few words again, because Fabius was saying, "—his granddaughter Julia Aemilii."

"What about her?"

"I don't know. He didn't say any more, and I didn't like to ask. He was in a terrible mood."

The mark on Naso's cheek jumped into prominence. "I noticed that, Fabius."

Fabius even laughed. "Yes. I imagine you did."

There was a long silence while for some reason they both looked at me. Finally Fabius said, "Well, I'll talk to him. See what I can find out. I'm no Messalla, but perhaps I can get him to change his mind. After all, it's not really politics. A love poem. How bad can that be?"

"That's right. How bad can it be?"

"And look, can you fix this?" Fabius had his back to us, searching in his cubbies. Presently he drew out a book. "Here. *The Art of Love.*" He unrolled it across the table.

"If any Roman does not know
The art of being loved,
Let him study here…"

He looked up, smiling. "Wonderful work. But maybe you could fix…clean it up a bit? You have to admit, there are some passages…"

"No," I cried. "He can't. It came to him from a goddess."

"It's all right, Pinaria," my husband said.

"But it's not. It's your *work*. You are a priest. You mustn't. You can't. You—"

For a moment I thought I had convinced him and he would refuse, but he took the book and began to write quickly in the margins:

"Here. How does this sound? Right here at the beginning:

"Girls with bound hair, modest and young,
Married women in ruffled dresses
Hiding your feet—
My songs are not for you.
I sing of secret love, but love the law permits,
And in my words there will be no crime."

"Perfect," Fabius said, rolling up the book with a snap. "I can go to him with this and show him it's just a misunderstanding. That you are not challenging his authority in any way."

"What about Audasius?"

"Well, what about him?"

"As my wife points out, he was selling my books. He had the new one: *The Festivals.*"

"Oh, I see. I can take care of that. We'll say that what Audasius is selling is a forgery. You never wrote whatever it is that is the problem in that book either. That should do it, shouldn't it?"

I suppose it was an example of Fabius' famous diplomacy and subtlety but it seemed very terrible to me. Before my eyes I saw Naso in his own library, binding his forehead with ribbons like a priest, and making an offering to the Venus, his special goddess. He believed in his poetry. He believed he was the confidante of a deity. I began to cry. "He's going to renounce his own book, Fabius?"

"Not the whole thing," Naso said. "Just a few passages." He smiled. Smiled. "I can write more."

Without taking his eyes from Naso, Fabius said, "Listen, Pinaria, why don't you go talk to Marcia? She might have some things for Naso to take with him or something—" He didn't really care if she did, but I could see that they wanted to be alone. Fabius did not look at me, but Naso handed me a square of linen for my tears and squeezed my hand.

I walked out into the peristyle garden. Here the shadows lay deep in winter quiet and the last of the sunset dyed the fishpond a cold transparent blue, sparked by the garnet and gold of the sky. Down at the end something was still roiling the pond, but the garden was empty.

So was the atrium, drowned in shadow and smelling coldly of winter stone and water. In the echoing dining room braziers and lamps were lit festively for a dinner party but the cushions were plumped unwrinkled on the couches, the plates bare, the baskets of bread slowly going stale.

At the room of Marcia and Fabius' young son Persicus I found a bustle of nurses and maids. The doctor—tall, bearded, Greek— stooped over the bed, holding the boy's thin wrist with a worried look. The little boy tossed and fretted, his voice a feeble scratch of sound. Maids shuffled in and out laden with linen, a kitchen boy came clattering in with a steaming pot—reminding me that Naso had had nothing to eat all day—the doctor's assistant was stirring some hideous-smelling stuff over a brazier.

But somehow the center of the room was the woman who sat in a kind of waking dream by the side of the bed. Her sea-colored eyes were on the opposite wall, and her head was tilted to listen to something no one else was hearing. There was something vague in her, even in her dress, that floated a bit, leaving her outline indistinct in the dim light of the room. Her hair too was constantly escaping from its pins, its soft gray tendrils curling around her face. Naso teases—teased—her and says it's blond, calling her "Minerva." He also says she's brilliant. I don't know how he knows—mostly she seems sweet and a little lost to me.

At last she rose and came to the door, embracing me gently.

"How is your son?"

"Better. For now." She sighed. "He's always sick, Pinni."

"Lots of children are, and they outgrow it. He will too."

"Perhaps," she said. "I heard about your trouble, Pinni. Livia told me. I'm very sorry."

"Thank you. There seems to be a lot going on. Did she say anything else?"

But Marcia wasn't interested in this. "Pinni, are you going with your husband?"

It jolted me. And suddenly I felt the floor hollow under my feet. "Of course. Of course I am. Can you—do you think Livia could talk to Augustus?"

"Yes, of course." She looked sad and sweet and a little blurry. "You have to go. He's your husband. It's your duty as a Roman wife. Oh, Pinni, have you thought? The Black Sea. We'll never see each other again."

The men had left Fabius' office and were deep in conversation in the colonnade.

Their voices were low, but I have quick ears. "Look what happened to Labienus," Fabius was saying.

Naso gave him his ironic smile. "I suppose it's a consolation. We can always try that if we need to."

"Try what?" I cried. "Do you mean parading a false funeral through the Forum? No, I see you don't. What...what else has happened to Labienus?"

Fabius' voice was suddenly loud. "Ah, there you are, ladies. Had a nice talk? Now, Pinaria, my dear, I want you to go home and

look after Naso tonight. Don't worry. Just go home and wait quietly
there. I'll send word as soon as I have gotten this ridiculous mistake
taken care of."

"But, Fabius—"

"I've already told your man: if there's a delay and he has to
leave—just for a short time, I swear it as a Roman citizen, Pinaria—
then you will come and stay with us. Isn't that right, Marcia?"

Marcia was looking across the atrium toward the dining room.
It seemed to take her whole attention.

"Marcia?" There was command in Fabius' voice. Sometimes,
trying to get Marcia to answer, I felt the same.

"But isn't she going with Naso, Fabius?"

"Yes," I said. "Of course I am."

"No," Fabius said. "She'll stay with us."

"Thank you," Naso said. "I don't know how I can ever repay
you—"

I was crying again. "But, my dear, I am going with you."

Fabius put his arm around my shoulder. "Anyway, it won't
come to that. You just go home now and wait. I'll let you know
as soon as I do."

Outside it was already evening and the air was chill. A star, remote and pale, hung low in the west, just above the embers of the
now-faded sunset, and in the east the full moon had risen. In the
shadows where the dying sun did not reach, its light was already
beginning to silver the stones.

Naso had started up the street.

"No, my dear. This way—here, let me take your arm. We'll
go home and get you some of that soup. You haven't had anything all day."

"What? Oh. No, I'm all right. You go home. I have to go see
Cassius."

I thought of the packing, the money to find, the servants that
would have to be told and the ones that would have to be chosen for
the trip. Naso's clothes, and mine. Food for the journey. So much to
do. And night was already here.

But five steps down the way I turned back. "What happened to Labienus?" I said.

"Are you sure you want to know?"

"Yes. Yes, of course I do. I'm not a child."

"My dear ch—My dear." I don't know why he tried to smile. I am quite a bit younger than he, but I am a married woman and a Roman matron. Failing, he gave up and patted my shoulder instead. "I assure you, you really don't want to know. I wish I didn't myself."

"Please tell me. I'll find out anyway, won't I? The whole city must know."

"Very well. Labienus said he had no wish to outlive his words. He has had himself walled up in his family tomb. He's dying there now."

Dying. Like the day. Like the night, that had already begun.

"Oh," I cried. "How you must feel! The packing will wait. I'll come to Cassius' too."

We came by back ways to Cassius' house, in case someone was following us. I didn't see anyone, but I suppose I wouldn't have. The streets were still crowded anyway.

Cassius had an atrium as big as an exercise ground, but decorated in the most understated taste: his walls were painted in delicate pastel colors of scenes at Baiae and Capri, and hung with pale curtains. The lamps were graceful, and the braziers burned applewood charcoal sprinkled with dried rose petals.

Cassius and his family must have been at dinner, for presently he came in, wiping his mouth on a square of linen so fine I could see his fingers through it. But Cassius close up was a shock: a huge man with a thick neck and a bald head, set on shoulders as muscled as a gladiator's. He had a fighter's broken nose and heavy, ridged brow too.

"Ovidius Naso," he said, coming forward and embracing him, "this is indeed a pleasure."

His voice was another astonishment. It was full and strong, as you would expect from his body, but it had a quality of such sweetness it seemed to take the fear and pain out of the day, so that all I wanted was to go on standing in his atrium, listening to him talk.

My husband embraced him as a brother, which, in misfortune they now were, but I could see that Cassius did not know it yet.

"And this exquisite creature is your wife? I always said you were a lucky man. Here, let me call my daughter-in-law: she's acting as my hostess these days—to what do I owe this honor?"

Naso's long mouth twitched. "It's not an honor, I'm afraid. Just the opposite—it's a shame that brings me here. I've just come from Fabius Maximus."

The great head lowered like a bull about to charge. "That's a shame, all right. Horrible man: half eloquent, half handsome, half rich: the only thing he is completely is completely without character of any kind."
"He's my wife's kinsman, Cassius."

I thought for a moment Cassius might hurl himself at my feet like a slave asking for pardon, but of course he had too much taste for that. Instead he bent over my hand. "Beautiful lady, I am a fool. I am a monster. Look at me—you can see that nothing intelligent could come from an ox like me."

"Think nothing of it, Cassius Severus." He and Fabius were old enemies, which is why I had never met him before. I had heard about him of course; Fabius disliked his extravagant style of speech. Well, extravagant it certainly was, but no one could have doubted that his apology was sincere.

"It's not Fabius we've come about, exactly, Cassius," my husband said. "It's Augustus. I—I can't say this, Cassius."

"Can't say what? Come on, old man, choke it out."

Naso was pinching the bridge of his nose. It did no good: I could see the glitter of water under his eye.

"He told Fabius—he told Fabius that he wanted him to prosecute you."

"Fabius? Prosecute me? For what? Because I said I knew Labienus' works by heart? All right, I grant you, Titus Labienus can be pretty forceful—'Titus Rabienus' I used to call him—but a Roman has the right to say what he likes. It's not a crime. It had never been a crime and Augustus, for all his power, will never get a jury to say it is. It's a novel thing, isn't it—this punishing literature by burning it alive? I do know Labienus' books by heart, and I'll recite them from beginning to end. In the Forum—all right, if he sends in the Praetorians again I'll do it in the Curia—the first chance I get. It's the only good thing in this whole ugly business—that Labienus knew that I would before he immured himself."

"It's not about Labienus. It's for treason."

"Treason?"

"I'm afraid so. I'm sorry, Cassius."

"Treason." Slowly Cassius' eyes began to bulge. His neck swelled. He clenched his fists. Hunching his thick shoulders, he began to pace around the pool, stamping his feet and dancing a step or two. Once he stopped motionless and stared straight ahead. Once he raised his arms and slammed his hand at his palm. For a while he just stood, bouncing lightly on the balls of his feet and working the muscles in his neck.

Presently he marched himself back. He was still glowering and his lumpy face was knotted like a ball of inferior wool, but he spoke very carefully in that beautiful voice. "And just what does Augustus think I've done that is treasonous?"

"You wrote some pamphlets."

"Well?"

"And he thinks they libeled some important people."

"They were supposed to. I can't stand Livia and all that Claudian crowd. A more arrogant bunch never peacocked through the City with an entourage long enough for a Persian satrap, let alone a Roman consular. And that son of hers, Tiberius…"

"I understand. But now it's a crime."

"It's a crime to dislike the Claudians? That's a good one."

"Or to write about them."

"I don't understand. Words are treason?"

"It looks like it."

"This is Augustus' revenge for Labienus, isn't it?"

"Labienus was the first of us, that much is clear. But I'm not sure…There's something more going on now. I'm a criminal too, did you know? For *The Art of Love.*"

"The *what*?"

"I know. It hasn't even got anything to do with politics."

Instantly Cassius said, "I'll speak for you at your trial."

"Thank you, Cassius Severus. Thank you." Naso turned his head away. "But there isn't going to be any trial. I have to leave tonight."

"What do you mean? How can there not be a trial?"

"I don't know. And it's not legal. Of course. But you know I have to go."

"What happens if you don't? What if you stay and defend yourself?"

But he knew the answer. He groped for a chair and lowered himself into it, looking suddenly like a gladiator who has heard the crowd calling for his opponent. "The proscriptions have come back, is that what you're saying?"

"I fear so."

But Cassius wasn't beaten yet. In spite of his gentleness, he was what he looked: a very tough man.

"I'm not sure you haven't some kind of weapon. Let's look at it. There has to be something political in it. Here, have a drink. We need it. Dear lady, a little water with that? Tell me when. So what's political in *The Art of Love*?"

Naso was drumming his fingers again. "Nothing whatever. Nothing. How could there be?"

"I know." Another sweet smile came over his battered face.

"...The years flow by like water to the sea
Neither, once it has gone, can anyone call back the wave
Or return the hour that has passed.
Enjoy your youth
It slips away on a quick foot
And nothing is as good later as it was at first.
These withered stalks, now white with age,
I saw here when they were violets:
From this thornbush a wreath of flowers was once given to me...

"Lovely thing. Who could bear to harm it?" He cupped the words in his thick hands, sheltering them.

"You know the poem?"

"Of course. It's one of those I've committed to memory. I know it's not political. But all the same, there has to be a reason."

There was a silence while they looked at each other. Finally Naso shrugged. "Fabius thinks he's becoming obsessed with morality in his old age. Maybe that's it. He does love lectures about old-fashioned Roman values. And remember that day he harangued us knights in the Forum about having children and being good solid Romans and all that?"

"Fabius." It was a snort. But he was too intelligent and too fair-minded to say he was wrong.

"Maybe so. But it doesn't explain everything. He exiled his granddaughter tonight. I heard it in the Forum on the way home."

"Fabius said he heard something about that too. What was it for?"

Cassius was studying him. "He said it was adultery."

"Did she commit adultery? I don't keep up with those circles much any more. I live quietly at home."

"Well, don't you think there must be a connection?"

"With me? How could there be? As I said, I live very quietly. I don't know those people."

There was a silence while Cassius stared at us. All the time his hands were flexing, as if he might like to strangle something. But when he spoke it was in a conversational tone.

"Do you know Decimus Junius Silanus?"

"Who?"

Cassius merely stared at him from under his heavy brow.

"Well, you know, I think I may have seen him at dinner parties. Do we know him, Pinaria?"

"I have met his mother, I think. His older brother is someone important, isn't he?"

"Yes, dear lady. He's close to Tiberius and that crowd." Cassius shrugged. "Someone named Plautius Rufus is accused of aiding Decimus in the adultery. He's been exiled. He never went home—just hired a wagon and headed for the port."

"Never heard of him. Junius Silanus is exiled too then?"

"Not so far. No."

"What is his punishment, then?"

"Nothing. Nothing is happening to him at all."

"Nothing? If he committed adultery with her isn't that strange?"

Cassius shrugged his heavy shoulders. "What about the rest of the family? You haven't had any contact with Augustus' grandson in exile?"

"Agrippa Postumus? No. How could I have? He's been on that island for a year."

"No letters, nothing like that?"

"How could I have? I don't understand what is going on at all."

"You don't?"

"No, Cassius. Of course not. I haven't any more idea than anyone else."

"Ah, well, my friend, if you don't, I certainly don't." The huge body shifted as he stood up. "I'm very sorry we had to meet like this. I know we haven't been close—I suppose it's because of Fabius—but I always admired you. I thought you might be the next Horace, you know. Make a splendid career out of your poetry. Earn Augustus' gratitude. My dear fellow, you deserve it. You have every advantage: You never write anything even remotely political, and your work is truly something for the ages. You are married to this beautiful lady, the cousin of Augustus' cousin." It was odd: he looked so sad when he said this.

"I thought I'd make a career like that too, Cassius."

"Ah, well. Things go wrong in this age of iron, don't they? Thank you for warning me. I will do what I can to prepare my defense."

His courtesy, and his courage, extended to sending an escort with us, for it was dark now, and the stars were appearing in a sky that only distantly remembered the blue of day. Gods and heroes strode silently overhead; down below we walked among pools of torchlight through streets where cloaked figures hurried to errands I could not guess and covered chairs were carried to unknown houses. In the darkness under porticoes women called in doves' voices and I could hear the chink of coins as we passed, but there was a note of desperation in the voices and the coins were few.

Our house looked like a beehive that someone has knocked over. The shops on either side had long since closed and shuttered, and no one had lit the torches at our entrance. As we approached the door was flung open, but the servant was one of the kitchen boys and gaped at us as if he had never seen us before. Inside I could hear noises: cries and thumps, and the crash of something heavy on the tile floor.

"Have they come already?" I cried, clutching my husband's arm. "We had till morning."

He patted my hand, but he was moving quickly, through the entryway and into the atrium.

There everything was truly chaos. Smoke hung in acrid rags in the air from something trailing out of a brazier. As we came in, kitchen utensils—of all things—that had been heaped on a bench slid gently toward the floor, making a tremendous clatter as they struck. I peered with stinging eyes through the fumes. Someone had started to pack loaves of bread and sticks of sausage, but run off in the middle of the job.

Naso's secretary Loricus was carefully arranging books in a case, but every now and then he stopped and stared off into the distance. Two maids came in carrying linens. When they reached the middle of the room they just dropped their burden with a slap and stood there like a pair of Niobes, clutching each other and weeping. Naso had started to cough.

There is nothing worse than a panic among the servants. "Here. Stop. Bring us some soup," I commanded.

"No," Naso said. "No food. There's no time."

"My dear, you have had nothing all day. You must eat. And the servants need something to do."

Slowly the chaos settled a little. The crowd of servants dispersed. We made our way into the atrium.

On the steps my daughter Perilla was waiting. Already at eight years old she was tall. I had been tall too at her age. Her small head was held up straight on a white and vulnerable neck. She did not like to show that she was afraid. But I felt her hand slip into mine.

"Mother, what is the matter?"

"I—I don't know for sure what it is yet. May I come tell you later? I have to ask your stepfather, you see."

Wise, she accepted this. I don't know if she believed me. But she hugged me, and allowed herself to be led away.

Someone was waiting for us: my heart leapt up. It might be Fabius' messenger. "Is there news?" I cried.

"News?" Emerging through the smoke was my cousin Pompeius Macer, Augustus' chief librarian and one of my husband's closest friends. He is a large man with pale emphatic features and a heavy mouth. His lower lip always looks moist and his expression tightly woven with concern.

"What news did you mean, Pinaria?"

"Oh, Macer, I'm so glad you are here. Thank you."

"Always glad to see you, Pinaria. Naso, I heard. I had to come."
Macer bent to embrace him.

"Please," I said. "Sit down. We can still find you a drink, in all this mess."

Naso sat heavily, but he smiled at my cousin. "You are the only one to show up tonight, Macer. No one else has cared. Or cared to take the risk."

I had been hoping he wouldn't realize that. There was, for example, no sign of Cotta. And all those young poets he had helped, the scholarly or literary men who thronged our dining room arguing about poetry and politics and whatever men talk about when the women aren't there, all the people who invited him to parties to hear his witty talk and his beautiful verse, all of them had stayed away. He was alone. He had been alone all evening, and it was getting late.

I had the servants send in soup and wine. Naso ignored it, then suddenly, taking his bread, ate everything before him.

Macer was asking what had happened, though I could see that he knew already. Perhaps he thought it would help Naso to speak of it.

"So, it's a poem. Well, you've written some wonderful ones.

"Arma gravi numero violentaque bella parabam....
Of arms and violent war
I was prepared to talk

33

Heroic subject, suited to my verse :
The second line was equal to the first.
But laughing Cupid, snatched, they say,
One beat away…"

Naso gave him a wicked little grin. "*The Love Affairs.*"

Macer too was smiling. "You are amazing. Not everyone would try a parody of *The Aeneid*—only the greatest epic poem ever written in our language…Arma virumque cano, Troiae qui primus ab oris…" He hummed a little more to himself. "But you can't expect Caesar to like it. He used it to make himself look good. Legitimate. Descended from Aeneas—"

Naso smiled. "You don't think Virgil meant it for that?"

"Maybe so. But then why on earth would Caesar like your parody—your mockery—of it really, however brilliant and joyous and amusing it is?"

Naso sighed. "Virgil would have liked it, though. I saw him once. He looked like a tough, you know? Not at all what you'd expect. I imagine he had a sense of humor after all. But whatever you think of it, evidently Caesar hasn't got a problem with that one. Or any of the others. Just *The Art of Love.*"

"Well, why? Don't you think that's strange?"

I thought that frightening vagueness might creep back into Naso's eyes, but Macer was wiser than I and I actually saw my husband smile.

"Well, a god, after all—who knows how a god might think? Or what offends them?"

Macer laughed and after a little began to talk of their travels in Asia when they were young. When I slipped away they hardly noticed.

Of course the house needed organizing. I found my housekeeper and gave some orders. Pretty quickly the house settled down: I think everyone felt better for having something to do. As I passed through the atrium I saw that my uncle Pinarius Rufus had arrived, and heard Macer say, "You'll be able to visit the site again," so I knew they must have been talking about Macer's epic "*Troy*". Naso was looking livelier too, even happy. I left before I had to see him remember why he would be traveling to the Hellespont.

I stopped at the door of my daughter's room to check on her. It was a good thing I did: the nightlight had gone out. In the disorder of the evening no one had refilled the lamp. "Mother?" her little voice piped out at me from the darkness.

I found the edge of the bed and sat down. "Yes, sweetheart?" Her forehead was hot and dry, and her hand clutched mine tightly.

"Are we going to Tomis, Mother? The maids said."

How do they know these things? But they always do.

"Why, sweetheart? Don't you want to?"

My Perilla is a grave child, thoughtful and deep. She considered the question. "Naso is going?"

"Don't worry. Your stepfather probably won't have to go. We are waiting to hear from Fabius Maximus, who is helping us. He's going to straighten everything out. It's just a mistake—we're just waiting for a word."

She had no faith in this. In fact, she ignored it altogether.

"And you? Are you going too?"

And there it was. I had a duty to my husband, there was no question of that. But equally I had one to my child. It tore me, and I thought I would rather be crucified than bear this pain. I could not leave her, I could not go. But Naso would be cast out in a wilderness, betrayed and alone. And among the people who betrayed him I would have to stand, my head forever bent in shame, and my heart a desert of loneliness.

"Naso says I should stay here."

She must have understood something of what I was feeling, for she said bravely, "Oh, no, Mother, we must go. He is—he is our friend."

Please gods, I thought, don't let me break down, not in front of the child. But tears were running down my cheeks all the same. "Yes. Yes, he is. But how can we? You must find a husband, you must marry and have your own home, your own children."

"That's all right, Mother. There will be loads of people there." But even her courage, which was like a small lion's, had run out. "Mother, are there bears there? Is it always dark? Is there snow?"

"Of course not. Why do you think that?"

"The maids said. They said they know a soldier who was there."

"Well, they're just making up stories. It's a—a very nice city. Ships go there, from Athens, and Alexandria, and all over the world. It's a little colder than here, but it will be fun. We can wear furs, and make a snow house. I've seen people do that up in the mountains. You'll see—" But all the time I knew I was lying, for how could I take her there, where there was no one and nothing for her at all?

I wanted to cry, thinking that life was going to be full of these tearings and sufferings now, and there was no time. No time to think of my family—or Naso's: he had a daughter and grandchildren in Libya that had to be told—no time to think of what life would be in a wilderness, or of what we would be leaving behind. If I went. If Naso went alone.

No time to make the right decisions.

I thought of Fabius and his promise to help us. But the night was passing, and we had heard nothing.

Suddenly I couldn't bear it any longer. I picked up a cloak and murmured to the doorman, "I'm going out for a while. Tell my husband if he asks. I will get back as soon as I can."

I do not think that ever in my life have I been in the streets without someone, even if only a maid, to accompany me. The darkness made the way unfamiliar and I could not be sure where I was. All around me I heard voices, noises, cries. I could not make sense of them. Every footfall seemed to me a pursuer, every glance a condemnation.

Over the eastern horizon the full moon was rising into a ragged hem of cloud. The air felt heavy and chill, and I could smell moisture in it. It would rain by morning. Here and there a tavern or a shop was open to the street, though the crowds passed and few people stopped. Occasionally a solitary workman drank at an open bar, and once I saw a woman also lift a cup to her lips. Somewhere a dog barked, uneasy in the coagulating air. Even the torches felt it, smoking in their brackets at corners or the doorways of important houses.

In the uncertain light, figures, cloaked like me, flickered in and out of shadow. Some were women, poor and shabby, but respectable—matrons with children and grandchildren at home, or young wives on late errands, too poor to afford a servant to carry their packages, or a torch. No one paid the slightest attention; the men in the street shouldered past them without comment or concern. All the same I could not shake off the idea that people were watching me: my clothes were too good, my hem too long, my shoes too thin.

Presently the crowd thickened and began to clot. People were all around me now. Under hoods or the edges of togas eyes flashed, iridescent as fishes turning under water. I heard breathing. No one looked at anyone else. No one spoke. All the same, as if by agreement, everyone was moving, all in the same direction. In a short time the crowd was too thick to fight, and I was carried along with it, wherever we were going.

Perhaps it was the darkness, lit so sparsely and intermittently by the torches, but I did not recognize any landmarks. We climbed a hill—an easy thing to do in Rome, but I could not tell which one this was. Buildings leaned over me, the entrance to a street loomed, filled with sighing and the close warmth of many bodies. I hesitated but an elbow struck me in the back; someone muttered behind me, my toe was ground into the stone. There was no way I could turn back.

The street was narrow and deeply rutted, filled like a river gorge from wall to wall. All the same, after a while I found myself near the front among hundreds of people. Every one of us was staring at the doorway at the end.

Unlike most this house had no shops on either side—just a high blank stucco face. Torches fluttered and crackled over the door. A Praetorian had planted himself squarely on his feet on the step. He wore a toga, as they all do: Naso has always said it was because they want to pretend that they aren't soldiers. But unlike normal civilians he carried a sword. His hand rested on the hilt now and his eyes went around the circle of our faces. The crowd muttered in response.

Beside me a woman wrapped in a man's cheap, rough toga balled her fist in front of her and shook it at the Praetorian.

"Excuse me," I said, taking a chance, "where are we? Whose house is this?"

Her eyes swiveled toward me and she clapped her mouth together hard. A man in a leather apron leaned forward and studied my face. "It's Caesar's granddaughter's."

"Julia Aemilii's? Fabius mentioned something—"

"Fabius? Fabius who?"

"I'm sorry. It's just that I've seen Julia going through the Forum sometimes, with her friends."

"We all have." The togaed woman let out her breath. It smelled of onions.

"And this is her house? What is happening?"

The carpenter, or whatever he was, shrugged. The woman said in a grating voice, "He exiled her mother. His only child. That beautiful princess."

He seemed prepared to argue this. "Well, she committed adultery. He had a right. The father is the head of the family."

I thought the woman was going to spit. "Head of the family? What family? Where are they? What has he done to them?"

"What *has* he done?" I asked, consumed with curiosity.

The woman snorted down her nostrils with contempt. "Ask yourself. All dead, aren't they? Or sent away. The mother locked away in the south somewhere, the brother in prison on an island. And now this one too."

From inside noises were coming. Voices, someone shouting. The crowd let out a breath like a wind issuing from a cave, and pressed a little closer.

"Out of the way," the Praetorian shouted, shoving us back. I was pushed against the leather apron. The woman in the toga disappeared, replaced by a pair of thinly dressed girls with tracks of black kohl running down their cheeks. No one spoke.

At the doorway appeared an escort of four more Guards, followed by what in the flare of the torches I first took to be a child. But it was a dwarf, a tiny man hardly as high as my hip, with a large head and short plump arms. When he saw the crowd he raised his fist at the backs of the Praetorians with his thumb showing in an obscene gesture, then grinned.

The crowd laughed uneasily.

Next came two more Praetorians; between them a woman, bareheaded, chin in the air. She was small and delicately made, her eyes large and intelligent, her face finely formed. She looked like the statues of her grandfather, and she had the same proud, level glance. When it fell on the crowd it did not soften, though they were calling her name, softly, so as to show they shared her grief: "Julia. Julia Aemilii."

Slowly she spread out her hands.

"My friends—" Her voice was as gentle as theirs.

"Move along," the Guard said.

She raised her head to give him a look of utter contempt. In the torchlight I caught the glitter of a single tear, flashing like a pomegranate seed on her cheek.

A path opened in the crowd, and she was gone, swallowed up by the backs of the Guards.

The crowd was sobbing now, weeping openly, crying at the Praetorians with anger. "Bring her back. Bring her back." In a moment they would be shouting.

The Praetorian at the door, finding himself alone in the street, shifted his weight, and I heard a little scrape as he drew his sword part way from the scabbard.

Behind him two more Guards appeared, naked swords in hand, their togas suddenly white in the gloom. They took up positions on either side of the door. Another escort came through, this time with a group: a tall, cloaked woman, obviously an aristocrat, and two or three female servants. With them came a young girl. Her they had also veiled, but the crowd knew who she was: "Aemilia," they breathed. She shot them a terrified glance from under the thin cloth, but they meant it kindly and she knew it. She was, after all, Julia Aemilii's daughter. She even managed a frightened little smile before they hustled her off.

"Is she exiled too?" I whispered to the woman next to me.

"Going to relatives."

"Poor child." It seemed worse than exile, and the tall woman had looked stern and unloving.

For a long time nothing happened. I don't know why we stayed. But the Guards had not moved, and the house still gaped open. There was something more to come.

The crowd knew it before I did. Their voices rose: women wailed, men shouted. I could see nothing. Around me the noise was rising in pitch and intensity. The sound beat against the walls, making a rhythm, a river roaring in darkness, tossed with a flotsam of shrieks and cries. The torches ripped, pouring shadow over us, the stars had been blotted out by the smoke so that we grieved in a cave now, not a chasm.

Then silence. It grew from us, where we stood near the door, traveling back through the mass of people, until the whole street was hushed. The torches hissed and stood upright, the light fell down on our cloaked forms like rain. From the house came a litter under drawn swords. The curtains were closed. As they crossed the sill the first porter stumbled. The curtains bellied out. The guard was shouting, but it was too late. We could see the whole litter now. On it a man's body lay. His eyes were open to the blackness of the sky. A trail of blood ran down his dangling arm, but it was dull and dark. It would never run again.

No one spoke. We knew who it was. Lucius Aemilius Paullus. He had been consul a few years before: we had all seen him in the Forum, proud and dignified. A perfect Roman. The husband of the Emperor's granddaughter.

Into the heavy sorrow the soldiers strode, raising our anger like dust with every step. The sound echoed off the walls as they marched down the street. We all watched. No one moved to close the gap behind them. No one said anything. But when they reached the end of the street and turned away, a roar came out of us, a bellow of horror and grief. They must have heard it on the Palatine. I hope they did.

Then it was over. Someone closed the door of the house. The rest of us stood a little longer, watching the blank wall. Then bit by bit we moved away down the street. Some were crying quietly, some were staring straight ahead, some of the men were swearing. All of us knew we had seen the death of more than a man.

It was late. Moonlight hazed through cloud, halfway down in the west. Past the ninth hour of the night, I guessed. Only a few men hurried through the streets now, and no women that I could see, though at the end of an intersection a litter passed, curtained in gauze and attended by torchlight and music. Someone going home from a party. The sound trailed away, leaving silence behind it. Silence and cold.

It was cold in our house too. No one had stoked the furnaces and the chill came up from the floor. A pungent smoke trailed through the atrium. In a brazier someone had been burning scraps of vellum.

"What's going on? What are you doing?" I could see the ends of a roll, hanging from the stand. He had been burning more of his books. "Oh, no, you mustn't," I cried, trying to pull them from the fire. I snatched my fingers back, putting their burnt tips to my mouth, but I was still holding on to the shreds. Bits of the smolder were still visible. Words winked up at me. "Kalends. July 1st." "Caesa...." Something that might have been "following" or "next..." "Son."

"What is this? It's *The Festivals*, isn't it? Why are you burning that?"

Naso was slumped on a bench, his deep eyes sunken in their sockets, his nose gleaming. Without looking at me he said, "It's nothing. Don't bother about it. Nothing."

But he was too late. Pompeius Macer was already saying, "He just thought the poem was a little dangerous, that's all."

"Augustus said so?"

"Pinaria, forget it," Naso said. "It doesn't mean anything. It isn't up to my standard, that's all."

"I always thought it was. And you never said that before—"

Pompeius stood up and took my hand. Like all that side of my family he is tall, and he seemed to loom over me. "Pinaria, I'm sorry. I seem to have worried you. And I have stayed too long. You must need your rest."

Naso got slowly to his feet. "Thank you for coming, Pompeius. So many would not have. So many didn't."

My cousin looked over our heads in the direction of the door. "I—ah, Naso, I—" He lowered his gaze and glanced at me, then back to my husband. "Look, I'll take care of it. What we were talking about. I'll see to it. Don't worry about a thing. No, don't show me out. I know the way."

I wondered if he was going to run down the hall to the door, but he recalled himself and embraced Naso as if he had all the time in the world. "Don't worry. It will all blow over. You'll be home before you know it."

Then he was gone.

"I'll know it," Naso said. "I'll know every hour of it."

"What did Pompeius mean, he'd take care of it? Take care of what?"

He turned to me. He wasn't smiling now. His cheeks had fallen into hollows I had never seen before, and his mouth was as hard as a carving.

"He said he would see to it that my books were not pulled from the public libraries."

"Oh, that's good. That's so good of him. I—I didn't like to think of—what might happen to them." Pompeius Macer was the custodian of the libraries that Augustus founded and maintained, except for the one in Augustus' own house, his personal library. So at least Naso would not have to see his own words destroyed.

"Has there been any word from Fabius?"

"No. Rufus has gone to his house to see if there is anything he can do. But I haven't heard from either of them yet."

I could feel him trembling beside me, touching my arm, my side. Our knees rested together.

"Did anyone else come?"

"Gellius—came to gloat. Your uncle Rufus. He cried. I wish I could."

His hand lay loosely on his thigh. I have always thought it beautifully shaped, the fingers flat at the ends and the whole hand rather square. A few dark hairs curled along the back and above the knuckles, catching the light like threads of gold. His wrist was thin and wiry. He was not a man you would call handsome in the conventional sense, but all the shapes of his body were very well made, his feet arched, his legs long and muscled, his shoulders wide. Even at fifty, growing more solid, he stood and sat with comfortable authority. But when I looked into his face, I did not know him.

"Come," I said. "Let's go to bed. We need some rest."

The servants were in our room, the clothes were still stacked everywhere. My maid, flushed under her dark skin, removed mine from the bed. Naso's servant was folding his toga with lavender and heading out the door.

"Where are you going with that?" Naso said between his teeth.

"I—master, I thought, since you wouldn't need…since you were…I was going to put it away until you come back."

"I will wear it. I am not a criminal. I am a Roman citizen. I still have my rights."

"Yes, master." He dropped it as if it burnt his hands.

At last they were gone. I drew the curtains and blew out all the lights but one. This I set on the table by the bed, a carved shell filled with rose oil. The room closed around us.

"I went to Julia's house tonight," I said. Always, in that room, in that safe space, I had told him everything. And always he had held me in his strong arms, protecting me.

This time it was different. He went very still. "Why did you do that?"

"You sound angry."

"Do I. I wonder why."

"Have I done something wrong?"

"I don't know. What were you doing there?"

"I didn't mean to go. I was just—out. Walking. There was a crowd, so I stopped to watch."

He did the one thing I would never have expected. He laughed. "And what did you find out?"

"I never got close to her. First there were all those people. Then the Praetorians were there. They led her away, and her daughter Aemilia. Her husband is dead."

He was not surprised, but I felt his attention leave me. I could not bear the loneliness. I wanted to shout to him to come back. Instead I asked, "What did you think I would have been doing?" My voice came out shaky and thin.

"Nothing," he said absently.

"Nothing? But you were angry just now. No, don't go away like that. Tell me. I have a right to know."

"I have to go away. I'll be killed if I don't."

"Oh, my dear, I didn't mean it. I just meant go away in your mind—I wanted you to tell me what you know—"

"There's nothing to tell." A strange smile stretched across his face. "Nothing at all. Come, my dear, it's time for bed."

He had undressed. In the dim light he was dusted with gold and shadow. The hairs on his chest shone, running down to darkness under his belly, and shadows pooled there, the color of wine.

He watched me pull the pins from my hair. "I should shave," he said, running his hand over his chin.

"That means calling the servants again and all that—it's not worth it."

"You won't mind?"

"What would Julia have told me?" I let fall my dress.

"Nothing. Ahh. No matter what, I am a lucky man."

"But don't you think it's strange that she's being sent away at the same time? Don't you feel that something is going on?"

He smiled. "No, why? He's sending away a lot of people, and prosecuting others. What connection could there be? Listen, Pinaria."

He sang a few lines from one of his poems—from a book he called *The Love Affairs*. The first time we lay together in one bed he sang it and now in the dark it came to me like the music of distant revelry, and I was ravished by its sweetness. It was not written for me, he first wrote it long before we met, but he said the woman in it he had imagined, and it was the work of fate that the name he gave her scanned with mine. So it is my song now.

"It was hot,
The middle hour had passed
I sprawled across the couch

One shutter open, one closed—
The kind of light you see in a wood..."

His voice was not like Cassius', so beautiful a stranger would be entranced, but it was pleasant and gentle, with an undertone of melancholy that never left him.

"Look, Corinna comes,
Tunic half-undone,
Throat half-exposed
By her loosened hair—
Just like this, they say, Queen Semiramis
Took herself to bed
And Lais was loved
By many men...
I tore away the tunic
Not much was harmed, for it was thin...
In all that flesh nowhere
Was a fault..."

He touched my collarbone.

"...What shoulders, what wonderful arms,
What breasts
So ready to my hands
And under them, a flat stomach.
What a lovely flank,
What a slender thigh.
Nothing I saw was not worthy to be praised...
May many such middays come to me,"

he whispered.

But his voice broke and he sat on the edge of the bed and held his head in his hands. "I—forgive me, Pinaria, I don't think I can manage anything tonight."

45

"Oh, my dear." I sat down beside him. "It doesn't matter. Here. Let us just lie down and hold each other for a moment."

Presently he felt better and we made love. I think he did not enjoy it much, but to me it was what it had always been and I did not want him ever to take away his arms.

I looked up to the breathing circle of the light, wondering what hour it was, and how much longer we had.

"We haven't heard from Fabius," I said.

"No."

His voice came from a long way away, and it was cold where he was.

"Oh, my love, I know it will be difficult, in Tomis, but we'll be together, that's what matters."

"Not 'we'."

"What? What did you say?"

"You're not coming. And neither is the child."

I was not sure I had heard. Then I was, and I grew angry.

"That's what you said at Fabius'. But it's not true. Of course I'm coming. How could I not be?"

He would not look at me. "I need you to stay here. And the child needs you here."

I put my hand on his chest. His heart underneath was steady. That was how I knew he meant what he was saying.

"But I *can't* stay here. I am your wife. 'Where you are Gaius, I am Gaia.' If you are an exiled man, I am an exiled wife. That's what I swore on our wedding day. I am a Roman, you can't ask me to break my oath. And anyway, how could I live apart from you? What else does my oath mean except that we are one person?"

He tried to smile but the grimace slipped a little to one side. "You are Gaia, but you are also Pinaria. And your cousin is Marcia."

"Yes. And—?"

"And her cousin is Caesar. Do you understand now?"

"But there are plenty of people who can help: Cassius…"

"Cassius is in a worse position than we are. He's going to be tried. If he's condemned—" He stopped because even by the light of one little lamp we could see that he was going to be. "If he's condemned he will have no recourse. But I have not been tried, I haven't even been accused of a crime. I can fight back. I can make them see that the whim of a tyrant is not a reason to relegate someone."

"Them?"

His eyes warmed, and he waved his hand.

"Well, who? Whom do you hope to persuade?"

"The Senate, the families. Maybe there aren't many left, not in the old sense, but there are enough. By Hercules, there are enough."

But I was still thinking of something else. "But, don't you love me? Don't you want me to come? I love you. I always have—"

"I—I—" He could not say it. "It doesn't matter whether I do or not. You just have to stay."

I became aware that I was running my finger over his thumb. I could feel the shape of it, the knobby knuckle, the thin, sharp, ridged nail. I could feel the energy in him, humming through the bone.

I cried out, "Surely others will help. Cotta. What about Cotta?"

"Cotta is very young, and very ambitious. Everything he is going to do he has already done."

"His brother."

"Also too ambitious. Too close to Tiberius. Why should he risk it?"

"Pompeius, then. He's Augustus' friend. He'll keep your books in the libraries. That shows he's willing to help."

He turned to me. "You really think he'll keep them in the libraries?"

"He—he said he would."

A little snort escaped him. "He'll get rid of them as soon as I'm gone."

In the silence I heard him thinking about the time.

The lamps had been kindled again, and we had put on clothes. The cloth twisted, I couldn't find my shoe. My mind kept trying to be with him, and it seemed an imposition to have to deal with fabric and leather.

"You must stay," he said. "Livia and Caesar Augustus are really our only hope, and you are the only way to them."

I tried one last time. "Marcia would go on working for us if I were gone."

"Yes, for a time. And then other things would intervene, and she'd mean to do it, and maybe once or twice she'd mention us to someone, and then after a while she'd forget to do even that."

I knew he was right.

He said, "You must stay. It's done. It's too late to change it now."

He took my hand and led me out into the atrium. "Oh, no," I cried, for in the opening the sky was as gray as raw silk. In the shadows it was still night. "Here. Wait, don't go out there—"

I had some foolish idea that if we stayed in the dark it would always be night and he wouldn't have to go.

"Listen, Pinaria. There's a few things I have to tell you—about the farms and the investments. I'm not dead, so you will not need a trustee. Don't let them try to appoint one. Say you are receiving orders from me, and keep control of the finances yourself. I can't trust anyone else. Don't let anyone persuade you to sell the iron works—it's been in our family for generations. It will make money again. And the apartment blocks in Sulmo need roofing—put Manilius in charge. If you need money, sell the villa." His beautiful voice cracked. "Well, I can't tell you everything you'll need to know. You'll have to do it on your own."

"But—" But how can I? I started to say until I realized that it wasn't fair. He had so much to think of just then; the voyage, his exile, his loneliness in a strange place. So I said nothing.

He knew of course. He patted my shoulder. "You'll do fine. I know you will."

In the atrium, the heap of boxes had grown smaller as the porters carried them out. I knew that on the street litters were waiting.

"Wait. Wait—maybe Fabius—"

"Not now. It's too late."

But the other servants had come, bunched together in the growing light by the pool. They were crying. The house echoed with it, and the pool gave back a metallic gasp.

I wanted to cry again too, but I could not. I had no tears. I thought I would never have any again. When I stepped forward to hold Naso he was a wraith of morning air in my arms.

"I love you," I whispered, hoping it was still true.

"My dear—my dear child—"

A porter lifted the last of the boxes. Loricus, the secretary, picked up his traveling hat and looked expectantly at us.

I tried to force myself to feel something. Nothing. Inside me was a desert, sand blew and nothing would grow. My heart was dead, and I wished he would go.

"Goodbye," he said. "Don't forget me."

Then he was gone.

I stared unbelieving at the space where he had been.

It was empty. It was silent.

Then suddenly I could feel. I was overwhelmed by feeling. Sobs tore through me. There were so many tears they blinded me. My eyes ran, my nose spurted water like a downspout. I thrust past our door, my shoulder slamming against the frame. Someone reached for me, but I shook him off. My face was as wet as rain.

The street lay open to the cool citron light of dawn. Down the way the houses slept behind their shutters; as I looked a torch guttered in its bracket and went out.

From edge to edge and as far down the way as I could see, the cobbles were empty. Violet shadows blushed along a wall, reflecting undisturbed in the puddles. If anyone had passed, no ripple remembered it. Not a scrape across a stone, not a drop of oil from a torch or a fragment of cloth trampled on the ground. Empty. Gone.

The light grew stronger and flushed with pearl. A flock of pigeons rose and circled, their wings like white scraps against the silence.

Far away down the hill I thought I heard a noise: perhaps it was a footstep, a creak of leather, maybe the chink of metal. But it might have been his voice. It might have been a word.

PART II

The servants half-lifted, half-supported me into the house. There they deposited me, unasked, in the garden. The dull day closed in. Far away, towards the port of Ostia, thunder muttered.

Presently one of my maids came out. "Mistress, do you want a cloak?"

My hands lay empty in my lap. There were no words to fill them. What I had of him was only what I could remember; he had taken away everything else.

Around midday they brought me some food. I forgot it as soon as they set it down.

The last dead bronze leaf of a rosebush floated in the pond, misting slowly with silver and pearl. I watched the current push it around. Once it caught on a piece of the coping and flashed like a tiny jewel in the lead-colored air. Once it traveled past my foot and I saw the thin crimson veins enlarged and distorted through the coagulating drops. Where you are Gaius, I am Gaia.

Naso, I said in my mind, where are you? Has the ship left? I saw him standing on the deck in the mist and drizzle. Perhaps it was only open sea around him, perhaps he could still make out the line of the coast and hear the soft shuffle of the beach.

The leaf passed under the splashing fountain, swirled, then sailed on, dragging its way on its long and meaningless journey.

In midafternoon, Loricus returned. Naso must have sent him, though I had thought he was taking him to Scythia. He came to the peristyle and waited, but by then I had traveled too far to speak to him. After a while he went somewhere else.

The thunder had drawn closer and more frequent; dark blue clouds had come down nearly to the horizon and greenish light seeped under them. It fell on my hands, and I saw that they were pale as marble and rimed with mist. Water appeared in my palm, first a splash, then another, then a little pool, shining like cold silver. Once or twice drops fell into it, shattering the surface, but when I did not move the water went clear again, and I could see the lines in my skin underneath, magnified and monumental.

Rain began to splatter. The earth blackened with damp and smelled of rust. The air grew colder.

The leaf continued its slow journey, passing eventually under a small shower from a twig. The weight of the drops spun it around. It rocked uncertainly, righted itself and continued its circuit, but it was riding lower now, and taking on water. Finally it sank, distending and collapsing as it twisted down through the chill and clarity.

From the house I could hear movement, the servants coming and going, the clack of a loom, someone grunting as he lifted a burden. And beyond that, the noises of the street. The city was moving, living, speaking. I have been—enclosed, I thought. In the garden. In my house. While in the city something happened last night. Something I do not understand.

The noises of the city disappeared under a sudden drum of rain; the surface of the pond grew pocked and pebbled. Through it I could see the leaf, lying on the bottom. Its shape was ruined, it was no more than a smear of darkness.

Dropping the sodden cloak I hurried toward the door.

Junius Novatus may have been a plebeian, but he was not a poor man. He had been at the baths, and now he came along the colonnade, appearing out of the dim and the drizzle in a small crowd of his friends and supporters.

I stood up. "Junius Novatus? I am sorry to approach you in a time of trouble but might I have a word? I am Pinaria Ovidii."

Novatus halted himself with a military snap. He was as crisp and pressed as his plain white tunic: a very young man with short hair and a small fashionable beard. He stood straight with his hands at his sides but I could see the rims of white around his eyes. From time to time he wiped his palms along his tunic.

"Thank you. I am sorry to come at a time of trouble, but I did wonder, you see, what exactly the trouble is. My husband, you may know, has been relegated—"

He snapped his fingers, and his friends, murmuring, melted into the shadows. "Right. Be careful what you say. There are informers everywhere."

I looked around at the unpleasant winter afternoon. The few people who were out went head down and quickly about their business, hoods and hats already dark with rain. "Really, Junius Novatus? I don't see—"

"They are here. He's got them everywhere, even in people's homes. I know."

"What has happened? What is going on?"

"Speak softly. Right. I have been fined. A large sum. We will have to sell property."

"I know. But I have not seen what you wrote. What was it about?"

"That's a lie."

"I—I'm sorry, what is a lie?"

"I did not write anything."

"I'm sorry. I thought Augustus said you did."

"I published something all right: a letter. He said it was a libel. About him. If telling the truth is a libel I guess it was. You notice though, he didn't dare take me to court. He just let me know that out of the kindness of his heart he would accept the payment of a lot of money instead of having me killed. Or whatever. Relegated."

"What did the letter say?"

"That Augustus took money and rights that belonged to his grandson. That his grandson was illegally and wrongfully exiled for objecting. That a friend was betrayed and a great man's legacy misused—"

"Whose?"

He sighed with impatience. "Marcus Vipsanius Agrippa's. His father. Augustus' friend. Once. Married to Julia, Augustus' daughter." He saw I did not understand. "Look, when Agrippa died he left an enormous fortune to his children, family money, I guess. And all that fortune he gained by his service abroad. You do know about that, right? How famous he was? Yeah. Well, four years ago his eldest son Gaius died. Lucius, the middle one, was long gone, dead in Gaul. Augustus had adopted them. Now he adopted Agrippa Postumus and made him his heir. Just what he ought to do. Loving grandfather and all that. Right. But wait: now Agrippa's legacy is legally Augustus'. And he began to spend it. "I found Rome brick and will leave it marble," he says. With whose money? And what happened to Postumus, the only man in Rome who dared to protest? Exiled, last year. His older sister went yesterday, her husband is murdered; the other is safely married to Tiberius's brother. His daughter is gone."

"And that's what the letter said? That Augustus was illegally spending his grandson's money?"

"Yeah."

"I see."

The rain was falling harder. It drummed on the roof of the colonnade, drowning his words. It was so dark the slaves had started to light the torches in their brackets on the walls. "I didn't write it. Agrippa Postumus did. He is my friend. I am honored to say. When I got the letter I did what it instructed: I showed it to the people I thought ought to see it. I thought it was important. I had to help Postumus protest. The Junii Novatii do not go back on their friends."

He wiped his face with a handkerchief. The linen flashed like a fish turning over in the dimness.

"Junius Novatus, when did Augustus adopt him?"

"Four years ago. The boy wasn't even fifteen, hadn't even taken the man's toga yet."

"Yes. I mean what day of the year was it?"

"The first of July. Why? What difference does that make?"

I was remembering the burning parchment. *The Festivals.* July first. "That is the boy's birthday?"

"That's right."

"Couldn't Augustus have meant it as a kindness. A fatherless boy?'

His laughter followed me out into the rain, ringing with the metallic echo of his fear.

Julia Aemilii's house was no longer guarded. The front looked abandoned; even the door gaped open. From it came a breath as cold and muddy as a river. Two bronze pennies wept on the doorstep. I reached down and touched them, and the color came away on my fingers. Not bronze: blood, now turning back to liquid and washing away in the rain. It must have fallen from Paullus' arm when he was carried out of the house.

I ducked inside. I had no feeling I was intruding—it was not like going into someone's home. When I shouted, my voice echoed down the passage, unrecognizable, not even human. No one answered, but my back crawled as if someone were watching me. But when I turned, there was no one there.

Along the passage the wrongness was worse. It rang with my footsteps. More drops had been scattered; a scrap of cloth lifted and fell. The place smelled of dead fires and rain.

I do not know what I expected to find, but whatever it was— some reason for their going, some connection to us—I did not find it. Without a torch it was difficult to see, but a little light wound through the colonnade. It was like walking through a forest. Drifts of air, small sounds, everywhere eyes hidden in the darkness, peering at me, watching, waiting. And never visible.

In the atrium the pool was splashing, and the rain thundered on the roof. Hangings had been slashed and lamps overturned; the family altar stared out, empty. The base of the altar had been splattered with blood, soaked in it, great gouts of it had splashed along the tiles as far as the wall. I could smell it, metallic and nauseating, and I had to sit down and put my head to my knees.

After a time I got up and went through to the first room.

A little light slid in through a shutter, enough to show me the chaos. It must have been a storeroom for clothing. Bed linens, tunics, dresses had all been slashed, even thick wool togas were now no more than rags. The boxes and chests themselves had been shattered so that the fresh wood gleamed in the dimness like broken bones.

Hastily I closed the door. But of course that did no good. All the rooms were the same. Everything that had not been mutilated had been taken away. Many of the rooms were empty, though I could see that they had contained furniture before. In one which must have held the looms, a length of cloth lay against the wall, ripped through by a knife or a sword. A bit of the design winked up at me too small to see what it had depicted, but it had been woven with silver threads. What had once been an office was now a vacant space; even the bins had been pulled from the walls. I could see where they had rested, but they were gone now. All that was left was a wax tablet crushed and unreadable, a scrap of red leather; the edge of a light purple cover and a bit of the ivory end pin from a book gleaming slightly in the light from the door. In the dining room every one of the deep green silk cushions had been slit and disemboweled, and the feathers blown about the room like a fall of snow. As I went past they rose and swirled in agitation, settling back almost before I had gone.

Out toward the back I came upon a kitchen storeroom. Like the linen closet, it was chaos. Jars had been smashed, and the contents—beans, grains, oil, wine—hurled across the floor. Heavy boots had trodden them into a slippery paste. I followed the prints out onto the flagstones of the kitchen garden.

There among uprooted trees and overturned earth a gray shape, vaguely human, was gliding in the distance. The rain fell between us, silvering the farther end of the path, and I thought it was a ghost. Well, I had nothing to fear from such a one now. I went closer.

He stared back at me through the grayness, then darted toward the kitchen hut. I could hear his feet squelching in the mud. A man then, an ordinary man.

I tore after him. "Wait! Wait! I want to talk to you—"

Through the kitchen—destroyed again; stones had even been pulled from the bake oven and smashed on the floor—out toward the wash house, through the blinding rain. He knew the house, and kept well ahead of me, but the silence of human absence hung over the place so thickly that I could hear his footsteps and his panting breath.

At last I cornered him, by the back wall. The gate had defeated him. Wrenched from its hinges it had jammed against a heap of overturned roof tiles. He was tugging at it as I came up. When he heard me he turned to face me, his face stiff with terror.

He wore a servant's tunic, much torn and dirtied, and there was mud under his nails. His heavy head was thatched with mud and straw so that it took me some time to realize that his hair was a fine light color. I thought he might be a Gaul of some sort, perhaps a Spaniard. He was as heavy as a carthorse; his nose was thick and broken, and under it his delicate mouth curled like a girl's. He was very pale.

"You," I said. "What happened here?"

"Mistress. I know nothing. Nothing. Mistress."

"I don't, of course, believe you."

"Yes, mistress. Believe me. Please, yes. I not from here. I from house over—there." He searched the horizon for a plausible residence, but the garden wall had made it hopeless. He let fall his hand. His powerful shoulders slumped.

"I asked you what happened."

"Yes, mistress." He was shaking with fear, but he recognized authority when he heard it. Laying his thumbs along the seams of his tunic, he drew himself up into something like a soldier's stance.

"They come. Guards. Yesterday. They take all people. I go to some place—" A crafty look came over his rather wooden face.

"To hide?"

He had been underground. Shreds of something rooty hung from him, and some grubs were clinging to his rain-sodden clothes.

He must have crawled into a pit or a compost heap. Given the soldiers' thoroughness, he was lucky not to have been run through by a sword when they were searching.

"Yes, mistress. Hide myself. They will torture—" He was looking at me now with naked appeal. I had to turn my head.

"They took all the furniture and things from the house too? Why did they do that?"

The girlish mouth trembled. "Please, mistress. Please. I know nothing."

"Were they looking for something?"

"I no know."

"You can guess."

"No. No guess."

I hated to do it. But I did not see any other way. "Just tell me. Remember. If it is legal for the authorities to have you tortured, so can I." I looked around in what I hoped was a very pointed manner. "No one would object."

He looked around after me. Then he looked at the ground. "Yes, mistress. They come ten days past. They take the papers, and the money, the mistress' jewels, the little mistress' too. They say to the master: you no go away, you stay in house."

"But they came back."

"Yesterday. Long time. Take all people."

"What did they want with them?"

"I know nothing."

"Yes, you do. Remember. No one here can protect you if I order—"

He sighed with resignation. Then, to my surprise, he drew himself up with a queer kind of almost military dignity. "They say mistress has lover. They say master to die. He say, why? I done nothing. They give him paper."

"What kind of paper?"

"With wax."

"A letter, then. With a seal."

"Yes, mistress. They watch him. I see their eyes. They wait. 'I done nothing,' he say. 'I no make treason.' They no answer.

58

"He kiss his wife. His little girl. He make them go outside. A soldier take them. They screaming and crying. Husband of mistress he take sword, put sword—" He was clutching his own belly. Under the rain his skin was green and sweaty, like a child about to throw up.

"I think that's clear enough," I cut in hastily. "They said it was treason?"

"Yes, mistress. Treason."

"But they didn't say what he had done."

"They say Mistress Julia she have lover. "

"That is not treason."

He shook his head stubbornly.

"Did they say who her lover was?"

"They say Junius Silanus."

"You know the name?" It was obvious he did. He spoke it more fluently than he had managed much of his Latin.

"He come here, much times. To parties. When I carry box— heavy box—for him, he give me copper money. Not all gentlemens do that. So I remember."

"I see. Is that your work, you carry packages, that sort of thing?"

"I am a free man, mistress. No slave. I free."

"Really? Who is your patron? Aemilius Paullus?"

"No understand."

"Who brought you to Rome? Who looks after your interests? Freedmen generally have patrons."

The pretty mouth trembled. "No understand."

"I see. And what was your work?"

"I wait. I see something, I do. Mistress, she say do, I do. Mistress give clothes, food. Maybe money, sometimes. Mistress—" His head swayed on the thick trunk of his neck and he lost his military bearing. I could smell his fear.

The rain fell around us. I wished I were somewhere else.

"All right," I said, sighing. I would have to find something to do with him. He was too dangerous to let wander. "All right. But you must swear that you will say that I found you lost in the street. If you don't—if you ever say to anyone, anyone at all, that I knew you come from this house—they will accuse me of treason too, and we will both die. But I will see to it that you die first, and badly. Very badly. Do you understand? Good. Swear."

He said something in his own language. Then he knelt down in the mud and kissed the draggled hem of my dress.

"Loricus, take care of him. I found him wandering in the street: he says he's free but he claims he doesn't know who his patron is. He doesn't speak much Latin. We—we need to make inquiries and get him back where he belongs."

Loricus gave me a shrewd look over the book he was rolling up. He was a man of much greater sophistication than I; I always felt a little countrified around him. His hands were gentle on the books that he was putting back in the bins, and he had devised a system to keep them in order that my husband always said was the best he had ever seen. He was a follower of Zeno the Stoic, whom he and my husband used to discuss for hours, but for all the austerity of his character, he had one vanity: his hair, which was very thin. He kept it combed over his shiny head where it lay most of the time, looking, I thought, rather embarrassed to be there. When it was disturbed it tended to stick straight out to the side, as if it were trying to escape. I always wondered what he stiffened it with.

His behavior was always very correct. "Yes, mistress. A very interesting problem. Do you wish me to make the inquiries about his origins?"

"No. No. Ah—I'll take care of that. You have enough to do. You just find him a place, until I—I find his owners." I had a feeling I was gabbling, and the look he was giving me sharpened.

He turned to study the new freedman. Then, to my surprise he spoke to him in a language I did not know.

The poor man brightened. I could hear that he was asking Loricus a question. Presently Loricus answered. The new man bowed, very deeply and respectfully, putting his thick fingers together in front of him in a gesture I had never seen before.

"Loricus, what did he—?"

"Yes, mistress?" Behind his dark blue eyes was a warning, and he had removed his voice to another room.

"Nothing, Loricus. Will you see to him? Send him to the country. It's better to get him out of Rome."

He bowed.

"Thank you," I said, with no irony at all.

The freedman had been led away, and Loricus and I were alone. I looked around my husband's study. Loricus had been putting the books that had not been taken back in their bins, but even so the place looked rifled, overturned, unfamiliar. It could have been the house on the hill, in the rain...

"Loricus, why did my husband send you back?"

"He thought you might need me, mistress."

I sat down. Loricus was more than my husband's servant, he was his companion, his critic, his helper. How was Naso going to live now, all alone out there with no one to talk to, no one to keep him company? "*I* might need you?"

"He thought you would be closing the house and going to live with Fabius Maximus and his wife now."

That was the obvious solution. I had gone back to them when my first husband died.

"And he sent you to help me? That was very thoughtful of him—indeed, it was more than that—" I had to stop to blink hard several times, "—it was very courageous. I cannot bear to think of his loneliness out there now."

"Yes, mistress. It is terrible." His fine head bent, and he looked lonely and defeated himself. Well, Naso had been his companion as much as he had been Naso's. Sometimes they had talked all night.

"There is one thing—" Loricus was anxious now. His hair was starting to come loose, and he passed his hand in its direction once or twice without actually touching it. He did not seem aware that he had missed it. "He wants you to be sure to keep control of his—of your—of the family accounts."

"Our what?"

"Ovidius Naso does not want you to have a trustee."

"Yes, he said that. But it's the law. I can't administer his property. Wouldn't someone have to be appointed? When my parents died, Marcia's father did it. My first husband appointed Fabius in his will. I mean, women can't. Can we?"

"That is interesting. Actually, no, mistress. Not technically. You are right, a trustee would have to be appointed. Ovidius Naso said, however, to remind you that you are not a widow. You are a married woman. And your trustee is your husband. Just in case, he drew up this—" From his tunic he drew a document which he handed me. In Naso's familiar calligraphy it laid out the terms under which I would be in charge, not only of my own money—my dowry and my inheritance from my parents and what had come to me under my first husband's will—but of everything Naso owned too. While he lived, Naso himself would be my trustee. After he died—I read the word, and my mind blinked away—I was to be emancipated, and could appoint a guardian for myself. Anyone I chose. Someone had witnessed it, whose names and seals I did not recognize. "A knight and a plebeian of good family we met on the road. It is perfectly legal, mistress. Ovidius Naso told me to tell you so. Since he is not a criminal—" His voice broke and he turned aside. His hair flopped down on his neck, but he did not even gesture toward it. "Since he has never been convicted of a crime, there is no reason he cannot be your trustee. Those were his instructions to me."

I looked at him, stricken. "I—I don't know how. I have never done such a thing—"

"Yes, mistress. He said that too. Perhaps I might help with that? I know the accounts, for instance. I have helped Ovidius Naso with them for years. That is why he sent me back."

So much kindness, so much care. I could not doubt my husband loved me. But all the same, the responsibility was overwhelming, and I went away and cried for an hour.

In the evening I went to dinner at Marcia's. I went openly, in a chair, with torchmen to accompany me. After all, Marcia was my relative. There was nothing out of the way in seeing her.

The rain had dragged itself off and the thunder was far away, over the Sabine Hills. Shops were open, releasing lamplight into the streets, but most had little to sell, and few people were in them. A pack of starving dogs ran by splashing among the puddles, and on a corner two beggars cursed loudly at each other over a space, though no one had passed for an hour who could have given either one of them a bronze penny. Up on the Capitoline Hill there were lights and movement, and the sound of singing drifted down on the fresh, cold air.

It was too chilly for the big peristyle dining room, so we ate in a small space off the atrium. Outside the wind had come up, and clouds were hurrying across the sky. The moon, just past the full, already shone in huge pale splotches among the columns. I could see them through the open arch, fading and reappearing with the movement of the clouds.

In the little alcove the servants had placed braziers at the foot of each of the couches and around the chairs. I drew back a chair but Marcia propped herself on her elbow on a couch.

"Marcia," I cried, "what on earth are you doing?"

"Reclining."

"Really? Like a man?"

"They do it in the best houses now. The princess Julia started it, but a lot of very nice people do it now too."

"They do? Really? And Julia started it? Julia Aemilii?"

"No, Julia her mother. Caesar's daughter. The princess."

"You know her? Knew her? Before she was exiled, I mean."

"A little. She was a terrible woman, Pinni. Wild and extravagant."

"What did she do?" I asked, fascinated.

"She ran with a very loose crowd. You wouldn't have liked them. The dregs of the old families. Drinkers and gamblers, bent on spending the last of their families' fortunes. She had so many lovers. And she used to make jokes about it."

"What jokes? Don't stop now."

"Well, once someone asked her how it was that all her children looked like Agrippa, her husband. She said she never took on a passenger until the cargo had been loaded."

I laughed. "That sounds rather witty."

She did not disapprove as much as she said she did, because her charming upper lip came down over her teeth in a little grin, and she giggled. "Well, I suppose it was."

"And that was part of her wildness? That she reclined like a man?"

"Oh, no, Pinni. Of course not. A lot of people do it now."

"Does Livia?"

Immediately she looked lost and a little anxious. "Well, no, not Livia. You know how conservative they are." Her little chin came up. "But Claudia Pulchra does and so do Paulla and Domitia. I'm going to. Do you want to join me?"

Amid so much that was changed, why not this? "All right. But what will Fabius say?"

But Fabius, coming in, was his usual smooth and unruffled self. He raised his eyebrows, but he said nothing, merely reclining on his own couch as usual. "So you will be staying here, Pinaria," he said, shaking out his napkin.

I thought Marcia looked a little put out. Well, I suppose if you set out to do a brave thing, and no one notices, you might be annoyed.

Fabius began on his soup.

"It will be nice to have you here. Company for Marcia. It will make it easier for us to look after you. My secretary is a good man; he can go over Naso's accounts and we can get started. You don't have to worry about a thing. I will send for the books in the morning—"

"I—Fabius, I can't." My mouth was dry. I took a sip of my wine. "Naso wanted me to look after our property myself."

Something flickered in him, like a lamp in a draft. "Yourself?"

"I— Yes."

"How can you do that, Pinaria dear?"

"He gave me a document. Giving me the authority."

"I assure you, a paper giving authority is not the same thing as managing an important estate. That takes knowledge, years of experience. Not quite as simple as reclining on a couch."

"Yes. I know, Fabius. I realize I don't know very much—"

"Good. Let me help you." He smiled gently. "It's nothing you need worry about. You concentrate on keeping up Naso's spirits in exile, and I'll see to it that he has something to return to. You don't have to worry about a thing."

"I have Loricus."

"He left Loricus?"

"Yes. To help me." I felt myself near tears. He was so kind, so anxious to help. If it had not been for Naso's wish I would have given him all my problems. He had looked after me so well when I was widowed.

He ate a little of his fish, frowning. "Well, bring Loricus, and I will give him whatever help he needs. Don't worry, Pinaria, we'll take care of it. And Naso, when we get him back, will be entirely pleased with the result, I assure you."

"Thank you."

"Fabius, did you—did Augustus—?"

"I only had a moment to talk to him, Pinaria. His house was packed this morning. Don't worry, we'll get Naso back. He'll enjoy a little vacation—Brundisium, maybe make it as far as Athens, see some people—they'll make a huge fuss over him there, you know how they love poets. By then I'll have had a chance to see what is going on. Don't worry about a thing." He wiped his mouth. "Will you be staying tonight? Please feel that our house is entirely yours. And go ahead and send Loricus to see me in the morning. I'll get your financial situation straightened out."

He threw down his napkin. "Now if you'll excuse me, my dear? Pinaria?"

He was gone in an instant. I watched him as he paused at the shrine in the atrium to leave a portion of bread for the gods of his house. In the tricky light he appeared and disappeared, first white as bones, then dissolved to darkness, then gleaming pale again.

Marcia leaned forward from her couch. "He did notice, didn't he?"

"Notice what?"

"That we're reclining."

"Oh, that. No. He wouldn't, would he? He's too well brought up. He'd be nice no matter what."

"Nice. I hate that," she sighed. "It's so demeaning."

There was still a little light left of the winter afternoon; as my chair climbed the Palatine Hill I could see the day going pale in the west. Long shadows lay across the street, so deep I almost missed the door I was looking for. It is famous, that door; huge, high, heavy, wreathed in oak leaves—the kind that may only be displayed if they are awarded by the Senate. But for all its magnificence, no beautifully dressed doormen guarded it: it took me a moment to see the two Praetorians in their togas still as water in the shadows.

I stopped my chair and gave my name. "I'd like to see Livia Drusilla, if you please. I know she's busy, but I will only take a moment of her time."

The Praetorian shouted something over his shoulder.

Then I waited. I had plenty of time to be impressed by the doorway. In fact, I had time to read all the plaques let into the walls to commemorate victories and triumphs, and to study all the veins in all the leaves on the wreaths.

The day darkened; the curtain of my litter began to snap in the little wind. It was a steady sound, like the beating of a heart, or the tramp of boots. It went on measuring out the time while the first stars appeared in the blushing sky, and the voices from the Forum far away below faded away as shops closed and people went home to their gruel and beans.

The Praetorians never moved.

I hugged my shawl to me, but I was shivering, with cold, with anger, with humiliation. I could not tell which. Only the thought of Naso, away in a colder place, made me stay.

Finally the door opened. A whisper was exchanged. The Praetorian said, "Livia Drusilla is not at home."

It was so obviously a lie I think I simply stared at him.

My silence worried him: maybe I was someone who could make trouble. He blinked at me in the near darkness. "Ah, mistress, ah, would you care to leave a message?"

"Oh. A message. Yes."

"What do you wish to say?"

How could I tell him that I'd come to beg for my husband's life? It would only make him sure that he didn't need to deliver the message at all.

He was snapping his fingers at his sides, growing impatient. "Mistress. Your message?"

"I—I will see Livia Drusilla's secretary."

"Demosthenes, the freedman?"

"If he is her secretary."

This required another conference. I waited, hardly daring to breathe. "Perhaps you would care to step inside?"

So I was led, escorted rather, by a servant of infinite silence and correctness, through a hall as imposing as the door. Long corridors, forests of pillars, a fountain splashing the quiet: we came toward the light of an atrium and my heart stumbled in my chest.

Over my head a monster reared. It was a skeleton, nearly scraping the ceiling. A huge misshapen head, a jaw of a hundred teeth like a line of swords, little claws clutched to its chest, hind legs thicker than marble columns. The bones were the color of hide, and it looked as if it would pounce from its low pedestal. The cruel claws would grab, I could feel the teeth in my flesh.

Dizzy, I leaned against the wall. "What is it?"

"The bones of a monster, mistress. Some farmers dug it up. Caesar Augustus has several more in his country house. They lived a long time ago, perhaps in the age of the heroes, the time of Troy."

"Indeed? So long ago."

"Yes, mistress. More than a thousand years ago."

Then, to my puzzlement, I was led outside. A garden? It was difficult to tell.

To my left reared up what was certainly the Temple of Apollo— though from the back, as I was seeing it, it looked smaller and rather strange. But the path wound on, and presently I was through another door, and in a different house. Very different. The floor was stone, not marble; the doors plain wood that gave onto cramped old-fashioned rooms painted in dark geometric designs in the fashion of sixty years ago.

"Where are we?" I asked the servant.

"This is Livia Drusilla's house. It was given to her by Caesar Augustus. It was once the property of Hortensius, the orator and jurist. Mistress."

Obviously the house had not been changed since the last days of the Republic, before Julius Caesar and the civil wars. I wondered how much we were supposed to think that Augustus resembled Hortensius in his plain republican dignity.

The room where the servant left me, though very small and nearly entirely undecorated, was pleasant in the last light of evening, and the maids brought me a bit of fried bread and a cup that turned out to be filled with plain cool water.

Presently Demosthenes arrived. A man in late middle age, he had the soft look of a freedman in an important household—he belonged to the other building, in fact, not this one. He was white-skinned and beautifully barbered, but his eyes were shrewd and cold. His servant followed him carrying a tray of books and writing tablets.

"You wished to see me?" He spoke in Greek, which was obviously his native language.

"Yes. I would like to make an appointment to see Livia Drusilla," I said in the same language.

"An appointment. Yes. You are—?"

"Pinaria Ovidii."

"Ovidii? The wife of Naso, the poet?"

"You know my husband?"

"Yes."

"I don't remember seeing you. Have you been to our house?"

"I—ah, no. That is, I used to know him."

"Used to?"

He took a square of very fine linen from his belt and wiped his brow.

"When I was a member of the household of Julia Caesaris, Caesar's daughter. I used to see him, when he came to sing. May I say, *kyria*, that I regard it as a great honor."

"Thank you. He sang at Julia's parties?"

"Oh, yes. Sometimes."

"And at the younger Julia's too?"

He rubbed his hands together. "I do not know. I have had no contact with the younger Julia. Not since she married. She was my pupil when I was a tutor at her mother's house—she and the two older boys. She was a fetching child, pretty, like all Caesar Augustus' family. And—"

He glanced around but there was no one with us except his servant, waiting by the table.

"Yes? She was what?"

"Oh. She was intelligent. That's all. A better student than the boys. In fact in natural philosophy I have never had a quicker pupil. And in mathematics—"

"She was like her mother then?"

He was wary now, looking sideways at me. "All Caesar Augustus' family are very intelligent."

"Just so."

"So you don't know why the younger Julia was exiled?"

His answer came quickly. "She committed adultery."

"Like her mother."

"That's right. Just like her mother. The elder Julia was a very wild woman. Uncontrollable. She had many lovers."

"Who?"

"*Kyria*, everyone knows who they were."

"I don't."

He began to count on his fingers. "Iullus Antonius, who was the son of Mark Antony, Titus Quinctius Crispinus, Appius Claudius Pulcher, Sempronius Gracchus, Cornelius Scipio."

"Were there others?"

"Oh, yes. Many, many others."

"Do you believe that?"

"Oh, yes. I know it for a fact."

"How? Did you see her making love with them?"

"Certainly. I was at those parties."

"Even the one in the Forum?"

"Yes."

"You must have been pretty far in Julia's confidence."

"Oh, yes. I was one of her lovers."

I think my mouth fell open. "You were what?"

"One of her lovers. She was not particular. Anyone who amused her…at least for a time…"

"And she was no longer amused? So you went to her father? Is that what happened?"

"*Kyria. Kyria.* This is bad philosophy. First you must make sure your assumptions are correct. I did not inform her father. He already knew. He asked me, and out of loyalty, mistaken loyalty, I denied my knowledge. I denied it for months."

Someone was making a clatter, and I was suddenly aware of his servant in the background, setting out the tablets and styluses. A battered little man with a twisted spine and a scarred cheek. He did not turn away from his task, but his bleached and puckered eye had rolled toward us.

Demosthenes had heard nothing. He was pacing in front of me, his chest thrust out like an orator in the courts. "Caesar Augustus, in his great generosity, forgave me. And Livia Drusilla has given me a position in her household, as you see. A position of dignity. I do not deserve it, and I am grateful, humbly grateful, for their goodness."

"They rewarded you for your mistaken loyalty?"

"They are very magnanimous, *kyria.*"

"Really? They were not magnanimous to my husband."

"Oh, no, *kyria*, you are wrong. I am sure they were. It must be that your husband did something so terrible that they could not overlook it. I see that you are angry and upset. But I know Caesar Augustus and Livia Drusilla, and I am certain they have been as generous as they could."

"Do you know what my husband did?"

"No, *kyria*. I have no idea."

"Neither do I. Neither does anyone else."

He shrugged. "It is after my time."

"I see. But you do know about Julia the Elder. Good. Was my husband one of the people in the Forum?"

He blotted his forehead. Then he blotted it again. But he was a freedman, he had once been a slave, and he had the habit of obedience. "*Kyria. Kyria.* He was there. Yes."

The slave was rattling the tablets again. Demosthenes' pale tongue came out and swiped his lips. More sweat had started on his face. "He was there, mistress. For a time. Not the whole time, perhaps. He played and sang a little. I don't remember how long he stayed."

"And that was all that happened? Some singing, some dancing, that's all?"

Oddly, he relaxed. He even smiled. Somehow this was not the question that he feared. "Oh no. It went much further than that. They made love, there. On the Rostrum."

"My husband did?"

"Oh, *kyria*. I don't want to say—"

"Tell me."

He was looking at me out of the side of his eye. "Well, yes. He was among the ones who made love with her."

"You are sure of that? You saw him?"

"Oh, yes. I made love with her too. So did all the others."

"I—I see." I was choking on my own anger and pain.

I could not get out of there fast enough. My eyes felt near to bursting with tears. "Tell Livia Drusilla, if you please, that I would like to speak to her. I wish simply to throw myself on her generosity. If she was so magnanimous to you perhaps she might consider the case of a poet in exile?"

If he answered I did not hear.

Naso was married the year the first Julia was exiled. Married six months by the December when she left. To me.

That night I slept at home. It was quiet, unnervingly so. In the morning I spoke to my daughter. "Would you like to visit your cousins in the country for a while?" I asked with a torn heart.

She is a biddable child, self-contained and a little conventional, like her father. "Yes, mama."

She glanced at me worriedly. "You won't mind being alone?"

"Oh, my darling, what a thing to say! You don't have to worry about me. I tell you what—I will go to Marcia's. Then you won't have to worry. How does that sound?"

Marcia had allotted me a set of rooms on the second floor. I had lived in these rooms before, when my first husband died. Before that they had belonged to Marcia's mother, who had given up her own house and come to live with her daughter when she got old. They were not large but they overlooked the peristyle garden on one side; on the other a fine long balcony ran along the whole outside of the house. It gave me a view of the roofs and temples on the Capitoline Hill, and in summer a lovely breeze through the pierced screens on the doors. There was a window on the balcony side as well. In winter solid shutters kept out the cold.

I took the second room along the balcony for a bedroom. My maid Philomela was already there, making up the couch with the coverlets from my own bed at home. A fresh gown was laid out across it, and my silver mirror and a plate of figs stuffed with cheese was set under a fine hanging lamp on the chest.

Philomela combed my hair and put me into my nightgown. I got into bed. She fussed with the objects on the dresser, straightening the mirror, shifting the little cup of barley water a little to one side, folding a linen napkin. It struck me that she was taking a long time.

"Philomela, what are you doing?"

She jerked as if I had hit her.

As she blew out the lamp I saw her, caught in a tiny pause by the light. The curve of her cheek, fuller than before, glowed as bronze as the mirror. I thought that she was faintly smiling.

"Philomela?"

"Mmm—mistress? Please. We are going home?"

Marcia's mother Atia used to say that people who were friendly to slaves were demeaning themselves and asking to be treated with undue familiarity, so I tried to be careful. But my maid has been with me since I bought her to help in the weaving room, a skinny, frightened child of five or six with huge black eyes and a headful of obdurate curls. A North African, I suppose. She did not speak and for a long time we thought she was mute, so Naso called her Philomela, but as she got older she began to talk. Now she is as fluent as anyone else. A few years ago I promoted her to be my maid: I saw she had a neat hand and a quick eye. And indeed she never snagged the comb in my hair or scraped me with the knife when she cut my toenails. She has a beautiful way with a hairstyle too, and has kept me well-dressed and reasonably presentable for years.

But she is still a silent young woman, and for her to say as much as she did was an effort. She stood panting like a hare, her enormous eyes fixed on me.

"Why? Do you want to? Is something wrong here? Tell me."

There was something in the way she was standing perhaps or in the texture of her skin, something I had not seen there before. There were crumbs on her tunic: And the figs and cheese looked a little skimpy on the plate. Hungry, then, though it was not long past dinner and I saw to it that my slaves were well fed.

I remember what that meant.

"Philomela, are you pregnant?"

Fear was rising in her. Soon it would cover her mouth and she would slide under into the silence that had claimed her as a child.

"Who is the father?"

She closed her mouth and stared at me with drowning eyes. Servants are all like that; they never want to tell, for fear you will separate them from their men or some such thing. Well, it couldn't matter much.

"Never mind, Philomela. You may go."

I heard the tiny click of the latch as she went out.

I lay awake a long time. The moonlight came through the ornamental screens, sliced into patterns as it lay across the bed and spilled onto the floor. City sounds—wagons rumbling toward the markets, voices passing, up above on the Capitoline Hill geese calling to a flight of migrating swans—floated to me on the milky light.

I was born in the city. I could just remember my parents' house, for they died when I was six. I remember the silence indoors, and the scent of lavender in a bowl by the doorway. My mother came in. Her hair was disordered and her face stained with tears, but she smiled at me. A lady and a beautifully dressed girl about twelve were with her. The lady I had met at family gatherings; she was Marcia's mother, whom I always called my aunt, though she was really some kind of cousin of my father's. Marcia I did not yet know—I was so young myself that I thought she was the same age as the women.

My mother gave my hand to the lady and said I should go with her. I did, of course, not at all sorry to leave the strangeness that had fallen over everything at home. I remember that my mother kissed me and held me a long time before she let me go. I do not remember if I looked back as I went. I hope so, for I never saw my mother again. Some time later my aunt told me that she and my father had died of a fever.

I do not know how I found out that it was not true. Some servant's whisper, I suppose, or another child at some birthday party—it might have been anyone. I asked my aunt, of course. She looked at me down her nose, a freezing glance, full of distaste.

"Was it—politics?" I asked. Someone must have told me that, too.

"We will not discuss it," she said in a voice like a saw in wet wood. Then she summoned a maid and had me taken out of the room.

For myself, I don't believe I thought very often of own parents. Children don't have much sense of the past, I think. The memory might have been a consolation to me, but sometimes then, and even occasionally now, something—a sound, a scent—reminds me of the woman who held me so long before she let me go. It stops me in whatever I am doing, and an odd feeling of shame comes over me, as if I were responsible for her death. I have never understood why this is.

As soon as she could, Atia sent me to the country, to my Uncle Rufus' house. There I was very happy—my uncle had a large library collected during his service abroad: poets, philosophers, mathematicians, astronomers—they were companions to me, and I never missed any other. My uncle loved them too, and we would talk about them when he had time.

Once I asked him what had happened to my parents.

"You are too young—how old are you? What, eleven?"

"Please," I whispered, as if Atia could hear.

"Well, why not? I suppose you must know sometime. What do you know?"

"Aunt Atia said it was a fever."

He shook his head.

"Was it politics?"

"Yes. I suppose. Well, yes. Your father had the wrong friends, that's all. And Augustus didn't like them, or him. So—"

He looked down at his own strong hands, marked with sun and scars. "So—he…your father…died."

"How?"

He looked surprised. "With his sword. How else would a soldier die?"

"And my mother?"

"She died too. With him."

"Why?"

"Because she was his wife."

"Where you are Gaius, I am Gaia," I said.

"Exactly. A good answer." To him it seemed perfectly natural. He was a soldier, and death was part of his duty. Why should it not be part of my mother's duty too?

Marcia was married two years after I went to live with them. Often after that I came to stay here, in Fabius' big, comfortable house. I know the way the sounds move and the light, I can feel the shape of the house around me in the night.

The light was bright and I did not feel much like sleeping. I thought of Naso, away somewhere on a ship, heading toward Greece and far beyond. I tried to guess where he was and what he was doing, but it did not seem real to me. My mind would not see him. Instead, I heard his voice, mingled with the city that he had loved. I could remember a bit of his verse:

This your Penelope sends you, Ulysses long delayed.
Do not write: come home.
Troy, hated by the daughters of Greece, lies in ruins,
But Priam and all that country were not worth this.

75

Oh, if only as they made for Sparta, that demented adulterer and
    all his fleet
Had been overwhelmed by the sea.
Then I would not lie down alone in a cold bed
Nor complain how slowly the day passed
Nor would I betray the endless night
With warp hanging from widowed hands…

When I met him this poem had only recently appeared. He sang me a little, one day as we were walking in the portico Marcus Agrippa had built in honor of his sister Vipsania. The scent of flowers had been everywhere, and the hum of bees had sung with him.

When I remembered this I cried, out of pain and fear and confused emotions, and for a time at least my mind was quiet.

Staying with Marcia had one practical advantage: I saw Fabius every day. And every day I asked him, "Has Augustus said anything yet?"

At first he smiled graciously. "It's a busy time. Caesar has had only a moment here and there. But I have spoken to him. Don't worry, Pinaria."

As the days passed his answers grew shorter, and finally, one morning as I passed his door and paused, he looked up before I even spoke. "Pinaria. Don't ask me again. I will tell you when I know anything."

Cassius and my husband had spoken of Junius Silanus: evidently he was the lover of Julia the Younger. It seemed a hopeless undertaking, but I thought I ought to go see him. After all, something had happened that night. Something strange. And Fabius wasn't having much success petitioning Augustus.

I had myself carried to Silanus' by a round-about route, in a plain litter: it belonged in fact to one of my clients, a woman who owned a linen shop. That night under the colonnade Junius Novatus had been afraid of informers; so had the military man at Marcia's dinner party. Now, thinking it over I thought their fear might have been well based: two years before, Augustus had appointed firemen—some buildings had burned in the Subura District. A good idea. But there were seven thousand of them and they were all still in the city, marching around and peering at the stalls in the markets or listening to the conversations at the bars. Perhaps the conflagration they were appointed to control was in fact smoldering in places like that.

I need not have troubled. Silanus' doorstep was jammed and more people were coming from the square all the time. There was no way anyone watching could have distinguished any of us in that crowd.

The doorway was wide enough to accommodate us all, and as fine as carving and balconies and ironwork could make it. Huge Herculean figures held up more ornate marble, and a wrought iron railing rippled over our heads.

The house was what the magnificent doorway had promised: carved and painted and filled with fine antique Greek statuary and furniture. Julia the Younger would have felt right at home—I thought in fact that the same painter who had done her house had done the murals on the atrium walls.

She would have recognized the atmosphere here too—for beautiful as the house was, it was in chaos, like hers. Like ours. Crude packing cases scratched the finishes of the tables and benches, heaps of clothes and books and equipment were strewn at the feet of the marble sculptures like offerings to some disorganized god. Chairs had been moved out from the walls to stand empty and lost in the middle of the floor.

But this house was far from empty. Men and women were packing themselves into the colonnades and the atrium as if it were rent day. Some carried gifts, some looked solemn, some merely dutiful. In their midst on an ebony and gold chair a beautiful elderly woman of great distinction sat like a chained eagle. She did not speak but her bright dark eye went everywhere. It rested on me for an instant; it was like being looked at by a lantern. I inclined my head with respect. When I looked up the eye had passed on and a man very like her in looks though much younger had appeared in the room.

He stood gracefully in front of her and bent to kiss her cheek, murmuring something that made the old face open in a smile, indulgent and affectionate. All the same I doubt she ever laughed.

The woman nodded to him with her eyes in my direction. He spoke to some of the women around him, embraced one or two of what were obviously his relatives, then hurried over. "Yes? May I help you?"

"I—I'm looking for Decimus Junius Silanus. Are you he?"

"Yes. And you are—?"

His presence was a little overwhelming. For one thing, he wore rather a lot of perfume, perhaps more than he had intended. And then he was so perfect. His teeth were even and very white, his fine-grained skin was tanned by the sun to a beautiful pale golden color, setting off his teeth and the whites of his eyes, but it was not the tan of the battlefield or trieme. Soldiers and sailors are marked by more than sun: their skins are roughened by weather and armor; their arms are white to the edges of their tunics, and then red; their necks and chins are wind-scoured and their foreheads creased. He was as even and golden as a clove of garlic in a pan, and oiled and curled and embroidered to the highest standard. Some slave Pygmalion had worked to create him, and like Pygmalion's Galatea he was a labor of love. I wondered whose love it was—it struck me that it was probably his own.

A line of my husband's came to me:

A pale complexion is disgraceful on a sailor
The sun's rays make him dark
Disgraceful too on a farmer, whose plowshare's always up,
Turning the earth over and over, under whatever Jove sends.
And athletes aiming at the olive crown are shamed if their bodies
     are pasty
But you who love, look pale: this is the complexion fitting to love
And your mistress, deceived, will fear you might be sick with love.

I thought, this man Silanus has read that poem. All the fashionable young men must have, for he would surely do nothing that was not the latest style. Well, if he knew my husband I had nothing to fear.

"Good morning, Junius Silanus. My name is Pinaria Ovidii. I am the wife of Publius Ovidius Naso."

"My dear. Really? *The* Naso? I am honored." He stepped back a pace. Everything he did was a little too much, a little too theatrical. And it was consequently a little unreal, like talking to a dream.

"Junius Silanus, I hope you will forgive my intrusion, and my frankness now. My husband, as you no doubt are aware, has been relegated, for a reason we do not know. I came because—"

"Because you thought I might know it?" He wore an amethyst ring that flashed now as his hand swept through the air. There were amethysts and gold beads on his shoes too. He was shaking his handsome head. "I have no idea. I've heard your husband's poetry recited at dinner parties—"

"At Julia the Younger's house?"

He didn't like to say. But he smiled at me to let me know he could have if he hadn't been so elegantly discreet.

"By my husband?"

"No. I regret to say I have never met him."

"I see. But you do know Julia? Isn't that right?"

"Well, since you already know—"

"I should think most of the city does by now."

He looked at me sharply. "What do they know?"

"That you are her lover. Forgive me, Junius Silanus, but that's what they say."

"Yes, that's what they say."

"Isn't it true?"

"Caesar says it is." He spread his hands. "Who am I to disagree?"

"No, no one disagrees with Augustus," I said.

"Not for long. But his granddaughter is pregnant."

I thought of her led through the street, the tiny tear on her cheek, the brilliant smile to the crowd. "She's married. Was married. Why shouldn't she be pregnant?"

"Indeed. But Caesar says it's mine."

"How does he know it isn't her husband's?"

He shrugged. "As far as I know, it is."

"If it's Aemilius' it's the child of a traitor. Perhaps Augustus doesn't like that idea. If it's yours, he needn't worry about it—"

"Perhaps." The teeth flashed. "Does he need reasons?"

I gestured to the crates and the preparations. "Has he exiled you, too?"

"He has formally withdrawn his friendship."

"Well, anyone's patron might do that. It's not a punishment. Perhaps he doesn't really believe you are her lover."

"Does it matter? It comes to the same thing. He's not just an ordinary patron. Obviously I had better get out of Rome. Some ambitious advocate with a plausible accusation—even a not very plausible one. Or some hero with a knife on a dark street. Who will care, if Caesar has said so publicly that he doesn't himself? My brother—" he gestured toward a slightly older man, more grizzled and serious in appearance, who was talking to the old lady in the chair—"my brother is Tiberius' friend, but even he—*suggested* is the word, I suppose—that I go." He tried to laugh but he was looking at the old woman, and there was pain in his voice.

I reached out and put my hand on his arm. "I'm sorry."

He looked at me then. Behind his polish and his gilded skin his eyes were very young and very frightened.

"It wasn't you who said something to Augustus about my husband?"

"I don't know anything to say to him."

"But you know his poems."

"Oh, certainly. Everyone knows his poems. But I never mentioned him to Augustus. Or to anyone else, so far as I know. I don't know anything to mention."

He had shown me his fear, which was real. I don't suppose he showed many people anything so honest. So now, about this, I believed him.

"Thank you, Junius Silanus. You've been very kind. I hope your trip will be safe and pleasant."

He bowed. When I left he had gone back and was speaking to the lady in the chair again. She was as upright and still as ever, but there was panic and defeat in every line of his slender shape.

Overhead the clouds were tumbling in their haste to escape the wind, and eastward long gaps had ripped open into blueness. My cloak bellied like a sail and the edge snapped at my cheeks. By the time I reached my house my face was raw again with tears.

There was no one in the atrium, though some of the mess had been cleaned up, and the little gods in the shrine straightened. In my husband's study what books remained had been put back on the shelves. The place was tidy and, oddly, calm. Motes danced in the long shafts from the window; wax gleamed on a stack of boards; pens cut and sharpened lay neatly in their tray. It was very still, the wind outside only a whisper, the faint cry of a ghost.

He might have been around the corner, just stepped out to another room. He might have been anywhere in the house. How could he have left me and gone away? Oh, Naso, my heart cried out, but the time for making a noise had passed, and I did not call his name.

For a while I stood in the silence. The room darkened and brightened as the shadows of clouds passed over the house. Nothing else moved. Finally I wiped my eyes.

I raised my voice. "Loricus?"

The quiet was not disturbed, though the motes swirled in agitation.

No one came.

In the back rooms, similar progress had been made. Linen was folded, beds and chairs were shoved back against the walls, clothes were put into the presses. The peristyle garden was swept. But the house was empty.

In fact it was not until I reached the kitchen that I found anyone at all. There the servants had clustered, keeping warm. They looked up, frightened, when I came in. The door slammed in the wind behind me.

I could smell bread baking and someone had ladled olives out of the jars. It was time for the midday meal. "Go ahead," I told them, pulling off a corner of a new loaf and dipping it into a bowl of sheep's milk curds and herbs. "You've done a good job cleaning up. Who told you what to do?"

They all spoke at once, cooing like the doves in the rafters. "Loricus, mistress. Loricus said you were coming back."

"How did he know that?"

They cooed in their gentle puzzlement, but there were no words in it.

"Where is he?"

They looked around, bewildered. "Here. Here. He was. Just before you came."

The herbs filled my mouth with the taste of summer, dried and gone. "Was he?"

"Yes, mistress. Yes. He was here." But they were not sure. They only said it because they thought it was what I wanted to hear.

When I got back to the study he had reappeared, standing in a shaft of light, a book in his hands. His hair was smoothed over his head, and his clothes were tidy, as always. But his cheeks were suspiciously red, and the chill of the wind came off him.

"Where have you been?"

He opened his eyes in surprise. "I beg your pardon, mistress. You have been looking for me?"

It was not quite insolence, and his manner was very polite. I didn't think—I couldn't see how to pursue—

"Loricus, I will be staying with Marcia and Fabius for a while. I will leave you in charge of the house. I will come back—every day if I can—" I nearly stumbled over this; my eyes had filled with tears.

I thought he knew what had tripped me. He looked away tactfully.

"You have done a good job with the servants so far. I will leave you in charge."

"Yes, mistress."

"And the accounts. I—Fabius wants you to show them to him. He wants to help you."

"And you wish me to do that, mistress? Show them to him?"

The sunlight cut the patterned floor into squares that glared in my eyes. I had to blink hard a few times. "No, I don't. But—he is my benefactor, Loricus. And he only wants to help."

He said nothing. He was waiting. I had a feeling he was waiting to see if he could still respect me, though that was impossible. Of course he would respect me: he was a servant, and I the mistress.

"My husband said I was to do them with you."

"That is so."

"And left me a document to that effect."

"So he did, mistress. I remember it."

"Well—ah, what if someone—what if Fabius *orders* you to show him the accounts. What will—what would you say?"

"Mistress, it is not my place to say anything." His eyes were very deep and very intelligent.

"No but, if he *ordered* you?"

He shook his head. "I would have to tell him—tell anyone, *if* someone asks—that they must speak to you about the matter."

"To me?"

"The decision is yours alone, mistress."

In my mind I saw Fabius' bright, smooth smile. It shone like Alpine ice and if you tried to grasp it your hand would slip away.

"And the document?"

"Yes."

"Is it—legal?"

"It is legal. There are precedents. When Cicero was—away— for example, he gave a similar power to his wife, Terentia. But in my opinion, you are within your rights to ignore it if you wish and find a guardian to administer the estate for you. Certainly no one would prosecute you if you did."

I looked around. The books in their bins, the pens ready on the table, the edge of the boards aligned so carefully with the corner of the table, just as my husband liked it to be. So often I had seen them together in this room. Two men, so nearly equals, so nearly friends, except for an accident of fate. And Loricus was holding himself faithful to that bond. He rolled up the book with delicate fingers and set it in its bin, straightening the tag so that the title showed. In case someone were to come in wanting to look up a poem. In case someone were to come back from Scythia to find a word he had left behind.

"Yes. All right. I—you and I will do the accounts. Do you think that's right?"

"If it is what you wish, mistress."

The squares were blurring at the edges in the light. The room had filled up with silence again, and with fear. In the long shafts the motes held themselves unnaturally still. I had thought that when I made a decision I would feel better, but I did not. Pontus was very far away, and my decision had not made it closer.

Loricus was watching me.

"Yes. That's right. Very good, Loricus. That is what we will do. We will tell Fabius—or *anyone*—that you and I will look after my husband's estate. And as Naso was looking after mine as well, we will administer that for him too."

He was careful not to answer. He did not even smile. Instead, very respectfully, he bowed.

In the room the dust motes made their own obeisance and danced away.

Marcia had ordered the lights lit. The hangings glowed and the shadows lay as soft as lambswool in the corners. The room smelled of the curling iron and the paste her maids ground so carefully to clarify her already white complexion. A cloud of these women hung around her, buzzing like wasps.

Marcia was staring into a corner, removed as far as was humanly possible from the fuss. One magnificent bare shoulder gleamed in the dimness. I had to call her twice before she swung around and saw me.

"Oh. Pinni. How nice to see you. We've got people in to dinner. Fabius is lining up support for the Cassius thing. I haven't even had time to find a musician these people haven't heard, or a dress they haven't seen a hundred times. Fabia's coming. I need to see her. And her little boy. So sweet. Don't you think so? Look at my hair. I have such awful hair."

"You look lovely." And indeed, with her curls half tumbled down on her neck she had a disheveled, dryad charm. What a pity she couldn't go as she was, but of course it was not at all what a political dinner party needs.

Sadly she tugged at a lock. "Horrible. Have you been out to get your account books?"

I was saved from answering by Fabius, who had put his head around the doorway. He was in his outdoor cloak. "Evening, ladies. Yes, Pinni, did you bring them?"

Not saved for long. "Ah. No. I didn't. I will do them myself. Naso wanted me to. I—I have a document—"

I expected an argument, but as always I underestimated Fabius. He smiled agreeably and spread out his hands. His air of polite interest did not slip. "Well, if you want any help, I'm always glad to oblige." I let out a breath I had not realized I was holding. "Thank you, Fabius. Thank you." I'm not sure what exactly I was thanking him for—I think it was for not telling me I was a fool.

His mind had gone somewhere else, dismissing me so completely I sat down abruptly, feeling my legs collapse under me.

Marcia slapped away the fingers of her maid. "Stop yanking at me, girl. Here, give me the hairbrush. So, now: what are you going to do, Pinni?"

I thought of the emptiness of my house. "I need to get him back."

"How?"

"I don't know. I haven't any idea why he was sent away. The only thing I can think of is to begin at the beginning."

"And what is the beginning, do you think, Pinaria?" Fabius said. He smiled at me as one smiles at a child.

"It's the exiles. All of them. They all go back to the first Julia, don't they?"

Marcia looked annoyed. "Oh, Pinni, how could they? It was all such a long time ago."

"Well, I know, Marcia. But what other explanation could there be?"

I thought that Fabius was not listening, but he answered me. "You won't find out anything. The ones in exile can't talk, and all the others are dead."

"Yes," said Marcia sadly, "that's true. Everyone is dead. We'll never know any more about it than we do now. Pinni, you won't be able to help Naso that way. Better to concentrate on using your connections now, don't you think, Fabius?"

"Yes, certainly. Marcia, I expect you in the dining room presently. And tonight, I think we will be more conventional. Do you understand me?"

Marcia had gone back to studying herself in the mirror. "Are you joining us tonight, Pinni? It ought to be good. We've got Publius Vicinius coming in. His father is a good friend of Caesar's—they play dice together. Maybe he can do something for you."

I went to dinner that night, feeling very little like eating and less like a party. My smile felt plastered on, and all too likely to crack. I pushed the food around on my plate, trying to look interested in it. And the Persian dancer seemed grotesque without being interesting, the comedian interminable.

I had not seen Marcia acknowledge Fabius' instructions, but she was sitting in a chair, next to her daughter, Fabia Numantina. Fabia's husband Appuleius reclined next to his father-in-law at the head couch. Marcia, as always when Fabia was around, was completely absorbed in her and hardly spoke to me at all.

It did give me time to speak to Publius Vicinius. He was young, but already very distinguished. "Speak to Caesar? I'd be delighted, if I have the chance. I'll mention your husband's case to my father." He smiled shyly. "I know all your husband's poems by heart."

"Every one?" I said, startled.

"Every one:

"Of bodies changed to unfamiliar forms
My mind is borne to speak.
Gods, breathe on this work
For it is your work too,
And from the origin of the universe
To my own time
Lead my unbroken song.

"Before sea and earth, and the sky protecting all,
Nature had a single face: Chaos was its name
Nothing existed unless it was heavy, weak, ill-made,

86

And everywhere, everything contended in a rough, disordered mass
No Triton yet supplied the earth with light
Nor Phoebe yet her crescent horns renewed
Neither had the earth been suspended in the surrounding air,
Balanced on her weight;
Nor was there any Amphitrite to stretch her watery arms around
*   the long shores—*
Earth there was, and water, and air, but all confused :
Unstable land, unswimmable wave, air in want of light;
Nothing kept its shape, all fought with each,
For they were all one body.
Cold warred with hot, wet with dry,
Weightless opposed those having weight,
A god, or better nature, resolved this quarrel,
For sky and earth and land he tore from the waves
And limpid heaven from the denser air.
After that he extricated darkness, and banished a large quantity,
And set things in their positions, bringing peace :
Weightless heat shone out in the sky
Next in lightness air, and next in place,
Then thick and solid elements were dragged beneath
And formed by their own weight to be the sphere of earth…

"He says it's the work of a god to bring order to the world, doesn't he? Well, hasn't Caesar Augustus done the same thing for us?" I laughed.

"You don't think so? He ended the civil war, didn't he?"

"I suppose. And banished a lot of people—just like the darkness in the poem. And set others in their places, if you think their places are as far removed from any real power as possible. Or of course, in the tomb."

On the next couch, a man with a military look was regarding me with deep interest. He cleared his throat.

"I think, my dear lady, you might be careful."

"Of what?"

"People report—"

"Report? Report what? To whom?"

He coughed and turned back to his wine.

"Is that true?" I said to Vicinius.

"Oh, no. I don't believe that."

"I can't see that anyone's paying the slightest attention to us. Not even the gentleman who just spoke."

"We're only talking about poetry."

"And this is my cousin's house. Her dining room. We are perfectly safe here."

"Of course."

He gave me his shy smile. But all the same he let his voice sink to a whisper. "Don't you think your husband must be a god himself? After all, he's doing the work of one, isn't he? Bringing order to the history of the world, 'From the beginning down to the present day,' he says."

"I know he says that. But it's so strange. That's just what he doesn't do, does he? Wouldn't you expect the poem to be chronological? But some stories happen in the past, some seem to be happening now...I don't understand why he thinks he's bringing order at all."

"But that's just it. He sees these events all at once. Everything happens at the same time. Isn't that the proof? Because that's how a god would see them, isn't it?"

"I don't know. It might be."

"But don't you think he's saying that? That he's a god too?"

It was in my mind to say that I had always thought there was something in my husband that was more than mortal, but there was something in the insistence of his question, in the way he was hiding his eyes from me, looking down at his plate. I glanced over at the military man, but he was not looking at us any more.

It might only have been shyness in Publius Vicinius' downcast look, but might have been something else altogether. I hesitated.

"Isn't he a god, too? Wouldn't you say?" he prompted me.

"Oh, no. The equal of Augustus? My husband would never say that. He is a priest, of course. All poets are that. But the equal of Augustus? Never."

"But your husband—"

"Is no more than anyone else," I said firmly.

He gave me a sweet, disappointed smile, and presently engaged himself in a conversation with his neighbor on the other side. I wondered if he would speak to his father for us after all.

Certainly I heard nothing further. No word came from the Palatine recalling my husband or easing his exile. Fabius began to avoid me in his house. My uncle urged me to redouble my efforts, but could not suggest how. One day in the Forum on my way back from a temple visit in my litter, a woman I knew cut me dead. Not more than a few days later I heard that several of my closest friends had gotten together for an evening of playing dice and chatting: it was the sort of thing I would have been invited to as a matter of course in the old days. Now I was excluded. There were few invitations to dinner parties too—it was almost as if I had done something scandalous in remaining loyal to my husband.

My cousin Macer took to calling at Marcia's in the mornings, at the hour when ladies receive their families and friends. In her pretty courtyard he would patiently hold the keys she was sorting, or exchange the gossip she so loved. But his eyes would linger on me, and he would keep his looselipped and over-moist smile trained on me as he cautioned me against false hopes. I could have said the same to him.

Marcia herself noticed. "You could do worse than Macer, Pinni. He's so well-connected. And so handsome."

"His connections haven't done us any good," I said. "Besides, I'm still married."

She set her upper lip on her lower and gave me a look.

"Are you finding anything out? About the first Julia?"

"No. Nothing. I don't even know where to look."

"You won't. Fabius is right. They're all dead. Or in exile somewhere. No one can get to them."

I thought about that at night. All those men who made love in the Forum, all those noble names: Iullus Antonius, the son of Mark Antony, consul and proconsul, dead. Even his sons were gone,

one to death the other relegated in another scandal a few years later. Titus Quinctius Crispinus, consul, descended from a legendary hero of Rome, relegated, no one would even say where. Appius Claudius Pulcher, another aristocrat, tribune, relegated. Cornelius Scipio, the last of that great family, relegated; Sempronius Gracchus, tribune, author of tragedies, in exile somewhere in Africa, silent as the tomb.

Then one day I went to a birthday party. I had been invited months before: the son of an old friend of ours was to be sixteen. But when my litter set me down at the door, the doorman, a huge Gaul with yellow mustaches, stared out over my head and refused to speak to me.

I repeated my name. "I have an invitation."

He shook his thick neck. The chain that held him to the wall rattled. He was so big it didn't look strong enough to hold him.

"Let me speak to the mistress of the house."

His strange sky-like eyes nearly closed as he looked down at me. He grunted something.

"Are you saying 'not at home'?"

He crossed his arms. The muscles bulged. The chain rattled again. Not another word did I get out of him, though I asked to speak to the mistress again, and the housekeeper.

He ignored that.

Presently I heard music from inside. I got back into my litter and went home to Marcia's.

"Marcia, I have to speak to you," I said, hurling myself into the back garden.

She looked up from something she was doing with the fishpond.

"Oh, hello, Pinni. What do you think of this? See the little earrings? Isn't it cute?"

I was so startled I forgot my errand. "You're putting earrings on a fish?"

"Well, just the mullets. Everyone does it now. Why? Don't you like it?"

I took a deep breath. "It's lovely. Listen, Marcia. I had to tell you. Lutatia Hortensii refused me entry to her house, to a party she had invited me to herself, back in May. The doorman wouldn't even let me send in a message. He obviously had orders not to admit me. What's more, the Hortensii felt perfectly safe insulting me. As if I had no more power than a slave."

She studied the little bits of gold and glass in her hand. She did not look at me. When she spoke her voice was very soft. "Well, they're right, aren't they? What power *do* you have, Pinni? Aside from your connection to us, what power have you ever had?"

Marcia was right. I had none. When my husband left, he meant to give me independence. Instead, he made me a slave. Powerless and outcast. The shame weighed me down during the day, and filled my nights with hideous dreams. I was as exiled as he was. The only difference was that I was still in Rome.

The afternoon sun was slanting down out of a sky like a pool of water. It picked out the edges of the stones and glowed through the marble columns of the big houses on the Palatine Hill. Only the shadows had warmth: they burned like coals, violet under the walls. The city noise and stink rose only faintly from down below: I could hear water splashing in gardens and somewhere a late-blooming rose puddled its scent in a patch of sunlight.

I had come in my best chair, hung with byssos silk the color of spun gold, and trimmed with crimson fringe. My gown was white, and my cloak scarlet and gold. My best jewelry weighed down my ears and my fingers. Maybe I had no more power than a slave, but I had no intention of letting anyone see it in my dress.

At the Palace door, again, I told the Praetorian, "I will speak to Demosthenes. If you please. And I am in a hurry."

This time they must have been impressed because very quickly I found myself led through that vast shadowy house, past the monster in the atrium, and through the garden, into the small house at the back. The twisted little servant bowed himself nearly in two when he saw me.

"One moment, *kyria*. I will fetch my master."

It was a useless interview. Demosthenes bowed and smiled and sweated himself around the little room, denying he knew any more than he had said. I didn't mind. It wasn't Demosthenes I had come to see.

The little slave's pace was slow, and he had an odd gait, a kind of dragging slide, rather difficult to adjust myself to. The garden nearly defeated him, but he did better on the marble floors of the Palace, though our progress was at best leisurely.

That was fine with me. I needed the time.

"What is your name?"

"Aesopus, mistress." He had a voice like a crow. It was painful even to listen to.

During the long winter nights it had come to me that it meant something that an immaculate and finical man like Demosthenes kept such a servant whose ugliness was so spectacular. It wasn't like keeping a dwarf, to amuse yourself or your guests. It was merely painful, and hideous.

"Have you been with your master for long?"

"Yes, *kyria*. Many years." His eye leaked and his mouth was warped, but his feelings about his master were perfectly plain. He nearly spat.

"He must be pleased with your service."

He stopped and stared at me angrily out of his one good eye. Even that ran with liquid.

"He has his reasons to keep me."

"What reasons? He's afraid of you, isn't he? Well, isn't he? I saw him sweat every time you rattled the things on the desk. Why?"

He gave me a shrewd glance, knowing and sardonic.

"Because of what I know."

"And what is that?"

Around us people passed, intent on their errands. Men lounged against the pillars or chatted in corners, footsteps slid through the narrow passages, but his ugliness was a cloak: people glanced at him and looked away. We might have been entirely alone.

"Nothing, *kyria*. I know nothing at all." He was winking and nodding, so it was not possible to tell if he meant what he said.

"You know something about the princess, about Julia the Elder? Is that what you are saying?"

He hunched himself over further, making a rattling sound in his throat that it took me a moment to realize was laughter. But it was a private joke. Under his breath he muttered something I thought was, "More than he does."

"More than whom? Demosth—"

"No names, *kyria*. In this place, they will be noticed."

We had come to the atrium. The monster loomed over us, all spine and teeth and claws, no more twisted and strange than Aesopus.

"Look, Aesopus. I can't believe that story about the party in the Forum. The lovers on the Rostra, and all that. Who would do a thing like that? I just don't believe it."

He snickered. "It was winter. It was cold. You think they'd do it on a piece of stone?"

"So it's false?" If that was, maybe it was false about my husband too. I held my breath until my ribs hurt.

Presently he began to whisper again.

"My master told what he didn't know. He made it up. My master was not her lover—he knew nothing at all. He was afraid, when he saw what had happened to me. "

"Saw what happened to you?"

"When they asked Demosthenes he said he didn't know anything. They didn't believe him. He must know. And perhaps I did too. After all, slaves go everywhere. Who knows what they see? That is how they reasoned." He rattled his throat again. "They were not philosophers, the interrogators. You cannot expect logic. So they went on with me. For a long time. A very long time."

"They—they tortured you?"

He twisted his neck and looked up at me out of a tilted eye but he said nothing.

"Who did it? Was it Aug—"

"*Kyria. Kyria.* No names. Not that one especially."

"But that is who you mean."

We shuffled along to the accompaniment of his muttering and for a time I could make no sense of the words. Finally though I heard him saying "He—" Again the utter contempt, so I knew he meant Demosthenes—"he had friends among the servants of…of the princess' father. They told him he was next, so he confessed. He confessed to what he never did."

"He was not Ju—her lover?"

"Him? She had better taste than that."

"Did you know who her lovers were?"

"I knew one. The son of the man who lost the sea battle, the descendant of Hercules—" I knew he meant Iullus Antonius, the son of Marc Antony. "And he was her husband by right. She had been promised to his brother once. Before the brother died." He gave me a nod and a wink. "A last grand alliance, to restore the Repub—the past. The past that had never been." He snickered a little and wiped his nose on his sleeve. "Still it was a beautiful dream."

"What about all the others?"

"They were friends. I cannot say if they were more, but I doubt it. And my master was never her lover. He only said so because he feared the pain. That is why he keeps me: so that I will not tell."

"Aesopus, why do you endure this? Why don't you just—"

"Die? Kill myself?"

"Yes."

He spat on the floor. "Hate keeps me alive. And I hate the Romans. I hate them all."

"Oh, no, surely not. Not all of us. We all haven't hurt you, and it looks to me as if Livia at least has been generous and looked after you. You cannot blame the whole Roman world for what happened to you."

He was doubled over making a peculiar scratching sound and holding his belly. More of his attempt at laughter.

"You think I can't, *kyria*? Then you are a fool."

"You do not have the right to speak to me like that," I said.

Then for a moment he looked at me squarely. "*Kyria*, I have what rights I take. I have paid for them." His hand gestured over his hideous shape.

He knew there was nothing I could do. He was not my servant, and who would I complain to? He gave me a little nod, seeing I knew it.

"So, *kyria*, I will tell you and you will listen to me. You don't know what you are. You don't know who anyone else is. Open your eyes. Examine your assumptions."

"Which assumptions? I don't have any—"

"Everyone has assumptions. Even you. Open your eyes."

"Why are you telling me this?"

"Do you remember a woman named Phoebe? No? She was the princess' maid. She killed herself. Caes—*he* said he wished Phoebe had been his daughter, instead of Julia."

"He wished his own daughter had killed herself?"

He sneered. "Are you surprised? Did someone tell you he was a nice old man? If you believe that—"

We dragged along to the door. There he stopped. He stood before me with his head bent and his eyes on the ground.

"Phoebe was my wife," he said.

"Slaves cannot marry," I started to say, but he looked up at me with such grief and anguish in his face that I was silenced. It was part of his sorrow that he knew that already.

He made me a little bob—I suppose it was meant for a bow—and started to shuffle off.

"Wait." I wanted to give him money, but I carry so little and I had left my purse with my servant at the door. I slipped a bracelet off my arm. It was too much, but I could not give him nothing at all.

It startled him. He held the shining bangle on his palm and studied it. Then he closed his fist on it. In the blink of that liquid eye, it had disappeared.

That night I was awakened by an uproar from the servants' quarters. Confused I sat up in bed, wondering what it was. The stars were very bright and the moon nearly down. Long shadows cut the railing of the balcony across the wall. Far away a pack of starving dogs was howling. The air smelt of dawn. But from the back of the house someone was crying and a voice shouted over and over for the doctor.

I waited to hear if someone would come, but no one did. I threw on my cloak and let my foot down onto the cold tile floor.

The garden was damp to the cheek and gray with dew. The scent of the rosemary hedges pierced the air. In the distance I could see the row of doors along the back. All of them, even at this hour, hung gaping open. A crowd of half-dressed servants moaned and cried back and forth, collecting like a colony of ants at one end. Lamplight fluttered inside and as I approached a scream shot forth, ending in a long bubbling cry.

The doorway was crowded, but I could see over the heads. A man was kneeling on the floor. I recognized him: it was the Greek doctor I had seen with Marcia's son. Beyond him I could make out the corner of a soiled couch. Blood and vomit had stained it. A foot, splotched nearly black and twisted at a painful angle, jutted past the end. Around the ankle a string of cheap blue beads was wound.

I must have gasped or cried out, because heads turned to stare at me. I knew the beads. Philomela. She had worn them when she came to us and every year she added to the string, bead by carefully saved-for bead: I used to give her some for a present at the Saturnalia. I had an idea that her mother may have put them there, in a last effort to protect her little girl, before they took her child from her.

"Let me past, please. Let me past." I shoved against the servants. They gave way, but others, crammed in front, flowed into the space, and I made no progress. "Here. Let me see. It's Philomela. I must see her. It's Philomela." They paid no attention, but I leaned my weight against an elderly gardener and craned my neck to see over the crowd.

The doctor rose to his feet and stepped back. Behind him, now revealed, two men, heads together, immaculate in their white tunics in that dismal cell. I stared in astonishment. One was Macer. I recognized his blunt profile, his blobby lower lip gleaming like an oyster.

The man he was talking to was Fabius.

Beyond surprise now I just gaped. Why would Fabius concern himself with the servants? But here he was, obviously having taken charge. He brushed himself off, spoke a word to the doctor, and looked once more at the pitiable creature coiled in the sheet.

And now I could see Philomela. I had known her foot, but there is no way I could have guessed who she was from her face. Black with congested blood, it was curdled in a grimace of horror and pain. The eyes, mercifully, had closed, but a rim of white showed under one and the lips had drawn up to show a row of teeth. The mouth was open in a last silent scream.

In the stench of the room Fabius moved in a glimmer of white. He rinsed his hands at a basin a servant was holding, speaking briefly to the doctor. Macer followed him, shaking his head.

Fabius glanced once more at the bed as he shook the last few drops of water from his hand. Then he turned to the door. His eye caught mine. His face went crimson with anger.

In two strides he was across the sill and had grabbed me by the arm. I could feel the pressure of his fingers in the muscle.

"Fabius," I gasped, "you're hurting me."

I doubt he heard. His brows were down and his eyes blazed under them. "Just what do you think you are doing here?"

"I—but it's Philomela. My maid."

"I know who it is. Why are you here? Go back to bed at once."

I could feel the heat from his body and smell the anger in him. His arm was around me, forcing me away. His fingers had dug so hard they pressed against the bone.

Tears of pain started to my eyes. "Fabius, what has happened? And why are you and Macer—"

"Go back to bed. Do you hear me? I order you—"

I writhed in his arms so that I could look him in the eye. "I am not a member of your household, Fabius. You cannot order me—"

He gave a roar of rage. I don't even think there were words in it.

"You cannot order me around," I finished.

He stared at me as if he did not know who I was. Slowly the glare in his eyes faded and his breathing slowed. He ran his hands over his hair, and shook his head. He was himself again, immaculate and calm.

"Come. I will show you to your room."

"I want to know what happened to Philomela. And I do not want an escort to my room."

"Well, you are getting one. While you are under my roof I am responsible for you. You will obey my orders. Is that clear?"

It must have been—either that or the grip on my arm, which he resumed—because he marched me all the way across the garden and up the balcony stairs. At the door to my room he glanced inside. "Go to bed, Pinaria."

"Go to bed? Why? What are you going to do?"

"I am going to bed too."

"Why is Macer here?"

"He is visiting me. Good night, Pinaria."

"But I want to know—what happened to Philomela? Why are you—"

"I said, go to bed."

He was disappearing down the hall before I summoned myself to call after him, "Fabius, what happened to Philomela? How did she die?"

His voice came back to me as he took the first of the stairs. "She seems to have eaten something."

"Eaten something? What?"

"They're turning out the kitchen now, trying to find it. Let's hope no one else ate it, whatever it was."

"She was pregnant," I said.

"That's right," Marcia said, appearing suddenly at my elbow. "She probably took poison. Didn't want to name the father. Isn't that right, Fabius? They don't want to, do they?"

There was a deadly little pause.

"Oh," I said hastily, feeling that I was interposing myself in a gladiators' duel, "she might have eaten anything. I was always hungry when I was pregnant, and I kept wanting the strangest foods. Even fullers' chalk from the laundry."

Fabius swore. "What does that mean? Do we have to go through the laundry too?"

"I've heard of women who wanted to eat charcoal, and even dirt."

He gave me a glare that plainly said he blamed me for all this. "Until we know more be careful what you eat."

"Really? Do we have to? Surely that's unnecessary, Fabius."

"Oh, Hercules. I give up. Go to bed, Marcia. Pinaria, good night. Do you understand me? Let's have no more disturbances. At least for tonight."

"As long as you are under my roof you will obey my orders." I lay on my couch, still dressed and entirely wakeful, while the daylight seeped into the sky and the city traffic began its morning clamor. In my mind I was listening to Fabius' voice and watching him as he swung toward me out of the chaos of Philomela's room. I saw his rage and his violence. He was nothing like the polished diplomat he pretended to be.

Aesopus was right. I lay there, more surprised than anything else, wondering why I had not known. It came to me that it was my husband's fault—if fault was the word. Naso was so fine a man, so gentle, so loving, so strong, he had made around me a place of peace and safety so that I saw through his eyes. He was Fabius' friend, so I had assumed that Fabius was my friend too. But now that Naso was gone, the light of the strange country I was traveling in had begun to show me people as they really were. And I did not think that Fabius was my friend at all.

Well, there was something I had to do. Obviously, I could not remain under the roof of an enemy. I would have to tell Marcia, as soon as she was up, and find someone to pack up my things. Then I would go home. It was where I ought to have been from the first.

Marcia was disappointed. "But Pinni, I need you. You have to stay here. How can I manage without you?"

It was always difficult to tell her things without hurting her feelings. "I'm sorry, dear. But I must go."

"But you liked it here—Is it your maid? I'll give you another. Yours wasn't very good. And pregnant—"

"Yes, I know."

"Well, sometimes they do—"

"Do what?"

"Kill themselves. If their protector is gone."

"What do you mean?"

She shot me a glance out of the corner of her eye. "Well, he is, isn't he? Gone, I mean."

"He?"

"Oh, Pinni. You know what I mean. They all do it. Your husband wasn't any different from the others. I doubt they even think it has anything to do with us."

"What has? Do you mean Naso was the father of her child? Is that what you're saying?"

Her eyes went vaguely to the fishpond, and she said, "Do you think the white mullets are getting any bigger?"

"No. Is that what you're saying, Marcia?"

"Well, he wasn't very nice, was he? His most famous poem is about how to trick women into going to bed with men like him. It's not very respectful of women, is it?"

"Not *trick* women, Marcia. He never said that. Persuade them, maybe. And the poor men in the poem are in love… Anyway, that was a long time ago and he wrote a lot of other things that are wonderful about women. What about *The Heroines*? Do you know another poet in Latin who has written a book from the point of view of women? Isn't that respectful?"

Marcia's charming upper lip came down over her teeth in that way she has when she is a little annoyed.

"Oh, Pinni, aren't you comfortable here? We could give you another set of rooms. And I need you. What about Persicus? He hasn't been well this winter. You know how worried I am—won't you help me? After all, we have tried to help you."

I gave up. "All right, if you need me, I will stay."

But she had already forgotten the whole discussion. "Oh, good," she said vaguely. Then brightening, "What do you think? The little speckled one is almost big enough for earrings, isn't he?"

The servants made Philomela a funeral, according to whatever rites they followed. I went and so did Marcia, though she plainly thought I was making too much fuss over a slave. We stood around in the farthest corner of the back garden, near the heap of broken pottery and kitchen refuse, and watched while the fire consumed the slender corpse. The column of smoke went up into a bright winter sky, where the breeze took it. In a few breaths it was gone.

Sometime later in the morning, as I was counting tunics into a basket, Marcia appeared, leading by the wrist an elderly woman.

"I know you don't have a maid, Pinni, so I thought maybe Artemis here could help. She is better than she looks. Aren't you?" She shoved the old slave forward. "She knows how to make a whatdoyoucallit—you put drops of it in your eyes and they look huge and bright—she tried to teach my girls but they never get it right. You could borrow her, until you find someone of your own. I don't need her any time soon—"

The old woman avoided my eye. She was clean enough, and her hands were steady, but all the same there was something about her I didn't like. Something hidden, discontented. Her mouth drooped and her eye had a sullen gleam. Sometimes someone like that can spread so much trouble among the other servants the whole house is disrupted.

"Thank you, Marcia dear. It's so thoughtful of you. But I think I will just wait until I find someone—I don't need much help right now."

Marcia never argued. Mostly she smiled vaguely and wandered off. That in fact was what she did now. The slave shot me a venomous look and scuttled after her.

From that moment when poor Philomela died, my safety seemed to vanish. Perhaps I had never been safe, perhaps Naso had created around me not a world but an illusion. People I had believed to be our friends turned and betrayed us. Cotta and his brother refused to see me. When I went to their houses in the mornings to sit among the petitioners in the atrium, one by one others went in to pay their respects and ask their favors, but I sat until everyone was gone and no one called to me, no one offered me a cup of chilled juice or a word of friendship. Angry, I waited until the servants began to stare, but it did no good. In the end I had to wrap my cloak around me and go home.

Vicinius, who knew all of my husband's poetry by heart, never came to the door, though he had promised that he would speak to his father—"Caesar's great friend, they play dice together on holidays," he had assured me. I waited, but nothing changed, and he never came. I doubt he had even raised the subject.

Macer, on the other hand, was always at Fabius and Marcia's, smiling and encouraging, holding my hand and calling me "Dear Cousin," telling me that he was sure my husband would be home in no time. For a time I believed him: he had charge of the public libraries and was close to Augustus. But it wasn't long before some well-wisher went out of his way to tell me that Naso's books were no longer available.

"Augustus ordered them to be removed?" I asked, fighting a need to sit down until the room stopped turning.

"No, Pinaria. But someone did it anyway. Someone who wanted to stand well with Augustus perhaps."

I gave orders that I was not at home to Macer.

It didn't stop the strangeness, or the fear. Marcia's house itself turned against me. The shadows seemed to grow deeper in corners, and whispers hung around them like cobwebs. Even in my own quarters I did not feel safe. My footsteps had echoes that padded after me, stopping a heartbeat after I stopped, starting again when I had turned away. But if I whirled to look, holding up a lamp or throwing open a shutter, no one was there, and the corners mocked me like grins, the passages stretched into vast distances, filled with cold winter light and inexplicable sibilance.

Things did not stay where I put them: some rolls of books in our own red leather covers had mingled themselves in the cubbies with Fabius' white and gold ones; a stack of writing boards left in order was a mess when I returned from a momentary errand; in my room my brushes and combs had been moved and my clothes were wrinkled, though I had watched the servant fold them flat. My rooms were full of people I did not know, coming and going on errands I had never heard of.

Loricus was the most peculiar of all. Of course he came every day to consult me about my own household, but I began to think he came at other times too.

One morning when I had decided not to go call on anyone I saw him in one of the gardens, where he was talking to a young man in a short tunic, none too clean.

"Good morning, Loricus. Who was that?" The boy, catching sight of me, had run off.

"Who?" he started to say, but he caught my eye. "Ah. Yes. That boy?"

"Yes. Whom did you think I meant?"

"He's nobody. Nobody you need worry about, mistress."

"I am not asking if I ought to worry, Loricus. I want to know who he is."

"Ah. Yes. Interesting." His deep blue gaze went toward the door where the boy had disappeared. "A servant we are trying out, mistress," he said. But the smooth head was beginning to gleam, and the strands of hair were working loose.

One evening after dinner, when the lamps were just being lit and shadows still pooled under the columns, I caught a glimpse of Macer, floating in and out of them, near Fabius' office. I was alone in the house: Marcia and Fabius had gone to dinner at Livia and Augustus'.

I made a dive, undignified, for the colonnade. Too late.

"Pinaria?"

His face was in darkness, but his voice came out to me, cool and soft, like water in a fountain. "Pinaria. How nice to see you." "Is it, Pompeius Macer?"

"Of course. It is always a pleasure to see such a beautiful woman."

His hand came forward into the light, manicured and white. I had a strange feeling that if it touched me I would be pulled down to drown under the shadows.

"I'm so sorry: Fabius is out. I'll tell him you called."

"I know. Never mind. I'd rather visit with you anyway."

"I don't think you ought to be doing that, Macer."

"My dear, we are cousins."

"Yes, of course, but—"

"But we could be so much more. I would like to help you, if you'll let me."

The way he helped my husband by removing his books.

"Thank you, Macer. You can. Please talk to Augustus about bringing back Naso. He wanted you to, and I know it would do so much good."

"Ah, such a loyal wife."

"I try to be."

"Don't let your loyalty go too far."

"What do you mean?"

The soft voice trickled on. "You must face facts, Pinaria. Naso will not be coming home. Not for a very long time."

"He would be if his friends were loyal," I said hotly.

"We *are* loyal, my dear. But the situation is dangerous. We cannot afford to be too closely linked with him. That is true for you too."

"I am his wife. I could hardly be more closely linked than that."

"Yes," he said sadly. "And you are in danger because of it. Your position, your wealth, you child's future, all are at risk."

"I know that, Macer. So does Naso. He is trying to protect us."

"You must think of yourself now. I can offer you security, and the standing which you have lost by Naso's disgrace. It would be a good arrangement, don't you think? With benefit on both sides. Of course I am devoted to you, and admire you—I think you know that—"

"How did you get in?"

The voice came out of the darkness again, untroubled.

"Ah, lovers know how to find a way. "Night and love and wine urge nothing controllable."

At that my anger swelled so that I could not keep it inside me any longer.

"Those are my husband's words. I know them: it's a line from *The Love Affairs*. And you are trying to use them against him. Against me. You may be my cousin, Pompeius Macer, but you are not welcome in my house."

I thought in the darkness he smiled. "This is not your house, Pinaria."

"Get out. Now. Or I will call the servants and have you thrown out."

"My sweet cousin," Macer said and I knew that he was smiling now. "Think about what I have said. The offer is open."

I thought about it, all right. Every time I did I wanted to wash my hands. I took to looking behind me when I walked and searching the corners of the street when I was out. I did not see him again, but I was sure he had been there.

When Marcia offered me another servant—a better one than the crone she had tried to give me before—I reacted with horror.

"But, Pinni, you have to have a maid," she wailed. "You can't go around like—like any old thing. You have to make the right impression."

"I know. And I will do something about it too. I just can't stand to have anyone around me now," I said, thinking it was a simple thing to say so that I wouldn't have to go to the trouble of making a decision. It was only afterwards that I realized it was true.

Then it was the day before the Saturnalia. Marcia, coming away from her son's sickroom, caught my arm. "They've moved Cassius' trial to today. When the holiday begins they won't be able to conduct any legal business. We've got some people coming to dinner, to talk about the trial. Fabius is prosecuting, you know. I don't know why he does this to me. Half the people I like in Rome are on the other side. How does he expect me to make up three tables for dinner? Why do men get so caught up in this politics thing anyway? What a waste of time. Do come down and join us, Pinni. I need more people tonight."

I had to smile, though there was nothing funny in the thought of Cassius' ordeal.

Cassius' trial was held in the Basilica, since the weather was too bad to sit in the Forum. The air was thick with the smell of damp wool clothing and the oil lamps guttered, sending shadows scuttling into the corners. In the smoky half-dark Fabius raised his arm and the jury on their benches leaned forward like people at the theater when the messenger comes onstage to announce the deaths. And indeed it might have been death Fabius was asking for. He listed the times Cassius had spoken against Augustus, he read a bit from the pamphlets that were going around, he argued from what everyone knew and he made it sound worse than it ever had before. His words flowed over the jury, bending them back and forth like grass in the wind. I began to fear for Cassius. I had thought that Fabius would deliberately lose the case: in private he had said that he and Cassius were on the same side. But he did not seem to be trying to lose. Indeed, I have never heard him speak better.

Cassius in his turn, pristine white toga notwithstanding, lowered his head and bellowed like an enraged bull in his own defense. Sincere, rough-spoken, powerful, he must have moved the jury, if anyone could. "Free men say what they want. *Romans* say what they want. Are you really going to let them rob you of that right?" he roared, and the audience around me hissed at villainy. The jury too seemed moved. They gave him back stare for stare, anger for anger, but his harsh laughter they did not answer. And I knew then that Cassius had lost, for before the whole city would have repeated his jokes, and the laughter would have echoed everywhere.

The jury filed up to the praetors' stand and dropped their ballots in the jars. The Basilica waited in tense silence. But when the verdict was read a long sigh, almost a moan, came out of the crowd. It was not surprise, I doubt it was even anger, but a kind of despair, bitter, sad, and resigned. Cassius was denied food and water anywhere in Rome—it was now a crime to give him anything, and anyone could kill him with impunity. He was no longer a Roman, scarcely even a person.

And for all his courage, Cassius felt it. His great head swung from side to side and he stared at us from under his heavy brow. In the thick atmosphere he glimmered, white as the ox they choose for the sacrifice. You could almost see the gilded horns and the gold cloth draped over him. He knew that too. The silence held. For a long moment he gazed at us through the lampsmoke and shadows.

Once he opened his mouth to speak, but what came from him was only a roar of pain, inarticulate and bewildered. Then a lictor stepped forward and led him away.

He vanished from Rome. I missed him. I think the whole city did. People went about their tasks in silent anger: shopkeepers served you their few provisions without a word; sullen crowds lingered on street corners or drifted through the nearly empty markets; tradespeople pretended they had not seen you, or stared at the floor with insolent intensity. The quiet was uncanny, especially for the Saturnalia. There were few feasts and banquets, for there was little food to spare in the city, and men when they celebrated the festival got drunk with grim determination. Even in the Forum that once rang with voices, people hardly spoke or muttered a word or two under their breaths as they hurried through. No one wanted to be seen to linger, for fear it might be thought that they would make a speech. It was so quiet that the tramp of the Praetorian Guard on the Palatine Hill could be heard all over Rome.

I lay awake at night, wondering at it. It did not seem possible that stilling one man's voice would silence the whole city, but the loss of Cassius was very serious. Slowly I began to think.

It was not just Cassius. It was Labienus too, whose books were publicly burned, and Naso, who was gone, and whose words so few could read now that his books had been taken from the libraries. It was Cotta Maximus and his brother, a disgrace to their outspoken father, and Macer in his sycophancy. It was Fabius, arguing so chillingly for repression in the courts, and so differently at home. It was Silanus, who had silenced himself by going away on his own, before something happened to him, and Timogenes the scholar, who turned against Augustus, but could do nothing more to express his anger than to burn his own history. And it was L. Aemilius Paullus, and Iullus Antonius, and Appius Claudius Pulcher, and the last of the Scipios, and all the rest of the dead and exiled, who could say anything they liked now, though no one still above the ground would hear them.

"Give it up, Pinaria," Fabius had said. "You'll never find anything. The ones in exile can't talk and the others are all dead."

"Think of yourself. It is hopeless, what you are trying to do," Macer had advised me.

I did not like Fabius, and I did not trust Macer, but all through those long December nights when I lay awake listening to the faint shouts of the revelers and the grind of military boots on distant stones I thought that they were right. And then on the last day of the holiday, as I stood in the garden giving out gifts of money to the servants, I suddenly remembered Marcia, reclining on her couch at dinner in a world turned upside down as if it were always Saturnalia, and I knew that they were wrong.

Julia the Elder and her mother lived in exile, that was true. But they lived.

As I closed up the coffer and handed it to Loricus, I thought: and all those powerful, political creatures, Fabius and Macer and the others, all those men who were so closely connected to Augustus, may have forgotten those women. But the Roman people haven't, the plain mass of us, whom the great ones so easily overlook. I saw their faces when we stood before her daughter's door. I could feel how angry they were.

If the women were still alive who else might not be? Among us, among the powerless and unnoticed, there might be many.

I knew one, the slave Aesopus. Hurriedly, in secret, I sent to ask him one last question. The answer came back in a word or two, along with my golden bracelet.

That night, the last of the Saturnalia, I left the house with a heavy escort. Bands of men were roaming the squares, arms linked, looking for trouble. I took ten slaves and a plain stout chair: I wore no conspicuous jewelry and kept my head covered and the curtains drawn. The streets are never safe during the Saturnalia but the night of Acca Larentia they are worse. Acca Larentia was the widow of a rich man—some say a prostitute—who long ago left her fortune to the City. Now her tomb is a shrine, and while it stands open, the dead walk. It is never a good time, and this year the city was already uneasy, famished and truculent.

It was a clear night, cold after rain and very still, with an immobile and monumental sky. The moon, three-quarters full again, spilled a long deep wash of blue against a silent barricade of clouds. In the streets torches passed, tossing shadows against the walls; voices were flung down alleys or out across the squares, repeating and distorting, from sources I never saw. In the Velabrum, where the priests were just closing the doors of Larentia's Tomb, I passed through clouds of incense. The last words of their chant died away, the smoke curled silently toward the sky, smelling of death.

I crossed the river, knowing I traveled among ghosts. It was so quiet I could hear the water running under the bridge, and far away now cries and shouts in the Forum, where someone must have been making a speech, in spite of the pervasive fear. Ahead the road was empty and the silence unnatural and frightening.

I told myself that once among the woven alleys that make up the Transtiberim I would be among living people, however foreign and exotic. But it was not so. The narrow streets were dark, and still water glistened with the reflection of moonlight between the cobbles. Famine was in the city, and there was no oil for lights—what they could buy the people of the quarter had eaten. Now and then we passed someone: a bearded Syrian in tapestried robes or a fringed and tasseled Jew, a small group of robed and hooded women swaying like columns. All of them stared from hollow faces and their bones gleamed under their hunger-roughened skin. Once from a doorway came the chant of people at prayer though they were singing in the dark; once the sputter of a cheap torch illuminated a room where men and women in torn clothing were sitting in a circle around a tiny corpse in white linen on a trestle. In another square I could see a pyre being readied amid the wails and cymbals of foreign music. Down a dark alley a procession was coming. "Hurry on," I commanded my bearers.

We came, by much stopping and asking, at last to a tiny square. In one corner huddled what I took at first for a street prostitute's booth, but it was painted and decorated like a country shrine. The smell of incense rolled out the narrow doorway. Offerings clattered on their strings as I ducked inside, and a voice singing tunelessly threaded me in.

Inside the aromatic smoke hung in folds, thick with dust. A few coals smoldered on an altar, and in the starlight of the doorway dimly I could make out a small pottery image—a wolf shape and what might have been a pair of men or boys. Dirty bedclothes spilled onto the floor and a pot of night soil added its odors to the smoke.

"Closed today. Go away. Acca Larentia," said a voice from near my knees. I looked down. Before me squatted a wide mass. It shook constantly with a motion like a calf's-foot jelly on a tray. In the stinging haze it took me a moment or two to see that it was in fact a woman, overflowing a three-legged stool.

"I am looking for a slave called Diana. I was told she once belonged to the household of the daughter of Augustus. Is that you?"

The woman ignored this. "No business today. The festival. Of Acca Larentia."

"Yes. I know. I passed the tomb in the Velabrum. Are you Diana?"

She turned up to me a face like a frog, plastered with white lead, her bulging eyes circled heavily with charcoal. "I am The Priestess."

"I see. And you are also or once were Diana?"

She shook her draggled head. "Busy. Busybusybusybusy. Must celebrate the rites."

"But the rites are over. The Arval Brothers have closed the tomb."

She spat on the filthy floor. "Men. Not for them."

"The rites are for everyone. Every Roman. The pontifex and the Arval Brothers make offerings there for all of us…"

"Hah. Hah. Hah. She was a lupa like us—"

I was a little shocked. "Lupa" is the street word for a prostitute. It means a she-wolf. My first husband said it was because they were so rapacious. But he reproved me even for asking. And Acca Larentia one of them? He would have been speechless. I was myself.

The frog-woman was crowing at my confusion. "Lupa. Lupa. Lupa. Hahahahahahaha. She was their *mother*."

"Mother? Whose mother?"

The figure quivered to life. Slowly it rose and, facing the altar, raised its shaking arms. She was as tall as I, though her great mass made her look short.

Gobbling in some dialect or language, she began to dance. Her hair tangled in her eyes, her clothes fell away from her jiggling breasts, her hips slithered and shook. It was strange, and frightening, and in an odd way very impressive.

She had obviously forgotten me. Her voice mumbled on, singing "lupa, lupa" and the huge figure moved in the half dark in some pattern of its own. I looked around. There was nowhere to sit but the stool or the bed, and I didn't want to do that. I would have liked a bit of water for my throat, for the smoke carried something drying and acrid on its fumes, but the flask I eventually found tucked under the stool held wine and was crusted with dirt.

"Lupa," she sang. "Mother. She was their mother. Hahhahhaha-haha." She shot me a glance under her greasy black knots. "Romulus and Remus!" she screamed in triumph.

I began to laugh. "Oh, no. That was a real wolf. She found them and suckled them. You can see the statue in the—"

Immediately there was a change. All the movements of her vast body shuddered once and stopped. Slowly she lowered her arms and deflated onto the stool. Her long lower lip swelled and under the curve of her forehead I could see that her eyes filled.

"Lupa," she said once, in a tiny voice like a lost child.

I thought this over. And indeed, I had to admit it made sense, if you ignored everything the priests and the teachers and the poets say.

Presently little sounds intruded themselves. The coals on her altar hissed, and her breathing began to rasp.

The noise grew louder until it filled the cramped space, grating back and forth in the reek. Now and then she mumbled and once she said clearly, "No. No. Please. No."

"Thank you," I said, putting a silver denarius on her makeshift altar. "I know you've told me what you can. I'll just leave you in peace now."

Her head did not lift and her body did not seem to move, but a small white hand, shockingly delicate at the end of such a thick waxy arm, reached out and snatched up the coin.

I stumbled to the door. It had shaken me to think of the priests as liars—or mistaken. It made me want to lean against the clean starlight and the solid black stones for support.

"Dancing," she muttered. "Pretty lady. In the Forum."

I turned back. "What? What did you say?"

"Dancing..."

"That's right," I breathed. "Julia danced. Her father said so."

"Ah, pretty," the woman crooned. "So beautiful. Naked. Flute-sandsingingandflowers. A crown of flowers she has. She is putting it on his head..."

"Whose head? Who was there?"

"A god. A god is there. Watching them."

"A god?"

But the moment had passed. She slumped on her stool, head down, hair hanging in strings. The choking air weighed down the silence.

"Diana?"

She looked up. "Yes, mistress. Diana is here."

I let out my caged breath.

"Sweetsweetsweet. Sweet mistress."

She had found the wine jug. Now she took a swallow and spat some out. She heaved to her feet and danced a bit, humming to herself. I think she forgot me. Poor thing, I hated to call her back.

"Diana. Where is your mistress now? Is she is in the Forum?"

"Yes. Dancing."

"Who is there with her?"

"No. Please. Nononono." Her voice rose to a scream. "Nooooo. No one there. No one there. No one is there."

"Calm yourself. No one will hurt you now."

"No?"

"Look. My hands are empty."

"Oh." She thought about this for a while.

"What is she wearing? Is she naked?"

"Only flowers. She takes off. Flowers. On his head." She made a kissing noise." Ummm. Lupa. Lupalupalupa."

"She kisses someone? Who?"

"Cold. Bronze."

"She kisses someone who is cold and bronze? A statue?"

She cackled with laughter. "Hah. Got you. Statue in the Forum."

"Whose statue is it?"

"Marsyas. The satyr. She loves Marsyas…"

"They were dancing around the statue of Marsyas? But he is a Paelignian—my husband sang of him. There is a statue of Marsyas in Sulmo, where he comes from."

"Yes. He is singing."

"My husband?"

"A priest? From Sulmo?"

I remembered Publius Vicinius. A poet may be a priest. It is the same word—"Vates".

"Yes, the priest. Was he singing while they danced in the Forum?"

Panic had seized her again. She waved at me, pushing me away. "No one. No one. No one dancing. No one kissing. No, please. Don't hurt Diana again. No one dancing." The tears ran down again now faster through the channels the earlier ones had worn.

"Diana, who was there with your mistress?"

"No one. No lovers. Only Iullus. He was her husband."

"Tiberius was her husband."

"No. Iullus. Promised to Iullus. Not Tiberius. Her father—No lovers. Not my mistress…"

"No lovers? Are you sure? Everyone has always said—"

Not everyone. Aesopus also had denied it.

"No. Nononono," she said in a sad little voice. "It was all just—"

"All what?"

"All just politics. It was only politics. She was chaste." But a tide of agony took her and she cried, "I told. I told. Mistress, forgive me, I told them…"

"What did you tell?" I whispered.

"Ahhhhhh." She was screaming, thrashing around on the stool, sobbing and shrieking. "Anything. Anything. Tell me. Tell me. I will say it. Anything."

My chief bearer put his head around the doorway. Behind my back I waved him away.

"Hush. Hush. It's all right. I am sure Julia forgave you."

"Forgave?" The eyes looked out through her hair like a frightened animal peering through leaves.

"Of course she did."

"She will forgive?"

"I am sure of it."

"Ask? Ask her to forgive?"

"We can't, dear. She doesn't live in Rome any more. She is gone."

"Not forgive?"

She began to cry again, this time very quietly. Finally she shook herself, and wiped her eyes. "Busy today. Rites." Then heaving herself to her feet, she started to dance. As I slipped out the door I could hear her behind me, chanting, "Lupa, lupalupalupa." Her voice sounded young, and entirely lost.

"I think she was telling the truth," I said to Marcia when at last I had a chance to talk to her. We were sitting under the colonnade with her daughter, Fabia Numantina. Down the way Fabia's little boy Appuleius was learning to play knucklebones from Marcia's son Persicus. They were playing for a heap of old beads, and Persicus seemed to be winning them all. The contrast between the boys was shocking: the sturdy little Appuleius with his fat cheeks, gurgling with delight; Persicus, languid and nearly green under his pallor. He had Fabius' dark elegance, but in his remoteness he reminded me of his mother. He had her charming pointed upper lip too.

Outside, the rain dripped off the roof, making a cave, cozy and filled with the aromatic smoke of the brazier.

"Could it be true, do you think, Marcia?"

Marcia hardly seemed to hear. When Fabia was visiting she rarely had time for anything else. I think that Fabia is the person Marcia loves most in the world. Well, there is nothing wrong with that—mothers ought to love their daughters. But it did make it harder even than normal to get her attention when Fabia was there.

Now she had turned her shoulder to me and was opening her mouth to speak to her daughter, but Fabia put out her hand to stop her. "You think the—the lupa—was telling the truth? About Naso?"

"Certainly about Naso. I never thought he was her lover."

Marcia's voice was so soft I could hardly hear her. "Oh, Pinni, you wouldn't."

"What? He loves me, Marcia. He wouldn't do such a thing."

"No. I—No. But you know, he married you because of your connection to us."

"He married me because he loves me, Marcia."

"Yes. Yes. Of course. Fabia, do you think it's getting chilly? Perhaps the boys need cloaks. Persicus does, and I think Appuleius does too. Really, Fabia darling, you ought to take better care of him…"

"Oh, Mother, please. Don't worry so. Appuleius is fine." Fabia turned to me. "What about the others, the ones accused of being her lovers too?"

"Evidently, this Diana and her sister were close to Julia. And why would she lie? Especially now? What would she have to gain? If anything, she would say what they wanted to hear. But she denied it."

"But Pinni, she is crazy. You said so yourself."

"All the same, I thought she was really remembering something. For example, was Julia really promised to Iullus Antonius?"

About marriages and betrothals, divorces, pregnancies, miscarriages, love affairs, Marcia could not be faulted. She was the Lucretius of this kind of information. And she loved to show off her knowledge. She did not let us down now. "Yes, I think so. When she was a child, she was supposed to marry his brother, Marcus Antonius Antyllus. They were the two sons of Mark Antony and Fulvia, of course, and Antyllus was the elder. It was supposed to be a big reconciliation between the supporters of Antony and the supporters of Augustus. The end of the civil war. It was all planned and papers were signed, but Antyllus died. We all thought she'd marry Iullus, of course, and I think there was a betrothal—I don't remember exactly, but I do believe there was—but then there was some problem with one of the tribes on the border somewhere, and her father betrothed her to some local king. She never married him either, but for a time it was a good idea, don't you think? Fabia, I'm calling the nursemaids. Your boy looks chilly to me."

"Mother—"

But Marcia had already called, and the servants were scurrying.

When calm had settled around us again, I said, "Diana, the former slave, said the meeting in the Forum was something political."

"Oh, no, Pinni. That's impossible." Marcia thrust some wool into my hands. "It's all such old news, don't you think? Here, wind this for me. Do you like this wool? It's something new—" But Fabia looked up with interest. "No, Mother, this is interesting. Pinaria, do you mean it was some kind of secret meeting?"

I thought about it. "It would have to be, wouldn't it? Otherwise why were the slaves tortured? If it were something ordinary why didn't they just say so when Julia and the men were accused of adultery?" Marcia was shaking her head. "But Pinni, don't be silly. Why would anyone hold a secret meeting in the Forum? I mean really, it's the most public place in Rome. It doesn't make sense."

"It makes as much sense as holding an orgy there."

Fabia laughed. "Mother, she's got you there. Why on earth would anyone want to have sex in the open square right in the middle of the city, where anyone might see them?"

"If they were drunk?"

"How drunk could they have been? It would still be more comfortable at home. You know who they were; they all had big houses with every comfort anyone could wish."

"I suppose they did."

"So," I said, feeling that I had secured a victory, "what would they be plotting about?"

Her eyes looked cloudy and sad.

"I said, what kind of political thing would they be doing, Marcia dear?"

"Yes, Mother. What kind of political thing?"

Her voice came from so far away. "I don't know. Boys, what are you doing? Fabia, look at them—what are they doing now?"

"They look fine to me, Mother. I have an idea. Let's ask Father. He knows a lot of things like that."

Marcia brightened. "Yes. What a good idea. Yes, let's ask him. Your father knows all that political kind of thing—"

Fabius was the last person I wanted to ask. "But he wouldn't know about this. He was away, wasn't he? In Spain? Marcia, wasn't he?"

She turned a look of concern to me. "Oh no. He came back early. Didn't you know? I thought I told you that. I didn't even have time to get the house ready. He was here at least half a month before that night. We can certainly ask him."

"No, thank you, dear. I won't trouble him. He's very busy, after all."

Fabia shook her head, and in Marcia's eyes the bewildered look came back. "But there is no one else to ask."

"Yes," said Fabia sadly. "It was a long time ago. They are all gone now."

Like Fabius, they thought it was over. Perhaps everyone did. The city was quiet, the voices had died. Well, then, I thought, I will go back to the ghosts and find the answer there.

PART III

When I was small and my parents died, I went to live with Marcia and her family. It is odd how children think: Marcia was six years older than I—just turning twelve when I was six—and though I knew she was still a child, I believed all the same that she was grown up, and a woman like my mother. Indeed as the memories of my mother faded, Marcia came to replace them in my dreams, and in a confused way I thought of her as both my playmate and my protector.

Her own mother was a cold creature. She was the granddaughter of Marcus Atius Balbus and Julius Caesar's sister, and far too grand to pay attention to a small child from a minor family like mine. Marcia spent a lot of time in her company, but of course Marcia, in keeping with her station, was being groomed for an important marriage, and a distinguished life. She was often required at some function, or to meet some other great lady who was visiting. So I played by myself until she was free. Then we had the run of the house, under the casual supervision of the maids. Marcia used to order them around as if she were her mother, a skill I admired but did not try to emulate. It was clear to me that when I was not with Marcia I was expected to keep myself as unobtrusive as possible.

Atia never addressed me except in anger. If she called aloud some pet name for a child—"Dear" or "Honey" or the like—both Marcia and I knew that only one of us was meant, and which one it was.

It was partly Atia's nature, I now know. Some terrible pressure welled up in her and sent her anger flying. Then she would accuse me of fantastic crimes: stealing from the kitchen, damaging her clothes, wearing her jewelry. Bewildered and enraged, I fought back, erupting like a fountain in shouts and tears, "But I didn't," I would cry, "I don't. I haven't. I never touched the dress…Lucius Marcius gave me permission to read in the library…I wasn't near the kitchen. I have never seen that ring—" I would shriek, desperate to be believed. It did no good. Atia would swoop down. "What is this noise? Pinaria be quiet this instant."

"But they—but I—"

"Quiet, I said." Her sharp nails would dig into my arm. But she would speak softly and shake her head. "What have we done to make you disobey us? We have taken you in, we give you everything anyone could want, we protect you with our name. And is this how you repay our love and our concern, with hatred and defiance?"

I had not thought I hated them. Or even that I was defying anyone. I only wanted to defend myself. My mother had taught me when I was very small that a Roman does not lie. How then could I agree that I had stolen or fibbed or disobeyed, when I had not? It was true that they had taken me in. Without them I would have had no place to go. I had no place now. I suppose even that they did their best for me. Perhaps Atia was right, perhaps I did hate them. If so I was vicious and ungrateful as they thought.

I have said that it is odd how children think. Well, it is. I knew that while I might be as bad as she said, I was equally sure that Atia hated me for no reason. Or none that I could understand. Confused and shocked, I could find no answer, and many times at night I lay awake crying in secret. Often I wished that I had gone with my mother and my father when they died.

Sometimes the disorder in the house was so great that Marcia felt it too: I used to hear her at night, stifling her tears at some encounter of mine with that harsh voice and frozen eye. It was such a sad little sound, I used to sneak in to her, slipping through the nighttime chill and silence to her room. There we would sit on her bed while I combed her long light brown hair, and she talked to me of her unhappiness. I think I liked listening because it made a bit of warmth in the terrible coldness of that house.

At first Marcia and I played together, but after a time her mother began to demand her presence more and more. Marcia's wedding was approaching. Alone, I spent some time trying to figure out what to do with myself, pestering the servants until they chased me off, whereupon I wandered out into the garden to kick disconsolately at the gravel on the paths or throw stones into the fish ponds.

One day I stumbled on a small room at the back of the house. Inside an old man with a long Greek beard looked up from a roll he had been annotating. I knew him, of course. He was Marcia's father's elderly tutor.

"Come in, little girl," he said. I think that like me he was lonely, for he would look up from his beloved rolls of Pindar and Herodotus as I came in and give me a sweet smile. I sat in the corner on a low stool, listening as he read aloud to himself. When finally I found the courage to ask to read the beautiful Greek myself, he taught me. I used to make a nuisance of myself I suppose, but the old man never discouraged me. Marcia came once or twice, and shared her knowledge, but when old Diogenes asked her a question in his ancient whisper, often she seemed not to hear him. After a while she stopped coming.

Her father I scarcely knew. His active political life kept him frequently from home, and on the rare occasions that I saw him he would frown in puzzlement when his eye happened to fall on me, as if he wondered what such a lowborn and ill-favored child was doing in his house. He had celebrated a triumph many years before, and the glory still clung to him. I was afraid even to speak in his presence.

Marcia's grandfather was Lucius Marcius Philippus. From the moment I saw him I loved him. He always had time for us children. When he saw us he would stop and talk, asking us questions that I had to puzzle over before I could answer. That interested me, but on those occasions a little frown would crinkle Marcia's fine curved forehead and she would look away. So in the end I think he talked to me more. He used to ask me what I read, and rather than have me recite, would tell me interesting things about the poets who sang the songs, or the occasions when he had heard them. Sometimes he would fetch me to stroll around the garden, which was, in his retirement, his great interest. He would name the plants to me, and tell me things about their growth or their properties or their literary history, always speaking to me as if I were a grown woman and my opinion worthy of consideration.

For my part I thought he was a great man. Now that I am older, I think so still. He was the stepfather of Octavian, who had become first Caesar then Augustus, and like the rest of Octavian's family he tried to persuade the young boy not to accept the legacy that Octavian's great-uncle, Julius Caesar, had left him. It was so dangerous, that legacy—already Antony and Brutus were at odds, and war was growling like thunder on the horizon. Octavian was only nineteen years old and had virtually no experience in military matters—or in any other matter, if it comes to that. It was probable that he and anyone who supported him would be killed before the year was out. Yet despite his misgivings Marcius helped his nephew: it was what a family did, he used to say. I remember once he took Marcia and me out to the garden, and directing twigs to be cut from a pear tree, gave one to each of us. He told us to break them, which we easily did. I still remember the little snap in the frosty air, and the bemused and puzzled look on Marcia's face. He bent down and handed us each this time a small bundle of the little sticks. "Now break these." But of course we could not even make them bend. "There. You see? That is what a family is," he said. "If we hold together, we are strong."

I had not thought that Marcia was listening, for her eye had gone away into the gray winter air in her usual dreaming way, but that night she came and sat on the end of my bed. "Pinni," she whispered, "let's never fight again."

I hugged her and said of course we never would, and I think we both cried. Perhaps we padded downstairs on frozen feet to swear in front of the night-shadowed family altar. Perhaps not. But in any case, though before that time we had the quarrels and spats that are common to children, after we never had so much as an angry word.

Marcia was married when she was fifteen, and the preparations for her wedding engrossed the house for months. Marcia's mother stalked the halls issuing orders to her secretaries and counter-manding them a moment later, her voice growing every day more and more hoarse and grating. Philippus hid out in his study, pre-tending to work on the marriage contracts. The maids huddled in corners crying, their legs and backs marked with red weals where they had been beaten. The rest of us kept unnaturally quiet, and every task was made more difficult by confusion and anxiety. But Marcia was marrying Paullus Fabius Maximus, a man of great dis-tinction and a close friend of Augustus'. He was then nearly thirty, and had been waiting for her for years. It was an important alliance on both sides. The household gods must have wearied of the peti-tions we all offered up—everyone feared the ill-omened word, the unlucky sign—but the ancestors would indeed have been pleased at the merger of the two families.

It was a beautiful wedding, in spite of our fears. Marcia was lu-minous in the flame-colored dress, with her mass of hair tied up with rosemary and fresh-water pearls under the veil. She could not keep her eyes down as she was supposed to, but gazed around her proudly as she walked under the torches to Fabius' house. People lining the street murmured with pleasure to look at her, and I think her mother too was pleased. Fabius certainly was: his grin lit up the feast, and when the dancing started he stepped out onto the floor with the eagerness of a boy.

All his friends sang poems they had written for the occasion. The best were by a dark-haired man with a huge nose and a deep voice. When he laughed, a great bellow of joy, everyone in the room smiled. He had a beautiful wife too—taller than he was, blond, and very elegant. She talked all through the songs he sang.

My own wedding five years later was much simpler. I was married from Philippus and Atia's house, of course, and they would not stint me, but it was a simple ceremony, as befitted a dependent of the family, not the daughter. Atia smiled in grim satisfaction through the whole ceremony.

My husband was Marcus Perillus, a knight many years my senior, actually quite well known in Rome though he lived almost entirely on his vineyards and seldom came to the city. He was an authority on Caecuban wine. A good man and a nice one. He was well-off, and when Marcia's father went over my marriage contract with me, he took pains to point out that our fortunes marched. "I wished you to know, Pinaria, that I am looking after your interests in a way I hope your own father would approve," he said, unrolling the scrolls with a little snap. We owned adjoining farms in the country near Fundi, south on the Appian Way, and some similar properties in other areas, including tile works and quarries, but mainly we had been in the business of making wine. It was the first time I had known that I had inherited anything from my parents.

My husband had no children by his first marriage, so he was pleased when I became pregnant and I believe still pleased when our child turned out to be a girl. I had a difficult pregnancy and was warned by the doctors not to try to conceive a second time, but my daughter was everything I could have wanted. Motherhood was a joy to me, from the first moment I saw my little girl, wrapped in thin linen and glowing like a rose in sunshine. When her tiny fist closed on my finger, I knew a happiness that nothing in my life had ever approached. Nothing has since either.

My absorption in my child concealed from me that my marriage, while pleasant enough, offered me nothing in other ways. I suppose it was the great difference in our ages. I had nothing to reproach my husband with—his behavior was always perfectly correct. But he was busy, and old, and had no interest in literature or history. He was good to my little girl, and until he died I lived dutifully and peacefully with him. I missed him when he was gone, too, and I hope I have honored his memory, and taught my Perilla to do the same.

But in truth my widowhood was not much different from my marriage. Marcia's father had died, and Atia had closed her house to live with her daughter; it seemed natural for me to do the same. Old Philippus, Marcia's grandfather, was failing, and I took it upon myself to look after him. He was very feeble and had to be assisted in even the simplest matters, but his mind was still as sweet and sound as a winter apple, and I only regret that I did not have the trouble of looking after him nearly long enough. It was only a few months before he too was gone.

When I began to go to dinner parties and festivals again, after my mourning had finished, I found the men interested in me in a way they had not been or at least that I had not known they were before I was married. A young widow with a large fortune is after all desirable no matter what she looks like, though I am pretty enough, I suppose. And if her guardian proves inconveniently apt to inquire into one's own finances and motives, the widow herself might be persuaded to apply to the praetor to have a new and more relaxed one appointed. So I found that rather a lot of attention was paid to me from the couches. At first I felt shamed by it, as if I had done something to attract it, but Marcia reassured me, and Atia made it plain that she felt it my duty to remarry. "You don't plan to be a burden on your relatives for the rest of your life, do you?" Atia asked me one day.

"Am I a burden? I hadn't realized. I suppose I could have my own house—"

"That will not be necessary, Pinaria. There is no need to make a scandal—a woman alone? With no grown sons? Don't be silly. No, you are still attractive enough to remarry. You are welcome to stay until you find someone suitable."

"Thank you," I said, and I felt sure she meant it, but I began to think of having my own establishment again, and to look with more favor on the men who approached me.

After a while I began to notice a certain similarity in the approaches. At dinner parties the unmarried men, and one or two married ones, would lounge as close to my chair as they could, making sure my wine cup was always filled and glancing at me hopefully to see if I was tipsy yet. Perhaps they thought I would like them better if I were. At the races or the games they would contrive to sit next to me, asking me what contestants were entered—as if it weren't perfectly obvious—and which I was betting on. These they would scrupulously announce they were backing too. From that they would progress to trying to remove bits of dust from my dress, or helping me arrange my footstool or my cloak. All the while I could see their eyes going to my ankles. They would find occasions to touch my hand or my shoulder. They applauded the statue of Venus when the gods went by on parade, looking at me out of the corners of their eyes to be sure I understood that they felt a special devotion to the goddess now that they were in love. One rotund plebeian noble who sat behind me at the games went so far as to groan with pain himself when a gladiator struck a blow. It took me a while to figure out that he was indicating that Venus had wounded him just as badly as the fellow on the sand below. Oh, dear. I began to think I would pass my life in widowhood.

One night I mentioned the silliness of these men at dinner, and Fabius laughed, saying they had all gotten these ideas out of a book.

"Really? Which one?"

"Oh, no, Pinaria. You're not going to read it. It's not suitable."

"Why not?" I started to insist, but Marcia kicked me in the shin and hissed that he was right.

Nonsense, I thought, I'm a grown woman, a widow with a child, not an unmarried girl: the next morning I marched myself down to the Argiletum and bought the book. It turned out to be called *The Art of Love*, by one Publius Ovidius Naso. I had to admit that it was naughty—obviously meant for men and the sort of women that they might meet in the arcades and around the entrances to theaters—but it was funny, and I began to laugh. I was still laughing months later when I met the author.

It was the singer of Marcia's wedding, the man with the big nose and the tall blond wife. He was singing again, at a party at a friend's house, a lovely song about the transformation of Narcissus, from a long poem on people whose lives had been changed by encounters with the gods. There was warmth in his beautiful voice, and humor. I watched him from behind my watered wine, and thought he was the most interesting man I had seen in many years. The blond wife was not in evidence.

It was a surprise to me that after his song and the applause and laughter and toasts in his name, he came and indicated the vacant chair next to me.

"May I? Thank you." He folded himself into the chair. I was immediately aware of his body: his gestures were elegant without flourish or ostentation, and his clothing was immaculate and very fine, but under it he was really as strong and sturdy as a bull calf. The joints of his hands were large, and his nose amazing: a great arched slope of flesh like the buttress of a bridge. He smelled cleanly of lavender. "I am Publius Ovidius Naso, by the way. I'm very sorry to hear about your husband."

"You knew him?"

"By reputation. I've even read his book. A very thorough job. I raise a few grapes myself. We don't make Caecuban, but it's drinkable."

He had dark eyes, very deeply set, large and liquid and full of secret thought. But whatever it was, the thought was amusing him: he knew a joke that he wasn't telling anyone. I discovered in myself a strong desire to find it out.

I was waiting to see what he would do, but he might never even have read his *Art of Love*, much less written it. He kept his hands to himself, and if he was interested in my ankles he gave no sign. Instead, he talked to me, asking me about myself and what I was doing. Was I interested in agriculture? Not really? In literature and philosophy? They were interests of his too: he had been reading a lot of Lucius Varius Rufus—his epic. Did I know it? I did not, but had seen his tragedy *Thysetes*. Really? What did I think of it? And so on. He listened to my answers with serious attention, and argued with me if he disagreed. I had not had such a good talk since Marcia's grandfather died.

Around us the party began to make the noises of people getting ready to leave. Couches scraped on the mosaic, outdoor clothes were called for, people shouted back and forth to each other. Naso looked up, surprised.

"Well, this has been very pleasant. Might we consider doing it again sometime? If you like I could lend you my copy of Varius' epic—"

"There is nothing I would like better," I said, and it was true.

"Good. I will call then, if I may, tomorrow afternoon, at Maximus'. He's an old friend, I'm sure he won't mind." He smiled around his nose, and leaned toward me. I could feel the warmth of his breath and smell the lotion on his hair. His skin was smooth where he had been shaved with artistic closeness under his cheekbone. He whispered, "I'm divorced, by the way."

By the time I had recovered from my surprise, he was at the head table surrounded by friends, with his back to me, as if he had never spent a moment in my company, or told me the secret in his eyes.

It wasn't all serious talks and literature: there were dinner parties and visits to the theater and the games, picnics with the children, and one well-chaperoned month-long visit to his country house in the Sabine Hills, at the conclusion of which he asked me to marry him. It was something of a formality for I had known since he had come to sit by me at the party that I would. The joke was that he had known it too, though I didn't find that out for years. I asked one night in bed, teasing the white hairs mixed with dark on his chest. "Oh, yes," he said. "I thought you looked so nice. So fresh and sweet. I knew I wanted to marry you. Why do you think I came over?"

"I thought it was to find out if you liked talking to me."

"Of course that."

"Would you have married me if I had turned out to be stupid?"

"Ah. Stupid. That's a difficult one. But you have such a sweet smile, Pinaria, and I might have—I might have indeed."

Little gestures captivate light minds:
Many a man who's found it profits him
To arrange a cushion with a nimble hand
Or use a letter board to stir a breeze,
And slip a stool beneath a tender foot…

PART IV

That winter, after Naso left, was full of hardship. People starved in the streets, crying in seagull voices for a scrap of food, but there was none. By spring there was a new horror: plague had broken out in the Subura and then a few days later in the Transtiberim. From those crowded quarters it quickly spread to the better neighborhoods on the hills, and all day the wailing of mourners and the bleat and shrill of instruments grated on the nerves. At night you could see the pyres smoldering in the distance, and every day you heard more stories of families discovered dead for days in their house, or wiped out in a morning. Anyone who could left the city and went to the farms and the villas by the sea.

I did myself: I had been in Sulmo for the festival of Mars and the old New Years' Day, which is still the first of the year in remote places, and important to the tenants and farm people. My daughter and I celebrated the Matronalia together, standing before the little

Juno in the farmhouse shrine, since we could not go to the Temple of Juno in Rome. With our hair and clothes unbound we made our offerings. I had the most curious sensation that the whole ceremony was hollow, and the words of our prayers echoed in the emptiness as if we were singing them in a cavern, but my daughter did not seem to notice anything wrong.

I had planned to stay away well into spring, but early in March a messenger came to tell me that a ship was in from Greece—one of my cousin Macer's, called the Helmet of Minerva. She carried letters, but the captain would not give them to anyone but me. I hurried back to the city, arriving on the Ides, and left again immediately for Ostia.

There I found myself standing on the great flat stones of the dock, while the port rumbled and roared around me. The breeze tore at my hair and tugged my cloak, but it smelled of the sea, and on it came the faint, ghostly mewing of gulls.

The captain came down from the deck to hand me the papers himself. He was a Greek, a thin, nervous man with one eye half closed by a scar. It made him wink, so that it looked as if he had entered into a permanent conspiracy with the world.

"*Kyria*, you are Pinaria Ovidii?"

"Yes. You have letters for me, I believe?"

His good eye opened in shock. "Please. Please, say nothing that may be heard—"

I looked around us. Beneath the brilliant sunlight of the first really warm days porters strained with bales of cloth or trudged down the quays; a long line of tall black men from the Nile sweated under huge amphoras of wheat or wine or oil; overseers shouted at them; brokers called out prices. Smacking and gurgling, little waves grasped at the stones. Birds shrilled. On the benches of a neighboring ship in from Massilia someone was releasing the rowers and near the next dock someone else was calling a name over and over. They were all busy, all preoccupied, and no one had a moment even to glance in our direction. We might have been invisible. The only people besides my own near enough to overhear us was the crew of slaves attempting to unload a racehorse from the

'Minerva'. It was taking all their concentration. The horse clattered and bumped, throwing up his head and trumpeting his fear and distress, the men swore and shoved, dodging around the heaving animal. I doubt they'd have noticed us if we had cried our news to each other at the tops of our lungs.

All the same he thrust the cloth-wrapped bundle at me shielded by his body. The little package felt warm, almost living, like a small child, and I clutched it to me.

"No," the captain muttered. "Don't do that."

"Why not?"

His eyelids fluttered at me, a frantic series of unreadable winks.

"Well? Why not? What's wrong with it?"

He bent and spat out the contaminated word. "Unlucky."

"Not to me." I held the packet tighter, protecting it. "To me it is valuable. It is from my husband."

His eyes blinked and the scarred one stayed closed. "He was an unlucky man. He nearly killed us all."

"What? He did? Naso? He's the gentlest man in the world. He never hurt anyone, much less killed—"

"A storm. We nearly wrecked. A very bitter night. We were driven back, almost to the Italian coast. I did not think we would reach Greece at all. And when we did, it was not the port but the rocks. We made our offerings and the rain took them. I doubt the gods heard us at all. It was Ovidius Naso's fault." He cleared his mouth and spat on the pavement the contamination of my husband's name.

"Why? How could it be his fault? He doesn't control the winds or the sea."

His voice had thinned itself so drastically that I had to lean toward him to hear it. He backed away. "A criminal. A condemned man. The gods hate such men, and evil follows them. I should never have agreed to carry him."

They say the Greeks know the gods very intimately. I caught my breath, almost in a sob. Perhaps he was right. Perhaps the gods had cursed us and all our lives we would be thrust away from safety and happiness, just when we saw them approach.

Desperate, I cried out, "No. That's not true. He is innocent."

It made me strong to say that. "You should remember something, captain. The gods hate inhospitality too, and they curse those that turn aside a traveler. So the storm was your fault, not my husband's. Good day to you. Thank you for the letters."

On the way home I was delayed. The festival of the Mamuralia was concluding and outside the city gate a crowd had collected. Priests carrying shields beat on them with their staffs. The procession stopped. Flutes skirled, drums thumped, the priests, solemn and pure in their robes, led forward a man wrapped in goatskins. They raised their sticks. The man cried out as the blows struck him. He was some beggar they had chosen to drive from the city: now for a few coins he would be thrust forever from light and warmth and voices, so that the city would be cleaned of sins he had never had a chance to commit.

Most years the crowd cheers each blow and throws stones and dirt at the poor wretch, but ours are not normal times, and the crowd, starved and ill, stared in silence. The priests were plainly uneasy, stopping their chant once and starting over—an unlucky omen. The only person who didn't seem to notice was the scapegoat.

The poor wretch just stood there, like a dog in a rainstorm, enduring his beating. Even when it stopped he did not move. The priests had to take his arm and turn him toward the road, another unlucky omen, which the spectators watched in deepening silence.

The bent little figure disappeared into the distance. The crowd let out a sigh, exactly as if it were one person and had been relieved of a burden, and began to move. It was clear they knew where they were going, though no signal had been given, no sound had been uttered. Within a shockingly short time the road was empty, the priests standing like islands in a receding flood, gaping after the great sluggish mass of citizens that had coagulated at the city gates.

I beckoned my chief bearer. "Is there another way into the city?"

"Of course, mistress. But we would have to go a long way around to another gate."

"How long?"

He shrugged. "Hours."

"Do you think we can get through this one?"

"I can try."

"Very well. See if you can get to Fabius Maximus'. It's nearer and the street is better."

But once inside the crowd had picked up speed and drawn closer together. My chair tilted and swayed as my bearers tried to keep their footing. I clung to the sides. All around us voices were rising. Faces, hollow with starvation or marked by illness, glinted in the darkening sunset. Tears. Some lifted their hands to the heavens, some just stared. Here and there a voice, burdened beyond bearing, raised itself to a shriek. All of them were crying aloud in a mass of noise like a spring torrent crashing through the narrow streets.

It took me some time to understand that there were words in the noise. And some time longer to understand what they were.

"Julia," they were shouting. "Bring back Julia the Elder."

"Why are they saying that?" I asked my bearer.

"They think the city is cursed because the family of Julius Caesar is all exiled, mistress. That is why they have no food."

My bearers dodged down a side street, and the noise faded behind us in the direction of the Forum. It was still muttering in the air, like an approaching thunderstorm, when I reached Fabius and Marcia's. "Julia. Bring back Julia." Caesar Augustus would have had to be deaf not to hear.

No one expected me at Marcia's, since officially I had moved back to my own house. I went looking for someone: in Fabius' library I found him. And with him, bending over a scroll on the desk, was my own servant Loricus.

"I—ah. I—ah. Ahem," I said. "Is there something happening here that I should know about?"

Their start of panic would have been laughable if I had not been so disturbed, and Fabius' uneasy smile made it worse.

"Ah—Pinaria—I—ah—I was worried that you were so late. Loricus—ah—Loricus came to tell me that you might be caught in the crowd. It's ugly out there tonight. The Mamuralia often is, isn't it?" He was gathering confidence in his lie as he went. "You went down to the port, I was told. Were there letters?"

"Yes, Fabius. Loricus, you came to tell him you were worried about me? Why?"

"Because of the crowd, mistress. Sometimes there are riots when they get like this."

"Like what?"

"Calling for Julia," Fabius said.

"Yes, mistress. Sometimes they call for her son Agrippa, in exile on the island of Planasia, too. Then it is usually more serious."

"Were they today? Calling for the boy too?" Fabius looked unconcerned, but Loricus' hair was standing out from his head.

"Not today. Loricus, what is in your hand?"

"Nothing, mistress." He held out his palms to show me. "And this—" he gestured to the scroll. "You see? Simply the accounts for an iron mine. In Albanum." He unrolled the beginning of it on the desk. Lists of diggings and shipments of ore for the last two years ago.

"That's one of our mines? I thought we—you and I—I thought we were going to do them ourselves."

Fabius said, "Ah, no, Pinaria. It's not yours. Why would you think it is? It's ours—well, Marcia's, actually. I hope you don't mind. Since he was here, I simply borrowed Loricus for a bit of help."

Loricus unrolled another scroll a short distance, making a gesture to show me. More lists, of slave workmen this time. I did not recognize it.

Fabius smiled at me kindly. "Now that that's settled, my dear, may I see the letters?"

"Oh. The letters. Of course. I am going to look at them now. I thought I'd just go home and—I thought I'd look at them alone. You won't mind, will you, Fabius?"

"Of course not. I understand perfectly. You show them to me whenever you are ready."

The two men looked at me blandly. By some sleight of hand the scrolls had disappeared. The desk before them was empty.

As soon as I reached my own house, I felt better. Calling for light, I took the letters into my room. There I sat in the chair by my dressing table, waiting for the courage to open them.

It was a thick packet, months of communications all bundled together. Some were written carefully, on good paper; some were no more than scrawls. One was still incised on waxed board: how that had survived the journey I could not imagine. Its thin wood showed white where it had been scraped and banged around, the wax was marked by a heavy thumbprint and something that looked like soot. But all of them had Naso's fine, minute careful handwriting. I had to wipe my eyes.

One or two notes asked after the household, and his children. He said he missed me, and promised to wear white clothes to celebrate my birthday. He said he would take a second ship for the Black Sea, as soon as one was available. But the large packet of poems, all carefully written on good parchment were poems describing his journey. With them came a brief note to me to have them copied and published.

He spoke of the night he left and for a little I cried to think of it, but the truth is I hardly recognized it, so differently had it appeared to him. He said I threw myself on the ground and kissed our altar, dissolved in floods of tears. Had I? I winced at the thought. It was undignified for the wife of a Roman citizen, who must bear happiness and misfortune with an equal mind. But I supposed I must have if Naso had said so.

He spoke, too, of the voyage, and the storm, the sight of the Italian coast, where it was death for him to land. It was terrible, and I was frightened for him as I read. I saw him roped to the mast as the water hurled itself back and forth over the deck. I heard the shouts of the sailors and the boom and roar of the sea. I saw him at last stand on the dock in Greece, shaken and pale but alive. He was a poet still. I went down and made a small offering to his genius in the shrine.

It was like praying for a sick man, a desperate hope. Something more terrible than a storm had happened to my husband. The little spirit that had protected him all his life had deserted us. All that was left on the altar was a lump of carved metal.

You could hear it when you read the letters. His voice was gone. A cringing whine, a moan of self-pity to the gods—it was horrible.

I would never have known who he was. He wrote like a slave. His wit, his passion, his satirical observation were swallowed up, and he embraced the knees of the man who had injured him.

> *Let the land of Pontus see my face.*
> *He orders it, and I have deserved it.*
> *Nor do I hold it right or respectful to defend a crime that he has*
> *   condemned.*
> *If, nevertheless, mortal acts never deceive you gods,*
> *You know that blame for crime is far from me.*
> *On the contrary, you must be aware:*
> *If I was carried away by my stupid mind, it was not to anything*
> *   criminal;*
> *If it is enough that insofar as it is permitted to the least of men,*
> *I have supported his house;*
> *If Augustus' public commands have been sufficient for me;*
> *If I have proclaimed this a happy age led by this commander;*
> *If to Caesar and Caesar's family I have burnt incense as to deities;*
> *If this is in my mind,*
> *Then spare me, gods.*

I sat up that night trying to compose a letter to him. In the distance I could still hear the crowd shouting for Julia the Elder in the Forum. Slowly they grew quiet. It began to rain. The lamp sputtered; the paper swelled.

I struggled with the letter. It had to speak across such a great distance, my voice would thin to a whisper, and he would not hear at all. I tried to tell him of my love; I pleaded with him to let me come to him; I begged him to tell me how he was, for I thought his health must have broken if he wrote in such a tone. There was no answer of course. All that happened was that the ink bled and the letter looked soaked in tears.

It was not until late the next day that it came to me to understand why he wrote as he had. I was standing in the linen room, rebuking a girl who had managed to tangle the warp on the loom so badly a whole day's work was lost. I was angry and she was in tears, begging me to forgive her, swearing I was the kindest and most just creature under heaven, that it was only my godlike generosity that kept me from having her whipped. My skin was crawling. But I understood.

He was no longer a free man, and he could not speak like one. In the circumstances he could be silent like Cassius, or he could find another voice. And what was there for him other than the voice of a slave? Indeed by choosing it he was saying that Augustus had reduced us all to the condition of slaves. For if we cannot say what we want, what else are we? We are not the citizens of a republic, but the bondsmen and women of one man.

It was a sign of his courage that he wrote at all, and for publication. He was fighting his war out there in the east with the only weapons he had. And under the meekness of the slave I thought I could see that his intention was to win.

Early in the spring Augustus convened the city at the Rostra—the great stone speakers' platform where his own daughter was supposed to have entertained her lovers—and made a speech to the unmarried men. If "speech" you could call it: "harangue" was more like it. It went on for hours, and I could hear the shouts of agreement or anger every time I stepped out into the garden. He told them they were destroying the state by their failure to produce children, and he imposed on them penalties and rewards to try to get them to marry at once. A few days later, the two consuls—who that year were unmarried men, as it happened—pushed through a bill in the Curia about adultery. It restated and strengthened Augustus' laws made years before, when he had taken away the right of a woman's family to judge her husband's accusations against her and given it to the state and the courts.

Those reforms he had ignored when he sent his daughter and his granddaughter into exile on nothing more than his authority as their father. In addition the punishment he had decreed for them was far harsher even than the new law prescribed. No one mentioned this when the law was discussed in the Curia. Indeed there was very little discussion of it at all. The memory of the near-riot at the Mamuralia, when the crowd had demanded the return of Augustus' daughter, was still present in everyone's ear and eye. This was Augustus' answer, for of course no bill was passed without his blessing. It was a slap in the face to the already sullen and truculent city.

To me it was a reminder and a goad. I arranged for the poems Naso had sent to be copied, and asked those friends I could still trust to make sure someone sang them at the appropriate occasions. I went around again to the people we knew who might have any influence, and pleaded with them to try again. If they refused to see me, I wrote to them, and I searched out others, friends or kinsmen of theirs, who might persuade them to help me. With a ship going out to Piraeus I sent letters to Naso with news of his daughter in Libya, of Perilla, and our home. I did not dare say much about what I was doing but concluded with only one sentence: "I am working. Have hope, my husband."

The spring passed into summer, and I was able to do less. Everyone left town for their houses at the shore or in the mountains. Marcia and Fabius packed up to go to Baiae where they had a beautiful place with a hot spring and a view of Capri across the clear, dark sea.

Marcia, with typical generosity, urged me to come with them. "But Pinni, you can't stay here. It won't do any good, and it's not healthy. There's so much sickness around and Persicus is so vulnerable. Come to us." Indeed the funerals still wound through the lower city, and the smoke of cremations hung over the squares. Wails and cries assaulted you at every turn and beggars clogged the intersections until the aediles drove them off.

"I'd love to Marcia, dear," I said, "but I can't lose the chance to see some more people. My father's uncle Pinarius is going to try to get me an audience with Agrippina. You know, the first Julia's other daughter. She is going to be in town next month…"

Marcia sighed. "All right, Pinni. I suppose I ought to try Livia one more time. Though it's difficult. If I do, will you promise to come to Baiae with us? Or at least go to the country for a nice long rest?"

"Yes. Oh, yes. Oh, Marcia, you are a darling. I will always be in your debt. Of course I'll come to Baiae, or wherever you want."

I had been at my uncle's, but he had no word of when exactly Agrippina was coming back. "It's difficult to say. Her husband's out there on the Danube, you know, and she always goes with him on his campaigns. But there's trouble there—tribal uprisings and all that—communication is poor and I can't find out more. I will let you know."

Tired and discouraged, I came home. The house was quiet at least, and the sun lay in clean silent squares on the floors. The servants had swept with lavender brooms and the scent, sharp and fresh, lingered as I passed toward the back of the house. I don't know why cleanliness makes a house seem so peaceful—it shouldn't make any difference and in theory a house could be peaceful if it's a dirty mess, but it never is. I don't know why.

But in this case I was wrong. The house wasn't peaceful at all: under the calm it was dangerous. As I came across the atrium I could see Loricus standing by the desk in the library. His hair was floating around his head, his tunic was flying, his body was bent as he raised his arm to strike. A slave boy knelt before him, weeping and pleading. "No," I shouted, but neither of them heard me.

Loricus' arm swung around. I could hear the blow as I ran up, and the boy, a look of surprise on his face, flew backwards, crashing into the rows of cubbies with a noise that was somehow unexpected. Books flew out: for a moment the air was filled with them. They rained down around the two slaves, till Loricus was up to his knees and the boy almost buried. Only his head showed, his mouth and eyes round with awe. Loricus' eyes were as wide, and he looked horrified. As the books settled, and quiet fell, Loricus put his knuckle to his mouth.

I stepped into the room. "Just what is going on here?"

Loricus gave a start and stared at me as if I had appeared by magic. "Mm-mistress." He swayed on his feet. I thought he might faint with shame. "Mistress, I—I forgot myself. I beg your pardon. I—" He knelt down before me and touched my shoes. "I most humbly beg your pardon."

Suddenly I was frightened myself. "Get up," I cried. "Oh, get up. What happened? Why are you like this?" I felt like a child abandoned by the adults, and my eyes stung with tears.

He rose to his feet. "Mistress, I—"

"All right, Loricus." I could see that nothing I said was going to make him feel any worse than he did already. His calm and dignity, which seemed so much a part of him, were destroyed, and he looked like death.

Then he was himself again and smoothing his hair across his head. "Mistress, the boy has damaged the books. I sent him here to dust, and when I came in he was standing in front of the desk— Here, look." He stood aside, revealing a badly torn roll. "Look," he cried in deepest horror, seizing it and thrusting it under my nose. "It has been—savaged."

Indeed the roll looked as if dogs had been at it: ripped across the fine lettering, the paper hanging in shreds. Even the cover had been slashed and scraps of leather strewn across the desk. Loricus was white with horror. From his place on the floor the boy began to blubber. "Loricus. Master." He shot me a look of terror, too humble even to try to address me, and too frightened of Loricus not to. "Master, I didn't. It was like that when I came. They were all—"

"All?" cried Loricus as if he had been stabbed.

And indeed as I looked I could see other books slashed and ripped in the same way. Pieces of their words were scattered everywhere, crying out from corners and across the floor. "Went." "Loving." "Father." "Stars." All the furniture had been overturned as well. A lamp had smashed. Oil had run from it, but had stopped. Some time before evidently. A long gouge had been carved across Naso's beautiful pearwood desk.

"I didn't. I didn't." The boy was weeping in the corner. His sobs were the loudest sound in the house.

"Loricus," I whispered, "he's telling the truth. He didn't do this."

"Of course he did, mistress. I will have him beaten until he confesses—" He was shouting with anger again, but it was fear that put him in a rage. I could see the knowledge of it come into his eyes as his voice died.

"Loricus, the person who did this had a knife, maybe a sword. The boy hasn't anything like that."

"He hid it," Loricus said, but without conviction.

"No, I didn't," the boy sobbed. Gaining courage, he stood up. "You can search me. I didn't. It was like this when I came in."

Loricus looked at him coldly. "I will search you, all right, you little rat."

"Please do, Loricus." I set a chair upright, and looking to see that it was unbroken sat down and waited.

When the search was completed, Loricus turned to me. "There's nothing here, mistress. He was right."

"Yes."

He looked around blankly. "Then who did this?"

"That's what I want to know."

They stared at me in silence. Presently I called a footman and told him to clean up the room.

I increased the guard on the house, putting a stronger, younger man at the door, and ordering a handful of bullies from one of the quarries to patrol the corridors at irregular hours. I thought of buying gladiators, but the sight of my own men parading with almost military order and discipline was reassuring. It seemed to help: everything was quiet again and Loricus restored order to the library, going around with a look of puzzlement and anger that I was not sure I quite believed.

Then on the day before the Ides of May, when the straw puppets are thrown into the Tiber in the great ceremony of purification, I was invited to luncheon at Livia's house on the Palatine. Marcia came for me in her huge, elaborate litter.

"It's going to be fun, Pinni. Livia's a good wife: they live very simply, because Augustus has an idea that it's more Roman and we ought to be like our ancestors, though why I can't see? Can you?"

"That's nice, dear. But I am not going for fun. I want to ask her to speak up for Naso."

"Oh. Of course. You won't say anything to ruin the party, will you?"

Really, sometimes her childishness annoyed me.

"Marcia—"

She peered out the curtains at the street. Without turning back to me she said, "No, of course you won't. You like a party just as much as I do, and you need to get out more. You've been moping at home too long, haven't you? This is going to be good for you—you'll meet some people, and there will be music, and you will feel much better. " She leaned back with satisfaction. "I know you will do just fine, Pinni. You'll be a credit to me. Won't you?"

This time we went directly to the small house.

"This is her own place," Marcia said, having pointed out the beauties of the Palace as we went past. "Augustus gave it to her."

Perhaps he was making sure she didn't live too well. Certainly his obsession with frugality and simplicity was honored in her rooms, at least at first sight. The walls were simply whitewashed and the floors plain tessellation without any elaborate mosaic. At the open window curtains blew in the soft breeze; they were colored like undyed linen, which at first I thought they were. But when I had a chance I looked closer: they were made of some material that shimmered like water, and yet was so delicate you could see through it. I wondered where it had come from, for I had never seen anything even remotely like it. The thread must have been very difficult to work, for it was as thin as a human hair.

But the surprise—or the bigger surprise, I ought to say—was Livia Drusilla.

She was smiling when we came in, very graciously, waiting for us to come up to her. She took my hand warmly in hers and, leaning forward, permitted me to kiss her cheek. She was shorter than I and very delicately made.

"Pinaria, why have you not come to see me before? We are cousins, are we not? Through Marcia here."

"I haven't dared, Livia Drusilla."

She laughed. She was still a very beautiful woman, dark haired with huge eyes in a small pointed face. Her voice was soft and very sweet, but the impression she made had no softness in it. Out of those wide greenish eyes blazed a formidable intelligence and a powerful sense of her own dignity. And though she was laughing, my answer had not displeased her.

"Livia Drusilla, you know about my husband, Publius Ovidius Naso, don't you? He is in Tomis now, and I wonder if you could, if you would, interest yourself—"

Marcia, next to me, seized Livia's hand. "Of course we are cousins. Pinni is some relation to my mother, Livia dear. How has your wonderful husband been, by the way? We are all fine: Fabius sends his greetings. Did you have a good Floralia? I thought the theatrical performance was good, but the games were dull, weren't they? Are you going to the country this year? We hope you will come to us in Baiae: my daughter Numantina will be coming, with her little boy. It will be fun. Could you come and stay with us?"

Livia, not a bit taken aback by this, simply smiled. "Come and meet some of the other ladies."

It was a long luncheon, for about twenty women, with some Greek musicians playing and lots of courses of the plain food. I was impressed by its simplicity, which wasn't simple after all: an asparagus soup, for instance, very clear and delicate, but even on a warm day in May the bowls were beaded with cold. Someone had arranged for snow to be brought down from the glacier in the Appenines to chill the broth. Not an inexpensive proceeding, and not one Cato the Censor would have approved. Nor would he have approved the little roasted birds stuffed into eggshells, the pale, tender, out of season peaches, the pistachios the size of thumbnails, and the dates as sweet as honey and as plump as plums. We were not offered wine but the water too had been cooled with snow.

Marcia and I were given chairs quite far down the room, so that I could hardly hear the conversation at the head couch, for Livia reclined along with two ladies from the Claudian family. The rest of us sat in chairs in the traditional way. I wondered if Livia would have reclined at a state dinner, and in the presence of her husband. In this, as it turned out when I asked Marcia, I underestimated her. She did.

The second surprise was the appearance, midway through the meal, of Augustus. A small, beautiful man, he was even in his seventies still blond and curly-haired and perfectly proportioned. He was obviously on the way from his bath: his hair was wet, and a slave was toweling him off as he strolled by and glanced in. Around his waist was a fine white cloth: I wondered if he supposed his wife had woven it. Another slave was dropping a tunic over his head, not before I caught a glimpse of the famous pattern of birthmarks scattered across his chest. It was said to be in the shape of the constellation of the Great Bear, though you had to be a priest to interpret it that way. It just looked random to me.

He leaned in the doorway. When he smiled at his wife, I saw that his teeth were very bad. "Hello, ladies. Excuse my informality. Good afternoon, Domitia. Metella. Servilia, my regards to your husband. Good to see you again." His eye went around the room as he nodded to his acquaintances and relatives. Marcia received a small inclination. I was still watching her frown of pleasure when I heard his voice in my direction. "And who is this delicious creature?"

I looked down at my plate, my face on fire, trying to pretend he was not staring at me, or that I did not know he was. I did not dare raise my eyes to Livia, who must have been furious to be so insulted, and at her own party.

Under her napkin Marcia whispered, "Oh, no, Pinni. How could you?"

"I didn't—" All I could see was the corner of the table, and the plain stone floor. In the doorway Augustus shifted from one foot to the other. He was wearing shoes with the thickest soles I have ever seen. They must have been as wide as three of my fingers.

I heard his breath in the doorway, the tiny chink of a cup midway down the room. A chair made a noise against the floor, like the clearing of a throat, as Livia rose at the head couch. I clenched my hand around the linen napkin and tried not to cry out with terror.

But her voice, when it floated down the room, was light and untroubled. "That is Pinaria. She is a cousin of our own Atia. Isn't she sweet? Why don't you join us, my dear? The servants will bring you a couch. Pinaria would be delighted to sit with you."

I believe I gasped. The rim of the plate cut itself into my eyesight against the cloth.

I could hear Augustus' own voice saying something trivial from the doorway. Over the rush of my blood in my ears I could not make out what it was. When I looked up he was gone. Livia's fine eyes rested on me a moment as she turned to the woman beside her. I should have felt relieved, of course. But I sat there on the chair at the end of the row, unable to eat, unable to move, more afraid now than I had been before.

"I don't know if it was a good idea for you to flirt with Caesar," Marcia said as we jolted through the Forum on the way home.

"But I didn't. Marcia, I was scarcely even looking at him."

"It didn't look that way."

"I know." Tears, hot and stinging, were pressing behind my eyeballs. It was horrible. I just want to reach my house and take a bath. "Do you think he will—do you think Livia will try to harm Naso?"

"Oh, I don't think so. She doesn't mind what he does, of course."

"Livia—Livia doesn't mind?"

"Oh, don't you know? She finds women—well, young girls nowadays—for him sometimes. She's a very good wife. Not like Scribonia. You know, his previous wife. She thought he was insulting her by his interest in other women."

"I thought so myself. After all, her own guest, at her own table, and in front of her friends, to openly admire another woman, to hint—"

Her shining eyes widened in surprise. "You thought it was insulting? But everyone knows. I mean, Pinni, men are like that. You know that."

"I don't think they are. Not all of them."

She pressed her full lips together and looked away. I thought she was angry. And presently she turned on me. "But really, Pinni, I was so embarrassed. As if you were a flute girl or something. Do you think you really had to go so far?"

"Marcia, I didn't do anything," I said, but it was useless. The tip of her upper lip had come down and rested on the lower. Marcia was very annoyed with me.

May, beautiful and flowery, slipped into June, and whatever the reason, nothing happened. Marcia, leaving for her house near Naples, had recovered her good temper. "Oh, I don't know if you did any harm at that luncheon, Pinni. After all, everyone's out of town. You can't expect anything to happen now. Wait until they come back in the fall. But I still think you ought to go out to the country yourself."

I sighed and thought of Naso far away by the sea that is always cold, and where the coming of spring means only that the raids by the barbarians would start again.

I kept putting off my departure. In June Augustus gave orders that his granddaughter's house was to be pulled down. "Not suitable for a Republic," he announced. The place was gone in month and the space planted with walks and gardens for the use of the public. It was as if he was trying to raze even her memory.

That same month I received a notice that one of my husband's cousins had applied to the praetor to have me removed as conservator of my husband's finances. I had to appear in the Basilica and defend Naso's instructions, so I spent the month, and most of the next, in the library, going through the accounts. Loricus had kept them in admirable order and bit by bit as I studied them my confidence grew. My uncle Rufus came often to help me, and by the time my case was called I felt reasonably well prepared.

I was nervous when I stood up, but the praetor, who was in fact the son of an old friend, encouraged me, so that I made my case. My voice shook, but I must have made an adequate defense, for his judgment was in my favor. I went home and sat in the library staring at the books, wishing I had never had to take on this responsibility. I would have been glad to give it to the cousin, though of course he meant to rob us.

I wrote an account of what had happened to my husband, and included it in a packet of letters that I had made up for a ship going out. I took it down to Ostia myself, and confided it personally to the captain. Then, feeling that I had attracted too much attention in the wrong quarters, I ordered the house closed and went to our own villa out toward the Sabine country. It wasn't Baiae, but it was the best I could bring myself to do, and from the terrace by the dining room, where Naso and I had spent so many hours, I could still see the city, and the traffic passing on the Mulvian Bridge.

So it was that I saw the chariots, before anyone in Rome had the news. A pair of them raced across the bridge, scattering pedestrians and raising a cloud of dust that trailed away slowly on the hot still air. They clattered onto the road and disappeared, but the eddy of their passing did not dissolve. People seemed to be hurrying after them. Presently I heard voices crying out, and shouts from the direction of the Forum. On the bridge, more people began to run toward the city.

I was just on the point of sending someone to find out what had happened, when my cousin Macer appeared.

"I think you'd better come back into town, Pinaria," he said, throwing himself into a chair and accepting a cup of wine. "There's been a disaster to the army in Germany—three legions lost. Who knows where the barbarian army is? It's not safe outside the walls now. Hercules, it may not be safe inside them either."

"*Three* legions?" It seemed an unimaginable number. "That's *thousands* of men."

"It looks like about twenty thousand. The Twenty-Seventh, Twenty-Eighth, and Twenty-Ninth, all wiped out. There were others too— six cohorts, and three squadrons of cavalry. It's unimaginable."

He blotted his face with linen square. He was red and disheveled, and I thought I was seeing him more as he really was than I had for years.

The news was worse than we thought. Three days later, driving fast horses, a courier arrived from Ariminius, the German general. They carried a burden so heavy it might well have delayed them on the road: it was the head of Publius Quinctilius Varus, our legate and the commander of our forces on the Rhine. As they approached the city, they hoisted it on a spear and paraded it through the streets, to the groans of horror and of fear from our people.

That day Marcia came by, pale and upset. I had to help her down from her litter.

Once in the house, fanned and cooled and restored with a plate of figs, she lay back on the couch. "Oh, Pinni, it was horrible. Horrible."

"What was, dear?"

"Caesar. I was at Livia's, you know how she is. Always the same, always calm, so I didn't think anything was really wrong. But then *he* came in, and his clothes were torn and he looked really wild. Staring off into space, and crashing around in the room. He had scratches on his face, like a mourner, so we all thought he'd been somewhere in the presence of the dead, at a funeral or something, and we looked away to avoid the contamination. But I could hear him, and he was moaning and every now and then he would hit his head against the wall. Livia got up—I looked out of the corner of my eye. I mean, wouldn't you? Of course you would. And she went over to him and shook him by the shoulders—he's not a big man, you know, and she rattled him hard. "Stop it," she said. And he would for a moment or two, but as soon as she sat down he started again. He kept crying, and saying over and over, "Quinctilius Varus, give me back my legions." Over and over. Finally Livia called a servant and had him led away. It was all so awful. Do you think he's insane?"

I just goggled at her. How could he be? Augustus? He had been our leader for my whole life, and longer. He had always been there. He had done an evil thing to us, but he was Caesar. The Augustus. The Father of Our Country. And as I thought this, I heard her voice, crying aloud my own fear.

"If he's gone insane, what will happen to us? Oh, Pinni, what will happen to Rome?"

Everyone must have had the same thought, because all day long silent crowds gathered at the Curia and before the doors of the modest house on the Palatine. By order of the Pontifex Maximus, no festivals were celebrated. German shops and businesses were closed, and lines of German residents' hand carts piled with bedding and cooking pots, poultry and household pets lined up at the gates to be inspected before they left. Even Germans serving in the Praetorian

Guard were ordered out. They marched through the Forum in their immaculate tunics though without their swords, heads high and jaws clenched in anger—a squad of tall, fair, pale-eyed, foreign-looking men with all the pride of Romans, and of Roman soldiers at that.

Once again the sounds of funerals wound through the city streets, as the families of the slain mourned before empty pyres. I went to two of these strange affairs myself, for not only the common soldiers had died, but many officers. I knew the wives of two of them: both men had been on Varus' staff and both had fallen on their swords when their commander killed himself rather than face the victorious tribes.

But when Augustus issued a call for volunteers to go to Germany to replace our army, the crowds melted away. The notices fluttered from their boards in the dry summer wind, fading gently, as if they had needed eyes to replenish their texts. But men and women passed them, heads turned away, in wide circles. Truly it was suicide to go, and everyone knew it. I do not think the praetors had more than a hundred volunteers, and most of them were either old men stiff with trembling pride, or young boys with eyes full of dreams and folly. A few were the city dregs, sick men, and drunks who roll in their own vomit in the gutters, men who would have enlisted to go to Hades for a soldier's bonus. They were all rejected.

"You can't expect the strong to go. Who knows when they might be needed at home, to defend the city?" Marcia said at dinner one night. Augustus, crying aloud in the Senate, had said that we might see the enemy from our walls within ten days.

Oh, no, I wanted to say, it will never happen here, not in Rome. But Fabius was shaking his head, and the look on his face was so closed and grim. We said nothing more for the rest of dinner.

Since Augustus could get no volunteers, he instituted a draft. Fabius helped to organize it, dashing in an out of the house at all hours followed by a cloud of secretaries, all checking lists and shouting at one another. It did not seem likely that order could ever come out of this. But one morning in the Field of Mars we saw the tables going up, and two days later they were done, and the urns in place. It looked as if they were preparing for a vote. But it was the opposite of a vote—instead of putting ballots into the urns, the long quiet lines of men under the eyes of the Praetorians drew them out. Every fifth man in the city under the age of thirty-five and every tenth man over that age was deprived of his property and franchise. Again lines went sullenly through the streets and squares, again shops were shuttered and houses closed, but this time there were no carts, and no pride, only angry muttering and crowds that averted their eyes as if at something unlucky.

Even this did not help. Many still refused to go, and there were not enough who could be intimidated into signing up to make up an army. Fabius had now disappeared from the house almost entirely, spending the nights on the Palatine and appearing unshaven and distracted at odd hours to issue a few orders in a voice hoarse with fatigue. The look of grim disgust never left his face.

Marcia was lonely, and often asked me to her house or came to mine. Thus it was that with Perilla and my uncle Rufus we stood together on my balcony to watch Livia's son Tiberius ride into town to head the new army.

"Only there is no army," my little girl said in her clear small voice. "There will be, honey. We will all be fine."

Tiberius rumbled past down below.

"I wonder if it feels strange to him, to be back in the city after so long," I said to Marcia.

"And without his wife," she said, with a malicious little grin.

I laughed. Augustus had divorced Tiberius from his daughter in Tiberius' name, but the great conqueror had never been happy about it—even pleading for leniency from his father-in-law on the princess' behalf. Why shouldn't he? She was his only real link to Augustus: his marriage had made him Augustus' son-in-law; without it he was only Drusus' son, the son of Augustus' wife.

At that moment the great conqueror lifted his face. The light fell on it, carving out the shallow sockets of his eyes, and throwing into relief his thick nostrils and small, prim mouth. He stared at the sky, arrogant and unsmiling, as he went by, until our view was cut off and he was swallowed under the shadow of the street.

Perilla shivered. "I don't like him, mama."

I could hear my uncle behind me, muttering. "No one does."

"Heavens, he looks very competent, doesn't he?" Marcia cried, riding over this observation with a smile a little stiff around the edges.

He did. With his magnificent toga with its purple border, his laurel-crowned head raised to the temples on the Capitoline Hill, he might have come to celebrate a triumph. Indeed he had earned one in his last command but had foregone it, since the city was in mourning. Instead he was now being driven to the Field of Mars where a tribunal had been set up at the great voting hall, the Saepta.

Slowly, with dignity that somehow implied reluctance, he mounted the steps. The Senate, ranged along the top, rose to applaud him. Augustus stepped forward and embraced him, and he was shown to the empty seat next to Augustus' ivory one. There Augustus made a speech praising him and expressing his confidence in his step-son's great generalship, after which Tiberius was led around to the temples and presented to the city's gods. It was very like a triumph. Except, that is, for the silence so complete we could hear above the speeches and footsteps even the calling of the birds across the empty sky.

Perilla of course was right. No one liked him. Not even Augustus, who it turned out, had struck a deal in exchange for calling Tiberius back and awarding him the trust of the city. He had forced Tiberius to adopt his own younger brother's son, who was also, not by coincidence, the grandson of Augustus' sister Octavia and Mark Antony. So now Germanicus was his own uncle's heir, and indirectly his great-uncle's as well. It was a popular choice, but no one imagined that Tiberius liked it.

That day Fabius came home from the Palatine. He would not speak to anyone; I wasn't sure he even saw us. He went into the atrium and lowered himself into a chair. There he sat in silence for a long time, fingering his sword. Marcia took one look at him and left him to himself. Fabius was my enemy, but I did not like the sickness in his eyes: I made myself inconspicuous on a bench where I could watch him. He had turned his shoulder to me, blocking my view of his face, but I was watching his hands as they considered the blade. He seemed to be studying the nicks and scratches in the steel. I was sure he was not aware of me, but Fabius was always a surprise, and after a while his hands went quiet and he said, "I am ordered to kill some of the citizens who will not accept the draft."

"Augustus ordered you to do it?"

"Yes."

"I—I'm sorry."

"Yes. So am I. I have never in all my life killed a Roman citizen, and I cannot bring myself to do it now."

"But it can't be legal. Cicero was condemned for it, a long time ago."

He looked out past me to something I couldn't see. "We have come a long way from Cicero." I knew he was thinking of the proscriptions and the many disappearances and executions since then. And I thought: Augustus came to power in blood, and he has maintained himself in it by blood and by fear, but I did not say it aloud, for nowadays even thoughts are dangerous. But I knew that Fabius heard it all the same.

"Well," he said, setting his sword carefully on the ground, "maybe this time he is right. The city has to be defended and we have not raised an army any other way."

"We are all afraid. My little girl cries at night," I said, which was true, but I said it to his painridden eyes.

He tried to smile at me. "Thank you for your help, Pinaria."

Fabius was always smooth: I knew very well how he really felt about me, and I thought he was shrewd enough to guess how I disliked him, but I could have sworn all the same that there was not the smallest trace of irony in his voice.

He forced himself to do it. A number of men were strangled, in public, in the Forum—it was done that way to avoid shedding the blood of citizens—and presently an army was cobbled together of those who had already completed their military service, and of freedmen. One of mine, a fellow who had been my first husband's dresser and now kept a fuller's shop, was sent with the draft. I watched them go, at their head Tiberius far in the distance visible by his white plume, then the ragged columns and the officers on their polished horses, tramping grimly toward the gates. They left behind them a cloud of settling dust and the silence of a double fear.

It was a long time before the city would talk about what had happened. Winter had begun, and with it a sparse and unquiet Saturnalia. At least the news from Germany, when it trickled back, was good. The Germans had been prevented from crossing the Rhine.

"Did they want to?" I asked an elderly general at a dinner one night, but he only looked annoyed and said, "Of course. Why wouldn't they want what we have? We are the envy of the world. That is why we must have the Elbe as our frontier." But I wondered. To the barbarians, surely, all they were doing was defending their country? Perhaps Rome had no attraction for them. Why should it? It was having less and less for me all the time.

Marcia came back from Livia's one day, looking a bit shocked. "He thinks a god has turned against him," she whispered. "He says he should have recognized the signs."

"What signs?

"Oh Pinni, you know. Only last winter the Temple of Mars was struck by lightning, and in June three Alps collapsed. Collapsed. And shot up flames. In the Alps, Pinni. How could that *not* be a portent? And last summer there were all those locusts in the city, eating the trees everywhere, and the Sacred Fig in the Forum. They just ruined our garden too. Until the swallows came."

"No one thought they were portents of anything before Varus' disaster."

"Well, but Pinni, we didn't know about that yet, did we?"

I gave up.

It was a difficult winter. Food was still scarce, and the sickness and death that had followed it still haunted the poorer parts of the city. Worse, the effects of the disaster remained: men were still being taken into the army, and drafts were going out almost every auspicious day, amid anger on the side of the population and suspicion from the authorities that sometimes built itself into little quick flames of riot, instantly stamped out by the Praetorians. The apprehension of the autumn had subsided, but the city still muttered with discontent under the winter rains and chills.

I spent the winter still immersed in the account books. It had seemed to me that though my husband's cousin had failed to get me removed as guardian of our wealth, others might think they had a better case. And of course I was not sure that those who were advising me were men that I could trust. So I asked my uncle Rufus, and became a pupil at his experienced hands.

At the beginning of spring another packet of letters came from my husband.

> ...*I beg you now, mildest Caesar*
> *Let my verse soften you toward me*
> *That it is indeed fair to me, and merited, I do not deny*
> *Decency has not fled so far from my mouth.*
> *But unless I do wrong, how can you pardon?*
> *My fate has given you the means for your kindness.*
> *If as often as men sin Jupiter sent his lightning*
> *In a season he would be unarmed;*
> *Now where he thunders the din strikes terror to the world*
> *But then he lifts the rain and restores the pure air.*
> *Rightly he is called Father and Ruler of the Gods*
> *Rightly he has inherited the world,*
> *Where nothing is greater than Jupiter.*
> *You also, have a right to be called Father and Ruler—Father of*
> *   Our Country—*
> *You should follow the god who has the same title.*
> *But of course, you already do,*
> *No one has ever ruled with more restraint :*
> *Your kindness has been called forth for an enemy*
> *Which he would by no means have permitted you*
> *If he had been the victor.*
> *I have seen, too, riches and honors increased*

To many men who had taken up weapons against you
And the day the war lifts, so does your anger,
And you both bring their gifts to the temples together.
And as the soldier praises you because he conquers the enemy
The enemy also has reason to be glad you have conquered him.
Yet my cause is better, for no one can say
That I have taken up weapons or supported enemies to your power...

    ...Thrown out among enemies
Farther from home than anyone
I alone am sent to Seven-mouthed Histria;
Under the icy Parrhasian Virgin and the Pole Star
I have been driven
Among the Iasyges, the Colches, the Teretea, the Getae
The Danube insecurely holding off their uproar—
For graver cause others have been driven into exile
But no one to a farther place has been sent to die.
Beyond this there is nothing, unless only ice and enemies
And the cold constricts the sea.
Rome goes no farther than the left bank
Closer the Bastarnae and the Sauromatae rule.
Here we are at the margin of the Empire,
Hardly clinging to Roman law.
From here, on my knees, I beg you, to make me safe
Remove me from the fear of the savage tribesmen,
Whom the Danube itself can only barely hold off,
And not to allow a Roman citizen to be captured by enemies.
The law of heaven forbids that anyone of Latin blood and birth
Should go in barbarian chains, while Caesar can prevent it.
I was ruined by two crimes: a poem and a mistake
Of one offense I will be silent
For I am not so significant that I should renew your wound,
    Caesar,
When to suffer it once was far too much.
The other part remains: that by a lewd poem
I stood accused as a teacher of foul adultery.

Sometimes thus even the minds of the gods may be deceived
And many things are too insignificant for your notice—
Like Jupiter, who watches over lofty heaven,
Your attention is not to be squandered on some insignificant detail,
For on you depends so much, while you ponder the whole globe
Lowly things must escape your notice.
Certainly the Princeps of the world could not forsake his post
To read the unequal lines of an ill-made song?

Also in this packet there were some personal messages for the children, which I passed on, and a short, sad, brave note to me, to remember him, and that thoughts of me were always with him among the snows and heats of the end of the world. He had been ill the previous spring when he arrived in Tomis, where he was going to live. The native doctors were strange, but effective, and they had brought him through the fever and cough with potions of willow bark and poppy, and he was stronger now that it was summer and the harvest, such as it was, had come in. The hope of his return kept him alive. I could not tell if he had received any of my letters at all, or if he knew about his cousin's attempt on his property. Nor did I know if he had sent messages to anyone else: I suspected he had, from the odd glance from Macer or the sudden silence when I came into a room, but it is easy to imagine significance to these things when one doesn't know, and since no one spoke directly to me, I could not tell. I wish now that I had known, of course. I do not know if the disaster that became our lives could have been averted, but it might have been. It was in the hand of a god, and perhaps Augustus was right, and he had turned against us.

One morning in August I was working on the accounts again. As I sat there in a shaft of hot, dry sunshine, looking at the books still spread across the pearwood table, it came to me that I had seen them like that before, and in circumstances that had made me uneasy. I was feeling uneasy now, though why I could not say, since I had won my case. But the books looked wrong. I could see one that was unrolled to a page of numbers, all in neat columns, the yield from some almond trees. In my ear I head Loricus saying, "Simply the accounts for an iron mine in Albanum." And Fabius saying it wasn't one of ours, it was his.

I scrolled back to the beginning. It wasn't for a place in Albanum, it was evidently in Sulmo. I thought I recognized it—it lay just alongside a farm whose tenant I had just been interviewing. It belonged to us. Furthermore this book was covered not in Fabius' blue and white, but in our own crimson leather. And it was here, in our library, not at Fabius' house.

Suddenly it came to me: Loricus holding up a book, Fabius pointing to it, all smiles to show me that nothing was wrong, it was only the accounts that they were looking at, they said, and I had not believed a word of it.

I didn't believe it now. There had been something in Loricus' hand, and it had disappeared. I got up from my chair, excited now, and started through the book.

It was tightly rolled, and very long: the orchard it covered was a good producer and had been in my husband's family for generations. I shoved aside the other books on the table so that I could unroll it all the way. Whispering in protest the tough papyrus caught part way. I tilted the case to the light. Something was sticking out—an edge of thinner paper. With shaking fingers I slid my hand inside, working the scrap toward the front. My hands are smaller than Fabius' and Loricus' I suppose; at any rate, the paper yielded and slid forth. I could see my husband's fine small handwriting on it as it came.

It was part of a letter. There was no salutation, but the end of the word "greetings" stood guard at the top of the ragged page. The next part was missing, but it resumed with the fragment of a sentence:

"...might still work. Jove is not much worshipped here. I will talk to..."

Some words were missing here, but I could see that it had been the beginning of a list. A name and a fragment of two others were readable, and the odd thing was, I knew them. They were our neighbors in Sulmo and the surrounding countryside—owners, like us, of large farms and businesses, important men, from among the principal families of the Paelignians.

The list must have been long: perhaps a dozen men or so, judging by the thin margin that had caught in the roll.

A tiny wedge remained: "…see what I can do here…"

That was all. A farewell in a fading voice. If there was more, Fabius had it, or Loricus.

My first thought was to put the letter back in the book. But Fabius, or Loricus, might try to retrieve it. The list of names they had, after all, was incomplete—some of them were on this page. The first place they would look would be this scroll.

I turned the skimpy little scrap over in my hands.

Where did it come from? When was it written?

"…see what I can do here…" Where was "here"?

Well, that I might be able to figure out. It was unlikely to be Rome, for certainly no one would write "Jove is not much worshipped here" about the City. Even if "Jove" was a kind of code for "Augustus" you couldn't really say he wasn't worshipped in Rome.

Could he have written it from Sulmo? It was certainly possible, since it named prominent Paelignians. But somehow I didn't think it had been. Why say it, whatever it was, "might still work" if he were in such close contact with his friends? No, it must have been written somewhere else.

Somehow, too, it didn't look like Sulmo. The papyrus was thin and a bit ragged, not of good quality. Naso's papers, his vellums, all his writing materials, were always the finest that he could buy. But this looked in fact like the papyrus in the packet of letters I had just received.

Had he sent it, then, privately to someone? To Loricus? To Fabius himself? Or to someone else?

Given how little Fabius had done to have Naso recalled, given his obvious dislike—hatred really—of me, it wasn't going to be Fabius that Naso was confiding secrets to. Whatever the secrets were. Fabius must have intercepted the note somehow.

Then who was it written to? I wondered if I could figure that out too. Meantime I had to find a safer place. But where?

My room was open to the servants. Of course I had boxes of valuables that I could lock, but they could be smashed open if someone were really determined. In the end I decided to tuck it into my belt, in the little pouch where I keep my keys.

I pulled it out: the ring of keys, clattering on the table; a knot of wool I had been meaning to match; a scrap of red leather. Why had I been carrying that around? I couldn't imagine. The little thing lay there, melting in the brilliance of the sun, scarlet where the light lay on it, crimson where it curled into shadow, liquid of as a drop of blood. I stared at it, and then I remembered where I had found it.

"Red," my husband had said, that day when he came down from the Palatine Hill, after he had seen Augustus. "It was red." I had thought he meant the blood from his wound, but it was a book he had been talking about. His book. *The Art of Love*. Loricus had known that. And now, I knew it too.

PART V

The big house was still guarded by the Herculean statues and the ornamental iron work, and the doorway was as crowded as ever. Even its luxury hadn't suffered.

Inside a servant took my shoes and brought me slippers; another, an Egyptian from somewhere south of the headwaters of the Nile, dark-skinned, liquid of movement and well over seven feet tall, glided away with my message.

I had time to study the fine Greek statuary and remember Junius Silanus, packing to go into his voluntary exile. I wondered where he was, and if he felt safe there. It was giving me prickles of unease just to be in his house.

I waited a long time. I thought it was deliberate, a kind of insult. Well, the old lady had no reason to love me. I had been in the house the night her son had left: most likely my name brought back the painful memory.

She came, a woman still very distinguished, draped in black with her black veil over her head. She walked slowly, with great elegance, her back straight and her steps long, like someone carrying a very full jar of water on her head. Though of course Manlia Silanii had never done such a menial thing in her life.

"Yes?"

"Manlia Silanii, I came because I hoped you could help me. My name is Pinaria Ovidii and my husband is in exile—"

"I know who you are."

"Thank you. You are most gracious to see me. I wondered, you see: I found this, and I don't know what it means." I held out the little scrap of red leather. "It came from our library, but I found it at Julia Aemilii's house. And Caesar Augustus seems to have known it was there. From something my husband said I gathered that Caesar was upset—"

She went rigid, her parchment face white, so that the lines stood out around her mouth like a spiked wall. Her eyes fixed on the scrap.

"I have no idea what you are talking about. What is this, this piece of what? Leather?"

"I don't know, exactly. It looks like the binding of a book. We use this color in our own library. But why I found it at Julia Aemilii's and what exactly it is, I have no idea. Her books were evidently violet. That's what I came to ask. I thought perhaps you would tell me."

"I do not know what you think you are doing by coming here. I know nothing about this."

"I think your son did, Manlia Silanii."

"Nonsense. I will not allow you to involve us in your schemes. You will leave my house, young woman."

"What scheme?"

"Do not lie. A Roman matron should never lie. Oh, no, don't shake your head at me. You know perfectly well. Tell me, didn't you ever think what would happen if you went on with your plots? Didn't you care? And now because of you the child is dead."

"I am sorry. That is terrible news, but I don't know what child you mean."

"My son's child. *Our* child. The Junii Silanii's. It was a little boy, and it died. He had the baby taken away and exposed—left to die. My grandchild."

"Manlia Silanii, *who* did? *What* baby?"

She wanted to slap me, but her training held her back. "Julia's. Julia the Younger's."

I remembered, now, Decimus Julius Silanus saying that Julia had been pregnant. "But your son said it was not his—"

"Of course it was. Why else would the grandfather have it killed? He fears the Junii—why not? It was a Junius who killed Julius Caesar—Junius Brutus. My husband's father was his half brother."

"I hadn't remembered that." The Junius clan is enormous and has both patrician and plebeian branches. The Junius Brutuses are plebeians, as was the man who circulated the pamphlet that Agrippa Postumus wrote—though, he belonged to a different branch. Many of them, patrician and plebeian, are among the richest and most powerful people in Rome. Powerful enough to assassinate a man in the Senate itself and walk away, for instance.

"*He* never forgets it. He fears us all, all of the great families."

"But he would want the child killed if it were her husband's too. The child of a man he had accused of treason and gotten rid of? Why would he want that man's son to live?"

Rage and pain and pride were rising in her faster than she could control. She was visibly shaking. "Go. Get out. Go away. Never come here again. You have done too much already."

"I'm sorry, Manlia Silanii. I am sorry. I have done nothing to harm you, but of course I will go. Only tell me, what does this little piece of leather mean?"

She walked away. But her straight back wished me dead.

"Please, mistress," I said after her, kneeling on the floor like a suppliant slave. "Please. For the sake of the exiled men we both love."

I did not think she had heard, but at the arches she paused and turned, staring down at me with ruined eyes. Then, to my astonishment, she made a sign the country women make when they put a spell on an enemy.

"Find her mother. The wolf. The bitch. The whore. May she burn, may she freeze, may she starve in the sight of food and die of thirst in a river. She's the one that started it. The daughter of the greatest man on earth. She knows. Much good did it do her." And horribly, pathetically, worse than anything I had feared, she began to laugh.

It was a long way on the road, and longer the way I had come, traveling slowly from farm to quarry to village where I had properties, but always working my way south. It was longer that way, but I did not want any question or comment about my journey. Now I lay back in the carriage among the cushions, trying to ignore the babble of the slave Diana from the wagon behind. Every now and then she let out a yelp, and I guessed that the other maids had pinched her.

The sun made the linen canopy virtually transparent, so that I wondered what good it was doing. It bounced and flapped with the lurch of the wheels. My men jostled along, muttering and singing. The road was full of ruts and smelled of stone and the sharp dry vegetation of the south.

It was too hot to think: the last idea I could remember having was buying Diana from her pimp, back in Rome. It was a good thought so far as it went but I was beginning to regret it now. To make her come I had had to tell her that we were going to see Julia. I had made her swear a terrible oath of secrecy, but I was by no means sure she had understood, or remembered it now. I kept listening, but I could make no sense of her croons and gabbles. I only hoped no one else could either.

Most of the day I drowsed, for there was little to do, and I could not plan. I tried, but I found myself thinking instead of my husband. I had a book unrolled across my knees, but I did not need it: I remembered enough.

One evening before we were married in a conversation that began after dinner in the garden of Naso's country house, he spoke of his young manhood. "It was my father's idea that I should make a career in Rome." The swallows were weaving a stitch of sound through the fading sky. We had dined pleasantly, and now my uncle Rufus, brought along to make everything proper, had, very properly, retired to his room.

"A political career? Because my family has never been involved in politics. Never. My cousin Atia used to tell me that. We're just country people, living on our estates. Or soldiers, like Rufus."

He turned his head, following the sound of the bird. "It's hard to avoid politics in Rome."

"I don't think our branch of the Pinarii came often to Rome."

"Neither did we, for a long time. But my father had ambitions for us. My brother had died, and so they fell on my shoulders. He wanted me to carry the fortune and fame of the Ovidii from Sulmo to the Forum of Rome itself. Not that I didn't agree. I had no wish to stay in Sulmo. My father had made himself an important man in a provincial city, but I thought I was destined for greater things. I saw myself making speeches that saved the Republic; that urged a nation to war, to peace.... A Cicero, in fact. Why not? He hadn't any advantages that I didn't have myself."

I laughed. He didn't pursue the point, and we watched the sunset darken and die, chatting of other things. Servants came and lighted the lanterns among the plants. Stars blossomed overhead.

He seemed interested in it all, aware of the colors and the sounds, even the small movements of the scented air. He breathed deeply, his fingers caressed the edge of the cool stone table, he tilted his head to listen to the small garden sounds. He was as relaxed and alert as a forest animal, and more alive than other people.

"What advantages did you have?" In a relationship so new I hesitated to advance such a personal question, but the light in the garden was gone now, and the jasmine-scented dark was all around us, full of warmth, and secrecy.

"Well, you know the kind of thing. Our name. Our history. The backing—financial and political—I could count on. It really wasn't much less than anyone else. Enough, certainly, for a Senatorial career. And then, I wrote poetry. I couldn't help it. It seemed to well up from me like a spring—even my school essays came out in meter." His smile in the lamplight was ironic, but his voice was humble and a little sad.

"Is that an advantage? It doesn't quite sound like it. Maybe if one is very young—"

"Cicero wrote poetry."

"That is so. Was it any good?"

"His or mine?" He was laughing again.

"Oh, his. I know yours is."

He shrugged. "It wasn't wonderful. His speeches are better. As for my own poetry, it was about what you'd expect. As you say, when one is very young—"

All of a sudden the garden noises were very prominent. I heard the first notes of a nightingale, and the quiet splash as a frog slid into the pool. Neither of us spoke. I was waiting for him: I had an idea he was deciding if he could trust me. It was an important moment, and I sat as quietly as I could, not liking even to reach for my wine, as one might wait without moving to see a bird reveal itself in a tree, or a child take a first hesitant step.

"It turned out to be an advantage though."

"What do you mean?"

His breath was quick in the dark, and his hands, with their broad knuckles and manicured nails, resting loosely on the edge of light, tightened. His eyes were in shadow but I knew they were fixed on me.

"You know that times have changed, don't you? We no longer live in Cicero's age. Then, a man could advance by standing for something. By speaking for what he believed before the people. That is what a republic is. That is what our Republic was."

I waited. But I knew what he was going to say. "It isn't any longer. Augustus can put his friends in wide-striped togas and call them senators, he can dress up his Praetorian Guard like civilians—though when civilians have been allowed to carry swords in the city I do not know—he can deny that he is—whatever he is…" He made a gesture of vagueness and laughed. "But everyone knows the truth. Even to a young man just starting out, it was obvious. There was no advancement through a political career, except as a—as a friend, shall we say?—of the victor of the civil war, and I—I couldn't accept advancement on those terms."

"Of course you couldn't," I said, warmly. "Besides, it is a dangerous profession now. You might find yourself on the wrong side."

"I wouldn't have minded the danger. Perhaps it would even have appealed to me. I was young." He laughed a little at himself. "What I couldn't stand was how pointless it was."

"I just wasn't good at it. I irritated the people I was supposed to please because they irritated me, and I spent too much time and attention on the ones who couldn't help me, because I thought they had something to say. I couldn't get the hang of the right way to do things, and when I did, I was so bored I spent my time making up verses in my mind instead. And I know I failed my father by my own failure, though he had too much generosity ever to reproach me. And on top of it all, I didn't want to go home. I am a Paelignian, and I am proud of it, but that doesn't mean I wanted to spend the rest of my life in Sulmo.

"So I looked around, and it seemed to me that it might be possible to advance in another way. Cicero was not the only provincial who won glory for his name in Rome. There were the poets, Virgil and Horace, for example. I never met Virgil—I saw him once—but I heard Horace sing, and nothing closer to immortality have I ever listened to in my life. I thought my heart would fill and run over, not with grief, though it felt like that, but with beauty, with a surfeit of beauty."

He paused and remembered that. The night deepened and grew still. Even the nightingale was abashed before his memory. "Well. Be that as it may." He let out his breath. "Virgil and Horace had found favor with the mighty, and risen in the world. Virgil had won the restoration of his family estates, a thing few of the others on the losing side were able to do, and Horace had become a gentleman, a landowner. They say his father was once a slave. I doubt it, but all the same he was certainly humble enough. And while I might be another Cicero, I didn't think I was another Virgil, much less a Horace, but still, I might try. People seemed to like the poems I wrote. Augustus himself likes them—he has seen a mime I did of *The Art of Love*, and laughed. The ladies of the highest circles enjoyed them especially—I wrote a few things for them: *The Remedy for Love*, since they asked for an answer to the other, and a book of the stories of famous women. So I became—" he looked up at me and laughed—"what I am. I don't know if my father understood, but I hope so."

I smiled at him and poured us out another cup of wine. "Oh, he must have been proud."

He put his hand over mine. "You are very kind."

Later, when the lamps were guttering and the stars had moved, he said, "I even thought—you know, Virgil wrote a kind of *Iliad* for our own history—I know I made fun of it, but all the same I have a great deal of respect for it, it's a beautiful poem. Of course, very much in support of Augustus." He smiled at me in the darkness. "Be that as it may, I thought perhaps I could do something similar, something about our gods, and our traditions. Something that might help people to remember how long our history is, and who we are, and at the same time, perhaps Augustus…Well, you know. It's a subject he talks about himself: that the Republic lives, that we are the great Roman people going back eight hundred years, with our simple and democratic values…" His hands went in and out of the lamplight, believing part of what he was saying. "All advancement comes from Augustus now, so I must think of that."

"Is that what you are doing now? I've seen you writing in the mornings while we've been here…"

"Ah. I thought perhaps a long poem about the calendar—our holidays and festivals, that kind of thing: now that Augustus has taken so many of the rites and priesthoods into his own hands…" He grasped the air with his own strong fingers. "Who knows? Perhaps he will be flattered, and not see…"

"Not see what?"

The hands fell to the table, closing over a thought to keep it hidden. Perhaps he did not know me well enough to say. But he smiled at me gently, so that I would know he still liked me. "We must not forget who we are. If anything will save us, it will be that." His voice was so sad. It murmured under the words, "Nothing will save us, we are lost," and the loss was doubled in the ripple of sound from the fountain, and the rumors from the leaves.

"Oh, well, truthfully, it's very dull, that poem. Most of the time I just fool around with another idea I had: a long poem about people who have been touched by a god. I love those stories. I don't know why. The gods…Who knows? Maybe they care about us after all."

"But you don't believe that?"

He laughed. "It is expedient that the gods exist. So let's believe they do."

I had never heard such talk. But somehow I was not shocked. It was all part of the night and its freedom, a world suddenly full of love. "I would like to hear the poems."

"Oh, my dear." I heard a little snort of laughter beyond the lamp. "You are making a mistake."

"I am?"

"Don't you know? You must never say that to a poet—not unless you mean it."

"I mean it," I said. In the dark garden he began to sing.

> "The palace of the sun rose up on tall columns
> Brilliant with flashing gold and fire-red bronze
> The roof was covered with gleaming ivory
> Silver doors shone back the light.
> And the work surpassed the materials, for Vulcan himself
> Had carved their leaves.
> In the middle the globe of the earth, and over it arching heaven,
> The blue-green sea holds the water gods:
> Sonorous Triton, Proteus of changing shape,
> Aegeon with his immense arm
> Pressed across the backs of whales,
> Doris with her fifty daughters:
> Some seen to swim, some to sit on rocks, drying their green hair,
> Some carried on the backs of fishes.
> Their faces are not all the same, nor altogether different
> As is fitting for sisters.
> The earth bears men and cities, the forests wild animals,
> And over the earth is set of the brilliant image of the glowing sky
> With six signs of the Zodiac on the right hand panel, and six on
>   the left.
> As soon as Clymene's son had climbed the steep path
> He came forward toward his father's presence,
> But there he hesitated, unsure of his own birth,
> And at a distance stopped: he could not bear the light of the god's
>   face.
> In crimson robes Phoebus was sitting on a gleaming throne
> Flashing with emeralds..."

It is beautiful—I have loved it since that night. It is the beginning of the great story of Phaeton, who drove the horses of his father the Sun to disaster.

"...Nor force the chariot through the top of heaven
Higher flight will scorch the roof of sky,
Lower will burn the earth.
The middle is the safest way to go..."

I thought: Oh my love, why didn't you follow your own advice? It was not until I woke in the middle of the night in my country house near Nola that I wondered if there was also a warning in that story for me.

Summer had declined into the hot dusty gasp of October when we came down out of the mountains of the south. We jolted through a narrow pass, the white haze from the road blew aside in a sea-scented breeze, and I saw the town of Rhegium in the distance, with the mountainous shape of Sicily across the strait, almost lost in the glare of the horizon. My men set down their burdens and wiped their faces. The horses rested their weight on one haunch and jingled their bits for water. From the wagon behind, Diana sat up and said clearly, "Mistress? Princess?"

"Quiet, back there," I said, too late of course. Well, I thought, we have announced our presence here. Now what?

I had sent my servant on ahead and he had rented a house for me. He had found one not far from the center of Rhegium on a slope behind the sea wall and promenade, where the breeze was cool and pleasant, at least in the evening. It was a cheerful little place between a bar and a flower shop, and had the benefit of a side door around the corner, wide enough for a wagon. Awnings in bright stripes fluttered at the windows, and from a balcony at the side one could look down to the water. The steep little street was busy, and I did not think anyone would notice our comings and goings.

I began to drive along the promenade, as indeed many others did, or took the air in litters or on foot. The sea walk was a favorite spot for the important people of the town: the wife of the prefect and her entourage; those of the local council with theirs; the richest courtesans with longer ones, and more beautiful turn-outs;

prosperous merchants, rusticated aristocrats, soldiers, all paraded up and down, admiring the view and shooting envious glances at one another's clothes. But not the women I had come to see.

Presently, and I hope discreetly, I wandered through the town. I was not sure what I was looking for, but I thought I would know it when I saw it. I hoped so, for it would be far too dangerous to ask. But all around me the little port hummed and bustled with its own business, and I saw nothing and met no one.

October faded and the nights grew chillier. In the evenings, clouds stood up on the horizon, and once in a while a wind flapped among the wavelets on the shore, bringing a smell of mud, spiced with the distant, unpredictable scent of Africa. Still I had no success.

Finally, one crisp fragile afternoon, I saw them, on the promenade. The crowd parted and slowed to stare as a litter, so anonymous and plain it might have been hired in the town's small forum, swayed into view. Two ladies reclined in it, gazing silently out over our heads. No one spoke, no one tried to get near them. Naturally not. They were surrounded by a troop of guards.

They went past me. I could see their faces, calm as gods, and their pale complexions, their plainly dressed hair and their simple clothes. They did not much resemble each other, but nothing was clearer than that they were mother and daughter. Their dignity and composure were regal, and their sharp glances alike in intelligence.

As their litter swayed down the promenade, I bent down and whispered to my servant. "Follow them. I want to know where they live. Don't let anyone see you."

I went to see the house, a big villa in a square near the edge of town, but it was closed. Rather old-fashioned and a bit run down, it lay back from the road like a country house behind a high iron fence; it must have taken some searching to find it in a city. Like its mistress it was guarded, and though people went in and out, their names were taken and their packages inspected. I did not see Julia or her mother, and the windows on the second floor were shuttered all day.

I went back to patrolling the promenade, through days of wind and salt foam, as the autumn deepened. I hoped to see them again, perhaps speak to them, but they never came. Finally I had to admit that they would not—no one would. Cold winds lashed the sea into waves that topped the cornice and soaked the road. My bearers shivered and moaned, until I took pity on us all and went back to my warm little atrium.

I began to watch the house. I sent my porters to drink in the bar in the square, my maid lingered over sandals at a shop, I had myself carried through in a closed chair often enough so that people assumed I lived in the neighborhood. I took care that they never saw my face.

It was all so dull and so regular: the guards changed twice a day, marching around from a compound at the side, where they appeared to live in a little hut just behind the gate. They were never seen on the street, and to the annoyance of the locals, never drank at the bars, or bought any of the merchandise for sale in the neighborhood. From time to time the smoke of cooking came from their compound, but from the house there was no sign whatever. No maid ever shook a dust mop out the door, no porter carried in a package from the gate. The windows were shuttered all day, and the one small aster in a pot forgotten on a balcony grew drier and drier until it died.

One morning, as I was passing through, I saw a wagon pulled up to the gate, loaded with food and big terracotta jars of wine and driven by an elderly peasant as wrinkled and brown as a walnut. Two guards came out to inspect. One of them slapped the driver on the shoulder, and I could hear a burst of laughter echo across the square. The driver waited outside the gate while the soldiers carried the provisions inside. There under the narrow shade of the guard-house roof, they were divided, and some of them—the smaller portion, and none of the winejars—were taken into the house. The rest the soldiers carried into their own quarters.

No one else came or went, though once I saw a maid spreading laundry to dry on a clump of lavender near the back wall of the house. The white cloths lay on the bushes all day, and no one came near them. The next morning they were gone.

Finally, on the fifth night, my senior porter came for me in my atrium. I slipped on a cloak and hurried out. The moon was up early and the street white with its light. Presently though, a wagon creaked toward me. It passed behind the fountain and lurched to a stop at the gate, a painted cart, gray in the moonlight. Four women sat in it. I could hear them talking among themselves.

Several soldiers came out, and they all moved into the guards' hut, voices trailing after. I heard the clatter of wine jars, and now and then a trickle of laughter.

Under the silent flood of moonlight everything grew quiet. The elderly cart horse dropped his head and slept on one haunch.

The moon had begun to decline and the shadows had shifted when I thought of leaving. Nothing looked different. Music was coming from the hut, but there were no lights. Plainly the inhabitants were going to be occupied the rest of the night.

I leaned forward to my bearers. As we lurched out of the square, I looked back. Stretched out on the driver's bench was what I had taken to be an abandoned cloak. Now I saw that it was a person, wrapped in rags and sound asleep. I could see the jut of a nose and the hollows of the eyesockets. The mouth was open. I strained my ears and almost managed to believe I heard a single snore.

The women went out again at the Kalends of November twelve days later. I watched them depart from the little street near the port amid the jokes of the men hanging around the taverns and the curious stares of the children.

A few days later I went and spoke to their pimp, an ancient and suspicious freedman with a sty in one eye and an unfriendly look in the other. It was hard bargaining around those eyes, but in the end he agreed.

On the Ides of November, I went to the port again. In Rome they were celebrating the Plebeian Games and the festival of Feronia, where slaves who were to be freed were presented to the deity. In Rhegium the first of the winter rains was falling, a thin drizzle, making the women in the little cart huddle under their cloaks.

I gave the brothel keeper two more denarii. I could see him thinking about putting them between his teeth to see if they were real, but he contented himself with giving the little silver coins a look of profound distrust. Unlike a Roman, he was unaccustomed to doing business with strangers and it made him uneasy. Though I had told him that I wished to make an offering to the Goddess of the cost of the evening, he was less than happy with the explanation. I had let him overcharge me by at least half, which seemed to improve our acquaintance, though you could not have called us friends.

Now at my insistence he helped me shove Diana up onto the driver's bench beside me, and waved us off. As we lurched around a corner I saw him still standing there, doubt and worry sitting on his shoulders, ominous as owls in daylight.

It was a long trip. The horse was slow, the street rutted and buckled, the drizzle just enough to make everyone bad-tempered. Though I had often driven a small cart around the farms when I was young, I had trouble managing this clumsy vehicle. The women clutched the sides and leaned their weight at all the wrong angles, and Diana—it would have taken Hercules himself to hold the cart steady when she wriggled.

And she wriggled constantly. Occasionally she nudged me with her vast soft elbow. "Mistress? Going to see mistress?"

"If you are good, Diana. If you do exactly as I told you. You do remember what I told you, don't you?" Sometimes she smiled at that, but sometimes she just looked confused. I did not dare to say more: the three women in the back had leaned forward and their chatter had quieted. It may have been just the weather.

Behind the shoulder of my familiar fountain I drew the horse to a stop. The cart jerked, the women fell against each other, everyone swore and Diana slid along the bench crushing me against the side. The only one happy was the horse. He lowered his head and began to graze for weeds among the cobblestones.

"Mistress," said one of the women, "what are we waiting for?"

A chorus of complaints and demands for wine followed.

"Quiet back there."

Presently fat raindrops spattered us. Diana looked puzzled; she put out her hand as if she stood in a doorway. The women groaned.

"Mistress, can't we go yet? We're wet."

"Not yet. Quiet."

The drops increased. Soon they were pattering down in that sound they have that is almost a rhythm but not quite, so that meaning seems on the point of being revealed, but never is. Still I waited.

The water began to soak through my clothes and trickled down the back of my neck. With a gust the smoking lanterns sputtered and went out. One of the women gave a tiny scream.

"Hah," said Diana, but I did not know what had pleased her. I could not think of a thing.

Slowly the features of the world came back. Silvered with water a few stalks of the metal fence stood up out of the darkness. Above them the house loomed, smeared at the top into the sky. The air smelt of water and stone.

Enveloped in noise we huddled in the cart. Even Diana was subdued. It rained harder, though I would not have believed it could. The chalky square pocked and bubbled. The gutters sang. A few feet ahead the world dissolved.

"Now," I said, and pulled my cloak over my head.

We arrived at the darkened gate. It towered over us, rattling in the wind. Water streamed from it. It did not look as if it ever opened.

I twisted to the back. "You. Get down and tell them we are here, will you?"

Six eyes stared back at me in mute insolence.

"Down, I said."

The youngest and most garishly made up tossed her dyed blond head at me. "Why don't you pull up right to the gate? Then we wouldn't have to go so far."

I tried to ignore the fact that we were alone in a town where no one knew me, and everyone knew them. "I said, get down."

There was a long pause. No one moved. The rain slashed down. No one looked at me.

It was Diana who saved us. Disturbed by the hostility in the wagon, or simply bored, she began to heave herself about on the seat. I put out my hand to hold her. "Diana, stop—" Then I saw that she was trying to get one foot on the step.

The wagon swayed, then tilted. In the back the women screamed.

Diana, tongue sticking out in concentration, swung her foot behind her. I clutched the side.

"Make her stop." The blond was shouting. They were all grabbing at the sides and tumbling on top of each other.

"Someone has to go," I said reasonably.

She threw me a poisoned glance. "All right. All right. Just make her get back in."

She splashed through the gutter, muttering what were surely curses. I gave Diana my hand.

We waited. The rain beat down on us. The gate remained closed though the woman I had sent was plainly shouting at it. "Diana," I whispered under the drumming of the rain, "remember what I told you. You may keep any money they give you. All of it. Just make sure you don't mention the princess, or say why we are here, or who I am. Can you do that?"

The woman tramped back to the cart.

"Diana, can you?"

She was staring off into the distance. I couldn't even tell if she had heard.

The gate gave a shriek and began to open. Huge in the flare and shadow of the water, a man marched out. The rain streamed off his helmet and blackened the shoulders of his cloak, his boots squelched through the puddles; on he came, with all the discipline that had conquered an empire—a salt-and-charcoal veteran, short-bearded and scarred. Pulling my hood forward to hide my face, I hunched myself low on the bench, trying to look like the old slave who usually drove.

"Late tonight, aren't you?"

"Weather," I muttered to his knees. I saw the edge of his armor, the tunic hanging a bit below, dark and dragging with water. On one hip he wore a dagger, on the other a sword, suspended from crossed belts bristling with studs. The sword filled my eyes. Long, narrow, the scabbard dented, it was clean, it even shone with polishing. But it had seen hard service and the inside of many people. I wondered if any of them had been women.

His hand descended into my view and rested on the dagger. It was as huge and ugly as a foot, puckered and seamed with scars and thick with wet black hair. The nails were cracked and yellowed. The dirt under them must have come from all over the world.

"Look at me when I talk to you."

All around us the rain fell, there was no help from it, there was nothing but rain. No one came along the street, no one called from inside. "Goddess," I whispered. "Feronia." But no help came. Only the rain, drumming down in the dark.

I twisted my neck upward as little as I dared, grimacing and squinting to look old. As his eyes came toward me to peer, the edge of my hood flapped forward against my cheek, hiding me from him.

"All right. Inside." Perhaps the goddess had heard me after all.

Then, to my horror he levered himself up onto the footrest while with shaking hands I picked up the reins and drove us through the gate.

Once inside he stepped down. I felt his eyes go over me again, but it was a cursory glance. His attention had gone immediately to Diana, who was busy licking the raindrops from her lips.

Under his beard his mouth curled at her, and he let himself linger on the mass of her flowing curves.

She gave him a long slow look in return before sticking out her tongue to taste the rain again.

He leaned over my head to check the rest of the women. I could smell the wet wool of his cloak, and his armor pressed into my arm. I did not dare cry out.

The women tumbled out of the cart as fast as they could. They pulled up their dresses and splashed toward the doorway, where the rest of the guards had assembled. Two of the men grabbed at them, but the others were interested—too interested—in us. I could see their eyes in the lamplight, shiny and hard.

The soldier got down off the footrest. He went around to Diana. "Here, sweetheart. Let me help you down."

She had a new game, now, tilting her head back and letting the rain fall on her face until her mouth and eyes filled up and overflowed. She did that for a while, blinking under the drops.

I nudged her. My elbow sank into her: she was as boneless as a heap of feathers.

"Come on. Get down," said the soldier.

I lowered my head and tried to speak without moving my lips. "Diana, go with him."

Slowly, with massive stubbornness, she began to shake her head.

"You can keep all the money, remember?"

Her head went on shaking.

The soldier clicked his tongue and threw back his head. "Inside. You think I want to stand here all night?"

The men at the door were laughing so hard they had nearly fallen down. "Got problems, trooper? Need help?"

His face looked like a boulder eroded in a waterfall, and his hand was hovering over the dagger.

"Diana. Go." I dug so hard into her side I felt her ribs. She unfortunately did not seem to feel anything.

"Diana, if you want to see your old mistress—"

Slowly Diana surged to her feet.

I let out my breath.

Too soon.

"Lupa, lupa, lupa," she trumpeted, "Lupa."

"That's right, sweetheart," the soldiers called. "Lupas are just what we want. Come and see us."

"Nonononono," called Diana shaking so hard the wagon rocked. "No lupa. Diana no lupa."

"Really? Look like one to me," the soldier said. "Come down off that wagon and get to work."

"Won't. No lupa. Priestess. Mistress knows."

From her height she looked around, over everyone's head. I knew who she was looking for.

"Feronia. Goddess." I was weeping with fear. "Not that. Don't let her say that. Not that."

"Princess," shouted Diana at the top of her voice. "Princess. Mistress."

"Feronia," I cried.

The men in the doorway were still laughing. "That's right, girlie. You're a priestess. Come and conduct the rites with us."

With a little scrape the soldier slid the dagger out of the sheath.

"Princess. Want to see princess," Diana was bellowing. "You promised—" Rainwater ran from the dagger and dripped like molten gold in the lantern light.

"Get down," the guard shouted.

"Diana." I was hissing in my terror. "It's our only chance. Go on. That's an order."

She eyed the blade, shaking her head so the rain scattered over us, and shouted, "Not lupa. Lupalupalupa."

"Wait till I get you inside," the guard swore.

Diana flinched. The huge mass of flesh trembled and the small head drooped like a tired child's. Tears leaked out under her eyelids.

All of them, all that suffering. Aesopus. Philomela. Even the oily and terrified Demosthenes. I couldn't do it. "Diana, all right. Sit down. You don't have to go with him."

"No?"

I looked at the sword again. "No. Not if you don't want to."

My poor crazy servant crossed her arms and hurled herself into the seat, nearly shattering the bench and making the cart shudder so violently I had to clutch the side.

I am a Roman. I prepared to die.

The soldier stared at us.

"All right," the soldier roared in disgust. "Stay there in the rain if you want to." And he turned on his heel and squelched himself back to the guards' little barracks, slamming the door behind him.

At the corner of the house I stopped and looked back. Across the rain-soaked night I could just make out the cart. The heap of rags I had arranged on the seat looked lifelike enough from this distance. Whether it would deceive anyone looking closer I could not guess.

"Diana," I called softly, "keep right behind me, will you?"

She was frightened by the open space, and clung to me as we made our way through the streaming mud. I had no idea if they had left a guard at the door on duty or where he was. All I could do was hope that the house was between us and him: it was impossible to hear footsteps over the pounding of the rain, but even in the dark we were exposed as we slipped around to the back of the house, Diana lifting and setting down her feet with exaggerated care. It took me a moment to realize that she was tiptoeing through the clinging mud.

I stopped. "Diana. Here's what we have to do now." I explained with as much care as I could. Diana's eyes shone like lamps in the darkness and went out.

At the back of the house a light showed, leaking dimly through shutters. I knocked. It was hard to make myself heard over the rain, but at last a shadow moved across the gap, and I heard a door somewhere to our left. "Go on Diana, say what I told you to," I whispered, giving her a shove in that direction. Hoping I looked like a humble and wretched slave, I hobbled after her.

Diana, for once, did what I told her. She stood on the doorstep, drawn up to her full height, which was considerable, and chattered like an ape to the doorway. I heard her say her name several times, and the name of her beloved mistress. Once she said, "Phoebe, Phoebe," and tears stood in her eyes. Of course, Phoebe: her sister, who had killed herself rather than compromise her mistress.

Presently the toothless old slave stepped back. Diana, magnificent in her triumph, lifted herself over the doorsill and surged into the house. I edged myself around the doorway after her.

"Wait," the old servant hissed.

The water dripped off our cloaks into a spreading puddle. We were in a back hallway, cluttered with baskets and garden implements, and stacked precariously with ceramic jars. From somewhere nearby I could smell ashes and cold grease. A kitchen. I wondered what they ate in this household. The great families are sometimes surprisingly austere, and her father made a byword of his old-fashioned ways, but this could not have been what they were used to. I wondered if they even kept many servants. The place was clean enough, but it was very quiet.

It struck me that their lives must have been very difficult, buried alive here, with only each other for company. They went out very seldom, as I knew, and in all the time I and my servants had watched their house no one had called. A mother and daughter, alone together, for years, with nothing to share but loss, loneliness, powerlessness, fear. They must hate each other by now. I began to think it had been a bad idea to come.

Beside me Diana sighed like charcoal settling in a brazier. She had been very quiet. She looked puzzled, too.

"She's here, Diana. Don't worry."

She pursed her lips.

Finally the old slave came back, mumbling and muttering. We followed into the front of the house, Diana ahead, I hunched over under my still sodden cloak. There had been no fire anywhere, though it was a chilly night and the house was cold.

The room was large but plain, more like a provincial dignitary's than the country place of an important Roman family. There was little furniture and only one lamp—a simple affair of tripods and dangling pots. It shed only a small circle of light, and the two women rising from the solid old-fashioned wooden chairs had been sitting in near darkness. At least they had a fire, a tiny thing more smoke than heat; yet it was smoldering in a brazier so beautifully proportioned and decorated it could have graced the finest room in Rome.

They set down their work—one had been winding wool on a spindle while the other held the skein—and in the half-dark floated toward us.

As I had noticed in the town, they were very different: I don't think I would have guessed that they were mother and daughter. The elder, Scribonia, was very tall and slender. She walked slowly, bent forward a bit at the waist though a discipline like a centurion's held her shoulders flat and her back square. Nor would it allow her to lean on a cane; very unobtrusively she paused and rested her hand on the back of a chair. She must have been about eighty years old. Her skin was pale, and clung so tightly to her cheekbones they were hollowed underneath. There were discolored patches under her eyes. I guessed she had been ill. She looked at us calmly, though we were certainly a startling interruption to a very dull routine. She did not smile.

The other woman stepped quickly toward us. This woman was a great beauty—more beautiful even than her portrait on the Altar of Peace, which I had gone to look at before I left Rome. She had her father's small, compact, elegant frame, his perfectly oval face and large, brilliant, rather prominent eyes. Middle age sat lightly on her, as it had on her father, and though I knew she was fifty-one she could have passed for a woman in her thirties. Intelligence and energy flamed from her, her personality would have struck you like a force from across the Forum of Rome. As it was, the room did not seem large enough to contain her.

Beside me Diana felt it too. "Mistress?" she whispered, obviously puzzled.

The younger woman had stopped to wait for her mother to catch up. At the sound of Diana's voice she swept us with her dark, powerful gaze again.

My poor servant gaped. She blinked once at Julia and again at Scribonia. I saw her eyes go over the women's heads, panic making them rimmed in white. Desperately she looked around the room. When she spotted the door, she turned.

"Diana," I said, grabbing after her, "this is the princess. This is Julia, Caesar's daughter." Her eye rolled toward me and she began to thrash her head back and forth. "No. Nonononononono."

"What is this, please?" Julia's voice was cool and entirely calm.

"Your pardon, mistress," I said like a slave, for she was very great. "This is Diana, who was once your servant. She is the sister of Phoebe—"

Julia waved me to be silent.

Diana began to thrash her head back and forth.

"Diana." I made it an order.

"No," she shouted. Flailing her arm from my grasp she hurled herself toward the door.

The princess stepped forward. She grabbed Diana's hands and turned her. Holding her lightly but firmly, she stared deeply into her eyes, like a groom steadying a nervous horse. "Diana. Of course. Phoebe's sister. How kind of you to come and see me."

At the sound of her name, Diana's huge white mound of flesh jumped once, then slumped. I thought she had fainted. But slowly she subsided toward the floor, and I saw that she was kneeling. "Mistress. Princess." And she began to cry.

Julia stood still and watched her. Diana wailed and snuffled and sobbed; water poured from her, her nose dripped, her eyes flooded and drowned. She wiped her face with her cloak, but new tears fell faster than she could deal with them. Years of suffering were in her grief, years of unimaginable loneliness. Her slavery in the little shrine, her prostitution, her dead sister, her madness, her dreams. Diana was an exile too, and now she had come home. No wonder she cried.

At last she stopped. For the first time the princess turned to me. "You are not her servant, are you? My porteress said you were, and my mother thinks you may be, but I do not think so."

I pushed back my hood. "No, mistress. No, I am not. Forgive me—it was the guards I was trying to deceive, not you. I am Pinaria, the wife of Publius Ovidius Naso."

The two women bent their heads together. The princess turned back to me. "Of course. The poet."

"Yes, mistress."

"Julia."

"Yes, thank you—Julia. Julia Aug—Caesaris. I have brought you something."

"You mean something besides my old servant?" She smiled as she turned her open hand toward Diana, who appeared to have fallen asleep on the floor.

"With your permission." I tugged at the strings of my cloak, and as it fell handed her the wine jug I had been clutching to my ribs since we had gotten down from the cart.

"*Wine*. Heavens, we haven't seen wine for years. Have we, Mother? How did you know?"

"I heard in Rome that...that your father had forbidden it. And I saw that the deliveries of food did not include wine jars."

"My father. Yes. He thinks I am a drunk. Or he pretends to." Behind her Scribonia caught her breath. "What harm can it do to say so, Mother? What more can he do to us?"

All the same, she changed the subject. "What a handsome present. I don't know when I've received one more welcome. Or by a longer or more difficult road. You must tell us all about your journey. You said you had been watching the house?"

We sat by the brazier in the plain, solid chairs while I tried to explain why and how I had come. Julia did not seem to listen, but had draped her arms along the rests; her small white hands, as beautiful as everything else about her, hung open and relaxed. Scribonia sat at attention like a general, and whatever she was learning about me came not from her ears but her eyes.

Presently the tray arrived, with a jug of water and three cups, all in the exuberant Greek style of the region. Julia set down the wine jar beside them, but made no move to pour. Yet she had said it was a welcome gift. And there was something in the careful way they avoided looking at the table...

Suddenly I saw. Muttering, "Please forgive my rudeness," I reached forward and grabbed the little jug, and tilting the cup slightly so that they could see that I had poured an honest measure. The raw wine seared my throat and tears started to my eyes.

Julia laughed. "Well done."

From her chair in the shadows Scribonia said suddenly, "A Pinarius was married to a connection of Julius Caesar, isn't that right?"

"I believe so, Scribonia."

"And I used to know another—Pinarius Rufus. Is that your father?"

"My uncle."

"I knew your father too, then. You look like him."

"I didn't know that. My parents died when I was young."

"Ah. Yes. So you are a kind of cousin of ours, Pinaria. You are very welcome here."

If it had been a test, I and my family connections had passed. Julia poured out the wine, mixing their portions carefully with water and handing the first cup to her mother. With obvious pleasure, they drank. I waved away a second cup.

The other two also drank only one. Julia set the cups on the tray and pushed them aside. "So. Your husband is Naso, the poet. Why did he not come with you?"

"He is in exile, now."

"Exile. What for?"

"I—I don't think Caesar Augustus actually told him. It seems to have had something to do with his book, *The Art of Love*."

The answer surprised them, both of them. "*The Art of Love*?" Julia cried sharply. Her mother gasped.

As if she were making no more than a literary comment, Scribonia said, "Wonderful poem. What could be wrong with that?"

"He seems to have seen something too. Or that's what he said."

The two women exchanged a glance. "Seen something?" Julia raised her eyebrow, and her mother, sharper, said, "Seen what?"

"He didn't say. He has never said."

"He gave you no hint?"

"No."

"Indeed." Their eyes met again, so briefly it was hard to be sure it had happened. Then Julia was smiling at me, her hands open in apology. "We get very little news. Since when has your husband been exiled?"

"Two years ago. Actually he was relegated. Augustus sent him to a place called Tomis."

"On the Black Sea."

"You know it?"

"I have been in that region, with my second husband."

She meant Agrippa, the great general, her father's most trusted confidant. He had been close to twenty-five years older than she. Perhaps in spite of that she had been happy with him. He was the father of all her children, and although the wives of many such men stayed home she had traveled with him all over the world. She must have enjoyed that: they say in some of the provinces she had been acclaimed as a goddess. When he died she married Tiberius. No one ever thought she had been happy with him.

"My father not only believes I am a drunk, he thinks I am a whore. He has forbidden any men to come to see me unless they apply to him for permission first. Needless to say, no one has. But he has said nothing about women. Not that any of them come either, or speak to us when we go out in the town. We might as well still be confined on that island." She gave a little shudder.

"He let you move because the people in Rome demanded it. There were riots in the streets on your behalf."

"Were there? You hear that, Mother? Riots. For us. What did I tell you?" She was pleased, I could feel it emanating from her.

Scribonia nodded. "Be that as it may, Pinaria, you could have driven up to the front door and been announced. Why did you come hidden and in disguise?"

"I thought the guards might take down people's names and descriptions. I didn't want them to have mine."

"Why not?"

"Because I know."

"Know what?" She demanded sharply.

"Yes. What do you know?" Julia asked suddenly very watchful under very lazy eyes.

"Forgive me. I do know. About the conspiracy."

In the silence a handful of wind spattered and died against the shutter. Charcoal gasped in the brazier, and from the floor Diana let out a tiny answering snore.

Julia seemed as indifferent as before. Even the white hands lay relaxed on the rests.

"I see. And what conspiracy is that, may I ask?"

I felt cold in the pit of my stomach, and my own hands were shaking. I hid them under my elbows, hugging them to me. My elbows were cold too.

The princess waited, her eyebrow raised.

Well, there was no help for it. It was what I had come to say, after all. Courage, Pinaria. Remember, you are a Roman too, just as they are.

"Some of it I have had to guess. I have tried, but I can remember nothing myself of the night it happened. My husband went to so many events—temple sodality meetings, and business dinners and all those things. Or said he did. So I don't know. I wasn't there. But I know the connection of the book with his relegation. And with you. I know what he saw—or some of it. I—I guess that the meeting in the Forum was not a party, but some sort of ceremony. What kind I don't know. Of consecration? To invoke the help of a god? If so, I know what god it was—Marsyas, who stands for the liberation of all Italy. I know that my husband was there, and who the others were—at least some of them. They are the men who were condemned with you, aren't they? Because they were not your lovers, they were your partners in the conspiracy. Iullus in particular. He was the son of Mark Antony. You and he meant to marry, didn't you? And take the succession from Tiberius. I think you looked for support among the Romans: so many of the men there that night were well known, and some had very great names indeed. The last Scipio. Your own half-brother. But I also think you hoped to raise the countryside as well. Was that what my husband was there to do? And I can guess about the wine: that was to bring the god down to help you. That's the real reason your father has forbidden it to you, isn't it? He guessed too."

"It wasn't wine."

"It wasn't wine? What was it?"

They did not answer. They didn't have to, because they could see I knew. Of course I knew. Catiline and his conspirators had drunk it too.

"Whose—whose blood was it?" I whispered, but even so my voice was too loud.

"All of ours."

"My husband's too?"

"Certainly."

"And mine." Scribonia licked her gray lips. "The taste is not as bad as I expected. Rather like copper, in fact."

Julia laughed. "Mother, you are incorrigible. No wonder he divorced you."

"Well, dear, I am just telling the truth. It does taste like copper. And a bit like ink too."

The laughter froze to death on the floor between us as Julia turned back to me. "You worked this out for yourself? That's very clever of you. You are almost right. But my father was right too, about one thing: we did make love that night. Iullus and I of course. He had been meant to be my husband from the beginning, until my father's stupid politics intervened. Iullus had been my lover for years—my husband before every god known to Rome, if not in my father's mind. Of course we made love that night. In the Forum, under the stars, and in the most sacred places in the city. But he was not the only one. That night I slept with them all. It was to create a sacred alliance. They are all my husbands now."

All of them? I wanted to say. *My* husband too? But I could not appear before her so impoverished by my pain. Not when she cared so little. "All of them?" I heard myself ask.

Julia raised her small molded chin. Suddenly I remembered a saying of hers. "My father sometimes forgets that he is Caesar, but I never forget that I am Caesar's daughter." She was very like him. I wondered if she even had the same cluster of birthmarks in the shape of the constellation of the Bear...

"Yes. I slept with everyone who was there that night."

"Well, not with me, dear. I went home early," her mother said. And then she said the kindest thing anyone has ever said to me. "I believe your husband left early too, Pinaria Ovidii."

I would have believed her—I wanted so much to—except that Julia laughed.

"What I don't understand—Julia—is what was to happen to Tiberius. Wouldn't he just fight back? Wouldn't there be another civil war?"

"So? What if there was? Iullus was quite certain we would win it. He was a general himself, and Mark Antony's son."

Scribonia said, "Tiberius has never been *popular*, you know. Not like my daughter."

"And not like Mark Antony."

"No, not like Antony." She said something to her daughter—I wasn't listening, because I had suddenly seen: Tiberius may have been an obstacle but behind him loomed a mountain.

I must have made some sound. Scribonia stopped talking and turned to look at me.

"Ah. I see, Pinaria Ovidii." She folded her hands in her lap and straightened her already upright spine like a woman preparing to say something distasteful. "I will explain something to you."

"Mother, is that necessary?" They were not women accustomed to explain anything to anyone.

"Yes, dear. She has guessed, you see."

Julia contemplated me. "Have you? How clever you are, Pinaria."

Scribonia regarded me. I had thought she was kind, but her eyes now were even more terrifying than her daughter's. "You are young, my dear, and of course you do not remember the civil war, though no doubt you know about it. But what you may not realize is how unlikely it was that Octavian—Caesar Augustus, as they call him now, but merely Octavian he was born—would win. He was nineteen years old when his great-uncle Julius Caesar died. He had no real experience with an army and practically no support among the factions. There had been a little fighting, and he had done better than anyone expected. Now he was looking for alliances. He married his sister to Mark Antony—quite an improvement in Octavian's circumstances. That alliance lasted of course exactly as long as Octavian felt he was still too weak to challenge his brother-in-law. But at that time he was still the weakest of all the contenders for the place that Julius Caesar had left so suddenly and noticeably vacant. He was young, but he was astute enough to see that he needed a marriage for himself too that would advance his interests. Specifically he wanted an alliance with the son of Pompey the Great: Sextus Pompeius, the admiral. He was protecting himself, you see, in case either of them won."

Julia, dropping the words like pebbles into the chilly little pause, said, "My mother is the great-granddaughter of Pompey the Great, and of Lucius Cornelius Sulla. On that side her family had been among the greatest in Rome for centuries."

Scribonia said nothing to this. There was nothing to say. Her
daughter was right.

"I agreed to marry him," Scribonia resumed. "I had been married before and had my daughter Cornelia, who was very little. It
was important that my family have its own alliances: in a civil war
it is not really possible to be neutral. And in addition, I was lonely,
and I was impressed. It was a remarkable performance for so young
a man. It was still very unlikely that he would win, but I thought he
might do well enough to put me in a position from which I could
advance the interests of my family and my children. He was—and
he is, I think—the most intelligent man I have ever met. He has
courage too. In any case, my family did not achieve its position by
reluctance to take risks.

"I got pregnant almost right away. He was pleased, my new
young husband. He had never had a child, and he wanted an heir.
Aside from that, it was not a good marriage. He had a mistress: the
beautiful young wife of Claudius Nero."

Julia made a little sound. "Oh, yes, dear, give her that. She was
very lovely."

Julia's nostrils closed in a small gesture of distaste.

"Like me she had one child—in her case, a son—and was pregnant with another. By her husband. It didn't show much except to
make her even more beautiful. Her pregnancy was certainly no obstacle to my husband. He was besotted. And she knew it: leaning
her breasts on his arm, gazing into his eyes, pretending she didn't
hear when I spoke. Once or twice I caught her looking around our
dining room—when she took her adoring eyes off my husband. She
looked like an auctioneer at a bankruptcy sale. She may have been
young, but she knew what she was doing. It was an insult to me and
to my family. And I told him so."

I swallowed hard. That must have taken some strength of
mind. Nothing I knew about Augustus suggested that he would
take criticism well.

"He wanted her. And she was so clever. She mooned and panted
and made a fool of herself, but she made him wait for her bed. And
wait he did: until the day I delivered. He came to see me after. The

nurse put the baby, my Julia, at his feet. He gestured to have her uncovered, to be sure she wasn't a boy. Still he hadn't picked her up, and I thought he wouldn't. I thought he would leave her to be exposed. He was thinking: I couldn't tell what was in his mind. Then he bent and lifted her in his hands. He never held her. He thrust her into the nurse's arms, and without a word or a glance at me, stalked from the room. I learned later that he had gone directly to his office and had his advisors draw up a divorce. He said I nagged him. Well, if he meant I would not tolerate his mistress preening herself in front of me, he was right. He forced Livia's husband Claudius to divorce her, and he married her himself before Claudius' second son was born. Two days later he sent for my baby—my beautiful little Julia—and gave her to Livia to rear."

She was panting as if with the exhaustion of her labor and her eyes were black with rage.

"Not to raise your own child," I said. "That would be terrible. So sad."

"It was the insult," Scribonia said again.

"So we will kill him," said her daughter.

The fire sighed and the last coals fell into ash. Distantly, outside, I heard the tramp of the sentry. For a moment I did not understand, and sat stupidly, listening to the muffled footfall. Why had I not heard it before? Was it closer? In my mind I saw the sentry now marching under the windows, listening to everything. Listening to Julia speaking murder, patricide, treason, listening while I said nothing.

The footsteps trudged away into silence. Foolish woman, they had not come closer; the rain had stopped. It was late, and I didn't have much time.

It did not matter about my fear. It mattered that I knew. I had to speak. "Julia, why was my husband exiled?"

"I told you. He was raising support for us in the country. Surely you must have known that. He certainly had meetings with the prominent men in the region. A lot of meetings."

"I thought they were talking about the crops."

Julia's lips curved. I could not tell if it was amusement or contempt. Probably both. "The Paelignians were the leaders in the Italian revolt. They are the ones that forced Rome to cede Roman rights to the country towns. They don't like tyranny much, and they are prepared to do something about it. Your husband was seeing to that."

"Sulmo supported Antony in the civil war," Scribonia said. "We thought his son would have special meaning for them."

"But Naso's father turned the city over to Octavian," I said.

"Because he was astute enough to see who was winning. So many were forced to do that, but it was not what they wanted to do."

"I suppose not. But why was Naso exiled now? All this happened many years ago—"

"One month short of ten years," Julia snapped.

"Yes. I'm sorry. I shouldn't have mentioned it. But why? Why wasn't my husband sent away then?"

"As to then, surely because my father didn't know. As to now: I haven't the least idea."

Her hands closed on the arms of her chair as she prepared to rise. It was going to be dismissal, and I had had no answer yet. "Then what does this mean, Julia, daughter of Caesar?" I thrust out my palm. On it, gleaming like fresh blood in the lamplight, curled the little scrap of red leather.

"I don't know. What is it?" There was hardly a heartbeat between my question and her answer, but I had seen the quick glance at her mother, the sudden rise of her little chin.

"It is a piece of leather from the cover of a book. It came from our library. I think it is *The Art of Love*, in fact. That volume is missing, for one thing. For another, my husband said that Augustus had the book, evidently in damaged condition—in fact he threw the pieces in my husband's face the day he relegated him. Naso was upset, and not very clear, but he said that the cover was red."

"So? Why does that concern me?"

"It's not a question of where this piece of leather came from. It's where I found it that matters."

"And where was that?"

"At your daughter's house, Julia Caesaris. At Julia Aemilii's. It was left behind when she was sent away."

"When was that?" Her tone—cold, conversational, indifferent—never varied. Not a hair on her head, not an eyelid, a fingertip, a muscle in her body twitched. Scribonia did not move. I have never seen such perfect discipline. The great houses of Rome play their games of matrimony and alliance for very high stakes. From birth their girls are players, and they learn the rules. And these women were experts. But I watched Marcia's education when she was small, and I knew: until I spoke they had no idea that Julia Aemilii had been sent into exile.

"When was that? When—when did you go to my daughter's house?" Julia demanded, covering the mistake by pretending this was the same question.

"Julia Aemilii was sent to the island of Trimerus on account of her adulteries, and her husband killed in December two years ago," I said, joining the pretense. "I saw them taken from the house. It was the night my husband was relegated. Others were exiled or punished the same night. I thought—I still think—there must be a connection. I went to Julia Aemilii's house to ask, but of course I could not. The soldiers kept us away, and there was a crowd. I went back the next day. The house had been ransacked, but this scrap had been left behind. I picked it up off the floor."

"Anyone might go to a copyist and buy a book."

"Indeed. But in that case, why did Julia Aemilii have ours, and why did Augustus throw it in my husband's face?"

"I do not know. All that I know I have told you. My daughter and her husband—all my children—have lived their lives...outside..." Without lifting her wrist she moved her hand in a small arc to indicate the world beyond their prison. "I have had a few letters—carefully scrutinized. Sometimes sentences have been scratched out. Sometimes sections are missing. He is letting me know." Her voice slipped a notch, and her mouth slid into hatred. It was the only lapse in her control during that whole long night. "That he is watching. That he has power over me. That he can kill me, and my mother, whenever he likes."

I had nothing to say. It was perfectly true. It was true of all the exiles. Of someone on the banks of the Black Sea, for instance.

"My granddaughter is exiled?" Scribonia's eyes had been following some thought into the middle distance.

"Yes. To an island in the Adriatic."

"And my grandson? Her husband is my grandson."

"He is dead. I couldn't find out if he was killed by the soldiers when they came to take your daughter away, or if they forced him to kill himself. But he is dead—I saw them take his body out of the house."

She did not flinch. "I see. And their daughter?"

"She was taken that night too, but not sent into exile. I believe she was supposed to marry Decimus Junius Silanus. But he has left Rome—voluntarily like you, Scribonia. Except that Augustus has withdrawn his friendship from Silanus. He is still traveling, as far as I know. Perhaps he thought it safer to go and left on his own. He didn't say when I talked to him before he left. But I think he was told to go."

After all, it was true that anyone might be killed, not only exiles but anyone, anywhere, even in Rome. It had happened before.

Julia moved slightly in her chair. "Mother, I think—"

Scribonia shook her head. "Tell me, Pinaria. *Why* was he told to go?"

"It was said that he was Julia Aemilii's lover."

"But you don't think so?"

"He was about to marry your great-granddaughter. It just doesn't seem likely."

"You are right, Pinaria. He was not her lover."

"Mother—"

Scribonia closed her lips.

I took a deep breath and said, "You must tell me. I have guessed, you see. Your granddaughter is part of the conspiracy, isn't she, Scribonia? She is your child as well as Caesar Augustus' and the insult is to her as well as to you. And your grandson, Silanus? Yes, I thought so. He is yours also, and not even Augustus', but descended from another marriage. They were in it together. Just what were they going to do?"

194

No one spoke. They sat like marble. Even their eyes did not move.

"Well then, I must guess more. They were going to bring Julia back, weren't they? The plan had not changed. You were still going to…assassinate Augustus and provoke a civil war, except that now you would have to have someone to replace Iullus. Because I believe you could do anything you set your mind to, Julia Caesaris, but I do not think the city would let you lead the armies into war."

Julia smiled. "No."

"Who was it, then? Tiberius would have to be destroyed. And your son Agrippa has no military experience. It would have to be a general, someone successful. A popular figure, well-known, admired. Someone who hated Tiberius, who felt perhaps that Tiberius had displaced him—"

I think I knew the answer before she spoke.

The circle closed. The conspiracy was complete. There would never be a way out now.

"It was Fabius Maximus," Julia said.

I had to make one last struggle against the trap. "But it is Fabius who betrayed you all those years ago in the Forum, Julia Caesaris. And your daughter, and her husband and Junius Silanus. He has been your enemy all along."

"Not Fabius," Julia said.

"No, certainly not," her mother said at the same moment.

"I'm sorry. I'm so sorry. I know for a fact that it was."

"How do you know?"

"He could not have known about us. He was legate in Spain in those years," Scribonia said.

"That is true. But he came back early from his command there. And a few months ago I caught him, conspiring with my own servant, a secretary. They had a letter from my husband they must have intercepted. It had a list of names…"

Julia closed her eyes. "I see."

Scribonia bowed her head and studied at her hands.

There was a long silence. I don't know what I hoped. That even at that moment they might change the plan, and it would still go through. That Julia would find someone else to help her restore the Republic or rule it in her father's stead or whatever it was she wanted to do. That the Roman crowd, who loved her so devotedly, would rise up and follow her against the arrogant and morose Tiberius. That there would be no war and Naso would not have to lead his fellow Paelignians against Roman troops loyal to Augustus and his all-too-evident heir, but would instead find his way back from the frozen world he lived in to his life of peace and honor, with me.

But it did not happen. Of course it didn't. It couldn't happen. There was no one else for her to find, they were all dead, or exiled, or silenced. And if there were still someone who would risk so much, even at this late date, there was no way to find out who he was, or how to communicate with him.

Finally I scraped back my chair. "Thank you, Julia, Scribonia. I appreciate your help. I'm sorry it didn't work out better."

Neither of them spoke but Julia granted me a little nod.

Tears were standing in my eyes, so that I nearly stumbled over Diana, still asleep on the floor.

Julia made a little gesture. I managed to speak. "Please keep her, Julia Caesaris. I meant to free her for her part in getting me here tonight. It is the Festival of Feronia after all. But I think now that she will be so much happier with you."

"Of course. I will free her in my will."

"I will go see your daughter, if you like. I think I could find a way."

Julia said sadly, "I would like to know if she is well."

No." Scribonia shook her head. "It is too dangerous. I could see from the window—the guard looked at her very closely, disguised as she was. The next time he will know her, and he may have sent her description to Rome, as she says. It's better if she stays away."

Julia sighed. "Well, thank you all the same, Pinaria Ovidii. Thank you for everything you have done for us. My mother and I would like to repay you, but as you see—" She swept her hand to show their poverty.

It was that, I suppose, that made people love her, for of course what I had done was bring her was the news that she would die in exile, and her daughter would too. Yet she thanked me. For everything I had done. For making her suffering deeper and more hopeless.

"There is something," I said. "I—I hope I don't—it's not impertinent—but could you tell me, Scribonia, how my parents died?"

"You don't know?"

"Atia would never tell me. No one would. My uncle said it was politics."

"I suppose you could call it that. It was during the time when my husband—the divine Augustus—had come back from the wars. He devoted his energies, which are considerable, as you know, to consolidating his hold at home, while pretending to renounce all the titles and special powers the Senate had voted him. He resigned his consulship, but somehow he managed to be appointed tribune and voted a right—proconsular imperium—that enabled him to control any province, whatever the governor there did or said. He had claimed to encourage free speech in the Senate—Rome was still a Republic, he said. But when your father and some other senators objected to the renewal of his powers, somehow they found themselves no longer members of the Senate. A few of the most outspoken were executed."

I swallowed hard. "And one of them was my father?"

"That's right."

There was a little silence.

"And my mother?"

She nodded. "She was a good wife, Pinaria."

"I am sorry, Pinaria," Julia said. "They died bravely, for Rome. And if we could have we would have avenged them. Their blood is sacred, and blood would have paid for it." She lifted her chin and gave me a cold little smile.

I looked back as I went out the door. She was gently prodding Diana with her toe. As I watched, she lifted her head and said something to her mother, smiling like a spring morning.

She deserved to ride at the head of a triumphing army and be hailed as a goddess. She deserved the cheers of the crowd and the loyalty of the people of Rome. She deserved to rule. She was so exactly like her father.

PART VI

It was a sad year. Augustus was sick again, and the city worried.
He was an old man now, with no sons. His heir was unpopu-
lar. In the city the seven thousand firefighters were suddenly
very noticeable, and at dinner parties people glanced at the servants mistrustfully and stopped talking when they came in. The
soothsayers, public and private, did a brisk business: Marcia went
every Ides and Kalends to a woman who lived in a cave and was
said to consult a spider. "You ought to come with me, Pinni," she
said, blowing through my atrium like Pomona in spring, her pale
son Persicus beside her. "She's marvelous. You wouldn't believe the
useful things she's told me—"

"Thank you, dear. But like Cato I think that when two soothsayers meet they must have a hard time keeping a straight face."

But she was staring after Persicus where he studied the paint-
ings on the walls and I doubt she heard me.

The rains failed again, and the ships, when they came at all,
brought poor grain, moldy and small in the kernel. People like us of
course were not affected: we lived well enough from our own farms.

But among those a little less well off there were stories of people freeing their slaves so they would not have to feed them, and indeed, you saw flocks of such hungry men and women begging in the streets in ghostly voices, or lying, too exhausted to raise their hands, against the steps of the basilicas or in the precincts of the temples. The public slaves removed them during the night, but there were new ones by daybreak, pathetic in their silence and patience, the dying waiting among the dead for the same fate.

I saw the same famished faces in my atrium every morning, praying in whispered misery for a gift, a loan, even a word of hope: freedmen we had set up in business, farmers desperate for another year, tenants and shopkeepers, managers of the temples and baths we had built in the provinces, widows, orphans, memoryless old peasants, and that strange anonymous crowd, so degraded by their need that they had lost all connection with rank or relation or trade and had become only 'the poor'. When I could bear it, I called them in, and sitting in my husband's chair, I tried to do what he would have done. But their spectral voices followed me, always begging for more—more than I could give, more than I had, more than I wished to see. Often I sat in the office long after I had told Loricus to send them away. Sometimes I put my head back, and gasping and weeping, I cried for my loneliness and loss. Those were the good days. The worse were the ones when I could do no more than sit, staring at nothing, until someone came and set down some food for my lunch or my daughter came in to show me her weaving.

Ghosts hung around other corners of the house as well. People came and went in ways I found difficult to follow.

"Who was that, Loricus?" I would ask, seeing a foot in an outdoor shoe disappear out the entry, hearing a murmur of conversation behind a door that closed as I approached.

"Oh, didn't he speak to you? It was Macer, mistress. It was Rufus. Gellius. It was a man from the bookseller. It was no one, mistress— just a servant. Fabius Maximus sent him," Loricus would say. I did not know whether to believe him or not.

Finally, I spoke. "Loricus, I do not want anyone here without my permission. Anyone who comes must see me first."

"Really, mistress? But you are busy; you have the household to run. I didn't like to bother you…"

"Bother me, Loricus. This must stop."

Some of the people I had to send for myself. My daughter was of age, and I had to find a husband for her. Again I had to sit in Naso's chair, behind Naso's table, and try to think as he did. But I could not. I didn't know enough. I knew who had sons of the right age, more or less, and Marcia could help me with that. But there was the more subtle question of politics and alliances. I was no Julia to think of marriage in dynastic terms, but in a world so dangerous, surely I ought to think of my daughter's safety? What if I chose a man no longer in favor or a family who had angered the palace on the hill? Would my daughter suffer? Or her children? There was the question of the dowry. How would I judge what to offer? Especially in view of the taint we bore, however unjustly, of the relegation of my child's stepfather? And whom could I trust to ask?

Naso. I trusted him. He had cared. He had worked so hard to find Perilla someone. All I needed now was to know what was in his mind.

So I sat, day after day, in the office, looking at the books on the wall. I took them down and read them—everything he had written: account books, notebooks, poems from the first book, *The Love Affairs*, to the last remaining page of *The Festivals*. Nothing told me much.

"Can I help you, mistress?" Loricus said, seeing me with the books unrolled in stacks on the table. "Are you looking for something in particular?"

"I am just trying to understand him. But the more I read the less I can tell what mattered to him or why he wrote. One poem says one thing, the next another. Here women are so frivolous that any man can seduce any of us if he knows the right way to go about it; there we are heroines and love devotedly, even to death. Here the gods are so powerful that an encounter with one destroys a life, or transforms it; there they are merely imaginary. Where is he? What does he believe?"

"Everyone feels that, mistress. He is a wonderful man, and a very great priest of the goddess, but his soul he keeps to himself."

The light caught the deep blue of his eyes as he smoothed back his hair. He looked momentarily very sad. "A very complex mind," he said. Then he began to sing.

"...Scepter and dignity having left behind
The father and ruler of the gods, whose right hand is armed
With three-pronged fire, whose nod shakes the world
Clothes himself in the shape of a bull and mingles with the herd.
He bellows in the pride of his beauty as he walks among the others
    on the tender grasses
As you would expect he is the color of snow, when neither footstep
Has trampled nor the rainy south wind loosened it;
His throat swells, his dewlap hangs with grace
His horns are bent, it is true, but as small as buds and as translu-
    cent as pearls,
So that you would imagine them the work of magic or of art.
No threat looms on his forehead, no terrifying light shines in his
    eyes.
Peace is in his face.
The daughter of Agenor gazes in wonder at his beauty.
No hostile intent, no menace, does she perceive...
But however mild he seems, she is afraid at first to touch.
Soon she approaches, reaching flowers to his glistening white
    mouth.
Wild with delight, and hoping for more, he slobbers kisses on her
    hands,
With difficulty he postpones the rest.
And now he frolics on the green and blooming grass
Now he lays his snow-white flank down on the tawny shore
And so little by little removes the fear from her breast.
When he offers his chest, she pats it with an innocent hand
Presently she twines his horns with a clover wreath.
At last the virgin princess makes bold to sit on his back
Unaware whom she is pressing.
His first deceitful foot he puts into the wave
From there going further beyond, far from the earth and dry land

Of the shore, into the middle of the level sea.
So he carries his prey, until, frightened,
She looks back at the beach, swept away and abandoned.
With her right hand she is clutching a horn, with the other his
    back,
Her clothing billowing out behind her in the wind..."

There was a silence between us, a little tribute to the poem.

Finally I said, "It's...it's so fresh. As if he saw it all newly made before him. The innocent girl, the flowers in the grass, the golden shore. Is that what you were pointing out to me?"

"It's one of the things."

"And there's a pun."

"Hmm? Oh, yes. 'Minetur'—'menacing.' I suppose it could be." He withdrew himself into his thought.

"Isn't it? It sounds like "minotaur," I said, a bit defensively.

"Oh, yes. It could be. More interesting perhaps is the word itself. It is derived from...mmmm...the earliest uses I can think of... hmmm...are the cries of cattle drivers. Threatening calls, to keep the cattle in line."

"Cattle again."

He looked at me with approval. "Just so. It's a word about cattle, and a pun about a half-man half-bull, and about a god disguised as a bull."

"So elegant and sophisticated. Yet my daughter loved that story even when she was very little. He used to sing it to her at bedtime. How does he do it?"

He shook his head. "You will never know. You cannot get to the bottom of him."

More mystery. Even Loricus, who knew him so well, did not know him at all.

"It's beautiful, though."

"Everything he touches is. Perhaps that is the clue. He loves anything... beautiful." He raised his eyes to me, a very direct look to receive from a servant.

"Yes," I said, and let the subject drop.

So I was left without an answer. But all the same perhaps the books had called up some spirit, some god or ghost that heartened me, for it came to me, one bitter gray morning in February that it was exactly as it had been with the accounts: no one was going to find out for me whom Perilla ought to marry. I would have to do it myself. Summoning a secretary, I sent a note to Marcia. I would give a small dinner party. I would start to learn.

Once I did I was amazed. The whole city was alive with politics. How had I never noticed? On the couches the talk was of virtually nothing else: who sat next to whom under the big striped awning at the Magalensian Games; what Tiberius' brother's son Germanicus was doing with his army on the Rhine; who had been to the sooth-sayers with Agrippina Claudii when they had spoken so anxiously about the health of Augustus, or to dinner with Furius Camillus the night of the dispute about the Republic; who had presented Augustus with a petition and received an answer, who had only been given a joke ("Hand me the thing, man. Do you think you are offering a penny to an elephant?"); and a hundred more rumors, whispers, guesses, sighs, complaints and hidden glances. It was like a huge flirtation, carried on by the whole city, not over love, but power. In fact, that night at Furius'—where I had been a guest—under the shouts about whether the Republic still existed or was nothing but a sham and a memory, an elderly ex-consul had leaned over and plumped his hand down on my thigh.

Startled I removed it, expecting an indecent proposal, but he merely wanted to breathe his winesoaked fumes over me. "Did you know, the seer said there is a plot to assassinate Augustus? Furius is running it, and some people who own a string of gladiators. It's supposed to succeed."

"Is it? How do you know?"

He tried and missed to put his hand back on my leg. "I'm in on it."

Some of the rumors at least must have reached Augustus, for a decree came down from the Palatine Hill, though everyone pretend-ed that it had been issued from the Curia: "SOOTHSAYERS ARE

FORBIDDEN TO PROPHESY TO ANYONE ALONE, OR TO PROPHESY REGARDING DEATH EVEN IF OTHERS ARE PRESENT." It must have been insufficient, because just before his birthday in the summer Augustus released his own horoscope. No one was surprised, and I'm not sure many were convinced, when it showed that he would enjoy a very long life indeed.

In the midst of my search for someone for Perilla, Macer came back into my life. Indeed it felt like an invasion of my house. Every time I came into an empty room it seemed that Macer was there. I felt like Penelope with fifty suitors, and all of them Macer.

Finally I lost my temper. "Macer, you have been a good friend to my husband, but do you think you are doing him any service now?"

"My dear. My adored one. He wouldn't want you to live alone. He of all people understood that."

"Understood, Macer? He is still alive, you know, and I am not a widow yet."

He bent his balding head humbly and took my hand. "It is so like you, Pinaria, to go on when..."

"When what, Macer? When it's hopeless? I refuse to believe that."

"Ah. Well, anyway, let me help you. I'll do anything. Let me advise you. I have done well out of my mines: let me invest something of yours in them. I can double it for you."

"I'd have to know a lot more, Macer."

"Oh, my dear. Don't you trust me? I only want what's best for you."

"Thank you, Macer. I am very happy with the advice I have had so far."

Oddly, Fabius also wanted to invest for me—not in mines but in a large concern that was buying up small farms in the region around Brundisium, and turning them into horse ranches run by slaves. "A very sound proposition, Pinaria, as I am sure you are able to appreciate. With a daughter to marry in a year or two, perhaps the money might be useful?"

"I'll think about it. May I see the books?"

"Of course. Of course. I don't have them here—I think I have them at our place in Baiae, but I will be delighted to show them to you. How much shall I put you down for? A hundred thousand? Really, a very fine investment, doing amazingly well. I'm sure Naso would be very pleased."

"I'll think about it, Fabius."

I don't know what made me mistrust these transactions—perhaps there was something in their voices. Or their eyes.

"Pinni, do you think Fabius is all right?" Marcia asked me one morning in early autumn as we jolted along in her huge litter to the Circus Maximus. We were going to watch the first day of the Roman Games: chariot races. My little girl stared wide-eyed through the curtains at the passing crowd, ignoring Persicus' teasing. Fabius was not with us: as a special favor from Augustus he had been allowed to sponsor a team—the Whites—and had gone early to talk to the trainer.

"Fabius seems fine to me. Why, is there something wrong?"

"I—I wondered. He's been selling a lot of property."

Perhaps he was in need of money: this little gift of Augustus' couldn't have cost less than a million sesterces. And there was the investment in the horse ranches: could it be that?

The litter slaves set us down at the door. Regally, Marcia stepped out, trailed by more servants carrying cushions, sunshades, baskets of food and drink, squares of perfumed linens, even rose petals to throw in the air if Fabius' horses won. We climbed to our seats and ranged ourselves along the row. Perilla, flushed with excitement, clasped her hands in her lap and leaned forward. Several young men in the next row nudged each other in the ribs and shot her glances out of the corners of their eyes. A god whispered in my ear: Hurry. You haven't much time.

Marcia sat very still, her eyes on to the small figures near the entrance gates; in the slanted golden light of a September morning I could see Fabius' dark smooth head bent to listen to a bandy-legged little man tattooed like a Thracian. They were studying the hoof of a fine chestnut thoroughbred, which did not seem to care for the attention. His beautiful eye rolled and his ears flattened. Once he reached out and nipped his trainer's tunic in an irritated sort of way.

Marcia clutched my arm so tightly it hurt. "I just wondered if his doctor has warned him."

Stupidly I goggled at her. "Warned him?"

She blushed. "I—I just thought. He might be sick." Then, getting hotter with self-justification she insisted, "He's raising money for something. Are you sure you don't know what it is?"

"He said something about an investment in a horse ranch. Why? Doesn't he talk to you about things like that?"

"Oh, no," she said, raising a dignified head. "Fabius had always protected me from worry about financial matters. I don't think it's quite nice for a woman to know too much about those things, do you?"

A roar of pleasure from the crowd drowned my answer. The chariots were coming into the gates. My daughter was shouting with joy—she had a child's passion for the driver of Augustus' newly formed Blue Team—she kept his miniature of him in the basket with her hair ribbons, and thought I did not know. I had done the same thing myself when I was fifteen.

The starting banner snapped down. The teams started, the Blues already in the lead. As I watched, Fabius' team challenged the leaders, the wheels ground along, the hoofs thundered like omens. Fabius' team drove closer, wheel to wheel. Perilla was jumping up and down, waving the blue scarf she had brought, even Marcia's hands had tightened into whiteness. On they raced, side by side. The beautiful chestnut thrust forward his head, foam flew back. Around the corner, Fabius' team on the outside, pressed so close to the leaders no daylight showed between them. Drivers crouched. Whips cracking. Shouts and cries and noise. Down the other side, lost in dust. At the pillar, hidden. Perilla grabbed my arm so hard I cried out. First out of the corner: the chestnut and his teammates, the Blue Team half a head behind. On they came. The banner fell. A huge groan of rage swelled from half the stands, while Fabius' supporters cheered and shouted and embraced. In a shower of petals, Marcia sat silent and still, her hands still clutched together, and I wondered: If Marcia is so well protected, why is she so anxious now?

With the autumn, Marcia's daughter Fabia Numantina came back from the country. She brought her son to see me. We sat in the colonnade in the late September sun, drinking chilled pomegranate juice and chatting. "I thought I'd open the house now," she said. "Appuleius will be coming home from Germany this winter."

"Is Germanicus coming too then?"

"My father says not," the boy said. He was a robust child, with big hands and feet and a clear skin, in contrast to his young uncle Persicus, Marcia's son, who still had a kind of transparent look, as if his childhood illnesses had thinned his blood and turned his bones to fine Egyptian glass.

"You admire Germanicus, do you, Appuleius?"

His eyes glowed with all the enthusiasm of his ten years. "Oh, yes. He's a great general. My father says he's a brilliant strategist, and his men love him. They cheer for him whenever they see him, and he can turn a loss into a victory by his presence. In Illyricum, my father said…"

He went on with his explanation, to which Fabia and I listened with more patience than interest, but it was plain that what the boy said was true: Germanicus had lost none of his popularity by his campaigns. I wondered what Tiberius thought of that. He had been forced by Augustus to adopt the young man, the son of his brother. No one in Rome thought he liked the idea one little bit.

When he had gone in search of Perilla, I told Fabia of my worries about her marriage.

"But I know the perfect person for her. He's a friend of my husband's—they served together in Germany. Nice young man. He was married before, but his wife died or married someone else, or some such thing—I forget."

"They wouldn't mind that Naso has been—sent away?"

Her clear olive skin flushed. "I think—well, you know, they haven't a great deal of money—"

"I see."

"A very good family, though. Your daughter would have position, if perhaps not an important establishment—" She turned her smooth dark head, so like her father's, to gaze at my garden. She, who had never known anything but the utmost of grandeur and richness. When she was married it was to the grandson of Octavia, Augustus' sister, and the house she went to was more magnificent even than her mother's. It was hard for her even to hide what she thought of my own place, though by any reasonable standard it is a large and beautiful place.

The return of the children meant I did not have to say more. I preferred not to. After all, Fabia is a lot younger than I, and it is hard to be really candid with anyone except one's own contemporaries.

But I didn't need Marcia to point out to me, though she certainly would have, that my Perilla's dowry was going to make a difference. I thought I had better look for places to raise the money.

Money is strange: One silver denarius is exactly like the next, and the portrait on its face passes from one hand to another in silence and obscurity. If you hold it in your hand, you cannot tell where it has been; if you give it to someone else you have no way of knowing where it goes. But all the same, if you know how to listen, it speaks.

Day after day as I sat in my husband's study, rolling and unrolling the accounts, the whispered voices came to me, each different. Here an old man, faint and rusty, creaked a tale of a family of slaves bought before I was born, there a tall young creature sprang from the paper in a burst of enthusiasm for an investment in a shipload of statuary around the time of my daughter's birth. Here, more recent, was Loricus' careful murmur, column after column of transactions all neatly recorded: rich brokerages in olives, oil, honey, wheat; there, bringing sudden tears to my eyes, Naso's beautiful chant, this time of contributions to temples and the construction of baths and roads and irrigation channels in the Paelignian country. Here a street of shops that came with my dowry, there a whole scroll of records of his grandchildren's inheritance. Recently sold—and for a handsome amount, a sheep farm in North Africa, quite a large one, really a very admirable and prosperous business. Unexceptionable. But all the same, I paused, and my heart thumped hard against my chest.

Puzzled, I held it with slippery hands to the light. There was something wrong with it. The record of the sale was not in Loricus' hand, nor that of any of his assistants, though the ink was fresh.

It was familiar, though. My heart shook me so hard I nearly dropped the roll. The letters blurred. But not enough. I could still see who had written them: it was Fabius.

I spent the rest of the day looking for the money the sheep farm was supposed to have brought. The light had faded and the books melted together into a heap of shadows before I admitted defeat. It had not been recorded in any of the current ledgers. Nor, as far as I could see, had it been the subject of a note on the stacks of wax tablets waiting for the secretaries, nor was there hint or indication of any kind that the money had ever been received. I raised my voice. "Loricus, get in here. I want you. Now."

If there were servants in the atrium at Fabius' I never noticed them. Crashing into the walls, shouting and swearing, I burst through the doorway of his library, Loricus trailing ineffectually in my wake. The big room with its bins of white books, so orderly, so polished, so filled with golden light from a hundred sweet-smelling lamps glazed back at me blandly. In the midst of it gleamed Fabius in front of his desk, a fine antique wine jug and an unrolled book at his elbow. I thrust past a chair. It made a sound like a cart overturning. I raised my voice to a shriek over the noise. "Fabius, what is going on here? Where is my money?"

Fabius waited a beat like an actor at the theater, then looked up. "What are you talking about, Pinaria, dear? Why all the fuss?"

"Fuss?"

"Yes, Pinaria. Fuss. I'm sorry, I haven't time to deal with this now. In fact, I am on my way out to dine with the consul—"

"I don't care if you are dining with Jupiter himself, Fabius. I want to know what happened to the money from this farm."

"Pinaria. Pinaria. Calm yourself, dear. Whatever it is, it can't be that bad."

"The farm, Fabius."

"What farm is that, my dear?"

"This one," I hurled the scroll onto the desk. It struck the desk with a loud clatter, and rolled open, coming to rest with one end swinging slowly over the edge, striking the side with a rhythmic little smack.

"Pinaria, let us not be vulgar now."

I simply goggled at him.

"That's better. Now, sit down and wait and I will be with you as soon as I have finished with—"

"Vulgar? You think I'm vulgar? I'll show you vulgar, Fabius."

I looked around. Beside the door a stand held small lamps about the size and shape of artichokes. I picked one up and weighed it in my hand.

Loricus was shouting something. Fabius reached out to grab my arm.

"No. Pinaria. Stop. That lamp is lit—"

I threw. The lamp hurtled off my fingers, spinning as it went. Oil flew from it, some of it catching fire in the air. Still turning, the whole burning mass slammed into the wall behind him with a truly astonishing amount of noise.

All three of us stared at it, open-mouthed. The oil dripped slowly down the wall, a small flame turned blue and drowned.

It seemed to say what I wanted to. I took a step closer. I picked up another. "The farm, Fabius." Fabius ducked. Crash. The lamp smacked into the wall, leaving another dripping trail of oil in the clean white paint. Now I was striding forward, picking up objects— vases, portrait busts, a whole stack of waxed boards—and hurling them at the desk. Most of them missed, shattering against the walls or the floor. Puddles of oil began to burn, and long splashes decorated the wall behind him. "I want—" crash— "to know—" crash— "all—about it." Crash.

Fabius, waking suddenly to the damage I was doing, leaped from his chair so suddenly it overturned and darted around the desk, hands out to grab me. "Pinaria, if you don't calm down I will have you put out of this room."

"Really? I don't think you will, Fabius." Moving fast, I shoved Loricus at him. "Tell him what you told me."

He froze in his place, his one foot comically still in the air. "Loricus told you something?"

My lungs were heaving, my hair had flown around my face. But my voice, amid the gasps for air, was strong and cold. "Yes—he told me something. He confirmed—that this farm—was sold on your instructions. Tell him, Loricus."

Loricus, completely unmoved by the chaos, made his little gesture to smooth his hair against his head. "I'm sorry, Fabius Maximus. I told Pinaria Ovidii that you authorized the transfer of the Marsyas farm. I told her how much you got for it. Pinaria Ovidii asked me what happened to the money, as she has asked you." He couldn't help it, a smile twitched and was gone. "But I had to say I don't know where the money went." He looked all of a sudden like an old man. "I'm sorry, Fabius Maximus. I don't see how I could do anything else."

Fabius stared at him, then waved him away. "It doesn't matter."

"No, it doesn't matter, Fabius. I don't need his confirmation." I picked up the scroll again. "I can read. I can recognize your handwriting. By what right did you sell something that belonged to me? How did you even manage it? Who would buy a stolen farm? And what did you do with the money?"

"Pinaria. Pinaria, my dear. I'm sorry you found out this way. But I assure you, no one has harmed you. There's no occasion for anger."

"Oh? You think not? Fabius. I trusted you—I've trusted you all my life—and you have stolen from me, and from a man who loved you and honored and admired you—"

"Pinaria. Please. Of course you are upset. Here. Sit down. Let's have some wine. I see you have been too clever for us. I will have to explain everything."

"I don't want to sit down. I want an explanation, and by heaven, Fabius, if I don't get one I will have the praetor on you. You have robbed me. Don't you understand?"

"No, I haven't. I acted on instructions. From Naso himself."

"Naso? I suppose you can prove that? You have some kind of document? A letter? Put that thing down, I don't want any wine."

It was a measure of how furious I was that ordered him around in his own house. It was even stranger that he obeyed. He set the jar down on the tray, taking care to avoid the splashes of oil and the broken shards, taking a long time over it. When he turned back to me, his dark eyes were serious and he wasn't smiling any more. "No, I don't have a document, or a letter. It would be much too dangerous for him to write one, or for me to have one. Do you understand, Pinaria? I am talking to you as equal now, a grown woman responsible for herself and her family—"

"I have been that for some time, Fabius."

"Yes, I know. I have been slow, perhaps criminally slow, to see it. But I see it now, and I am telling you—trusting you with a secret, really—"

"You are trusting me? Since when, Fabius? And isn't it really a question of whether I trust you? Which I don't."

He held up his hand. "Hear me out, Pinaria. I don't blame you for feeling angry at what you think was the nasty trick we played on you—"

"Trick? Is that what you call it? You stole, Fabius—"

"I only want to say that we are conspirators, Naso and I. Loricus has been helping us."

"Conspirators? Naso? And you?"

He nodded gravely. "And others I may not mention."

"Conspirators to do what?"

He nodded to Loricus, who went to the door, peered out then pulled it shut, standing in front of it with his arms crossed.

"What we have all wanted for many years. To break the power of Tiberius and the Claudian family. To bring back the Julians from exile. To restore the Republic, the real Republic, not the sham it has become."

I sat down. "Bring back the Republic? But how?"

He was already picking up his overturned chair and tidying his desk. The oil fires went on burning, and he contemplated them, obviously wondering whether I would break out again if he called a servant to clean up. Evidently deciding that I might, he turned his back on them and bestowed on me his most emollient smile. "Pinaria, I will pay you the compliment of talking to you as the politically astute woman you have become."

"Why don't you just tell me, Fabius? If I'm so astute I don't need the compliments."

He nodded. "The problem for us is this: how to mobilize opinion in the city. Not just us, our circle and our people, but the plebeians, who vote and fight. Even the freedmen—they have influence, you know. Caesar, you see, has always had his personal following—the fact that he has brought peace and order to the city, and the fact that he is Julius Caesar's adopted son and his heir. The Julians are still tremendously popular, as you know.

"Well, then what we have to do is find a way to counteract that. Both Julias command huge followings. Imagine bringing them back into the city. Imagine the popular rejoicing. One could capitalize on that—for a while at least, the city would be in our hands. And if it were managed correctly in that time a small band of devoted patriots, members of the old houses and men who had earned the right by their service to Rome—or who have ties with our country allies— yes, like Naso—those men would be able to reestablish the Senate as a real and functioning body, get rid of the scum and refuse that have disgraced it for so long. Don't you see, Pinaria? It's not a question of changing the constitution—our institutions are what they always were. It's just a matter of getting rid of the influence of one man. That's all that we would need to do. It's urgent, Pinaria. Caesar is old. If he dies and is succeeded by Tiberius, the cause is lost. No one who knows anything about the Claudians can doubt that."

"What on earth are you talking about? Who will capitalize on the time Julia is going to buy you? What band? Naso is relegated. He's gone. How could he conspire with you?"

"You underestimate your husband, Pinaria. He is right now the most active member of our group. Up there among the barbarians he is raising an army. They don't need much encouragement: they have hated us for years. But they do need money. I sold the Marsyas property and sent the proceeds—every last bronze penny—to Naso. No doubt he will use it where it will do the most good."

"But why? What for? You don't imagine the barbarians are going to conquer Rome, do you? They haven't a chance. And if they did win, why would they put you in power?"

"Of course they won't conquer Rome. They are simply a ploy. How else can we be sure that Tiberius is called away when we—on the day that we—"

"Assassinate Caesar Augustus," said Loricus.

Fabius was still standing, leaning against his desk, almost the same elegant Fabius as he had always been. Only now I felt nothing but contempt for him. Contempt and a feeling that he was hiding something. "Distinguished men, Fabius? Does that mean you?"

He smiled modestly. "I am doing my part."

"And what is that?"

"Look, Pinaria, I'm talking to you very frankly. Try to understand. The problem is that the city has to be defended. It needs for its leaders to be men of military experience, even expertise. There aren't many of us who fit that description and who are not at the same time so in Caesar or Tiberius' debt that they cannot act freely. I have the good fortune to be one. That's all."

"And you will lead the city in the civil war against Tiberius? Because how could you imagine that he wouldn't raise an army himself? He can afford it, and he is respected by the soldiers. Why would they trust you?"

"I would have Julia's backing."

"And the city would believe that?"

"Why not? They would be able to see it. She would be my wife."

It was all lies. So like Fabius, so plausible, so dishonest. The brilliant room swam around me, the light began to dim around the edges. I do not think that I have ever in my life been so frightened. Not the night of my husband's relegation, when what I felt was pain and anger, not the long time in the house of exile when Rome itself rejected me and I felt nothing at all, not when I thought the soldiers would discover what I was doing in Rhegium. Not even when my mother gave my hand into a stranger's and turned her back on me forever.

I don't remember how I left that room, that house. All I remember was standing in my own study trying to think of how to get word to Naso that he had trusted a traitor. I was already composing the note in my mind when I noticed Loricus, standing as still as a soldier in front of the desk.

"Get out, Loricus."

"Mistress, I am sorry for what happened. I was obeying Ovidius Naso's instructions. I hope you will see that I have always been loyal to him."

"That may be so, Loricus." I thrust off my cloak and let it fall to the floor anywhere, I was in such a hurry to begin writing. "But you have not been loyal to me."

"Mistress, you are his wife. Surely loyalty to him is the same as loyalty to you?"

Where you are Gaius, I am Gaia.
You may be Gaia but you are also Pinaria.

"No, Loricus. It is not the same thing. I am his wife. Of course our interests are the same. But I am a Pinarius too. And we are a great family, consuls, knights, citizens, soldiers, Romans. I am one of them. A freeborn Roman woman. And I have been, for the years that Naso has been gone, your protector. You owed me more than you gave.

"I don't want to see you. From this moment you are forbidden to come into this room. You are forbidden to open a book, to write a letter, to so much as pick up a pen wherever you find it. You will go immediately to my uncle Rufus, and there you will stay, doing whatever he tells you. You are to have no contact with anyone here, or with any member of Fabius Maximus' household, or any other member of the conspiracy. If there is one. I am giving you a note for Rufus to that effect. And you may thank me, and your gods if you have any, that I have not sent you to Elba to the iron mines. If I find that you have disobeyed me in the slightest degree I will do that. Is that clear?"

Fabius was a traitor no matter how much or how little you believed of what he said. On the one hand, if he had lied about his authorization for selling the farm, he had betrayed me, and stolen from me. On the other, if he was telling the truth, he was betraying

Naso too, pretending to help a conspiracy he had already exposed to the authorities. Not to mention Julia. Well, a god had put it in my mouth to warn her. She was safe now.

There was still the question of what I ought to tell Marcia. It was clear that she too was safe: Fabius had no intention of marrying Julia. Nor would Julia consider marrying him. I could not see any reason to tell Marcia about the theft. It would only distress her, and she was powerless to stop her husband. That I would have to do on my own. I resolved to say nothing to her.

But Naso, in his love, his trust, was waiting far away on the Danube, working amongst those dangerous barbarians, for a chance to strike at Rome. I had most urgently to get word to him, and I hadn't the least idea in the world how to do it.

In the end I wrote a letter and took it down to Ostia myself, since I had no one I could trust to send. It was a day of wind and bitterness. Dead plane tree leaves as big as curled hands blew across the quays. Out in the harbor the heads of the whitecaps were sliced into long sprays, and the sea chopping below them was the color of old stones.

The bustle of spring was no longer even a memory. The weather had turned, the sea lanes were closing: there would be no more race horses from Thessaly, or crates of melons from Africa, no wheat or fine statuary or oil, until spring. Far down at the end of the quay a single ship was still loading. The bearers I had hired so that no one would know where I was going set me down beside it. The hull towered over me: I cannot say it inspired confidence. It was battered and scraped and none too clean, listing like a sloppy old woman in worn-down shoes. Gulls glided over it like vultures, and indeed with its whitened ribs and fishy smell it was ready for their attentions. Even the crew, when they appeared to stare at me over the railings, had the look of desperate men on their last voyage. Some were badly damaged: a stump of an arm, a scar dragging upward a sagging lip, hollow cheeks, dirty clothing, missing teeth. I wondered if they were pirates. Well, as long as they took my letter and delivered it, I didn't care if they were sea monsters in disguise.

They lined the railing, scrutinizing me with an equal mistrust. I don't know what they thought—well, I do, of course: a veiled woman without an escort and carried by hired slaves. They must have wondered why I had waited so long to ply my trade. Indeed one of them shouted down to me, "You're too late, darling. We're sailing within the hour."

"I know. For the Black Sea? Yes? Good. I want to see the captain."

They conferred, eying me mistrustfully. The wind whipped, the leaves skittered, the sky retreated, high and cold. I waited.

Presently the captain appeared. I thought he was fat, but as he came down the gangway to me I saw that actually he was thick with muscle and solid with assurance. His skin was the color of the night sky and polished till it gleamed. A loop of gold glittered in his ear. Alone in all his ship he looked comfortable and well fed, alone he had prospered, but remembering the captain of the 'Helmet of Minerva', who had blamed Naso for his own bad luck so long ago, I wondered.

But what could I do? There was no other ship, and I had to get word to Naso somehow. I put the letter into his pink and black hand.

He studied the packet, looking a long time at my seal in the wax. I did not like to interrupt him for fear of making him reconsider, but I thought that the longer he looked the higher the price was going to be.

Finally I spoke. "How much do you want to take it to a Roman citizen named Publius Ovidius Naso, in Tomis?"

He weighed the letter in his hand, letting it bounce gently on his broad palm, but his fathomless eyes were on me. "*Kyria*, who are you?" he said in a heavy Greek accent.

"Who am I?"

"That's what I said."

"What—what do you care who I am?" I demanded, beginning to get angry. "I have to send a letter. I'm going to pay you, you needn't worry about that—"

He handed me back the letter. "I'm sorry, *kyria*."

"I am his wife. What of it? A wife can write to her husband, even if he's in Tomis, I should think. It's not a crime. If you are worried about carrying the letter, just tell me how much you want. I'll pay it. I haven't any choice, have I?"

"*Kyria. Kyria.* Don't upset yourself. I know Ovidius Naso. I have talked with him—this is not my first run to the Black Sea. I'll take your letter. I don't want any money..." And to my vast astonishment, he began to sing, in a deep, rolling voice. At first I did not recognize what he sang, for he was translating it as he went into Greek, but then the meaning came home to me:

Of bodies changed to unfamiliar forms
My mind is borne to speak:
Gods, breathe on this work
For you have done it too.
And from the origin of the universe
To my own time,
Lead my unbroken song.
Before sea and earth and the sky protecting all,
Nature had a single face:
Chaos. Nothing existed unless it was heavy, weak, ill-made,
And everywhere, everything contended in a rough, disordered mass...

So I went home, contemplating the uses of a fame that was certainly godlike, and hoping that I had been in time. There was nothing I could do now but wait for the news from Dacia.

In December Germanicus came home from the wars to be consul. With him came his wife, Julia's daughter Agrippina, and a large number of his aides, including Suillius Rufus. I called on Rufus' family, expecting to wait while they dressed and so on, but they welcomed me right away. Their relative poverty was obvious, and it made them uncomfortable, but my uncle had already discussed the terms of a marriage settlement with them. They had agreed to the form of marriage I wanted, and the amount of the dowry, so we did not have to talk too long about such things. But now, in addition, I had a stipulation to make, which they had difficulty understanding, but finally, and with the promise of another share in my first husband's largest importing business, they agreed. After that, we chatted a bit about our children, and in the end they invited me to dinner.

They had plainly gone all out for this party, to welcome back their son from the Rhine. Germanicus and his wife graced the head couch. I watched them with interest: Agrippina, pregnant and beginning to show, had not the beauty of her mother and sister: there was too much of her father, Vipsanius Agrippa, in her square chin and heavy cheeks. But all the same, she reminded me of her mother. Even as she reclined on a couch next to her husband—it took me a moment to realize that I was reclining too, that indeed it had become perfectly natural for women to recline like men—she resembled Julia: her arm lay along the rest and her hand fell loose, her head was raised in that typically Julian pride. She smiled graciously but said little during the meal.

Suillius Rufus struck me as an upright young man. Not handsome, he seemed straight and trustworthy. There was an air of intelligence about him. He had dark eyebrows that nearly met across his nose, and bright eyes looked out from under them, studying and weighing and keeping their thoughts to themselves. I could see that Germanicus thought highly of him, bending to consult him about facts in the stories of military life he was telling, and once laughing at a joke. Well, I thought, he will do, and then I wondered what my daughter would say.

For that was what I had bargained so hard for: that my daughter, who was her father's only heir, would not only keep control of her own money, subject of course to the rather loose control of the distant cousin we had chosen to administer it—but that she would also to have the right to say if she would marry Suillius. I myself was given to a man I had never seen, and though I was lucky to have gotten a man so kind, I had sworn on the still-damp head of my newborn child that she would never have to marry as I had.

On the day Suillius and his parents came to visit, I sent off the maids and held Perilla's hands.

"Do you understand what is happening today?"

She nodded solemnly. Her slender body stood upright before me, her new young breasts just swelling her dress, the ribbons in her hair lying along her slim and pretty neck. It was the first day she had worn her hair pinned up and she was very proud of it.

"You wait behind the curtain. I think you'll be able to see the family, but they won't see you. I'll come to you—"

For some reason I had a hard time swallowing. I went on holding her hands, unable to think of anything, just staring at her. Her huge eyes looked back at mine.

I saw that I was frightening her, and forced a smile. "Well, then, if we're all set, let us go. You look lovely, my darling. Don't worry about a thing."

The senior Suillii came in first, much on their dignity, holding themselves stiffly as they approached through the varied light and shadow of the winter afternoon. But they warmed visibly as they saw the size of our atrium. The pool glittered and the fine Greek bronze in the middle shone in the long slant of golden sunshine. By the time they reached my chair they were cordial.

Behind them came their son, his thick eyebrow drawn down and his step firm and military. He did not look around him, but marched forward through the bars of shadow and took my hand. His own was dry and his grip straightforward, neither shy not bold. I thought he made a good impression—an old-fashioned and correct young Roman. He did not speak until I addressed him, but he answered me politely in a gravelly voice that I thought people would remember. A useful attribute for a career in politics, which of course is what he said he wanted to do with his life. Well, my girl and her fortune were going to be very useful to him in that.

We all four drank our warmed juices and nibbled at the little cakes. Presently a maid came in and whispered in my ear—a signal I had arranged. I excused myself and followed her out, my legs trembling.

Behind the curtain Perilla stood waiting, half in shadow. The light from the atrium carved her cheekbone and turned her childish lips to coral. I could not read her expression.

"Oh, Perilla, what do you think?" I whispered.

"He's nice."

"Could you love him?"

Her shadowed eyes looked back at me, glints in the darkness.

"Yes, Mother."

"You are sure?"

She nodded.

"Perilla—" I thought I would cry out with pain. But the Suillii were just beyond the curtain. I forced a whisper through my teeth. "You don't have to. My baby. My darling. You don't have to."

"I must marry someone, Mother," she said reasonably.

"No—" I muttered, tears choking my voice.

She leaned forward into the light, and I saw that her mouth had curved into a small smile, private and interior. Fine golden down sprinkled her cheek. It had not been there last year.

"Oh, Perilla. Are you sure?"

She said nothing. Instead she reached out a tentative hand and took me by the arm: a gesture of consolation, of support. A woman's gesture, to another woman.

I brushed damp strands of hair out of my eyes. "Listen, my darling. It's all right. I have arranged that your money will stay in our family. If you want to divorce him at any time, you can."

Out of the light she said again gently, "But, Mother, he seems nice."

I thought: she is my daughter, but she is no longer my child. If I stretched out my arms to hold her I would not be able to reach her; she was like someone on a ship moving farther and farther from the quay, and all I could do was stand there and watch her go.

That night I threw myself into Marcia's arms and cried my heart into submission.

"It's all right," she said, patting me clumsily on the back. "I felt the same when Fabia married. You'll feel better soon. And wait until your first grandson is born. I don't think I was ever really happy before that."

That winter Augustus was sick again. He wrote a letter to the Senate, praising Germanicus, but he was too ill to speak, and Germanicus himself had to read it aloud in his fine commander's battlefield voice. It recommended Germanicus to Tiberius too. That was talked of at dinner parties: nobody knew what exactly Augustus had meant by this gesture, if Tiberius was now supplanted by his brother or not.

That winter too, the arrests began again. The guards marched through the city; at familiar houses doors swung open, crowds gathered, people were led away living or dead, books were burned again in the Forum including some satirical verses about Livia Drusilla and the pretensions of her family. I was pretty sure they had come from Cassius Severus, away in his exile, but no one would say so. No one said much of anything: at dinner parties, the talk of politics had grown vague and insincere—people were afraid to criticize Augustus, but under the false smiles and the chorus of praise the diners eyed one another on the couches, wondering which of us were the informers. We all knew of course that they were all over the city.

I forced myself to go out, I even gave parties myself, hoping to hear something useful, something that would tell me if Naso was still safe. Though there were rumors everywhere, I heard nothing to the point. It did not occur to me until much later how odd it was that I had come to consider Tomis safe in any circumstances.

The one person who might have told me something—Fabius—I could not ask. Nor did I dare say anything to Macer, though he had taken to coming to call even at the mornings when I saw petitioners and clients. I could not quite bring myself to tell the servants not to admit him: indeed, I felt that in such a crisis any friend we had, however ambiguous, might be useful, even necessary.

The fear never left me: the winter seemed unnaturally cold, and my dreams were full of darkness and the sound of rushing voices on the wind.

My daughter, at least, was happy. The house rattled with preparations for the wedding. The weaving room was never quiet, nor was the kitchen, and I think I ran the length of the house twenty times a day, summoned by some emergency at one end or the other. The soothsayers chose the date near the end of June, the most propitious month; Perilla's only male relative on her father's side, the elderly cousin and his equally ancient wife, arrived and were installed in the back garden courtyard; the weavings and garlands were hung in the atrium; Perilla tried on her dress, and we had a little party to celebrate. At last the day came. Perilla sacrificed her toys at the family altar, and stood with her young man, hand in hand before the company, saying as I had once before, "Where you are Gaius, I am Gaia." Macer, having pleaded for the privilege, sang the wedding song, the cousin handed Suillius the small golden cake which he divided with my smiling child, and before I knew it we were out the door into the starry summer night shouting the wedding cry under flaring torches while a crowd of onlookers roared jokes and obscene advice at Suillius. Under her fine flame-colored veil Perilla flinched. "Perilla—" I cried out, taking a step out of line.

A hand gripped my arm, pulling me back. Fabius. The torches chased shadows over his face. His mouth was pulled tight and the lines from his nose to the corners made a cave of darkness. "It will be all right," he said. "Look."

Suillius indeed had seen Perilla's discomfort, and was shielding her with his body from the worst of the noise and the calls. I could see him smiling down on her. She raised her veiled head and turned it toward him.

"Don't cry," Fabius said. "It's inauspicious."

"I won't."

"Good. I have news. The uprising has begun on the Danube."

"What?" I turned to look, but the procession had swallowed him up and in that shouting crowd I was left alone on the street.

All through the summer if you listened carefully you could hear the rumble of that distant war. Augustus heard it, up on the Palatine, and took to his bed, ill again. He was seventy-five. There were ceremonies for his birthday, elaborate and exaggerated in the fawning way that had become customary. He attended them, looking as green as an unripe apple and walking with difficulty. In the end he had to plead with the Senators not to call on him with their congratulations, giving the war as his reason, though everyone knew the truth. Something was on his mind, for he continued the arrests and the bookburning, and imposed more stringent controls on the exiles, forbidding them enough money or servants to live in any real comfort, and making those who were still on the mainland or nearby islands move further away. Nor were they allowed to cross the sea.

Relegated people like Naso and his own child and grandchildren he left where they were, but I heard that he had again insisted that his daughter be deprived of the right to drink wine. It gave me a chill: did he know, then, that I had brought her some? There were new call-ups to the draft: some of my own servants from the farms and some of Naso's from the mines were conscripted. I had a moment of horror thinking that if one of them killed Naso I would never be able to bear it, but in the end I learned that our people were sent to Germany.

In Dacia the war was short, and brutal. A commander on the Danube was sent, another joined him. We heard of a town on a ridge that surrendered only after a long siege, and battles along the river where the water ran red with blood. Whether it was Roman or barbarian the rumors did not say.

All through that summer I seem to have held my breath. But though at last, among the crisping leaves of autumn, we heard that the operation had been successful and the Getan uprising had been put down, no word came about a lone Roman poet and his secret hope for the wrong victory.

PART VII

That year I spent nearly entirely in the country with my daughter. She had gotten pregnant—early, I thought. Her husband might have waited, as many men do who marry such young brides. "But Mother, he had to go to the army. If we waited it would be for so long," she pleaded, so like the child she so recently had been. As if I could do anything about it.

"I only hope the goddess is watching out for us then," I said.

If she was she behaved in the typical fashion of deities: my daughter had a terrible pregnancy, full of alarms and discomforts. In the end the child, born tiny and very premature, turned blue in her arms and died. Perilla's grief was terrible: I thought I might lose her too. And to my surprise, my own sorrow, for a child I had not wanted in the first place, was nearly as bad.

Finally, when I thought she had recovered enough to face the world, I took her back to Rome and helped her reestablish her life in the big place Suillius had bought with her dowry on the Caelian

Hill. My own life caught me up again, and I lay awake in the lengthening spring nights, watching the moonlight paint the floor and hollow the empty shadows of the room.

I had a letter. Macer brought it, as he had brought many others. He appeared in my atrium one morning in the spring of the next year, among my patient and humble dependents all waiting for their turns to speak to me. He looked older. His eyes had sunk deep into their discolored sockets, and new lines had carved themselves into his cheeks, but his thickly sensual mouth still shone moistly under his beard. Though now his beard was entirely gray.

He stepped close to me and lowered his voice. "Do you have some place more private we could go, Pinaria?"

"Really, Macer, I have all these people to see. This is a very bad time to choose, and if you think I want to be alone with you anyway—I am a married woman, Macer."

He held out a packet of letters. "I know that, Pinaria. Dear. I brought these. Letters from Pontus."

I put out my hand. He weighed the letters back and forth from one hand to the other, but did not pass them to me.

"I don't want you to open them until you are alone. One of them is very—very—well, you know."

"How do *you* know, Macer? Surely you haven't read a letter from my husband to me?"

He was not even embarrassed. "Of course I have. He meant it for publication. He can write so powerfully, and I am sure it's not what he really thinks—"

"Not mean it? Mean what? Is it bad news? Is he all right? Is he—is he—?" I couldn't say it. But the bright morning was suddenly as cold as the Danube, and I thought: Naso is fifty-nine years old and his health is bad.

The letters had disappeared behind his back. "My dear. How like you to think only of him. You are so good. No, it's nothing like that. He's all right. It's just—"

"Just what?"

It must have been the shadows that were making his eyes look so pitying, so sad. He smacked the little packet down on my palm.

"I'm sorry, Pinaria. Read it when you are alone."

Uncharacteristically he made me a little bow and started to go, but not before, entirely characteristically I'm sorry to say, he had taken my hand and held it just a little longer than was necessary, or correct.

When I had seen my clients I took the letter to the garden, and turned my back to the house. It was a good thing I did, and I thanked Macer in my heart for warning me. It was the worst letter I have ever received in my life.

> *It is amazing that you have not succeeded better, spouse,*
> *And that you can keep back your tears at my troubles.*
> *What should you do, you ask?*
> *Ask yourself: you'll find the answer—*
> *If you really wish.*
> *A great role is assigned to you by my little book, spouse;*
> *There you are held up as an example of a good wife.*
> *Take care that you do not become unworthy, and that my praise is*
> *   true:*
> *See that you protect the work that Fame has done.*
> *Even though I bear my complaints in silence, Fame will complain*
> *   for me*
> *If you do not have all the concern for me that she owes me.*

It was horrible. I sat there, staring at it, unable to believe he would do this. Keep back my tears? Where did he get that idea? And that I didn't do enough?

There was more, much more in the same vein. He complained that he was ill and that the doctors couldn't help him—now I must pull the cart by myself. That was followed by instructions about how to approach Livia—as if he didn't know that I already had. I was to wait until she wasn't busy, no—she was always so busy she had no time even for her personal needs. But choose a good time anyway. I should throw myself at her feet, weep in an exaggerated way, tremble with fear. I should hardly dare to ask if he could move to a safer place. I wasn't to defend his actions—what actions?—because he was in the wrong. And so on. All of it was plastered with the most oily compliments to Caesar and his wife.

I looked at the letter for a long time; then, resisting an impulse to wipe my hands on a cloth, I told my maid to draw my bath.

I went to Marcia.

"That's the letter?" She tilted it to the light and read it with her soft nearsighted gaze. It was a dull day, the last moment of winter as it passed into spring, and the water had an iron look.

"Yes."

"He says you might dishonor me if you don't try hard enough."

"Do you think I will?"

"No, of course not, Pinni." Her short upper lip came down in that stubborn and annoyed little way. "Well…people do know you're connected with us. And really, Pinni, when it comes right down to it, what have you done?"

"It seems like a lot to me. I've seen all his friends, and all the important people he ever knew, over and over. Often they won't even see me any more. He doesn't seem to realize that. And he says I should go to Livia. But I did."

"Well, but you didn't do what he said." She tossed some more bread out of her basket.

"You mean throw myself at her feet? All that? Would she have wanted me to? Isn't it a bit—embarrassing?"

"Why? Maybe she expected it. You're not really her—her social equal, are you, Pinni?"

"I never said I was. But I am the wife of a Roman citizen. He can't mean it. Really he can't."

"He doesn't think he's humiliating you. He just wants you to do whatever will work."

"But it's so cold. There's no love in the letter at all. He calls me "spouse" as if it were some kind of legal document…"

"Maybe he doesn't love you. Maybe he just married you for your position."

"I don't know. Maybe. Maybe he did at that."

I don't know why I didn't tell her about his night with Julia. It must have been that upper lip. Perhaps if I had—but when I thought of it again, it was too late.

If I had thought I was finished with Macer, I was wrong. He was always at my house now: I could not bring myself to have him denied entry—he was after all my kinsman and Naso's best friend. But it was a trial to me to deal with him. His thick mouth seemed to be everywhere, talking at me, leaning toward my ear, glinting with concern under his beard.

"Pinaria, I know how you feel. But think how little he knows about what you have done, how far away—"

"I know, Macer."

"He doesn't mean it personally. He's just using you as an example, to show how unfeeling Caesar has been."

"Yes, I see that. That's precisely the problem, Macer. I'm not an example, I'm his wife. He's supposed to care about me, but he doesn't seem to mind at all if I am held up to shame."

"He didn't mean it that way. You have been wonderful to him, Pinaria—I wish—"

But it was all too evident what he wished. "I'd rather not talk about it. Now, if you'll excuse me, I have some accounts I have to see to."

"Let me help you, Pinaria. Here, if you like I could take a look for you—"

"No, thank you, Macer."

"I only want what's best for you, Pinaria."

"Yes, thank you. Now, if you'll excuse me—"

We seemed to have this conversation several times in the next half month. I began to see that wet, shining mouth in my dreams. Finally in desperation I sent to my uncle Rufus for Loricus.

I was surprised how glad I was to see my old servant. He looked the same: the lines in his face were no deeper, the white in the fringe of hair he combed over his skull no paler. In no time he had taken over the office and organized everything for me. It became a pleasure to go into the bright, clean room and see him at the desk, his head bent over the roll—there was never more than one at a time—his tall brow unperturbed. Sometimes I went simply to sit there in the chair across from him, listening to the tiny scratching sound of his stylus on the boards as he made and checked his calculations. He never failed to rise and bow to me as I came in, to consult me, to ask every morning for my orders.

The next time Macer came I had him shown into the office. He took one look at Loricus, standing respectfully behind the desk, glanced at me, at the stacks of letters we had been writing, and seated himself several feet away. His business did not seem to detain him long, nor did it require the usual handholding or expressions of esteem. Even better it didn't need him to come back for quite a long time.

One day I showed Loricus the letter. He read it with the same attention he gave to his work. When he was done he set it down before him and folded his hands over it. He looked very sad.

"A very painful letter, mistress. And if I may say so, not deserved."

"Thank you. He says he's ill. Do you think it might be…serious? He's not young, you know. "

"Perhaps. In any case, it's interesting. It may be a literary device."

"For sympathy?"

"Just so. But if I may say so, your concern—your pain—shows that you are indeed a good wife."

He said nothing more, and I could not go into it with a servant. But it was odd: the person who said the least was the one who helped me most.

Then for a long time, almost a year, nothing happened. That is, life changed, in that imperceptible way it has, so that you don't notice until everything is different and the children have grown up. Persicus turned sixteen and assumed the toga of a man. The party Fabius gave was lavish and beautiful and was talked of for a month afterwards. My daughter, who had been a bride, grew into a Roman matron of dignity and self-assurance. Where did she get it? Perhaps from her father; perhaps it was something that life, and her terrible loss, taught her. She dressed elegantly and managed her house well, she spoke in company, suddenly having opinions on every subject. When her health improved she took her leave of me—a moment of such sadness I had to conceal it from her, for she was going to Germany to be with her husband. Suillius was there, serving with his great patron Germanicus. She would have company: Agrippina had gone with them, taking the child she had given birth to in Rome the year my daughter was married. We heard that the soldiers loved the little boy, calling him "Caligula," after the little uniform he wore, right down to the tiny hobnailed boots. All those Julians had charm, when they chose to exert it. Evidently they had it even at two years old.

Perilla wrote often and I think she enjoyed camp life. She was one of the ladies around Agrippina, and her letters were full of chatter about the culture and wit of the princess.

I used to wait for her letters, as I had once waited for Naso's, hoping every day and wild with joy when one arrived, only to feel worse afterwards, for they made the distance seem so far and the time so long.

Naso still wrote of course, keeping up his campaign of hints and flattery, asking his friends to intervene, extolling Augustus in such lavish terms that you couldn't quite believe it and wondered what he really meant. He wrote to Germanicus, asking his help—four times— and the book of poems he called "Letters from Pontus" carried a graceful dedication to the great soldier. He never wrote to Tiberius. He did send a poem praising the two commanders who had put down the Getan uprising, but he also praised, in an indirect way, the Getans themselves. Even he, who could make anything sound good, could not make the barbarians sound loyal to Rome, but he made them kind and friendly, and said they liked him. You could tell that he liked them. He had learned their languages, and claimed to have written a song of praise to Augustus in one of them. I don't know if anyone else believed it, but I did—it would have struck him as an amusement, and a way to pass the time. He still sounded hopeful, though now he had been gone six years. He never wrote to me, though I had answered his letter, telling him how hard I had tried. I did not dare to ask if the letter I had sent by the Greek sea captain had ever arrived, and he never said.

Gradually the borders of the empire grew quiet. The fear of a few years before, when Augustus cried aloud in the Senate that we would see the barbarian armies from our walls within ten days had retreated; so had the famine that had so devastated the city. The dinner parties grew a little bolder, but the pamphlets that always circulated were fewer and more discreet. Execution and exile had taken so many that the rest had grown furtive or been silenced altogether.

Fabius had grown in power in those two years: now he was one of Augustus' closest friends—the Imperial couple had even paid him the compliment of attending Persicus' birthday celebration. On the first of January the following year, Fabia Numantina's husband Sextus Appuleius became consul, along with his cousin. I sat with Marcia and Fabia, just outside the Temple of Jupiter, watching the parade wind through the Forum down below. The white bulls for the sacrifice moaned, the brilliant clothes snapped in the wind, the air felt fresh on my cheek. Young Appuleius sat in front of us with Persicus, both of them pale with emotion and wide-eyed at the glory of the day. The procession passed us, with Fabius among the senators, and I averted my eyes, feeling that I had seen something unlucky. When I looked up, it was to see Marcia regarding me, but she said nothing. Presently she smiled at me, and went back to watching the ceremony.

After that I tried to pretend that nothing was wrong, but it was difficult to stay close to Marcia, for I could hardly bring myself to talk to Fabius at all. Often I felt his eyes on me at the parties I could not refuse to go to, or when I visited Marcia. I forced myself to see her as often as I could, trying to pretend that nothing had happened, but of course she had noticed. "You like Fabius, don't you, Pinni?" she asked one day. She was spending a month with me at our country place near Fundi. It seemed as good a way to avoid Fabius as any.

We were sitting on my terrace, listening to a Greek grammarian sing to the lyre from the *Parthenia* of Pindar. It was spring, the air was sweet with blossom, the sea below glittered under the sun, lunch would be brought to us in a little while.

I caught my breath. "Like Fabius? What makes you think I don't?"

Idly she tossed a handful of breadcrumbs to the sparrows. Her arm made a beautiful childish arc through the summer air, but the sparrows, chittering, rose for the sky. "Oh, I don't know. I just thought—"

"Thought what?"

She lifted her head. I could hear it too. There were noises on the road, shouts and tramping feet. Loricus dashed past in the colonnade, followed by a scurry of secretaries and what looked like half the household staff.

"I know you are fond of Fabius, Pinni. It's just that I just want so much for you and he to be friends."

"And you don't think we are?"

She watched the birds with shadowed eyes. "Oh, yes. Of course you are. Oh, Pinni, let's not let anything ever come between us."

"What could come between us?" I started to say but the noise was worse. Now it was inside the house. Men were shouting, women's voices rose in fear. Someone was making a dreadful hammering of some kind.

"What is it?" cried Marcia.

"I don't know." I was on my feet. "I'd better see to this. Excuse me—I'll be right back."

Behind me I heard her chair scrape on the floor.

I rushed for the entryway, where the worst of the noise seemed to be. A crowd jammed the corridor, yelling and shouting. The uproar was unbelievable. Down in front I could see Loricus with his hair flying over his shining head. He was shoving people aside, trying to get through the crowd. Beyond him, I could see the open door and a corner of the sky.

I caught my breath. The sky was clear, it was just past noon, but the day was growing darker, not brighter. "Loricus," I shouted, raising my voice over the noise. "What is this? What's happening?"

Some god must have conveyed my words to him, for he turned and started shoving, forcing a path through the crowd.

Panting and hoarse I arrived at the front. There I stopped and stared. "Oh, gods," I cried, "what is happening?" The air was thick and dark.

"Pinni," Marcia screamed right behind me. "It's him. It's him—"

"What?"

The noise swamped her voice. All I could tell was that her mouth was moving in her frightened face. The birds were shrieking in the trees. I could hear farm animals in the distance, lowing or braying or howling. Human voices were crying out too. Someone was beating on metal—a shield, a cooking pot, a brazier. The harsh sound shuddered through air. I gasped for breath.

A lock of hair had plastered itself across Loricus' cheek and a bruise was showing under his eye, but he had gotten my household huddled together in some sort of quiet. Men and women, farm people and house, were all crying and muttering, clinging together under the darkening sky. All the time more kept coming, running up the road or pouring out of the house—my maid, the woman I put in charge of the weaving room, the cook, leaning her huge arm on the reedy neck of the scullery boy. Even the swineherd, who had brought with him a small pig under his arm, and the freedman I had rescued from the destruction of Julia Aemilii's house, who had clapped a helmet on his head and grabbed a sword off the wall.

"It's an omen," Marcia screamed. "Something terrible is going to happen."

"It's an eclipse. Don't look at the sun," Loricus said, taking my arm. "Look down."

On the terrace the shadows of the trees looked wrong. What had been coins of sunlight through the leaves were now only half circles. Something was taking a bite out of them.

"Loricus, what does it mean? Is the sun dying?"

"Interesting thought. It might be."

I held onto Loricus' arm. "It might die? Will it come back?"

"Possibly. There are records in the histories—"

Behind me I could hear Marcia, sobbing with fear. I wanted to myself, but I had my people to think of. I straightened my back. "Well, if it's dying there's nothing we can do about it."

"That's right."

"But it's an omen. We must pray," Marcia screamed, and covered her head.

It seemed to me that if a god was encompassing our destruction it would not change his mind if we prayed, but all around us people were moaning their fear to the heavens. Only Loricus stood with his head unbowed. Marcia was muttering to her ancestress. Over and over she said the same words, but they made no sense. They did not even seem to be Latin. Perhaps they were some very old language, so sacred it could not be spoken any longer. I held out my hand to her, and gave hers a little squeeze.

The light worsened. And as the sky darkened it began to bleed. Lightning ripped across it, and huge drops of fire began to fall from the wounded sun. The shadows on the terrace burned purple and the light was red.

Behind me Marcia caught her breath. "Listen."

Under the crash and rip of lightning, trumpets were blowing and horses were stamping out on the road.

As one person we moved to the terrace wall, silent at last, to watch the road below. An elaborate wagon fringed in gold and curtained in white linen swayed out of the fiery gloom, led by outriders and driven by slaves in blue tunics. It trundled up our steep road between the hillside and the sea, music playing and horses snorting, a strange defiance to the sky. At the top the whole affair lurched to a stop, the curtains parted, an elegant white shoe glimmered toward the stones.

"Fabius," Marcia gasped.

He emerged, as usual looking like a man who had just stepped out of his bath, pale, clean-shaven, calm, but even he could not conceal that he was startled as he took in the darkness and the terrified crowd. His eyes went from face to face, stopped for a moment, flew open, then passed on to the gaggle of household slaves jamming the doorway, not disturbed even by Loricus' marked face and disordered hair, and his wife's tearstained pallor.

Calmly he bowed in his usual way over my hand. "I'm sorry to disturb you at such a time, Pinaria, but Marcia is needed at home—"

"She is? Because of this? Why? What is happening?"

"I don't know. It hadn't started when I left. Everything was normal in Rome."

"Then why did you come?"

"Persicus is ill."

Behind me Marcia said, "You see? I told you it was an omen. We have to go at once."

"And I told you, he was ill before this started. If this omen is for us, it is not about Persicus."

"What is it about, then?" I asked, wondering that both of them thought the sky should turn itself to blood for them. They were important people but if this was an omen it was for a catastrophe beyond our imagining.

"Get your people together," Fabius was saying to his wife. "The roads are jammed. Let us wait a little."

"But Persicus—"

"I know," he said. "Of course you are worried. But we won't get through now anyway. Go ahead. It will be all right."

But the sky sputtered and burned overhead, giving his quiet certainty the lie.

Marcia had gone to supervise her packing. Fabius planted his feet and looked over my crowd of people. I knew I ought to invite him in, but my flesh crawled at the thought: on such an unlucky day, to ask an enemy over the threshold seemed the very end and limit of folly. But he was Fabius, whom I had known most of my life.

"Won't you come in?" I heard myself say. Horrorstruck I began to gabble—"No, perhaps it's better if I have them bring you out some wine? Something to eat?"

I could always smash the plates afterwards.

"No, thanks. Pinaria, these are your own slaves?"

"Yes, of course. Some are freedmen and women. Who else's would they be?"

"Really? Who is that man there?"

238

"Where?" With a sudden feeling of faintness I realized that he had recognized Julia Aemilii's one-time servant.

"He's mine too. Of course."

In the gloom I saw him raise his eyebrows. "Where did you get him?"

My throat had constricted. Truly this was a luckless moment. All the horror of the day had been leading to this. "I—I found him. In the street. He was lost. He didn't speak any Latin and had no idea who his patron was. I—I just took him in. And when the freedmen were called up, he went. He is just back from Germany."

He turned on me a thunderous face.

"Pinaria, stop it at once. Stop these lies. What are you playing at with that man?"

"I'm not lying—"

"I said, what are you doing with that man?"

"I—Fabius, stop this. I don't know what you're talking about. And at such a moment, with the sun dying and my people in hysterics—"

"You're right, Pinaria. This is too public." He grabbed my arm and almost dragged me to the door, calling over his shoulder to the send the soldier in.

"Now. Just what is going on here?" He hurled me into a chair. My back smashed into the arms, rocking the chair on its legs. I leaped up to face him.

"Fabius, I don't know why you are acting like this, but this is my house, and you will observe proper decorum while you are here. If not I will have you removed. Don't think I won't."

"Why should I observe decorum, Pinaria? You don't at my house."

Well, that was true. I had broken up his library after all.

"I see you know what I am talking about. Now, what is this? What kind of traitorous nonsense are you involved in here?"

"I? Are you crazy, Fabius? You of all people to speak of treason to me? You betrayed my husband, who was your friend, and you tried to betray me too. You have no right to speak to me at all, let alone of treason. "

I doubt he heard me. He was jerking me back and forth on my feet, very gently but with a frightening persistent rhythm, like a mason striking a block of marble with a mallet. His fingers had dug so far into my arms I felt them grind against the bones. "Who is that man? What are you doing with him? You found him in the street? Don't make me laugh."

Horribly, he tried. His teeth gleamed as his lips pulled back. A strange grunting came from him. "Don't think I don't know something is going on. You avoid me, you pump my wife to find out when I am going to be away, you sneak through my house, ducking around corners when you hear me coming. Who is he, Pinaria? What are you doing?"

He was shaking me harder now, so that my teeth snapped when I tried to open my mouth. He didn't care. He was still talking and his voice had risen again. "What is he, some son of Vipsanius Agrippa by some slave somewhere?"

"I—I don't know. I have no idea. I told you, I found him."

He dropped my right arm but still gripped me in his left. Slowly he raised his free hand. The fist was balled up so tightly that the knuckles gleamed. "So you did, Pinaria. But you haven't told me where."

"Nor will I, Fabius."

We stared at each other, full of anger and hate. "By god, woman, you make it difficult." His arm was drawing back, so that I could see that it was going to swing toward me. At the same time he was engaged in a curious little struggle to force his fingers open. Once or twice he nearly succeeded, but then his fist would snap closed again. He did not seem to be aware of any of these movements.

I swallowed hard. "I—I'm not afraid of you, Fabius. Your ugly temper won't do you any good. I'm just glad to know what you really are."

"What I am? You haven't the least idea—"

Outside heavy boots shuffled toward us. Fabius dropped my arm and stepped back. The freedman slouched into the room, glancing around.

"Remarkable," I heard Fabius mutter under his breath.

The freedman was staring around the room. When he saw me he made a low bow, and his delicate, girl's mouth opened as if to speak, but as his eyes passed on, he took in Fabius. Glancing up from rubbing my arm I saw a change come over him. He pulled back his shoulders, clicking his heels together and clapping his arms straight to his sides. His thick chin jutted forward, his eyes fixed straight ahead.

Shouting into the empty room, he said, in his odd foreign Latin, "Fabius Maximus. Imperator. Ave."

"Hail, soldier," said Fabius pulling himself upright imperceptibly in return. "Name?"

It was comical, but neither of them was amused. They had managed to pretend that my pretty atrium was some kind of parade ground, and they were reliving some moment of military glory in it.

"Miles gregarius, Second Legion Augusta, Imperator." He shot a look at me under his eyelids.

"I didn't ask for your rank and unit, soldier. I asked for your name."

He was frightened again and mumbled something quickly, his head down.

"What? Speak up."

"Telephus. But, Imperator. General. Chief. I am Clemens now. Called Clemens. After this lady. She kind to me."

Fabius raised his eyebrows. "Really. And just how has she been kind to you?"

Sweat stood out on the man's forehead, darkening the thatch of straw-colored hair. His eyes looked drowned in terror and his little mouth was clenched over his teeth. He was trying to keep them from chattering, but I could hear them even where I stood.

Fabius curled his lip. "Enough of this display. Stand up, soldier. That's an order."

Clemens pulled himself into a semblance of his former posture. Tears stood in his eyes.

"I am freedman, Imperator." Under the pressure of his fear his scant Latin was breaking down, and it was hard to understand him. "My father Roman. I Roman too."

"Indeed? And he freed you? What was his name?"

The soldier looked at the floor.

"I see. You don't know. In fact you are not a citizen at all, and you had no right to serve in the army, is that right?"

The soldier raised his terrified eyes. "I citizen. I free. Yes, free. Father Roman—"

"Never mind. I think we can guess who you are. You look like him. And how did you meet this lady?"

Again the eyes. Again Clemens ignored the question.

"Imperator, when you come home, I march with you. Cannot stay—I fought against my country. So, I come to Rome. My father, he dead. I go to his house. They say, his son has—"

"Yes? Speak up. His son. That would be Agrippa Postumus. Is that right? What does he have of his father's?"

Clemens said quietly, "He has the slaves."

"I see. Yes, he did, for a time. Until Caesar decided that the great general's children were under his own protection. Then he confiscated their inheritance. That would include you, I suppose?"

"Maybe, Imperator. I work for the young son in cobbler shop."

"How long?"

"Long time. Two years. One day cobbler send me to grand house, do job for lady there. So I go. Maybe house sold. I don't know I stay there—lady very nice. I stay one year."

"I see." Fabius seemed to be counting. "That was this lady here?"

He mumbled something to the wall behind Fabius, sliding his eyes to see if Fabius had heard.

"What? Speak up, soldier. You went to whose house? This lady's? Her name is Pinaria Ovidii, if you don't know."

The soldier stood up straight and closed his eyes. He said nothing. All those years ago, I had threatened him that if he told anyone where I found him we would both die. He remembered.

Fabius was getting angrier. His hand went to his side, looking for the sword he was not wearing. Clemens began to tremble again.

"Soldier—you know the penalty for lying? You know that I can force you to tell me? Have you forced to tell me. Think about it, soldier. The fire, the iron, the hooks—"

"Yes, Imperator," he whispered. Under his closed eyelids tears had begun to leak.

"Oh, for heaven's sake, tell him," I shouted. "I can't stand this any more. Just tell him."

As if I had cut a string that was holding him together Clemens fell to his knees. "Lady, I no tell—"

I thought I might scream.

"No, Fabius," I managed in a reasonable voice. "It wasn't my house. It was Julia Aemilii's. That's where I found him."

At Julia's name the soldier had raised his head. His drowned eyes looked at me. "Lady," he said. "You save me, long time ago. I no tell. I die before."

"Thank you, Clemens. I know you would. Thank you for your help. I hope it won't be necessary. I will take care of this.

"Fabius, you might as well know the whole story, since you have heard part of it. He came from Julia Aemilii's house."

Fabius' mouth fell open. "Julia Aemilii? Is that right, soldier?"

Clemens' eyes swiveled to me. "That's all right. Tell him."

"Yes, lady. Thank you. Yes, I was at her house. First her brother, then her."

Fabius turned to me in astonishment. "I didn't know you knew her, Pinaria."

"I don't. I didn't. I went to Julia Aemilii's the night Naso was—Naso was relegated. After Naso and I left you. He went home, but I thought she might know something about why he was sent away. I was wrong, Fabius. I never got to speak to her, and there was nothing in the house. Nothing."

He was shaking his head. Perhaps it was disbelief. My stomach clenched with fear. It was so important that he never suspect what I now knew about her.

He was looking at me curiously. "You guessed about Julia Aemilii? That's very clever of you, Pinaria."

"Guessed? Guessed what, Fabius? I told you, I didn't find anything—"

"Nothing?"

"I don't think so. I would have remembered if I had—"

The soldier said, beaming with helpfulness, "You have piece of book. You pick up from floor. I see you."

"A book? Is this true?"

Past speech, I nodded.

"I don't understand. What book?"

I thought the walls themselves might be bending forward to listen. But what was the use? Fabius would have it out of me. "*The Art of Love*," I whispered.

Fabius reached behind him for a chair. "So you know."

"I know nothing. Nothing you can ever use to do any more harm to my husband or those poor banished and imprisoned women or anyone else. You may be a traitor, Fabius, but you cannot use me or anything I say to hurt anyone else."

He stared at me with his mouth open. Twice he started to speak and failed to find words. I think it must have been the only time in his life that his glibness failed him. He just rested there, half-seated, half-upright, goggling at me like a mullet, until the silence in the room swallowed us up.

Finally Fabius said, "What I don't understand is why you think I am a traitor."

Then I was angry, really angry. Before I had been hot, boiling inside and hardly able to speak for shouting out my rage; now I was cold and the words snapped out of me so smartly I did not have to think. They might have been welling up inside me for years, waiting for this moment.

"Because that is exactly what you are, Fabius. You are the poisonous little crawling serpent who saw Julia Caesaris and her friends in the Forum that night in December eighteen years ago and told her father. You are the one who gave him the names of her friends, who knew that it was a plot, but who, for all I know, connived with Augustus to pretend that she was a shameless adulteress, to help him ruin her name as well as her life. You are the one who betrayed Iullus Antonius to his death and the others as well, the sons of the greatest houses in Rome. You were jealous, weren't you? You've come a long way in your own career, but really you are not one of them, are you? Well, you cut them down to your own size that night—"

"Pinaria, stop. You've got it all wrong. They were betrayed all right, but I was not the one who did it. I have often wondered since who it was. I was not part of that plot. No one asked me and I would not have joined if they had. Caesar had shown me great favor, and I

244

owed him my loyalty. Indeed, I think I had a right to expect a great deal more from him. I was after all a member of his own family, married to the daughter of his cousin. I had every reason to be loyal to him—listen to me, Pinaria. Don't interrupt. Anyone with the slightest knowledge of political life would have known better than to ask me. Julia Caesaris and her mother—oh, yes, didn't you guess? Her mother was the center of that conspiracy, why else do you think she went into exile with her daughter?—would never have asked me, at that point, to join them.

"No, in those days, after the destruction of Scribonia's plot, I kept away from Caesar's family. Whatever you think of me, Pinaria, you cannot think I am a fool. And only a fool would throw away a chance to be Caesar's heir for the sake of walking in the shadow of the grandson of Mark Antony for the rest of his life."

"So you got rid of Iullus Antonius."

"No, Pinaria. I did not. I knew nothing at the time of Julia and Scribonia's plot."

"At the time. But you found out."

He rubbed his hands over his hair. "Well, yes. Later I did find out. In fact, I have been very actively trying to help the two Julias return. They have the prestige, you see, to bring back the Republic—"

"That story again. Yes, we all know how much you care about the Republic, Fabius. What happened? Why did you change your mind—?" But even as I asked, I knew. "It was because Augustus adopted Tiberius, wasn't it?"

He nodded. "Surely you must realize that the assumption by Tiberius of all of Caesar's powers means the death of the Republic. Beyond any hope of revival. We will have a dynasty of kings again, five hundred years after we had a revolution and threw them out. It will take five hundred years to get rid of them again."

"So you say. But all the same, I know you betrayed Julia Caesaris, and all the others. You saw them that night, didn't you?"

He was shaking his smooth head. "No, I didn't. I was not here. I was still in Spain. My term did not expire until the end of the year, and I didn't come back until well into February."

"No, that isn't so. You came back early. I know you did."

"How do you know?"

"Everyone does, Fabius. It wasn't exactly something that could be kept secret from the city, was it?"

He was shaking his head. "You've got it wrong. Somehow you've gotten it very wrong indeed."

It was Clemens, helpful again, who broke the impasse. "February, mistress. Feast of Ovens. Tables in Forum, foods for gods—"

"The Feast of Ovens?"

"That is in February, Pinaria."

I felt behind me for a chair, for I was sure my knees would not support me any longer. My head felt very far from my body, and Fabius' face seemed to be changing under my eyes. For so long it had seemed as stiff and false as an actor's mask, but now I saw in it the strain of keeping himself to his obligations. He was no monster of egotism and ambition; he was merely an anxious and burdened man, who had been working too hard.

"And the money that disappeared, and all the other things, that wasn't because you were betraying us?"

"The money went to Naso. To raise support for his uprising. He asked for it himself."

All those years of tension and distrust. All that fear. All that loneliness. I began to cry. "And my maid, who was poisoned, and the people in my house, and Macer with his marriage proposal, and all the other things? That wasn't you?"

"No."

I blew my nose and wiped my eyes. "Then who was it?"

He had come to the end of a long road. He lifted exhausted eyes to me. "I thought it was you."

"No."

"That is why I was watching you."

"It wasn't me."

"I know that now, Pinaria."

"Well, then, if it wasn't you and it wasn't me, who was it? Loricus? Macer?"

He shook his head.

"Who then?"

His eyes were sick. The journey had been too long, and the burden too heavy. "What made you think I had come back early from my command in Spain, Pinaria?"

"Oh, Fabius, I told you. It was common knowledge. Everyone said—"

"Everyone? Did they? You asked around? You checked with people who know me: Messalinus, Gellius? Marcius? Macer?"

Had I? I tried to think. I had visited them all, asking for help, but had I asked about Fabius? "I—well, no. I thought—someone told me, Fabius. I don't remember who it was. "

"Someone. It must have been someone you trusted if you took just one person's word."

And I remembered. The afternoon in the garden, Fabia Numantina and her mother, the little boys playing knucklebones. Sunlight on leaves, and scent of roses. "Yes," I whispered. "Someone I trusted."

Voices had risen in the hallway, boxes clattered, someone gave a smothered order. Fabius turned his sick eyes to the noise.

In the doorway, tall and ever so slightly disheveled as usual, stood Marcia.

"Oh, there you are," she said, smiling cheerfully. "The darkness is passing. I think we can go now. Have you had a nice chat?"

All the times we had held each other in the dark, listening to Atia raging up and down the house, all the moments of happiness with our tutor when he showed us the secrets of the natural world, all the whispers and giggles, the games, the jokes. Even the anger and the tears. All gone. All blown away like dust. I was alone, and a stranger was standing in front of me.

"Why are you staring at me, Pinni? Is something wrong? Do I really look that bad?" And indeed she touched her hair. I almost laughed.

"I—no, of course not. I'm sorry, Marcia. You are right, it is getting brighter in here, isn't it?"

She gave me a quick smile. "Dear Pinni. The sun is growing again. Anyway, that's what your secretary, that Spaniard, says, and he seems to know. So, everything is going to be all right. Here, I have an idea. Why don't you come with us? Something must be happening. Don't you think we ought to see what it is?"

"I imagine I'll find out here just as quickly. If it's important."

She wasn't being stupid—I could see that now. She wanted something. Naso was right, she was very intelligent. He had even warned me, though of course I hadn't understood.

Her fine brows came down and she looked at me sadly. "Oh, Pinni, how could you refuse? I'm worried about Persicus. You will be such a help to me. You owe it to me to help me. After all, we looked after you."

I didn't go. I suppose it might have been the first time Marcia asked me for something and I failed to do it. It is strange how childhood persists in us: even with all I knew my sleep was troubled with remorse. Her son was really ill, after all. Nevertheless, I stayed where I was, waiting.

Day after day we listened to the road, but there was no news. Persicus clung to life, and slowly improved. Rome was quiet. The borders seemed secure. So perhaps Loricus had been right: the eclipse was not an omen at all.

"Do you think the gods care about us, Loricus?" I asked him one day.

"No, mistress. I cannot imagine why they should."

"People say they do. They pray to them to be healed of illnesses and things like that, and they say the gods answer."

"But they never think of who made them ill in the first place."

I thought about this for some time. At first it frightened me. Then, as I got used to the idea, it began to seem a liberation.

The spring was beautiful and I enjoyed the fine weather, the sailing, the long days of little to do. My daughter visited me, creating a festival by her presence and a void when she left. And one day near the end of June, Fabius stopped in.

"How is Persicus?" I asked, when we were seated on the terrace.

"Better. Marcia is a good nurse, you know."

Out on the bay a boat was making toward Capri, its oars moving all together like the tiny beat of wings.

Fabius turned on me a face white with fatigue and strain.

"I am out of favor, Pinni. Do you know what that means? I am no longer Augustus' friend."

"How do you know? Has he sent you away?"

"Not yet. But it may come. I went to see him as I always do, first thing in the morning, like everyone else in Rome, everyone who counts. When I was shown into his room, I said, "Hello, Caesar." He lifted himself off his couch and said, "Goodbye, Fabius." I left immediately of course. But it was already too late."

"Why did he change to you? Does he—does he know?"

"I have been trying to find out." But his head was shaking as he spoke. "I have no idea. Anything is possible. Augustus is ill again. And there have been more omens. Lightning struck the statue of Caesar on the Capitol and destroyed the letter C. The seers say that since the 'C' stands for one hundred, and the rest of the word 'aesar' means 'god' in Etruscan, in one hundred days Caesar will enter into some divine state. And when the Senate tried to meet to offer some prayers, the building was closed and an owl blocked the entrance."

"An owl? In daytime?"

"I can hardly imagine a worse omen."

Out on the bay the sun-dazzle swallowed the little boat. I waited until it emerged, still on its course for the island. "Is he seriously ill then?"

"He doesn't look well. Last month we held the ceremony to conclude the census. Thousands of people packed into the Forum to see him bury the old era and inaugurate the new one. A lot of us remember the first time he performed the rite. That was more than forty years ago."

"You can't have been very old yourself then."

He smiled. "You don't know what he was like then. He was a young man in the first flush of his power. Solemn as a priest, and straight as a soldier. You would have thought a god had indeed entrusted him with our future."

He raised his head, looked away over the mountain toward Rome, paused, shook his head, then tossed down the wine. The past was gone; he was looking at me, all in the present. "I tell you, Pinaria, the contrast was pathetic. This time he could hardly speak, and when the priests handed him the tablets to take the vows for the coming five years he gave them to Tiberius. I was standing right behind them. His voice was very weak, but I heard him plainly: he said he couldn't take vows he would not live to perform."

The boat beat on toward the island, drawing a line across the dark blue water. Dividing it. Harbor. Sea. Past. Present. Augustus had been the leader of the city since before I was born. All of a sudden my sunny terrace felt as cold as winter.

"Maybe it won't amount to anything, Fabius. He's been ill many times in his life. Nothing has ever come of it."

"I know. But he's old now. Very old. In August he will celebrate his seventy-sixth birthday. If god wills it." He poured out his last drops of wine. But this time the wish was different. The drops made little spatters on the marble. They looked like blood.

He looked up and caught my eye. "I see you understand. It's time, Pinaria. Do you still have that slave, Clemens?"

"Yes, of course, Fabius. What do you want him for?"

"You've noticed the resemblance, of course."

"Resemblance? To whom?"

"Come on, Pinaria. What are you playing at? Of course you know—"

"Know what? I assure you I have no idea what you are talking about."

"Really? You just took him in because he was so pathetic, without thinking of using him for this?"

"For what, Fabius? "

He sighed and set down his winecup. "I suppose I must believe you. But he might be the twin brother of Caesar's grandson, Agrippa Postumus. He'd have to grow a beard, of course, to make it really certain. Everyone remembers Agrippa Postumus' little beard. But even without it, I don't see how you could have missed the similarity."

"I don't think I've ever seen Agrippa Postumus, Fabius. Perhaps when we were children, but not since then. I lived mostly in the country and didn't go out much when my daughter was small, and by the time I did Postumus had been sent to Planasia."

"Yes. Of course. I see. I never guessed that you were telling the truth. Now it's hard to get used to."

"It is, isn't it?"

He passed his hand over his face to smooth away the past. "Yes. Anyway. Clemens. You see what an opportunity he represents? Lend him to me. I want to get Agrippa Postumus to his sister and brother-in-law in Germany where they will be safe. I don't like this situation. Caesar is traveling with Tiberius right now—they're in Capri, I think, where I hope Tiberius is letting the old man rest. Then they're going to Naples, where some sort of birthday event is planned for Caesar. And after that, Tiberius is going out to the army. It's too much. Caesar ought to be at home, under the care of doctors, not marching around the countryside with his adopted son. We haven't much time, that's what I'm saying, Pinaria. I think I can arrange for Clemens to be substituted for young Postumus on Planasia. They may not discover the deception, at least for a while. And once I have Agrippa Postumus I can get him up to the army. Germanicus will protect him. Indeed, I think Germanicus will be very glad to see him."

The little boat had reached its destination. The sail was down, the oars standing straight up, motionless and white as a ribcage. "Fabius," I whispered, looking around to be sure no one was within hearing, though why now, when we had been talking treason all the time the little vessel had been making its way across the bay, "are you trying to start a civil war?"

"Of course, Pinaria. I've been trying to do that for the best part of ten years. I don't see any other hope for us. Do you?"

A day or two later I had a message from Marcia: would I come back to Rome? Please? It was urgent this time. I was about to refuse, when I saw that she had added a note from her daughter Fabia Numantina: Fabia's son Appuleius was sick.

For a moment I goggled at the tablet. But indeed it was not the fragile Persicus, who was ill, but the robust Appuleius. And though Fabia was trying not to say so, it was obvious that she was frightened.

The road was crowded; under the meager shade of the cypresses that lined it, hundreds of families had gathered. Many had been there some time: the remains of meals were scattered over the ground, and some people from the nearby farms had even brought out blankets or couches. As we proceeded the crowds grew thicker, until the road was all but blocked and my servants had a great deal of trouble to clear the way.

Presently in the distance we heard trumpets. All of us who could pressed to the sides, amid the shouts of the people already there. My servants drew close around the sides of my wagon. But it was a good-humored crowd, friendly and at ease, though excited.

The trumpets drew closer, followed by the measured and stately sound of hoofbeats. In the distance plumes were tossing and light glanced from bronze helmets. Fathers lifted their littlest to their shoulders, while the crowd made way for the older children to perch like a row of birds on the gutters.

The horsemen came into sight, a detachment of cavalry on matched black thoroughbreds. They rode with their scarlet capes spread out on the horses' rumps, their armor blinding in the sun, their horses' necks arched. A pretty sight. Behind them came not a chariot, but a litter.

The light and the heat glared off the stones, but the man in the litter had not drawn the curtains though he was as pale and shiny as an unpainted statue. It was of course, Augustus. He lay back on his cushions, raising his hand from time to time in an exhausted gesture of acknowledgement to the cheers of the crowd. Behind him rode Tiberius, dark-haired and dark-eyed, like all the Claudians, against Augustus' Julian fairness, and scowling with disdain, his eyes raised above the crowd. Augustus, who could not see him, was smiling.

"Where are they going?" I asked my servant, who turned to the crowd for an answer. "Naples, mistress. There is to be a celebration of the Augustus' birthday there. Gymnastics and games."

The procession drew opposite us. It was too late to close my own curtains, and it would have been an insult. All the same, I found myself leaning back in my cushions, wishing that like some god I could simply disappear.

Disappear I did not. Augustus passing me, lifted his head, staring. He looked surprised.

"Pretty woman. I know her, don't I?" His voice was as thin as a breeze in reeds.

His slave said, "She is Pinaria Ovidii, master."

"Oh, yes. With the talkative little maid." He flopped his hand weakly around his head. All the same it was a vivid reminder of Philomela's wild hair. "Cousin told me—what's her name?"

"Marcia Fabii, master."

So Philomela had been an informer. I couldn't imagine why I had never guessed. No wonder she had taken poison. She must have thought I had found out. And Marcia had known it, and never said a word.

Augustus fell back on his cushions, gasping.

"Pretty woman. Husband's a fool."

I think I must just have stared.

"Thought he'd start a revolution. Social Wars again. Paelignians. Fool. I bought them all years ago." He lifted his hand. "Most important men." His fingers closed around the prominent families of the country towns. "Promotions, friendship, marriages, position. That's all they want. Fool—thinks I didn't know." There was a pause filled with his wheezing breath. "Pretty woman, though."

As the litter jerked onward, he lifted his head and smiled at me again. Tiberius drew his brows down further, and lowered his eyes to study my face as he went past.

The procession jingled and tramped down the road, the crowd surged after it, and I let out my breath, realizing with astonishment that I had been holding it since the litter had come in sight.

In that time the whole of Rome held its breath. Everywhere people seemed to be listening for news from the south. Certainly the city was quiet, the fountains in the squares splashed straight into their basins, the little noise making the only sound. Leaves hung on trees unmoving, covered in summer dust; the stones of the temples and apartment blocks radiated such heat it made me gasp. The crowds in the streets were silent, the Forum echoed to footsteps, not voices.

I leaned out of my litter as we passed through the stillness, thinking: As it is in Rome it is all over Italy, and beyond. The whole world was waiting.

The only exception was at Marcia's. There they were waiting too, but for other news. The whole family had come to hear it: I recognized several distant cousins in the atrium, staring sadly into the pool, their heads covered against an unlucky sight. Marcia rose from among them when she saw me, and dragged me behind a pillar. Marcia's looks never showed much of what she was feeling, except to become more disorganized as she was upset. Now her hair was tangled, and a smear of ash from some family offering lay like a scar across her cheek.

When I embraced her she felt like a bag of bones. "How is Fabia?"

"Lying down."

I was crying, thinking how they felt. I don't think I had yet understood that I was losing someone I loved in Appuleius too.

"And you, Marcia. How are you? Are you all right?"

She thrust me away, turning her head with an angry snap. "What do you think? Glad it's not *your* grandson?"

"What?" In the old days, I would have thought I had not heard her right. Or that such bitterness was after all only natural. Now I wondered: perhaps she wished it was indeed my child who lay feverish under the covers in a darkened room. If so it was an evil wish. Even to say the words brought unluckiness.

I looked around the room. I had been in it thousands of times, since I was married. I had even seen it like this crowded with relatives, when Marcia's grandparents died, then when her parents did. Only now did it seem strange. I thought: I would not know my way from this room to the others, the furniture would bump against my shins, I would crash into the pillars, or fall into the pond. Everything is different. Now that I know. Everything is unfamiliar. Now that I know.

But I could not help it: she was suffering, so I said, "Marcia, I'm very sorry."

"Oh, yes. Yes, of course." She gave me a little smile, the old Marcia again, sweet and childish, so that my heart relaxed. "It's horrible, Pinni. Fabia is out of her mind. I had to give her something to make her sleep."

I murmured something, hugging her to me. Even her scent was familiar to me, and the warmth of her body in my arms. It felt safe, and sad, and like falling asleep again.

But it was not safe at all, and Marcia was no child. Her whisper was like a little knife, pricking me, making me lean back to see her. "Pinni, something worse has happened."

"Worse?"

"Well, not worse, but bad, Pinni, very bad." She was watching me closely. I wouldn't have known that either, before. I would have thought she was dreaming under her heavy eyelids. But now I saw that in fact her eyes slid toward me then darted away as she spoke. She pulled me aside, behind a pillar. "You know Caesar is ill?"

"Yes, I know. I saw him down near Baiae. He looked terrible."

"You saw him?" Her eyes flew open, candid as a child's.

"Yes, on the road. His cortege passed me. I could see that he didn't look very well."

She didn't believe me. I think that was the oddest thing of all. She was sure I was lying. She looked away, thinking hard, then turned back, watching me under those thick lashes. "He can't speak very well either."

"Yes. He only said a few words, and those were difficult to hear."

"What did he say?"

"Nothing much. I told you—he passed me on the road."

I could see the glimmer of blue under the pale lids. "I'm surprised Fabius didn't tell you how ill Caesar is."

"Did Fabius see him?"

That startled her. I could see the little jolt go through her, though she looked away quickly. She looked vague and distant, as so often before, but now I knew that she was thinking before she spoke. "Oh, yes, Pinni. Why not? He's Caesar's friend."

So she didn't know that Fabius was out of favor.

"He took Caesar to see his grandson. I thought he might have said something to you about it."

"Agrippa Postumus?"

"Yes. On the island. Planasia. They had a big reunion, hugs and tears and promises and all that."

"Marcia, are you sure?"

"Yes, of course I am. He told me. Fabius did."

"I see." What I saw was that she was lying.

"And Fabius didn't say anything to you about it? Are you sure, Pinni?"

I wondered if she knew about Fabius' visit to me. Perhaps she was only hoping to find out if there had been one. In any case I was not going to tell her.

"But Marcia, Augustus exiled Agrippa Postumus years ago. He hates him. Why would he go and see him now?"

Now she was sure I knew something. I'm not sure what she thought it was. It was astonishing how clever she was. Naso was right. I could see it now. She was furious with me. Her beautiful, full lips opened to blurt out an angry response. But amazingly, by a great effort of will she stopped herself. I saw her do it. She took a breath and let her eyes go vague and dreaming. "Oh, Pinni, you know how people are. Caesar is ill. He's old. Of course he'd want to see his grandson."

"Yes, of course. How wonderful if Augustus can have his family back. And another Julian leading the city—"

She wasn't interested in that. "You're sure Fabius didn't say anything to you about this?"

I shook my head.

"Really? I'm surprised, Pinni. You and he are so close, always whispering behind the doors, and talking in the library. I thought you were his best friend—"

So that was it. She was jealous. I wondered what she actually suspected Fabius and me of having done. "If Fabius has been good to me, Marcia, it is entirely for your sake. He undertook to look after your dependents when he married you, and he has done exactly that. For your sake, and for Naso's, since Naso is his friend."

She simply turned her back on me and walked away without another word. I stood staring after her black-draped figure as she passed down the colonnade, moving through the slanting sunlight and the violet shadows until she had disappeared. I don't know when I have ever been more astonished in my life.

I made a chance to see Fabius, very briefly. He was sitting in his library. The lamps had not been lit, and the fading light of evening was making the corners of the room dim. No book or tablet lay on the desk. He was simply sitting there.

"Fabius, I saw Augustus on the road, the day before yesterday. He said he knew about raising the country towns. He knew it was Naso. He didn't say anything about you. Do you think he knows? Is that why he said "goodbye" to you?"

"I doubt it. He might have guessed something, I suppose. That would explain it. But if he had really known anything he'd have ordered me into exile, or had me murdered."

That was true enough. I only wished Fabius cared.

"Did you take him to see Agrippa Postumus?"

"Where did you hear that?"

"Marcia."

He shook his head. "She made it up. It's not true."

"That's good. And I'm glad Augustus doesn't know about you—"

He was staring into the gloom before I left.

The news out of the south continued to preoccupy the city. The rumors were everywhere: Augustus had felt better, had felt worse, was ill, was recovering. He had accompanied Tiberius part of the way on the road as Tiberius set out to take up his command in Il- lyricum. Augustus was dead, was dying, was recovering, had recov- ered; that he had embraced Tiberius, or rejected him, recalled his will from the House of the Vestals, or reassured himself that it was still safe there, had taken to his bed or to the road, had been poi- soned, had been cursed, had been miraculously restored to health. Most of the stories died in a day, but one or two persisted, and some were even true: that he had accompanied Tiberius part way on the road for instance. I heard that one confirmed by a young friend of my son-in-law on his way to Germanicus in the north. Marcia, now going to dinner parties again, hinted that she knew something, and presently people began whispering that Augustus had gone to see Agrippa Postumus on Planasia. That rumor was very circumstantial: the young man and his frail grandfather had embraced, tears were shed, promises made, though never specified by the tellers of this tale. Fabius' name was never mentioned. I wondered if Marcia was the source of all of this, or if she had simply taken advantage of it to try to find out what I knew.

With every rumor the tension in the city grew worse. People took to standing where the old daily digest had been posted, though Augustus had long since abolished it. When a senator passed they would clamor after him for news.

Then there was another story: Augustus had gone to Nola, a little town south of Naples, where he had a house he had inherited from his father. Tiberius was rushing back to be with him. I was in the Forum one hot August morning when Livia, in a closed wagon, rumbled through in desperate haste, the outriders already at a full canter before they had rounded the corner of the Temple of Castor and Pollux. The city was so quiet I could hear the wheels and the hoofbeats all the way to the Circus Maximus.

All that day we waited. The whole city seemed to have crowded into the Forum, standing patiently in the hot sun, the taste of the southern dust in our mouths. No one spoke. We were listening, all of us, for a word. When night fell we went home, only to be drawn back again the next morning.

That day too passed, hot, still and silent. In the evening a small breeze awoke and rattled the leaves overhead in my garden. On its unslaked ripple came Fabius, cool as snow, gleaming white and purple under the lamps. "Clemens is on his way," he murmured, accepting a cup of wine. He had grown wary, like all of us, and glanced around him in the darkness before he spoke. "He left this afternoon for—that island."

"Then has Augustus…stopped living?" Even I, who hated and feared him could not say the unlucky word.

The cup flashed a tiny silver signal in the shadow. "Not yet. He is sinking. He has not spoken since last night, and his eyes are closed now. But he is still breathing."

"Did Tiberius come in time?"

"Not to hear him speak, though Caesar knew he was there. He blinked several times and his eyes followed Tiberius around the room. Or so they say." He swirled the wine in his cup and drank it off. "Well, I must be off before Marcia misses me. She's got people coming to dinner, as usual." For a moment he looked very sad, and I knew he was missing his grandson. "I'll let you know about Clemens. If you have any prayers, say them to your family gods now, Pinaria. Everything depends on the next few days."

I sat late in the garden that night. The lamps guttered and blew out, but I did not call the servants to refill them. Overhead, among the leaves, the stars moved in their slow dance, destiny and human fate all unreadable in their glitter. I thought of Naso under the northern star that never sets, the pole around which all the others turn. I thought I could see him, silvered by that foreign light, but waiting as I was. I thought of the other exiles, Cassius, Julia, her strange mother, her daughter, her son. Waiting. They must know by now. They too must be waiting for the word.

Toward midnight Loricus came out of the house and stood in the darkness under a pillar.

"Did you need something?" I asked.

"A breath of air, mistress."

Suddenly I wanted company.

"Come and sit down. Have you heard anything?"

Soberly he shook his head.

We spoke a little, of indifferent things, neither able to say what was on our minds. Around us the city breathed slowly in the darkness, but there was no other sound.

It was noise that woke me, though at first I thought it was light. Sunlight was flooding the garden, the morning breeze was lifting the edges of the leaves. Someone had draped a light shawl over me and perched a pillow behind my head. I shook my head, bewildered. My mouth was dry.

All around me a confused sound was rising: wails and cries, the clash of shields or pots and pans, shouts and moans. I thought at first it came from the house. I stood up.

Now the house was moving: servants ran past me in the colonnade, shouting or crying. A maid, blinded by tears, crashed into me. I raised my voice to shout at them, but it was hopeless. The noise was too great.

Up on the second floor, it was worse. I stepped out onto a balcony. The sound was everywhere. The whole city was crying out, shouts and groans going up to the sky. The stones themselves seemed to shudder. Down below me a mass of people moved slowly through the street, and more joined them all the time crowding slowly toward the intersection. I guessed they were making for the Forum, or the gates. Soldiers on horses tried to force their way through, moving like islands in the viscid mass; under the voices and the shuffle I could hear a drumbeat of marching boots. I guessed the consuls had called out the guards.

All day the noise continued. It was hot: I thought the sun itself must hear the city's agony, for it reflected down on us until the stones shimmered so they seemed about to fall.

I fidgeted from one room to another, trying to settle, but it was impossible. My head ached and my skin felt like sand. The seats in the gardens burned to the touch, the balconies overlooked the noise, even the weaving room, usually an orderly and peaceful place, was a chaos of weeping maids and screaming children. By afternoon I was ready to scream myself. The worst I think was that I could not leave my house, nor could anyone get through, and I had to guess what was happening.

Finally, in mid-afternoon, I came to the library. The door was closed. It struck me that it was the only room in the house where that was true—the others had all been hurled open as the servants ran back and forth in their excitement and distress. I put my hand on the panel. It felt hot under my palm, but when I pushed, it opened into a haven of quiet. The roar from outside was no more than a whisper here, and the stone floor was cool. Sunlight fell in long, motionless bars through the grating, pooling on the table.

A book lay unrolled floating calmly in its shadow on the gleaming wood. Behind it Loricus, just as tranquil in his spotless tunic, made a little gesture to rise, which I negated. Instead he inclined his head politely.

I sat down. "How do you do it, Loricus? The rest of the house is in an uproar."

He spread his hand to show me the book. It was the *Pyrrhoneia* of the skeptic Aenesidemus. "Philosophy is a great consolation at a time like this."

He looked different somehow. The sunlight sculpted him, giving dignity to the depth of his fine eyes. Now they glimmered blue as a distant sea under his eyelashes. The shape of his head was very strong, a beautiful curve. I saw with a little shock that he had cut his hair, so that his baldness showed. He had trimmed his beard too, revealing a quiet and determined mouth, the corners gently tucked into the pleasure of his thought.

I let him read for a little, looking around the room, enjoying the peace he had created for himself.

Presently he looked up. "He died in the same room as his father, fifty-seven years ago to the day he took office as consul for the first time."

"The same day? Do you think it means something?"

"What kind of thing?"

"Is a god at work, do you think? Perhaps an omen, for our plan?"

"Anything is possible. But we must not look beyond our evidence. It's a coincidence—it's interesting. That's all." His voice was undisturbed. He might have been talking about some figure from history: Tarquin or Aeneas or the first Scipio. The calm of the room remained untouched.

"Is that how you do it?" I said. "You just think of things as interesting? You don't try to act on your ideas? Shouldn't a good man try to make the world better? Plato says he should, I believe."

"'The price good men pay for refusing to participate in public affairs is to be ruled by their inferiors.' It's in the Republic."

"Yes," I said.

He gave me a shrewd glance. "The trouble is, it is very difficult to say what makes the world better or worse. For example, look at Caesar. It is true that he has been cruel and bloody, it is true that he has damaged, if not destroyed, the Republic we knew. But he has raised up other men, unknown men, of unknown families. And he has brought peace from a civil war, and kept our borders secure for more than two generations. Which is he—bad or good? Does anyone know?"

"But surely one must protest the evil he does—did? Shouldn't one try? Even if you are wrong? What good does sitting and thinking about it do?"

"Ideas are important too. And those who think of them are as valuable as those who act. An idea might change the world. Plato's have."

"Is that why you do this, then? Read, and study, and so on?"

His eyes flashed blue before he lowered his lids, but when he looked at me again, he was speaking quietly. "In my own country my father was a priest, an important man among our people. I would have followed him: it was the calling of our family. Well. Chance happens to us all, and in this house, I am a slave. I must do another's bidding; I am confined to another's place, in a country that does not belong to me. But here, in the books, I am free. I may go anywhere, anywhere I like. To Africa. Gaul." He gestured at the book. "Greece."

"Alexandria," I said. "Aenesidemus taught in Alexandria."

"So he did," he said, but I thought that under his beard his mouth twitched into a smile.

Slowly the city grew calmer, but it was not peace that silenced it, it was grief. The crowds still stood in the streets, but now they bent their heads and cried. From every street came a different note blending together until the city itself groaned with pain.

Through this strange sound one day the senators walked to the Forum, dressed as simple knights, their heads lowered and their eyes on the ground. There, from the Rostra, Pompeius and Sextus

Appuleius the consuls, still in their purple-bordered robes, swore allegiance to Tiberius. Appuleius looked straight ahead, expressionless. If he seemed less than happy about his oath, people no doubt remembered that his son was very ill.

Next the crucial officials, the chief of the Praetorian Guard and the Superintendent of the Grain Supply, swore the same allegiance, then the whole Senate, in voices made ragged by what might have been sorrow. I tried to find Fabius among the senators but he had made himself inconspicuous, and his head was covered. Next, the consuls asked the army, represented by the ranks of the Guard, who, more willingly perhaps, lifted their voices in affirmation. Appuleius and Pompeius acknowledged this with bows and nods. Then turning to us they cried out, "Let us all swear. All the citizens." At that the voice of the city went up into the sky in a shout. Those of us who were in the Forum could hear the noise as the side streets then the hills and the districts further away added their support.

The sound continued. Day and night the city cried aloud. There was no way to escape it, even indoors. Marcia and Fabia and I were disturbed by it as we sat all day in young Appuleius' room, trying to hear the child's nearly inaudible breathing.

His eyes and cheeks had hollowed and his skin seemed first loose over his bones, then too tight. Every day he grew weaker. I did not think he was aware of us any longer, but Fabia still tried to talk to him, or to get him to eat or drink. He would accept a drop or two of water without opening his eyes, but food no longer interested him, and he paid no attention to her desperate and pathetic offers.

For a time Marcia stayed with us, but as the child sank further she spent less time with him, until one day I saw her stop in the doorway to study the wasted little face in her usual little way. But this time, instead of coming in she nodded once to herself, and slipped away. After that she did not come back again. I don't know if Fabia, distracted now with terror and grief, had noticed.

Sextus came of course, as did Fabius, but they were busy organizing Augustus' funeral, and it seemed an unlucky thing to bring into the room of a sick child. Mostly they stood in the doorway for a little, like Marcia, then disappeared. Persicus himself came once in a while, and left quickly, drawn away by his mother, who said she needed him to help her with the callers who thronged the atrium asking for news.

The next day we heard that Augustus' body, accompanied by Tiberius and all the dignitaries of the towns along the route between Nola and Rome, reached the little town of Bovillae not far south. On account of the heat, they had been walking only at night, leaving the body in the main temple or the principal building of whatever place they came to at daybreak. The entire order of knights, thousands of men, mustered in the Forum and marched off to meet it. We could hear their tread even in Appuleius' room.

The senators, still dressed as knights, and the consuls and other magistrates in black went with them as far as the city gate, where they waited to escort Augustus to the atrium of his own home. On his way out the door, Fabius stopped in to glance at Appuleius, but Sextus, already wearing mourning, would not even let Fabia see him. A feeling of evil luck hung over the house as it was.

That night the city fell silent, an unfamiliar and uneasy quiet after the constant commotion of the last days. Appuleius' breathing suddenly became audible again. That night I stayed on a couch in the same room with Fabia. I did not see Marcia or Persicus at all.

All the next day Appuleius continued to sink. The city seemed quiet, though the Senate was meeting. "Convened by Tiberius," Sextus said, stopping by before he dressed to hold his son's transparent little hand. "In his capacity as tribune. He won't say he's the Emperor—he's to be called only Caesar. Nor will he allow any debate about anything—only the reading of the will."

"Why not?"

"Who knows? Mysterious man."

He set his son's hand down on the coverlet as carefully as if the boy still felt it. He smiled at Fabia, but he ducked out of the room with his fingers pressed across his eyes to stop his tears.

Around noon I went up on the balcony and watched the distant procession of the Vestal Virgins carrying the will to the Curia. As always when they appeared, an awed hush surrounded them. I watched until the last of their escort had disappeared into the Forum.

The city remained quiet, except that in midafternoon a shout went up and echoed through the streets. Startled, Fabia looked up. I took the moment to try to get her to eat some of the food the servants insisted on bringing in.

It was nightfall before Fabius and Sextus came home. Marcia was with them. She was smiling. It was so long since I had seen anyone smile that I did not understand what I was seeing. And indeed, as they approached Appuleius' room her face went blank. I thought I ought to leave them alone with their family, but as I was going out the door I asked Fabius about the noise.

"It was the will. Just like a normal rich man's will. Except that he gave each of the soldiers serving in the cohorts composed of Roman citizens three hundred sesterces—that's more than a year's pay per man. The Praetorian guards got a thousand sesterces each. Oh, and he left the people and populace of Rome forty-three million five hundred thousand sesterces."

"Forty-three *million*?"

"That's what they were cheering about."

"Forty-three *million*."

Fabius gave me an ironic look. "Of course, he left the larger portion of his estate to Livia and Tiberius. I have no idea how much *that* actually amounts to."

I didn't know what to say. My husband was a rich man, and Fabius was a very rich one. I myself administered a very respectable family fortune. But that was what we had been fighting. I had had no idea.

Marcia said in a voice of sweet complaint, "He arranged for Livia to be adopted into his own family. She's to be called "Augusta" now." She glanced into the room where her grandson lay. "I must go and congratulate her." And she smiled.

Tiberius kept the city under lock and key. He issued a proclamation warning the city against what he called "the enthusiasm that had marred the obsequies of the Divine Julius." He meant the speeches of Brutus and Antony, of course, and the civil war they ignited, though no one said so. Just to be sure we got the point, he would not let Augustus' body be burned in the Forum, but insisted it must go to the altar Augustus had constructed, in the Campus Martius. Though it went through the city accompanied by all the magnificence of music and incense, ancestor portraits and honorifics, it went under an armed escort. The pyre, loaded with valuables and perfumed with riches, was nonetheless surrounded by a guard, watchful lest someone besides Tiberius and his son try to make a speech.

"What is he afraid of?" I asked Loricus when I got home that night.

Loricus was always pithy. And he always knew. "Germanicus."

For several days the Senate debated. Or pretended to debate. They begged Tiberius to take the sole power. He refused.

"Why, Fabius?" I asked. "Is it still Germanicus?"

He unwound himself from the black cloak he had taken to wearing. No one wanted to wear the toga now. Not until Tiberius went back to wearing his.

"That's right. Germanicus and the armies. Nothing reassures Tiberius. Valerius Messalinus even proposed that the oath of allegiance be repeated every year. Tiberius asked him if he, Tiberius, had told him to say this. Messalinus swore before the entire Senate that he had thought of it himself. This from a man whose father stood up to Caesar when Caesar tried to make him City Prefect: This fawning and lying is the only independence we have left. This sham."

"But Messalinus is Cotta's brother. Our friend. His father was as close to a patron as Naso ever had."

"Friend," he said, tasting it, like a word in a foreign language.

Another day, I whispered as we passed in the atrium, "Have you heard from Clemens?"

"Nothing, except that he left some time ago. He should have been there by now."

The whole city lay under the brilliant September weather as if a cloud of sadness and apprehension were pressing it down. The stones were quiet, and though people went about their business they did not look at one another, or speak more than a few words. Most people kept their heads covered, as if they were still at the funeral. Rome was like a city under siege or a plague, abandoned by her gods, and left to the mercy of the crows.

And for us in the family there came a worse day: Appuleius slipped silently from sleep to death. For days his breathing had grown slower and slower. It was plain what was happening. The servants knew, and came to check on us several times a day; Marcia sat with us again, keeping to a chair by the door and studying the boy intently. We seemed to hear nothing but the occasional whisper of air from the bed.

It had begun to seem that we would go on like that forever, three women sitting like statues in a darkened room, listening to something that was no sound at all, when all at once Fabia let out a scream and hurled herself at the bed, trying to seize his last breath with her lips. The little yellow face did not move. Fabia began to cry. I took her in my arms, holding her rocking body to me, shaken by her sobs. Just before my own tears came I noticed Marcia. She was sitting in her chair, her hands in her lap. Her eyes were dry and her expression remote. And as I bent my head to Fabia's sweet-scented hair, my cheek wet already with my own grief, I thought: in all the time I have known her, I have never seen Marcia cry. I wonder if she can. Then the sorrow took me, and I did not think of anything else again for a long time.

So the house sat, chairs grouped in the atrium around the small body wrapped in his child's cloak and lying on a flower-strewn couch. In the silence the smells of the gardens came to us, and the rumor of sound from the city beyond the walls. Every day and almost every night, the most important people in the city trooped through the atrium to show their respect—for a child's funeral it was impressive. The wives sat with us, but if you got up from the atrium and went into the house you would find their husbands clustered in corners drinking wine and talking politics. When they saw members of the household, they would stop talking and bow gravely.

It was from them that we learned, a few days later, that not one but two different armies, having heard that Augustus was dead, had rebelled. Germanicus' command in Germany was one of them, but the other was far away from it, in Pannonia on the upper Danube.

"They could not have made a worse move," Macer was saying in Fabius' atrium, taking my hand as I went by. "Dear lady," he murmured into it, before I could pull it away.

"Indeed." Sextus Pompeius, Appuleius' colleague in the consulship, put out his foot for his outdoor shoe. "If they wanted to assure that there would trouble here—"

Fabius lifted his whitened face. "Tiberius will accept the Imperial power now."

"And we will do well to look cheerful about it." Pompeius, perhaps to illustrate this, stretched a ghastly grin across his cheeks.

Fabius shook his head. "That I cannot do. It's the worst thing that has happened to the city in five hundred years. I cannot pretend otherwise."

"Well, then, let us hope your excuse—" Pompeius swept his hand toward the atrium—"is good enough. Be well, Fabius."

They were right, of course. Tiberius accepted the supreme power that night, sending his son Drusus to Pannonia, accompanied by many distinguished men, two Praetorian cohorts and a large group of Germans serving with our armies.

I heard them go, very late, from my own house.

"Interesting," said Loricus, standing beside me on the balcony. The stars were clear, the moon, only a sliver, had long since set behind the Temple of Jupiter. Down in the streets the dust of marching feet slowly fell back into quietness.

"What is?"

"He didn't send anyone to help Germanicus."

That was so. I wondered now why no one had noticed. "Why not? Do you think Germanicus doesn't need help?"

In the soft light his eyes were twinkling. "You think not? It would be just as dangerous for us to lose those provinces as to lose Pannonia. More dangerous, actually."

"Oh. Well, why then?"

"I think you can guess."

"No, I—Oh. He hopes Germanicus will lose?"

He wasn't twinkling any longer. "There's no one who poses a greater threat to him right now. Not even Agrippa Postumus. Germanicus is a very great general, and his troops are loyal to him."

On the eighth day after his death we carried Appuleius to his father's family's tomb. There, on a beautiful couch covered with green leaves and flowers, he was burnt, and the smoke went up to reproach the heavens. At any funeral it does that, but the death of a child requires an explanation that the gods have never bothered to vouchsafe. I came away, thinking of my daughter's baby born so tiny and blue, and the little bodies in the streets of the poor at night, the children of slaves, and those like Julia Aemilii's, put to die among the stones and scrub outside the walls of towns. And I thought: if the gods permit that, then I do not care if the gods exist or not.

But then it began to seem that the gods—if there were any—might have relented to us: at the Ides of September a few days later, word came that Agrippa Postumus had been seen at Cosa, in Etruria, strolling along the causeway, and under the portico of the baths. A huge crowd had quickly surrounded him.

"By heaven, he did it!" Fabius cried, bursting in on me at home. His face was full of joy, more expressive than I had ever seen it. In his exuberance he gathered me into his arms, a thing that even with our close family ties he had never allowed himself before. He smelled of lavender and spices from the lotion his slave put on him, and his cheek against mine was smooth.

"Why has he showed himself? I thought we were going to smuggle him to Germanicus and Agrippina."

But my voice was muffled in his shoulder, and he was already exulting. "I'm on my way. I'm going to him now."

"Take care," I whispered to his back as he flung himself out the door. "We have enemies everywhere."

We had friends too. From all over the city men poured out to see the prince. I saw Senators and knights in chariots or carriages, young men on horseback, flocks of plebeians, who had always loved the Julians, jamming the gate and the road north. It was like a festival, and they all felt it. I myself was infected by the joy of the city. I went about the day humming. Macer came by that night, saying, "Pinni, come with me. There's a dinner party at Calpurnius'—really, a meeting. You ought to be there."

I went but no one knew anything, except that Agrippa Postumus had been seen briefly and at night, in several of the towns along the coast. He seemed to be working his way south to Rome.

Two days later the Senate met. Among the honors lavished on Augustus was that he be recognized as a god. To no one's very great surprise the resolution passed. His adopted father had become the Divine Julius, and certainly Augustus, whatever one thought of his tyranny, had done as much for Rome. There was a saying going around: on his deathbed he was supposed to have said, "I found Rome brick, but I have left it marble." It was very nearly true.

I heard nothing from Fabius: Cosa is almost a hundred miles away and he would hardly have time to get there and back. But towards evening Marcia stopped by. She had Persicus with her. He stood behind her chair, glowering over her head at the topiaries in the garden.

"So," she said, settling herself with much bustle into a chair, "do you think it's true?"

Well, I thought, two can play that game. "Is what true?"

She gave me her vague and brilliant smile. "Oh, Pinni. That Agrippa Postumus has come back."

"Come back?"

"There's a rumor that he has. I can't believe that you didn't know."

"Oh, no one tells me anything. I live very quietly. You know that."

"Well, you wouldn't be happy if he did come back, would you? I mean, his father relegated your husband."

She studied my face; I studied the wall.

"Really, Pinni—"

I gave her a large smile. "I have some new wool from Gaul. It doesn't seem to take the colors well. Could you take a look for me?"

"Another time, Pinni dear. I had better be going—we have to call on Livia Augusta to congratulate her. Don't we, Persicus? The vote was unanimous."

"Of course it was. What else?"

"What do you mean?" Her gentle voice rose to as close to sharpness as it ever came. Persicus bestowed his glower on me.

"What do you think I meant? That Augustus' real nature has been plain to everyone for some time, don't you think?"

"Oh. I see. Where did that girl put my cloak? Oh, dear. Persicus, darling, did I have a cloak when I came in?" She beamed at him. He seemed to take it as no more than his due.

I waited, but again I heard nothing from Fabius. We heard a lot about Agrippa though; the whole city seemed to be talking. His progress was reported, along with many stories. Tiberius was asked about him in the Senate, but he said he had heard nothing but rumors: he could not act on mere fables. But he acted all the same, fable or no: he had stationed the Praetorians at the northern gates. They did not seem to have any orders—certainly they made no arrests— though they scrutinized the faces of the more prominent people coming and going. Were they looking for someone? Did Tiberius know whom to look for? Perhaps he was simply unsure what to do: it could not be easy to imagine a way to go get rid of the last of Julia's sons without bringing on another civil war.

And a civil war seemed all too imminent. From Pannonia the news continued of riots among the troops. And in Germany a strange story had started: the soldiers there were rebelling because they wanted to swear allegiance to Germanicus rather than Tiberius. He had refused, very properly, very nobly, but that did not seem to have quieted the troops. In desperation, Germanicus announced he would commit suicide—and to my horror I heard that many of the men were willing to accept his offer. Finally Germanicus had read them all a letter, from Tiberius he said, granting them all their demands.

"Interesting. It has to be a forgery," said Loricus.

"How do you know?" I asked.

"The evidence. Look at the evidence. There hasn't been time to send a letter, and Tiberius doesn't act that quickly anyway."

"No. He's not a quick thinker, is he?"

"Even if he were, it won't solve the problem. The army can count the days of a journey from Rome as well as anyone."

So I had two things to worry about: my son-in-law up in Germany with Germanicus, and Fabius somewhere on the coast north of Rome, escorting Agrippa Postumus to whatever dangerous fate awaited them. I waited for word from Fabius that he was all right, that Agrippa was well, that our plan was still secret, but no word came.

Two days later, amid huge crowds cheering and waving garlands of late-blooming daisies, Agrippa Postumus arrived in Ostia. If Fabius was with him, no one said so, and I did not dare to send anyone to find out.

That night the city reveled. I heard the singing in the streets, the shouts and smashing crockery in the wineshops, the dancing and the music and the geese up on the Capitoline Hill yammering; I watched the torchlight swing over the walls and smelled the dust kicked up by the hurrying feet.

For myself, I did not know whether to be happy or frightened. As soon as I sat down, I got up; as soon as I found myself in one room, I needed to be in another. And nowhere was the answer to my fear. I did not go to bed, but sat in my garden, sure that Fabius would come now.

I must have slept a little for I woke to see the sky already bleached with light. The dawn breeze was rattling the chestnut, and from the fountain a few drops blew across the path, pushing before them a handful of dead leaves. The air was chilly: summer was over.

Far away in the streets the morning had begun. I could smell the smoke of cooking fires, shutters creaked, voices called. A little of the celebration still sounded: drunken voices passed outside raised loudly in song, and a pot turned over and crashed. Soon my clients and dependents would be arriving at my doors too. And still Fabius had not come.

I had indeed a crowded atrium to deal with, filled with flutter and bustle, and though every movement jerked my eyes to the door, Fabius never came. How could he? I told myself: it is too public here.

But news came to find me all the same. In the second hour Loricus burst through the colonnade. He looked gray around the mouth and he slumped against a pillar as if his legs were shaking.

His lips were blue and he had trouble forming the words. "Mistress. It's Fabius."

But the news was already in my house, it had been there all morning, blown in on the cold gritty wind that had awakened me to an empty garden. "Fabius?" I said. It was a stupid question.

He nodded.

"He's been arrested, hasn't he?"

"He's dead, mistress."

The autumn had come to Marcia's house too. Even in the doorway—which for some reason stood open—you could hear the air whining through the columns inside the house. A crowd had collected, apparently to listen to it, craning their necks and blinking against the blowing dust. Marcia's doorman was trying to make them move off. "Citizens. Citizens, please. Have some respect." His voice whipped away, and the crowd paid no attention.

Inside, the turbulence had kicked over all sense and order. Servants were running back and forth; some had been blown like dust into the corners, where they huddled, moaning and sobbing. One or two had blood on them. A basket of linen rolled on the floor, the fine weaving shuddered and flapped among the dirty footprints. As I watched, a little slave boy wearing nothing but a string around his neck came running from the atrium. Unable to see in the sudden shadow, he tripped across a bench. He lay there, collapsed into a trembling heap, and began to cry. As I passed I picked him up and set him on his feet.

In the atrium everything had sunk back into chaos itself. I could not see the altar, and perhaps the gods had gone, perhaps it was the beginning of the world again. Nothing made sense. The light splashed down from the hole in the roof over a mass of variegated color crammed from wall to wall. Men and women, children and infants, had jammed into the space, all swaying, flapping their hands, swirling like grains of sand in stirred water. Some had clambered onto the furniture, some even waded into the pool. One toothless old man had covered his eyes and was blundering through the room, caroming off footmen and treading on the bare feet of the maids. No one noticed. They were not looking in one direction, but everywhere, as if they did not know where to look, and more of them were pouring in all the time, shrugging on tunics or wiping their hands on their fluttering clothes. The noise was incredible, and over it all came the shriek of the wind.

I leaned back and let out my voice as loud as it would go. "What is going on here?"

The tumult was instantly still. All the faces turned to look at me. "What has happened here? Where is Fabius?"

Still silent they turned and opened a path to the altar. There on the floor lay two figures in a bright splatter of crimson.

"Both?" I cried. Where you are Gaius, I am Gaia. I ran forward.

Blood had spurted everywhere. Fabius lay in it, staring up at the sky. He had wrapped himself in his embroidered toga, the one he had worn when he had celebrated his triumph. It had been, of course, the greatest moment of his life.

Now he lay in his beautiful robe with his sword in his chest, in front of the altar of his ancestors. He had already joined them: he lay as still and his face had the same marble look. It would never move again. The lips would never open. He would never tell me why he had died.

Near him a woman had crumpled into a heap. Her gray hair was matted with blood and I could not see her face.

"Marcia," I called softly, not liking to disturb her if she was dead. But her pulse was strong and did not flutter under my hand. I slid my palms under her shoulder and turned her over, frightened that I would hurt her. Her eyes were closed. She was very pale. But her mouth was open, and the shriek that I had thought was the wind was coming from her.

"Marcia." Her eyes remained closed and she did not stop screaming. The sound sliced open the air. Murmurs fell out of it all around me, soft exclamations of surprise.

I ran my hands as lightly as I could along her body. She did not appear to be injured. The blood was all over her clothes; her face was smeared with it and some was in her open mouth. But I did not think it was her own—it was drying even as the air touched it, turning brown like the leaves.

"Marcia, it's Pinni." Her lids shivered open. Her sea-glass eyes stared at me.

Very slowly her mouth closed. The screaming stopped.

In the sudden silence I said, "What happened here?"

She swallowed. "Fabius. Dead."

"Yes, I know. Why? Did someone kill him?"

She closed her eyes and turned her face away. She appeared to have fallen asleep.

In the silence the servants' voices fell around me like rain. "He did it, mistress. He did it. He killed himself."

I gave the orders: the servants seemed grateful for them. Marcia was carried to her room, bathed and put to bed with a sleeping draft. Fabius I had lifted onto a table with his feet to the door: from somewhere someone found a coin to put in his mouth. Grabbing a servant I turned her toward the colonnade and sent her to get Persicus.

I sat in the first of the chairs that had been set out, contemplating the wind as it glittered among the victories on Fabius' crimson and gold robes. Of course he would wear his toga to go to his fathers. But his magnificence meant more than that. It was a criticism too, a reproach, and a memory of the Republic as it had once been. Fabius' ancestor had built the first triumphal arch in Rome. Fabius himself was the last of the great generals to celebrate a triumph: after him all the honors went to Augustus, no matter who had been in the field. It was a joke, a solemn farce, but even Tiberius had gone along with it, graciously pretending that Augustus had deserved the credit for his own military brilliance. Now Fabius was showing that he had not accepted the lie.

"Farewell," I said, "Farewell," repeating the ritual, but it was more than that. Even in death, Fabius was still fighting.

After a while the doctor came in and removed the sword. Bloody as it was I laid it on the altar. Let it be sign: I was still fighting too.

The funeral eight days later was as magnificent as Fabius' triumph had been. All the pomp of the old days was in it: he was carried standing upright out of his house into the blaze of sunset to the accompaniment of torches and music. Mimes and dancers followed, then a parade of his relatives wearing portrait masks or carrying busts of his ancestors; it took more than two hours for the gilded chariots that carried them to grind into the Forum and assemble before the Rostra. Next came his son Persicus, his eyes cold and his mouth hard, like the sort of horse you do not want to buy, surrounded by consuls. Fabius' dependents and friends walked behind him, all the way from the greatest senators to the lowest freedmen, a huge family. Tiberius came: an even more signal honor: Livia led the procession of ladies, leaning on Marcia's arm. I could see their veiled heads bowed together under the heavy silence as Fabius' distinguished brother stepped up to make the oration.

I suppose he said the usual things. I was not listening. The sky was clear and behind the buildings the full moon was rising. It was silvering the shadows and turning the sky the same deep blue that Fabius used for the covers of his books and the decorations of his house. Under its light Fabius' brother gestured in the conventional way and the massed family listened respectfully. I saw Tiberius, standing first among them in the place of greatest honor; he was looking over the vast mass of Fabius' retainers and friends. We filled nearly the whole Forum, and of course in Rome any public event draws people from every street and alley for miles. Nothing could conceal Tiberius' unease, and the sneer in his lip was more prominent in the tricky light. I wondered why he had come, if he feared the crowd so much; then I realized he had feared not to even more. But even his soldier's discipline could not make him stop shifting his weight nervously from one foot to the other, and his big square hands played constantly with the folds of his toga.

Finally the speech was done. The procession began again, moving out under the torches. It must have been two hours or more before we had all passed under the gate and had come to Fabius' family tomb. There the huge pyre was already built, aromatic with rare woods and herbs in the cool autumn night. Fabius' body was laid on it, and his beautiful toga removed and folded with as much reverence as if it had been a legionary standard. It would be used to dress the statue of Fabius that would in its turn be carried through the Forum in the funerals of his family. Though I wondered, watching Tiberius as he usurped a kinsman's privilege and put the torch to the wood, whether he would ever again allow such a public display of a great family's power. I thought not: he was already eying the crowd again as he straightened up and went back to his place beside Persicus and Marcia. I saw him bend to say something to her.

The fire, when it came, ate greedily through the pile and reached up into the sky, blotting out even the moon. Fabius' clothing blossomed into flame, billowed like sails, fell back, curled and blackened. A wall of flame and smoke roared up, hiding the body. The priests threw on more incense. Down in front I heard Marcia begin to wail. "It's my fault. Oh, Fabius, forgive me. It's my fault." Her voice was rising. I ran forward and grabbed her arm.

"Marcia, hush." I was trying to hold her, but she was thrashing wildly in my arms.

"Fabius. I betrayed you."

"No, of course you didn't. No one betrayed him."

She was screaming now. "I did. I did." Her face shone and her body writhed, but her eyes, oddly, looked sensible and intelligent. I turned my head to see where she was looking. She was staring straight at Livia. After a moment the elder lady nodded; pulling her veil to hide her face with a trembling and arthritic hand, she turned to say a word to Tiberius.

"Hush," I said, holding Marcia as she grew quiet in my arms. "It's all right. No one betrayed anyone. There was nothing to betray."

"Listen to me, Marcia. There was nothing to betray." I must have said it ten times as we went home, and now I was saying it again an hour later in Marcia's shuttered bedroom. The dark walls flickered with chalk and ochre as a single small lamp sent ripples of light across the ceiling. Marcia lay on the couch, a cloth soaked in scented vinegar over her eyes.

"You don't think so?"

"It doesn't matter what I think. What on earth are you doing? Trying to make people talk?"

"But Fabius is dead now, Pinni."

I had that familiar feeling that I was talking to someone in another room. "Marcia, you didn't betray anyone. There was nothing to betray."

"Oh. But what about his visit to Planasia, Pinni? With Augustus. You know."

"Nonsense. That wasn't true—it was just something the Julians and their friends put around."

"Perhaps it was true and perhaps it wasn't." Under the shadow of her arm her full lips curved in a private smile. "But the other is true. He went to see that fool in Etruria a few days ago."

"To Etruria? You mean to see Agrippa Postumus?"

She pulled the cloth off her eyes. "Really, Pinni. He came and told you he was going, didn't he? When he called at your house that night."

I just goggled at her.

"Why do you think I don't know? I make it a point to know everything about Fabius. I had him followed."

"You spied on him? Your own husband?"

"Of course. Everyone does it. Don't tell me you never did."

"It never crossed my mind," I said, with truth.

I was looking at her eyes. They were large and beautiful, a fine light color with a glint almost like water but I had never noticed how shallow they were. I wondered why I was only noticing it now.

"What are you staring at? It wasn't for me. You know I care nothing for myself. It was for Persicus. Ever since he was born he has been the most important thing in the world to me."

"Persicus?"

"Of course. You wouldn't understand anything like that, Pinni. You never had a son." She flashed out in triumph for an instant, like a bird darting suddenly from a tree. It was true. And I regretted it. But both my husbands had loved my little girl and no one had ever thought I was a failure because of her sex. Marcia, however, plainly did. And she was prepared to make sure I knew it.

"A son is something really special, Pinni. You really wouldn't have any way to know how deeply I love him."

"Persicus?" I repeated, dumbfounded. I couldn't tell if she believed what she was saying, or simply hoped that I would. Whichever it was, it was plainly false. All the time he was growing up she had done little but criticize and neglect her own little boy. All her attention, all her love, had been lavished on her grandson instead. "What about Appuleius?"

She seemed to have a little trouble remembering who that was. "That's very unfeeling of you, Pinni, to remind me of another grief, when I am so overwhelmed by this one."

I was rapidly losing contact with this conversation. All I could grasp was that it was suddenly my fault that she had done something dishonorable.

With her usual acuteness her manner changed. Her voice softened and she looked vague and sad. "Oh, Pinni, it's hard to be born into a political family. You are forced to do a lot of things you would rather not do."

"Well, that's true at least. I suppose it wasn't easy. I used to watch you getting ready to go out with your mother, to see the great ladies. All that fuss about clothes and curling irons, about what to say and how to sit and who was going or not going. I used to wish I was going too but perhaps it is better that I wasn't wanted."

She said plaintively, "Oh, yes. You had the best of it, Pinni."

"I did?"

"Oh, yes."

"You don't mean that. You knew how Atia treated me. She was never so harsh to you."

She said nothing, but her upper lip was down.

"I know you were sometimes unhappy. I tried to help, Marcia. Don't you remember? I suppose I wasn't very effective, but I did try. I smuggled you food if you were being punished, and I made offerings for you in secret to the Juno. I used to come in and comb your hair. I felt sorry for you."

"You felt sorry for me? *You* felt sorry for *me*?"

She was so angry I could hardly hear her voice, and her eyes had gone so unfocused I thought she might be about to faint.

"You felt sorry for me? Who are you, Pinni? The daughter of an obscure senator that never got further than the praetorship. A man who had to kill himself to avoid disgrace or worse. A nobody. Scarcely even related to us."

"I know. Atia made that abundantly clear, didn't she? All through my childhood. And she couldn't wait to marry me off to the first man who asked."

"We took you in. You ought to be grateful."

"I always have been, Marcia."

"So you should be. We were very generous, more than you deserved. You were always making trouble. You still are. I was right to make sure I knew what you were up to."

"What—what do you mean? Did you have me followed too?"

"Don't be silly, Pinni. I just made sure your maid told me everything that went on."

"My maid? You mean Philomela? You got her to spy on me?"

She would not meet my eyes, but she nodded.

"Only for a little while, Pinni."

"What do you mean?"

"Well, I had to get rid of her. She was going to tell you—she was afraid if you found out she'd be sold. And she was pregnant. Some fellow who works in your garden."

"You got rid of her? You mean you poisoned her?"

"You don't have to look so shocked. She was just a slave, Pinni."

I could not think of anything more to say. Perhaps I had thought like that once. "You mean you knew all along that the father of her child wasn't Naso? Why did you tell me it was?"

She turned to look at me then, her strange eyes glaring, her silver hair loose and tangled. I could almost see the tendrils raise their heads and hiss. Not Minerva, Medusa.

"It was my family, Pinni, not yours. You had no right to be there."

There was nothing now that could be said between us. The depth of her jealousy and hatred shocked me into stone.

Marcia picked up her comb and leaned to look into her mirror. "Of course, I told Livia about Fabius."

I could hardly find my voice. "Livia? When?"

The triumph was permanent now. She could hardly keep from smiling. "The night he left to go to that fool Postumus, of course. And when he came back, Tiberius ordered him to call."

"That's why he died, then."

It was not her nature to accept blame, even by implication. She gave me a tragic look. Then, with that softness of manner that had deceived so many people—including me—for so long, she lowered her eyes and whispered, "Oh, Pinni, I had to."

"You had to?"

"She was going to find out anyway. They are having that house in Ostia watched. I had to let her know that Persicus was not involved. You'll never understand how much I love Persicus, Pinni. You'll just never understand."

The road to Ostia lay white under the full moon. Cypresses barred it with black shadows and a small white cloud of dust rose under our wheels. I thought of Naso, far away under the moon. The moon had been full the night he left too.

There was no one on the road. Even the docks were bare, and the ships slept on their anchors with long slow breaths. But in a small square in the town a crowd still lingered, spotted with shadow under the plane trees. They sat on benches or strolled slowly past the fountain, but they were all watching one house with an open door.

Loricus pulled the wagon under a wall. He was the only servant I had brought with me—the only one I could now trust. It felt odd to travel almost alone. "Don't announce my name," I said.

"No, mistress. I recognize some of these people. Not all of them are friends."

I pulled my veil over my face and let him escort me inside.

The little house had an atrium so small the pool took up most of the room. Beside it, on a bench a young man lolled on his elbow, his face lifted to the moonlight. He wore a small decorative beard around his mouth—I remembered his friend's that night long ago under the portico when he had been fined for publishing Agrippa's letter. It must have been the fashion in their circle.

No lamp or torch shone anywhere. A small tray of food lay on the floor beside his slippered foot, but he was drinking the wine. He had evidently had a good deal of it before I came, and I did not see a water flask anywhere.

His clothes were rich. The slipper alone was covered in beadwork that flashed in the moonlight, and his tunic in better light would have been crimson. Now, in the half dark, it was mostly black.

Men and women were passing in the darkness. Some stopped to whisper a word to him, at which he nodded or shook his head. One or two kissed his ring. Under the little beard he smiled at them. I didn't hear him say anything.

I went forward, bowing. He raised his eyebrows.

"Julius Caesar Agrippa Postumus, I am honored to meet you—I came to tell you—yes, Loricus, what is it?"

Loricus was squeezing my arm. The young man on the bench had straightened up and was waving his hand at me.

Loricus was staring at him. "He wants you to remove your veil, mistress."

"Oh. Yes, of course." I fumbled with the length of fabric.

Loricus was saying, "He wants us to come with him—into another room? Yes, of course. We are coming. Mistress—"

He took my hand.

In a little room the light flickered in a shallow dish, so dim the furniture was no more than a few random glints. He gestured to me to sit, but I forgot that in my haste.

"Julius Caesar Agrippa Postumus, I have come to tell you: Fabius Maximus was betrayed by his wife. She says you are being watched."

The bearded face leaned a little into the light. I stared at him. The same heavy jaw and prominent chin the beard did little to conceal, the same high cheekbone, the thick bent nose. He looked like Vipsanius Agrippa, certainly. All the same, there was something wrong. "You—you aren't Agrippa Postumus, are you?"

He was smiling again. "No, mistress. I Clemens. You can see."

Behind me Loricus let out the breath he had been holding.

From under the couch Clemens lifted a plain undecorated funeral urn and thrust it into my arms. "*This* is Agrippa Postumus."

"What—what is this?"

"Remains. Remains of the prince. Of Agrippa Postumus. As you say, I went to the island. But the boat, the freighter, it was too slow. Agrippa Postumus, he already dead. A tribune was burning the body. These are his ashes. I gather them. After."

"Why did he do that?"

"He have an order, from a man named Sallustius Crispus."

Loricus' judicious voice came from out of the darkness. "Sallustius Crispus is a friend of Tiberius'."

"So Tiberius already knows," I said.

"And Livia."

"Is correct, mistress. More. Sallustius Crispus order him to be—" He made a gesture squeezing his hands together.

"Crispus ordered him strangled?"

"Yes, mistress." Clemens bowed his head, and suddenly he didn't look much like Agrippa Postumus any more. He looked humble, and sad. "I asked the others. The others like me. Slaves. The tribune showed them the order."

"Did they say who told Crispus to send it?"

"Some say The Augustus ordered it when he died. Some say Tiberius. The slaves, they do not know. Maybe Crispus do it on his own. To make Tiberius happy."

"If Crispus did that, he would still tell Tiberius."

"Yes, master—" Clemens said, calling Loricus by the name in his own language that he had used in my house. "How else would Tiberius be happy?"

"Just so."

I looked around the little room. It seemed smaller than when we had come in. "So we are all still in danger. Clemens, you especially. Why are you still here?"

He drew himself up and looked at me with a deep unreadable eye, this strange man who was at once a slave, a soldier, and a prince.

"Once you save me. I waiting for you, mistress."

The lamp was getting low and smoke was beginning to curl from the wick. There was not much time left.

"Clemens, now I can't help you. You must save yourself. You must get away."

"Yes, mistress. But you must too. I wait to say that. They will arrest me. Maybe they know who I am. Maybe not." He looked at me proudly. "I not tell. I give my word. I die first. But maybe they know already. So you must go."

I had not thought so far. But he was right.

"Do not go to your house. Go from here. Get a ship. Go. Do you need money? Many rich men give me gold."

"No, thank you," Loricus said. "We can send for it."

I do not think that ever in my life I had imagined that a slave would offer me money.

"Bring me paper," I said.

"Mistress, we must go."

"Yes, Loricus. But first I must free Clemens."

"We do not have time to register it at the temple—"

"No, perhaps not. But if he has a document it might be enough to save him from being tortured."

Clemens had tears on his face. "I—I thank you. But your name—it must not be on a paper."

I did not know what to say. I just stared at him. Then I reached out and put my arms around him. I do not think that ever in my life had I embraced a slave. And I was crying harder when I did.

Something was wrong with the moon. It still sailed in the sky, so brilliant that the stars were paled around it, and it glared the road like a fall of snow, but something had cut almost halfway into it. I thought of the coins of sunlight on my terrace, the day the sun went down in blood.

"Loricus, what does it mean?"

"It is an eclipse. It may help us, if the night becomes darker."

"Will it?"

"I think so."

"Something is destroying the moon?"

"For a while. I'm sure it will come back."

"You are?"

On a breath he let out his anxiety as if he had been holding it a long time.

"Oh," I said. "I see."

He squared his shoulders. "The sun came back."

"That is true. And you said it wasn't an omen."

"It wasn't. A purely natural event."

"But not long after that Caesar Augustus died."

He frowned and let his square fingers play over his chin. "A lot of things happened not long after that. Why was it not an omen of them?"

It made me smile. He was so easy to tease.

His brilliant eye fell on me, and if it had not been getting so dark I would have sworn he blushed. "Humph. At least we can take advantage of this—purely natural—event. We can turn off the road. There are villages along here where some fisherman can take us to a ship. It will be less—less conspicuous—than going directly to a port—"

"I'm sorry, Loricus. It's a good plan. But we can't do that. We must go south, as quickly as possible."

"South?"

I showed him the corner of the urn. "I must take this to his mother."

"But, mistress, I think you are in peril—"

"I know. But I must. There is no one left to tell her. Fabius is dead, and who knows what will happen to Clemens…"

Even as we had been speaking the night had grown darker and the moon looked worse.

Three days later we were in Rhegium. The month had turned, and the year was failing. Dead leaves blew in the streets, and on the seafront the shops had folded their awnings. The water chopped in the straits, gray as slate under a threatening sky.

The wind nagged at my clothes as I hurried through the town, I did not even pause to go to my own house. We had come as quickly as we could in growing anxiety and now my haste was desperate.

Loricus felt it too. He leaned forward on his seat in the carriage, his hands clasped between his knees, saying nothing but keeping his eyes on the road behind us. He had been sitting like that the whole of our trip. If he had seen anything he had not said, but we both knew that hard as we had pushed ourselves the Imperial Messengers would have been faster. As we rumbled into Julia's little square I heard him catch his breath.

The space was empty, except for the leaves. A few had found their way through the open gate and were skittering across the cobbles. A few pigeons picked among them, moaning gently and gazing at us out of their pomegranate eyes.

"No guards," Loricus said.

"Yes, I see that. I'm going in."

He held my arm to restrain me. "No. Pinaria, please. Not till we know what this means."

The tall house stared back at me across its courtyard. The shutters were closed, the statues made their blank little gestures on the roof.

"I know what it means," I said.

I found them in the atrium. They had drawn close to each other on the chilly bench. Julia was lying with her head in her mother's lap, her fine chin, sharper than I remembered, pointed at the sky. Scribonia's hand lay across her eyes. Neither of them moved, but only one of them was dead.

The house smelled of ashes and cold damp stone. An earth smell, an underground one. A thread of light twisted its way into the hall. The air rang with vacancy and silence.

"Scribonia—"

The old lady lifted her hand and curled it gently in her lap. "Pinaria. Do come in." She turned back to her daughter. Julia's eyes were closed, the lids still thin and blue, the lashes dark against her pallor. "I found her like this an hour ago. There is no one else here. Not even the servants."

"What happened?"

The discolored eyes looked at me squarely. Nothing would ever make this heroic old lady flinch from the truth. But her lips were thin with pain and her voice was stiff. "About a month ago, the soldiers ordered me out of the house. They did not say why, though I demanded to know."

"Augustus had died."

"So I found out later."

She bent her head to her daughter and gazed at her. "She made me go. She insisted. 'But, Mother, perhaps you can help me—outside,' she said." Scribonia snorted down her delicate nostrils. "Liar. She knew what it meant.

"Every day I have come to the house, trying to get in to see her. The guards pushed me aside or pretended not to hear me. One of them drew his sword against me. Against *me*, a Scribonius Libo, the sister and wife of consuls." She paused to catch her breath. "Well, but I forget. Why should I be different from so many others?

"So I have sat outside in the square all day, watching the house, trying to find a way in. Last night at midnight a horseman arrived. After that the soldiers disappeared into the house. Presently all the servants came out and were led away. Then the soldiers packed up and marched out. They left the gate open, and I came in."

She stroked her daughter's body. "She was still alive. Barely. They had given her no food. Not for more than a month. She was strong, my girl. He may have despised her, but she was as much a soldier as he was."

I knew who 'he' was of course. I would have known even if she had not spat out the word.

"When I found her, she was lying over there—" She pointed to the coping of the pool. "She had been trying to drink. Her hand was in the water."

"And you lifted her up to the bench?"

"Oh, that was no trouble. She was very light."

"Yes," I said. "I imagine she must have been."

"She died an hour ago."

"Scribonia, I am very sorry."

"Thank you."

Together Scribonia and I laid out her daughter on a table. She knew the work and did it without comment or fuss, folding Julia's hands over her breast and wrapping her in a white dress out of a chest in another room. Her composure wavered only once: when she could not find a coin to put in Julia's mouth, I handed her one: a silver denarius. She glanced at it, glanced again, opened her hand and dropped it on the floor.

I bent to pick it up. Under my fingers the tiny portrait glared into a ring of misshapen letters. "Caesar Augustus Father of His Country." I straightened up to see Scribonia's eyes swimming with tears.

I felt like hurling the coin on the floor myself. "Oh, heaven, please forgive me Scribonia—I am so clumsy—"

But I underestimated her. They were tears of rage. As they splashed over and ran down her cheeks she lifted her chin. Her lips moved, and I heard her whisper, "By Juno, I will make them pay. They won't forget her. I will see to it."

I sat with her for some time. Finally I gave her the urn with Agrippa Postumus' remains in it.

But she was prepared for this. "Yes. Thank you. They told me in the town yesterday that he was dead."

"Evidently he was killed right away, as soon as Augustus died. No one knows who ordered it done."

She took the pottery out of my hands and held it to the altar. Then, very carefully, she laid it at her daughter's feet. She stood a moment with her head bowed and I knew she was praying again, repeating in her heart her promise to her dead.

When she looked up she was as composed as ever. "How did you get this, Pinaria Ovidii?"

"My servant Clemens, who once belonged to your grandson, gave it to me."

Under the probe of her gentle questions I told her the story. When I had finished she folded her hands. "I am sorry, Pinaria. Your servant has been captured. I heard it in the town: the news arrived two days ago. He was taken to Tiberius. When Tiberius asked him how he had become Agrippa Postumus he said, "The same way you became Caesar." She smiled thinly.

"I don't suppose Tiberius was amused."

"No. He ordered Clemens tortured. I'm sorry. No doubt he was a useful servant."

"I will miss him," I said, truthfully, though I didn't mean quite what she thought I did. My stomach was clenched with pity, thinking of his suffering. He had kept his word, even though I had not been able to keep mine.

Scribonia's spider voice was whispering at my side. "My husband would have laughed at the remark. For all his faults he was human. My daughter used to say, 'Sometimes he forgets that he is Caesar.'" The wrinkles in her face suddenly showed, like erosion in stone. "She would always add that she never forgot that she was Caesar's daughter."

"Tiberius never forgot it either."

"And he killed her for it. Well, I will make him remember that she was my daughter too."

"My daughter was a serious woman even though *he* didn't think so," she said at one point. "All those stories about her affairs. They were meant to deceive. Sometimes she wore revealing clothes in front of him—to make him think she was frivolous and thought of nothing but love. Then the next day she'd be serious again. He rebuked her, but she was too clever for him. "'Yesterday I dressed for my husband,' she would say. 'Today for my father.' But it was all a blind, a way to hide what she was doing."

I said nothing. He had found out anyway.

It was morning now: there was light in the atrium, and the sound of doves on the air. "What will you do now, Scribonia?"

She lifted her old face to the pale dawn. "I will burn my daughter. Of course. Then I will go back to Rome. There is nothing to prevent me. I was never exiled. And I will see who remembers the Scribonians. What will you do, Pinaria?"

"Loricus says I must leave Italy."

"Loricus?"

"My husband's secretary. He believes it is too dangerous here. Even before we knew Clemens had been captured—"

Little lines appeared around her mouth and her fine nostrils pinched. "Pinaria, a word of advice. He is only a slave. You cannot rely on these people, and it is not a good idea to let yourself become attached to them."

"Clemens was always very loyal. I don't believe he would have said anything."

"Clemens." She raised her eyebrows.

"Yes. He swore he would die rather than betray us. Didn't you mean that?"

The little lines were very sharp: so was her glance. She looked as angry as a hawk. "Remember what I said. I do not usually give advice." She knotted her old fingers in her lap and I knew she would not say anything more.

"I am honored, Scribonia," I said, puzzled.

Loricus had gone off somewhere. I came out of the house to see my carriage empty and a street child holding the horses. People were passing in the square, shutters were open in the shops and men were on their way to make their morning calls. Down the way a line was forming for admission to the public baths. The smell of cooking drifted out on the crisp autumn air.

I wiped my eyes. I could still feel Scribonia's last grasshopper embrace and the touch of Julia's hand.

Presently Loricus appeared. He had a basket of hot breads and a flask of wine, which he handed me. "Are you ready now, Pinaria?"

"I like that. I've been waiting for you."

He did not smile. "Let's get out of here."

He tossed a coin to the child and took up the reins. "I don't even want to go to your house."

"Why? What has happened?"

He shook his head. "Later. Let's go."

We were through the city gate and out on the road before he spoke again.

"Where are we going?" I asked.

He looked terrible: his face had a grayish cast and his hair had flown around his head. "That is just the question, Pinaria."

In all the hurry and trepidation I had never thought of this. "I—I suppose I could go to my daughter in Germany. Or to Naso."

He was shaking his head. "We cannot do either."

"Why?"

"I went shopping. I thought I might go to the Forum and look around a little." He indicated the bread. "Eat. You haven't had anything since we arrived."

Obediently I tore off a piece of bread.

"Swallow. Go on. Good. Take some wine."

"But—"

"Drink it."

I did as he said, but I was starting to cry. "Why are you doing this? Where are you taking me? Why aren't we going to the port?"

He turned to study me. "Pinaria, I'm sorry. It's just that I heard your name in the town."

"That's natural. I have a house here—"

"It was soldiers. They were looking for you. They asked where you lived."

The bread flew out of my throat, the raw wine went with it. I bent over the side of the wagon, retching and gagging on my empty stomach. The road rolled by under our wheels and the ruts scraped. So Scribonia was right, and Clemens had broken under the pain.

I pulled myself upright and tried to compose myself, but the tears were running from my eyes.

"My daughter—"

"She's all right. She's with Germanicus after all. They can suspect what they like, but they won't touch one of his people—he's too popular, both in Rome and with his army. And if we are careful, they may not make the connection."

The countryside was running away past me, liquid with speed and tears. It was all going, and I could not follow it.

"Naso—"

"I doubt they know anything about him. He's probably safe enough."

"But we don't know what Clemens told them. He might have named anyone."

"It wasn't Clemens. They tortured him all right, but he never spoke."

"He didn't?"

"No. That was in the town. Tiberius gave up and had him killed in some secret part of his palace. It got out, of course. I heard they buried him under the kitchen midden. And so far there has been no hint of an investigation."

I made a little sign to apologize to his ghost. He was a brave man to the end, the soldier he had wanted to be.

"How do they know then?"

"We must have been recognized."

"Or Marcia told them. One of her lies, which happened to be true."

Loricus slapped the reins on the horses' backs.

Late that night we stopped. I jolted out of a doze to see the cobbles of a courtyard and an old slave holding a lantern while two younger ones unharnessed the horses. Someone had wrapped me in a tattered cloak and there was dew on my cheeks and in my hair.

Loricus was hunched over the bench. He was studying me.

"How do you feel?"

I shook my head to clear it. The journey seemed to have gotten into it and my mind was full of rumbling wheels and dusty landscapes.

"Where are we?" I said.

"Don't you recognize it? It's a property of the Ovidii's. I took a chance and stopped here."

"Is it safe?"

"They say soldiers came yesterday, but have not been back. Not very safe, I'd say. But we can stay the rest of the night, if you like. How tired are you?"

"Where are we going?"

"Brundisium. There are ships there from all over the world. It's a busy port."

"But it's far."

"Yes. Even if we push it we will need three or four days."

"I can go on."

"Good. It will be a bit of time here—perhaps you'd like to wash, or lie down, or something? I'll call you."

Towards dawn we drove into a chilly little wind. The moon, restored now and a bit past the full, rode low in the sky, its light fading, revealing the stars. They spilled across the sky, a glitter of cold dice. Fixed stars and moving ones, wheeling like us through the night, but towards a different sea.

"Loricus," I said. "Where are we going? What are we going to do?"

"That is for you to say, mistress. I have not thought past Brundisium."

"My daughter, then."

"No. Pinaria, I am sorry. We cannot risk calling attention to her."

"Oh, Loricus. Not to see my own child?"

He put his hand over mine, a quick warmth in the wide cold night.

I thought of Scribonia, with her daughter dead in her lap. Then for a time I do not know what I thought.

We had gone some distance along the road, and the stars seemed fewer in the eastern sky ahead of us. Loricus' shape, featureless in its cloak, still loomed up beside me, comforting in the darkness. "Loricus, do you think Naso is a god?"

In the darkness his eye gleamed down at me. I don't know how I could tell it was amused.

"No," I said. "Neither do I. Do you think he loves me? Ever loved me?"

"Why do you ask, mistress?"

"Marcia always said he didn't."

"Marcia."

"I know. But she might be right about that. And there was that letter he wrote."

He thought a long time. "Perhaps. I don't think it matters. What matters is if you love him."

Though it was not a question, he seemed to be waiting for an answer.

"I—he is my husband. I gave my word. Where you are Gaius, I am Gaia."

He said nothing. After a time his let out a breath, and I heard his even breathing coming from him as before.

We rumbled on through the darkness. "Loricus, if we went to Naso, what would happen?"

"To him? I don't know. If the route were roundabout enough perhaps nothing. It took Ovidius Naso nearly a year, don't forget. I doubt that once you got to Tomis anyone would think of telling Tiberius, and if they did, he might not care that much, not after so long a time and from so far away."

Exile then. Gods, give me strength.

"Very well," I said. "That is what I will do."

The stars had mostly gone now in the aging night. Dawn was coming. I could see the shapes of cypresses and parasol pines cut out against the sky, and here and there the rough texture of a field or the gleam of water in a ditch. They seemed infinitely beautiful as they swept away, a coastline abandoned into darkness behind us.

"Loricus, can you arrange everything for me? Money, servants, passage on a ship, all that sort of thing?"

"Yes, of course." His hand still rested on mine.

"I will free you when we get to Brundisium."

"Thank you, mistress."

"And of course you will not have to come with me."

"If I am free, I may go where I like."

"That is so, Loricus. You said that once before." We rode along in silence. "Where did you think to go?" I asked around what felt like a stone in my throat. "Once you said you had started out in life to be a priest of your people. Will you go back and do that, do you think?"

As always he gave me a serious answer. "The time for that is past. I cannot go back any more."

"Because your country has changed?"

"Because I have. 'All things are in motion and nothing is at rest. They are like a river, and you cannot step into the same water twice.'"

"Heraclitus," I said.

In the growing light I saw him smile.

"So," I said, not understanding why this question was so difficult to ask, "what will you do?"

"You don't know? I will come with you."

"Oh, no. You mustn't. Tomis not a good place for anyone."

"It is where I want to be. It is the only place in the world that means anything to me at all."

"For Naso's sake?"

He shrugged. "Besides, you will need my help."

"Help?"

"Publius Ovidius Naso is an elderly man now. And we have not heard from him in some time. He may not even be there any longer."

"Where would he go?"

He looked sadly at the road passing under the wheels. "He is nearly sixty. And his life has been hard. His health has suffered. You might find that he…"

For all his philosophy he would not say the unlucky word.

The day had dawned, a chilly mist that shrouded the horizon and made ghosts of the trees, but I could see the glint of a river as we rumbled across a bridge. Somewhere near at hand a bird began to sing.

"But Loricus," I said, "that doesn't mean you have to come. You are free now, and I release you from your service to us. To me. You can go anywhere you like."

"Yes. I can."

"So?"

Behind his neat beard I thought he smiled. "We'll see."

"Yes," I said. His cloak billowed out against the sky, a wall between me and the cold gray morning. "Yes," I said, suddenly happy. "Yes. We will."

ACKNOWLEDGEMENTS
AND THANKS

To Dr. Elaine Fanthom, Professor, Princeton University, for help with women's issues and for sharing with me her fascinating ideas about Marsyas, and what really happened the night the princess danced in the Forum. The idea behind this story is my own, but it is better for her critique.

To Dr. Judith Hallett, Professor, University of Maryland, for the suggestion of who Demosthenes and Aesopus might have been; for help with women's names though I am not sure she would agree with my choices here; and for her constant and generous help in all aspects of this work.

To Susan Kelly, novelist *extraordinaire*, who read this book in ms, and whose comments were uniformly helpful and encouraging, as always.

To Maj. Michael Sherwood, USA Ret., for information on how long it would have taken the slave Clemens to grow a beard. Maj. Sherwood is an expert on the matter, growing a magnificent specimen every year in his capacity as the Santa Claus at a shopping mall.

To Ian Cameron Smith and his wonderful website (http://www.hermit.org) for information on moon phases and eclipses both solar and lunar. The ones in the book correspond as nearly as he can make them with the historical information we have. (See note below: ECLIPSES).

To Dr. Allen Ward, Professor Emeritus, University of Connecticut, grateful thanks for the suggestion about Augustus' formation of the Blue team, and Fabius' possible sponsorship of either the Reds or Whites; for help with women's names, though my solution must not be thought of as endorsed by him; and for reading this book in ms. His vast knowledge of Roman history he has so generously put at my disposal, and my gratitude for his help cannot be sufficiently expressed.

To Dr. Martin Winkler, George Mason University, for help and encouragement, especially about translations. A note about a particularly brilliant effort of his will be found below.

ENDNOTES

Why was Ovid relegated?

The reasons for the relegation of Ovid have been and still remain one of history's most tantalizing puzzles. His relegation is not mentioned by any historian, and what we know comes entirely from him. He left clues, but no narrative. He says, in a famous phrase, that he was condemned—rightly, he adds—for "carmen et error"—"a poem and mistake."

The lines I have quoted from that poem, *Tristia* 2:

that by a lewd poem
I stood accused as a teacher of foul adultery.
Sometimes thus even the minds of the gods may be deceived
And many things are too insignificant for your notice—
Like Jupiter, who watches over lofty heaven,
Your attention is not to be squandered on some insignificant detail,
For on you depends so much, while you ponder the whole globe

Lowly things must escape your notice.
Certainly the Princeps of the world could not forsake his post
To read the unequal lines of an ill-made song?...

can surely be read as a challenge to Augustus to recall the poet or to say frankly what the real reason for his relegation is. (If they are, of course, we have no record of any answer Augustus may have made.)

Ovid also tells us that the poem was *The Art of Love*. He says he saw something he shouldn't have, but it wasn't a crime and it wasn't a crime to see it. He says Augustus was right to be outraged both as the Father of His Country and as the father of a family. Beyond that is all speculation. For those wishing more information, the guesses of historians for the past two thousand years are neatly summarized in a little book called *The Mystery of Ovid's Exile* by Thibault and published by University of California Press. They range from the charming medieval notion that the poet must have seen Livia in her bath, to the more recent hypothetical affair between Ovid and Augustus' daughter—Thibault by the way feels this is unlikely since they would both have been over forty. The book was published in 1966 and since then many historians have looked to other reasons. Very current nowadays—though by no means universal—are political reasons. Sir Ronald Syme, for instance, (in *The Roman Revolution*) says that the men condemned with Julia the Elder were "not innocent triflers or moral reprobates but a formidable [political] faction."

That Ovid was part of it is, of course, the argument of this book.

Why in the year 8 AD?

I have suggested a number of reasons in this book, but there is one more I would like to mention:

It is unlikely that Ovid ever had a patron—he was himself a rich man, perhaps a very rich one—but he did have important friends. One of the earliest was the great Marcus Valerius Messalla Corvinus, who died in the year that Ovid was relegated. His younger son Cotta had property on the island of Elba, where Ovid was visiting him, either when he, Ovid, was told of his relegation or shortly after he learned of it.

Elba was not then a place of exile, but an island rich in iron which was mined in ancient times. Sulmo, where the Ovidii were an important family, was known for its ironworking, so I imagine that Ovid's acquaintance with the family of Messalla came from their mutual interest in this business. Messalla was one of the few people in Rome powerful enough to stand up to Augustus: early in Augustus' assumption of power in Rome he asked Messalla to take the office of Urban Prefect, a Republican office which Augustus had enlarged to allow the use of force against citizens. Messalla resigned after six days, saying that he could not understand the application of the powers he was asked to assume (or, according to St. Jerome, that it was an unjust form of authority). Augustus took no action against him, but Messalla effectively retired from political life after that.

As I have indicated in this book, the year 8 AD was a very troubled one in Roman politics, seeing many deaths and exiles. That is perhaps sufficient to explain Ovid's relegation. It is interesting to speculate, however, that the death of Messalla left Ovid without the protection that this great man's friendship may have afforded him.

The death of Augustus, the succession of Tiberius, and the death of Agrippa Postumus:

Did Tiberius see Augustus before his death? And did Livia poison him? Depending on the source, Tiberius either spent a day in consultation with Caesar or arrived too late to see him alive. I have chosen a compromise in the book. Tacitus tells us that Livia poisoned Caesar to prevent his disinheriting her son Tiberius. Very few modern historians believe this story, and I have not accepted it myself. As for the visit to Planasia, it is reported by both Velleius and Dio as fact, but by Tacitus as a rumor, and as a rumor I have treated it, though it does not strike me as totally implausible. Some modern historians accept it as fact, though many do not. The story of the slave Clemens is given in considerable detail in Tacitus, and as a fact, not a rumor. Whether Fabius was involved is a much more complex question.

Tacitus tells us that Marcia, Fabius' wife, was heard to say at her husband's funeral that she was responsible for Fabius' death. Ovid himself says in a letter (*Ex Ponto* 4.6.5f) that *he* was responsible, and while that does not mean that Fabius was party to a visit to Planasia (that may or may not have taken place), it suggests that Fabius had a deeper involvement than simply trying to plead with Caesar on Ovid's behalf for a safer place of exile, or some such relatively trivial matter.

These three considerations have led me to the solution in this book.

Was Ovid involved in a conspiracy?

What was to happen after the death of Augustus was a question that must have preoccupied both Augustus himself, who left no son of his own (Julia the Elder was his only known child) and the Senate and Roman people as well. There was no provision in Roman precedent or law for any kind of succession, Rome having elected its officials since the expulsion of the Etruscan kings hundreds of years before. Indeed the pretense that the Republic still existed and Augustus' position was based on elected offices was kept up until his death and after.

Over and over during Augustus' lifetime conspiracies against his life or his rule came to light. Many are mentioned, some in considerable detail, in the histories that have come down to us and they are especially thick on the ground around the time of Augustus' death. I have combined several of them, since they seemed to me especially closely related to the descendants of Julius Caesar. Telephus and his part are mentioned in Suetonius while Clemens and his are in Tacitus. It is my idea that they might be the same person, for their aims are similar, and the dates of their plots must also be, though Suetonius does not tell us when the Telephus affair occurred. All the same, if the young Agrippa Postumus was to be taken to Germany surely that would have happened after the death of Augustus and before the revelations around Clemens. Who Clemens might have been is my own hypothesis.

That Fabius was in any way connected with them is again my own invention: he was well-known for his loyalty to Augustus, but the modern historian Sir Ronald Syme remarks that he had reason to resent the preferment of Tiberius. Many in Rome did. Fabius fell out of favor and died before the date that Tacitus gives us for the conclusion of Clemens' conspiracy: I have altered that for dramatic purposes. His fall from grace is well documented, as is his wife's friendship with Livia and her behavior at her husband's funeral, though I have tied these events to a different scandal from the one Tacitus mentions.

Much of my reconstruction, if that it is, depends on dates which are either unknown to us, or the subject of controversy among the scholars—very thorny questions. One or two examples will have to suffice:

When, for instance, did Julia the Younger's husband L. Aemilius Paullus die? At the time of his wife's relegation in 8 AD he may have only been exiled. Among those who believe he died, it is not known whether he was executed or committed suicide, and the date is often given by modern scholars as earlier than 8 AD. Sir Ronald Syme, in his book *The Roman Republic* lists him as consul in 1 AD with a question mark. He also has a very elegant argument to show that the date of his exile or death is 8 AD. Yet in *The Augustan Aristocracy*, a later book, Syme has changed his views, and felt that Aemilius must have been exiled. According to the scholiast on Juvenal, the younger Julia's husband was put to death when his wife was banished for adultery. Syme thinks he was still alive in 14 AD when a 'L.Paullus' was replaced on the list of Arval Brothers, a priestly college in which membership was for life. I have stayed closer to Juvenal.

When was Cassius Severus' trial and exile? The date given is 12 AD in Dio Cassius, but others including Rogers (*Journal of Roman Studies*, 1959) and Syme (*The Augustan Aristocracy* p. 411), for various reasons think it must be 8 AD. Here I follow them. "The widely accepted date of 12 is arbitrary and unsupported"—Rogers (paraphrase) and "Nothing forbids and everything encourages the year 8..."—Syme.

The date of the uprising in Dacia which is discussed in this book (there were others) is sometimes given as 6–8 AD but Syme (in a book called *History in Ovid*) says it was 12 AD. That means that it would have happened while Ovid was in relegation in Tomis.

And so on. In all cases where I have been in doubt I have as always tried to follow the more explicit ancient sources. And one thing that struck me most forcefully in them was that the conspiracies around Augustus so often involved the descendents of Scribonia, the wife he divorced to marry Livia, and the mother of his only child. That child, Julia, was relegated for flagrant and persistent adulteries—at least that was the official reason. Many modern historians think it is the right one. To me it sounds like window dressing, a charge trumped up to hide a more serious and indeed more devastating reason—and some ancient historians tell us this is so, particularly Dio who mentions Augustus' unhappiness at the efforts of his daughter to assassinate him. Indeed I cannot think of another reason why Scribonia wanted to go into exile with her daughter. Historically this has been seen as the gesture of a true Roman mother. Perhaps it was. But Scribonia was far more than that, and I have tried to show something of what I think this amazing woman was really like.

METEOROLOGY

Dec 1, 8 AD was a full moon, most probably, though modern calculations leave out the adjustments to the months that Augustus made that year.

The first of December was also the first day of winter.

The eclipse of April 12, 14 AD presaging the death of Augustus appears in Dio Cassius, the ancient historian. He was writing about 200 years after the event, and his sources are largely unknown to us. "...the sun suffered a total eclipse and most of the sky seemed to be on fire; glowing embers appeared to be falling from it, and blood-red comets were seen..."

To find out if this might have been a real eclipse I enlisted the help of Ian Cameron Smith, a web expert on eclipses. It is his opinion that the most likely candidate for this eclipse was one we know to have occurred five years later, in 19 AD and most likely visible in a wide swath from Russia all the way across Southern Europe. Given the lapse of time and the dramatic events involved, Dio's mistake seems very plausible to me.

The lunar eclipse that ended the revolt of Germanicus' troops also has a real counterpart, and would very likely have been visible in Italy. This information I also owe to Mr. Cameron Smith.

Ian Cameron Smith's website is http://www.hermit.org. It is absolutely fascinating.

Real people and fictional

OVID'S WIFE

Ovid tells us he was married three times, but we do not know the names of any of these ladies. It is the third who was his wife at the time of his relegation. As to who she is, there has been much scholarly speculation over the years. Pinaria is my own choice, for the reasons below:

Many authorities think that she must have been a relative of Fabius—including the editors of the Loeb Library edition of the *Tristia and Ex Ponte* (2002) and Henze. But Syme thinks she is a relative of Marcia's. There is evidence that may be understood either way:

In the poem *Ex Ponto* 3.75–78:

Line 75: hoc domui debes "this you owe to that house" de qua censeris "by which thou hast thy esteem." In the Loeb translation by A. L. Wheeler 2002 the footnote says this refers to the Fabians, but it is followed,

Line 77: nisi eris laudabilis uxor "unless you be a praiseworthy wife" non poterit credi Marcia culta tibi "it will not be believed that you have honored Marcia."

I think this must be the line on which Syme relies when he says Ovid's wife is a relative of Marcia's. I find it a very plausible interpretation in any case.

The Pinarii were a distinguished clan, evidently large, and connected with Augustus' family, though it is not necessary to suppose that the daughter of any particular member of it would have been close to the Imperial family on her own.

Perilla is almost certainly the daughter of Ovid's third wife by a previous marriage, though we do not know anything about her father. A very charming letter (*Tristia* 3.7) is addressed to her. Ovid had a daughter by another marriage, and she evidently had a child or children. We do not know their names.

LORICUS

Loricus is a purely fictional character. His origin in Spain I have signified by his name, which is that of a hero of the local Celto-Iberian people in the wars against Rome.

DEMOSTHENES, AESOPUS, PHOEBE AND DIANA

The first three are real, mentioned in the ancient historians as implicated in the story of Julia the Elder. Diana is invented. I am deeply indebted to Dr. Judith Hallett for the suggestion as to what position Demosthenes (and, it follows, the others) must have occupied in relation to the Julian family.

SCRIBONIA

The descriptions of Scribonia that have come down to us, though varied, strike me as in the highest degree unlikely. She was the daughter of a powerful political family and before her marriage to Augustus she had been married to two ex-consuls, leading men in Rome. After Augustus divorced her she did not marry again. It is ancient historians who tell us that she asked to accompany her daughter Julia into exile, though she had other children living. A reason for this I have suggested in this book.

She is recorded to have outlived Julia by at least two years, though perhaps not much more than that.

If as I speculate she was an active member of a faction against the Claudians, the death of Julia was not the last arrow in her quiver. About two years later, her nephews Lucius and Marcus Scribonius Libo were tried as conspirators against Tiberius. Scribonia advised Marcus not to commit suicide but to wait for his fate. It is a shockingly tough-minded view.

There is a very excellent article about her, by the way, by Ernestine F. Leon, published in 1951 (in *TAPA*), though it does not address the question about faction and conspiracy, which are my own invention. Leon calculates Scribonia's age in 16 AD as "over eighty-five," a dating I have followed. She points out that Scribonia would have been "near the end of her days. Had she lived many years longer, Pliny would hardly have failed to note the fact in his list of prominent long-lived women."

A word about some words

DOMINA

Often translated "my lady," it is what the servants called the woman of the house. I have chosen "mistress" to represent it, since "my lady" seems to be to refer to a different and more modern social system, and does not bring out the fact that the servants in a household were usually slaves.

I have, however, used the word "Princess" to designate an Imperial or (in one case royal) lady. This term was not in use at this period, I believe, but it is derived from a title that was used of Augustus—"Princeps," designating the senior senator and the leader of the Roman world in civilian affairs—so it seemed appropriate for the women of his family. "Emperor" is derived from "imperator," a military commander.

NAMES

Among men, few first names were in use in ancient Rome, and a man was generally known by his nomen, his family name: i.e., Ovidius. Julius, for example, with us a first name, is the family name of a clan; Augustus' family name, after his adoption by his great-uncle Julius Caesar, became Julius. Often a man inherited or was awarded an additional name, called a cognomen: i.e., Naso, or Caesar, or Augustus. Men had first names too: Julius Caesar's was Gaius, as was Augustus. Ovidius Naso's first name was Publius.

Girl children were named after their clan. That is, their name was the feminized form of their fathers' family name. Ovid's daughter was therefore called "Ovidia." In the earliest days of Roman history that would have been all there was to it, unless there was more than one daughter, in which case the girls would be identified by birth order: Ovidia Major and Ovidia Minor, for instance, if there were two, Ovida Prima, Secunda, Tertia and so on if there were more. They did not change their names when they married.

By the time of this book, a woman's formal name included the abreviation of her father's first name and the addition of his cognomen. Thus Julia the daughter of Augustus would be formally "Julia C[ai].f. (Filia) Julii Caesaris Octaviani /Augusti." This works out to something like "Julia daughter of Gaius Julius Caesar Octavianus Augustus." Naturally some simplicity had to creep in somewhere along with a good deal of variation.

Some historians think this reflects a growing liberty and status for women (growth which in fact I have tried to show in this book). Sometimes for instance in this period we find women taking their family name and their father's cognomen declined in the feminine form; thus, for example, Ovid's daughter might have called herself "Ovidia Nasa." Augustus' wife Livia called herself "Livia Drusilla." Or it appears they might use it in the genitive form—as "Julia Caesaris"—"Julia (of) Caesar" i.e., "Julia, Caesar's daughter." Some women were called by a grandparent's name: for instance Julia's daughter was called "Julia" (the Younger) though her father was a Vipsanius. When they married they were often informally identified by their original family name with their husband's family name added on, though their formal name never changed: thus, the granddaughter of Augustus when she married Lucius Aemilius Paullus could be called "Julia Aemilii" (i.e., "Julia of Aemilius" so to speak), though her official name remained her father's and her original clan's no matter what her marital status.

Throughout this book I have allowed myself to be ruled by a principle of simplicity and clarity in this very arcane and complex matter, and considered what would fall most naturally on modern ears accustomed to other conventions and a different language. For instance, it seems likely to me that a wife called her husband by his first name—"where you are Gaius, I am Gaia," she swore at marriage, and "Gaius" is a masculine first name, not a family name. Therefore, most probably Ovid's wife would have called him not Naso but Publius. For obvious reasons that is not a place I wanted to go. Julia the daughter of the Emperor I have referred to as Julia Caesaris, and under that name many modern historians refer to her as well, though there is much disagreement on this point. Elaine Fantham, for instance, in a recent book refers to her as Julia Augusti, but that name has political connotations I have only hinted at in this novel. As I say, it's a complex subject, and to anyone wishing further information, I recommend the Wikipedia articles on Roman Names.

AUGUSTUS

"Augustus" is not a name but a title, conferred by the Senate on Octavian early in his career. It means something like "the revered one." He is often referred to by his name "Caesar" which he received when his great-uncle Julius Caesar the dictator adopted him.

MINETUR-MINOTAUR

I owe this pun indirectly to a book called *Metaformations: Sound-play and Wordplay in Ovid and Other Classical Poets* by Frederick Ahl, and to discussions about it with Dr. Martin Winkler and Dr. Allen Ward. Anyone reading Ovid must be struck I think by the complexity, ambiguity and wit of his language, and Dr. Ahl's discussion, while going further than I can follow, brings out many ways in which Ovid uses wordplay and puns.

This pun, if it is one: MINETUR ("it seems to be menacing") and MINOTAUR, the name of the half-man half-bull Cretan monster, is not one of the puns mentioned in Ahl's book, but my own addition. It appears in the line :

...quod proelia nulla minetur

Which I have translated:

No hostile intent, no menace, does she perceive

Dr. Winkler offers the wonderful :

Nothing hostile, nothing *minatory*, does she perceive....

The discussion of time in the *Metamorphoses,* by the way, is also based on a chapter in *Metaformations*, though the idea that Ovid is saying that Augustus is a god because he has brought order to the world, and that he himself is a god the equal of Augustus for the order he has discovered in these stories, I owe to Dr. Lou Bolchazy.

Tisanum Barricum

A recipe for the soup Ovid might have eaten on the night of his relegation.

For Lou Bolchazy, in memory of a very fine soup.

Of the many cookbooks of antiquity only one has come down to us: Apicius' *Art of Cooking.* Published sometime in the mid-400s of our era, it appears to be a compendium of many books and pamphlets. We do not know who this Apicius was, but a famous gourmet of that name lived in Tiberius' time. No one knows if any of the recipes in the cookbook go back to him, and there were other men of the same name known to be interested in food and cooking: in fact the name itself came to be a general term for a gourmet. In Italian cooking today it still denotes a style of cooking involving richly flavored sauces with many herbs and spices and often the addition of fruit, especially dried.

The book is written loosely, evidently for a professional cook, with little in the way of instruction and no amounts given for the ingredients. Several modern scholars have made translations designed for people who want to try making Roman dishes, among them *Apicus: The Roman Cookery Book,* by Barbara Flower and Elizabeth Rosenbaum, published by Harrap in London in 1958, a scholarly work but still useful to the cook. A lovely little book called *Roman Cookery: Ancient Recipes for Modern Kitchens* was published in 1999 by Serif, London. The author is Mark Grant. He has used recipes from many ancient sources besides Apicius. There are many sources on the web as well.

The soup that follows is adapted from Apicius. It is very nutritious, even without meat, which may mean that this soup was a meal in itself, perhaps a light lunch, or the supper of a poorer family, or a richer one that adhered to the tradition of simple living. Apicius calls this version

TISANUM BARRICUM
Barley Broth

> 1 small head of Green Cabbage, chopped. I like Savoy cabbage in this recipe.
> 2 Leeks washed and chopped, white part only
> 1 small bulb of Fennel, bulb sliced and leaves chopped
> 1 tbsp Fennel Seeds, ground**
> 1 tbsp chopped Cilantro**
> 1 tbsp chopped Dill**
> 1 tbsp dried Oregano or a small handful of fresh chopped Oregano**
> 1 small handful fresh Celery Leaves or Lovage**
> Pinch of Asafetida (also called "hing" and available at Indian groceries)**
> 1 small handful Beet greens, chopped**
> 1 cup Barley soaked overnight
> 1/2 cup dried Chickpeas soaked overnight
> 1 cup water
> 1 tbsp or to taste Nuoc Mam*
> Olive Oil for sautéing

NB: Another Apician barley soup uses a roast pork leg: if you wanted a meat soup that would be fine here. I would use a leftover with more bone than meat. Cook it with the barley, and remove it before serving.

Sauté the cabbage, the sliced bulb of the fennel (but not the leaves), and the leeks in olive oil until they are translucent and just beginning to brown. Remove them to another pot and add the beet greens. Boil this gently in a few teaspoons of water until the cabbage is soft.

To the first pot add a little water, scraping up any browned bits from the vegetables. Add barley and chickpeas and cover with water. Cook until they are soft and the water has been absorbed. Add more water as you go along if necessary. Transfer to a serving bowl.

Pound the fennel seeds, dill, cilantro, oregano, asafetida, chopped fennel leaves and celery leaves with the Nuoc Mam. Stir this into the cabbage/fennel bulb/leek/beet green mixture. Pour this combination over the barley. Drizzle with a little olive oil.

Serve with crusty Italian style bread or focaccia (some things don't change much). The soup should be thick enough to sop up with the bread. Spoons were not used at table in ancient Rome.

*The most important seasoning of Roman cookery in ancient times was a fermented fish sauce called garum or liquamen. Mark Grant in his book gives a recipe for making your own. I find that the Vietnamese fish sauce Nuoc Mam (or Nuc Nam or Nam Pla), available in Asian groceries, makes a good substitute. Some recipes call for anchovy paste: to my mind Nuoc Mam has a taste closer to fermented fish than anchovy paste. If you use anchovy paste, you might try mixing it with a little balsamic or red wine vinegar and a touch of soy sauce to get something of the depth of the Nuoc Mam. In that case be especially careful of the salt.

**All the measurements for the herbs are meant only as guides. You will want to alter them to your taste. Since Apicius gives no measures himself, you will have the rare and delightful experience of being right no matter what you do.

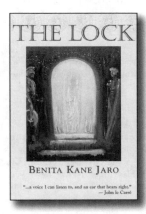

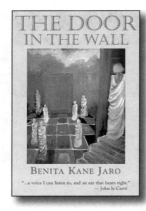

BENITA KANE JARO

"...a voice I can listen to, and an ear that hears right."
— John le Carré

The Door in the Wall

Benita Kane Jaro

xiv + 250 pp (2002) Paperback ISBN 978-0-86516-533-5

Political intrigue:
a novel on the life of Julius Caesar.

Marcus Caelius Rufus, a young politician, has holed up in a country town in the midst of a bloody and prolonged civil war. Great forces contend for Rome, and Caelius has ties to them all—the charismatic Julius Caesar, his beloved teacher Cicero, the hero Pompey the Great. Which side is he on? He must choose. Now he must reconsider who he is: his childhood and education, his loves and friendships, his complex relationship to Caesar, the man who has come to dominate his life. Before he is done, he will discover the shocking truth about Caesar, about Rome, and about himself. This book is a vivid and exciting read.

Reviews

"*The Lock*, by Benita Kane Jaro (281 pages, June 2002), is the third in a trilogy of vivid historical novels set near the end of the Roman Republic. *The Key* (1988) focused on the poet Catullus, while *The Door in the Wall* (1994) revolved around the intrigues and relationships of Julius Caesar. *The Lock* centers more on the Roman senator Cicero and his attempts to prevent the collapse of democracy and thwart the machinations of Pompey in his bid for sole control of Rome. Written engagingly and with a clear grasp of the complexities of Roman politics, *The Lock* shows how the ancients came to grips with some of the same choices and challenges that we face today."
—**Stephanie Orphan**, Editor, *C&RL News* (October 2002)

If there is to be a worthy successor to Mary Renault, or to Marguerite Yourcenar, it may be Benita Kane Jaro.

—**Doris Grumbach**

"Through her deft use of dialogue and descriptive detail, Benita Kane Jaro imaginatively brings to life the personalities and political intrigues of ancient Rome in the turbulent days of Julius Caesar. She is especially successful at recreating the smells, sights, sounds and tastes experienced by her characters, and thereby summoning up the physical texture as well as the intellectual substance of lived reality."
—**Judith Peller Hallet**, Professor of Classics, University of Maryland

"Benita Kane Jaro recreates the major characters and events in the waning Roman Republic with a solid command of the ancient sources and the kind of disciplined imagination that brings history alive. Through the eyes of Cicero's witty and perceptive protégé, Marcus Caelius Rufus, we are presented a compelling picture of the folly, corruption, and ruthless ambition that destroyed the Roman Republic and replaced it with Caesar—who is portrayed with deep insight into his essential nature."
—**Allen Ward**, Department of History, University of Connecticut

"...assiduously researched, intelligently written...readers interested in the period will find this book more lively than the...sagas currently on the market."
—*Publishers' Weekly*

Vergil's *Aeneid*
Hero • War • Humanity

Translated by G. B. Cobbold

xviii + 366 pp (2005) Paperback ISBN 978-0-86516-596-0

One of the pillars of Western literary tradition, Vergil's *Aeneid* is also a terrific read: the story of a man whose city is destroyed in war, and of his journey to find his place in destiny. This epic has it all: adventures on the high seas, passion, battles, monsters, magic, meddling gods, and struggles that test the moral fiber of both men and women.

The *Aeneid* has been deemed one of the most influential poems in world literature. And yet, a translation with wide appeal has been lacking—until now. G. B. Cobbold joined with Bolchazy-Carducci Publishers to produce an *Aeneid* that gives the epic its due as the rousing and moving story that it is, while remaining true to the spirit of the Latin original. This an Aeneid like no other: a fresh, page-turning rendition that reads like a novel, but has the vividness of poetic language, with attractive and accessible reader aids. Sure to become a prized standard!

Cobbold's command of Latin and commitment to a strong narrative line have produced an *Aeneid* for everyone! Features include

- Introduction to the *Aeneid* and Vergil
- Vivid novelistic rendition with sidebar running summaries and dynamic in-text illustrations
- Map of Aeneas' voyage
- Glossary of characters
- Family trees of main characters and gods
- Book-by-book outline of the plot of the *Aeneid*
- Timeline of significant events in Roman history
- Reading group discussion questions

Reviews

"Part of the reading experience includes spending some time with the classics and G. B. Cobbold has made that much easier with his new translation of Vergil's *Aeneid*. The author's knowledge of Latin and this classic story has permitted him to retell it as a novel, rather than its original text as a poem about a man whose city is destroyed by war and his long journey to find his destiny. In the process, there's plenty of high drama, passion, battles, monsters, and meddling gods. It speaks to every new generation in a very special way. This new version makes the story especially accessible in many ways, including a glossary of characters, a timeline of significant events in Roman history, and other aids."
    –**Alan Caruba**, *Bookviews*, My Picks of the Month, *Bookviews* June 2005
                        http://www.bookviews.com/

"*Vergil's Aeneid: Hero, War, Humanity* is an impressive English translation of Vergil's classic work of literature. G. B. Cobbold renders Vergil's *Aeneid* into a novel format, with sidebar summaries, which reads very much like an exciting modern adventure story! Enhanced with illustrations, a map of Aeneas' voyage, a glossary of characters, family trees of main characters and gods, a book-by-book outline of the plot of the *Aeneid*, a timeline of significant events in Roman history, reading group discussion questions, and much more, Vergil's *Aeneid* truly makes classic literature come alive. Highly recommended for study and discussion groups, and a welcome alternative interpretation for those who are more familiar with Vergil's *Aeneid* in verse-by-verse form."

                        –*Midwest Book Review*

www.BOLCHAZY.com

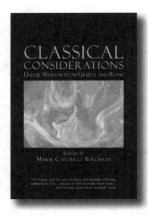

Classical Considerations
Useful Wisdom from Greece and Rome

Edited by Marie Carducci Bolchazy
Illustrated by Thom Kapheim
viii + 128 pp (2006) Paperback ISBN 978-0-86516-618-9

The ancients knew that wisdom comes from sharing ideas with each other and with those who have gone before. This book is such a sharing: 53 quotations from ancient Greek and Latin authors, with English translations and accompanied by a brief essay, poem, or explanation of context. Contributors to Classical Considerations are a richly diverse group: classicists, reporters, students, professors, teachers, a psychiatrist, a judge, Vietnam veterans, a publisher, a minister, and a football coach. They show how the words of the ancients have connected with their own understandings of the world. Themes considered include fate, character, art, war, redemption after suffering, and time.

Reviews

"Have no worries. This isn't *Chicken Soup for the Modern Soul – Ancient Greece Edition*. It's not a self-help book, nor is it a dry, academic read. It's a pithy, sometimes trenchant, collection of quotes and collected wisdoms, which is buoyed by contributions from Penn State coach Joe Paterno (attributing his coaching philosophy to Vergil), Stephen R. Covey (the author of *The 7 Habits of Highly Effective People* using Aristotle to probe the unconscious) and professor Timothy F. Winters (explaining why reading Homer can help kids learn about softball and life). Editor and Barrington resident Marie Carducci Bolchazy's aim isn't so much to review the wisdom of Greek and Roman literature as it is to show how that ancient wisdom can still prove useful to modern readers."
—*Northshore Magazine*, August, 2006

"*Classic Considerations: Useful Wisdom From Greece And Rome* by Marie Carducci Bolchazy is a compendium of reflection on the thought and philosophical vision of the ancients made available in translation and applicable to the circumstances of contemporary readers. Introducing readers to an understanding and compelling glimpse of the core of Western humanities, *Classic Considerations* consists of wisdom from a psychiatrist who works with Vietnam veterans with post-traumatic stress disorder, a journalist, a famous football coach, a judge, college students, a renowned business and personal development speaker and writer, and a minister for a wide understanding of the interconnecting world of modern philosophy and interpretive study to completely provide an encouraging outlook on life and society. Showcasing the original Greek language quotations, *Classic Considerations* is very highly recommended to all readers with an interest in Latin or Greek philosophies and their continuing relevance for the present day."
—**James Cox**, *Midwest Book Review*, *The Bookwatch* 28.5

"Just a short note to thank you most sincerely for sending me a copy of the book you edited, *Classical Considerations: Useful Wisdom from Greece and Rome*. I enjoyed very much reading the quotations; a number of them were already familiar to me. I enjoyed even more seeing them collected with the comments you brought together.

   "It is not often that I get a chance to go back on some of the elements of my own education, and your book has been the means for me to do that. I have already taken a lot of pleasure in the selections, and I thank you for that. Perhaps we will have an occasion to meet. In the meantime, you have my gratitude and prayers."
—**Francis Cardinal George**, O.M.I., Archbishop of Chicago, April 17, 2006

WWW.BOLCHAZY.COM